BEN BOVA

Titan

HODDER &
STOUGHTON

First published in Great Britain in 2006 by Hodder and Stoughton
A division of Hodder Headline

A Hodder & Stoughton Book

1

A CIP catalogue record for this title is available from the British Library

ISBN 0 340 82396 8

Typeset in Plantin by Hewer Text UK Ltd, Edinburgh
Printed and bound by Mackays of Chatham Ltd, Chatham, Kent;

Hodder Headline's policy is to use papers that are natural, renewable
and recyclable products and made from wood grown in sustainable forests.
The logging and manufacturing processes are expected to conform to
the environmental regulations of the country of origin.

Hodder and Stoughton Ltd
A division of Hodder Headline
338 Euston Road
London NW1 3BH

To my the memory of my friend,
the truth-seeking David Brudnoy.
And with special thanks to Dwight Babcock,
who coined the 'Lazy H' name for one of Titan's seas.

It is only by risking our persons from one hour to another that we live at all. And often enough our faith beforehand in an uncertified result is the only thing that makes the result come true.

William James

24 December 2095:
On the Shore of the Methane Sea

It was nearly dawn on Titan. The thick listless wind slithered like an oily beast slowly awakening from a troubled sleep, moaning, lumbering across the frozen land. The sky was a grayish orange, heavy with sluggish clouds; the distant Sun was nothing more than a feeble ember of dull red light smoldering faintly along the horizon. No stars in that smog-laden sky, no lightning to break the darkness; only the slightest hint of a faint glow betrayed where the giant planet Saturn rode high above.

The ice-covered sea was dark too, with a brittle, cracked coating of black hydrocarbon slush that surged fitfully against the low bluffs that hemmed it in. At their bases the bluffs were ridged, showing where the feeble tides had risen and then fallen back: risen and ebbed, in the inexorable cadence that had persisted for eons. In the distance a methane storm slowly marched across the sea, scattering crystals of black hydrocarbon tholins like a blanket of inkdrops swirling closer, closer.

A promontory of ice suddenly crumbled under the relentless etching of the sea, sliding into the black waves with a roar that no ear heard, no eye saw. Slabs of frozen water slid into the sea, smashing the thin sheet of blackened ice atop it, frothing and bobbing in the water for a few moments before the open water began to freeze over once again. All became still and quiet once again, except for the low moan of the unhurried wind and the ceaseless surging of the waves. It was as if the promontory had never existed.

Titan rolled slowly in its stately orbit around the ringed

planet Saturn just as it had for billions of years, as dark and benighted beneath its shroud of ruddy auburn clouds as a blind beggar groping his unlit circuit through a cold, pitiless universe.

But this slow dawn was different. A new kind of day was beginning.

A sudden thunderclap boomed across the ice-topped sea, so sharp and powerful that shards of ice snapped off the frozen bluffs and tumbled splashing into the dark crust below. A flash of light lit the clouds, casting an eerie orange glimmer over the shore of the sea.

Through the clouds descended a thing utterly alien, a massive oblong object that swayed gently beneath a billowing canopy. It descended slowly toward the rounded hillocks that edged the dark sea. As it neared the icy surface another flash of brilliant, searing light burst from beneath it, with a roar that echoed off the ice mounds and across the wavelets of the turbid sea. Then it settled slowly onto the uneven surface of one of the knolls, squatting heavily on four thick caterpillar treads as its parachute canopy sagged down to droop over its edge and halfway to the black, encrusted sea.

The creatures living in the ice burrowed deeper to escape the alien monster. They had neither eyes nor ears but they were delicately sensitive to changes in pressure and temperature. The alien was hot, lethally hot, and so heavy that it sank through the soft surface mud and even cracked and powdered the underlying ice beneath its bulk. The ice creatures moved pitifully slowly; those directly beneath the massive alien were not fast enough to avoid being crushed and roasted by its residual heat. The others nearby wormed deeper into the ice as quickly as they could, blindly seeking to escape, to survive, to live.

Then the black tholin storm reached the cliffs and swirled over the alien monster. Silence returned to the shore of Titan's frigid sea.

Oral Diary of
Professor James Coleraine Wilmot

'Today, Urbain and his science chaps land their probe on Titan. The real work of this habitat will begin.

'Ten thousand men and women locked inside this orbiting cylinder. In the two years it has taken to arrive in orbit around Saturn we've survived one murder, one execution, and an ugly spot of police brutality. We've had an election, of sorts, and established a government – of sorts.

'The scientists are happy. They've been studying Saturn's rings and made some startling discoveries. Now they're sending that ponderous landing vehicle of theirs down to the surface of Titan. Bloody monster's going to trundle around the place under control from up here in the habitat.

'I've been moved out of power, of course. It's better that way. If Eberly hadn't pushed me I would have removed myself. Nasty bit of blackmail, though; not pleasant at all. Nevertheless, my task here is to observe these people and see what kind of a society they ultimately produce for themselves. An anthropologist's dream: watching a new society being created.

'Ten thousand men and women. No children, of course. Not allowed. Not yet. Exiles, most of our population. Political dissidents and disbelievers who fell foul of their faith-based governments back on Earth. Locked into this artificial world, this man-made habitat. It's pleasant enough, physically. Better environment than most of them had on Earth, actually. But I wonder. Many of these people will live here permanently; they won't be allowed back to Earth.

Ten thousand hotheads and nonconformists. Physically they are adults, but they behave much like teenagers. Few of them accept responsibilities; they run from one fad to another: their latest is taking some form of enzyme injections to turn their skins a golden tan. Silly business, but typical of them. They live to play, not work. Except for the scientists, of course. And the engineers, I suppose. Actually, one shouldn't be surprised by their adolescent attitudes. What with their long life expectancies and the rejuvenation therapies that can stretch their lifespans into centuries, why shouldn't their adolescent years extend into their forties and fifties?

'But it troubles me. It would only take a few of these aged adolescents to cause enormous troubles. They could spread dissatisfaction and rebellion through the whole population like a viral infection. A few malcontents could wreck this habitat. A handful. Perhaps only one. How can they protect themselves against the outbreak of that kind of disease?

'It's going to be interesting to observe what happens.'

24 December 2095: Habitat *Goddard*

'*Titan Alpha* has landed!' the mission controller sang out. 'She's down safely.'

With a loud howl of triumph he yanked the communications plug out of his ear and tossed it to the steel-beamed ceiling of the crowded control center. For the past six days the tele-operated *Titan Alpha* had spiraled through the radiation-drenched vacuum between the massive habitat *Goddard* and Saturn's giant moon, cautiously orbiting Titan a dozen times before attempting to enter its thick, smoggy atmosphere. Now it had landed safely, and it was time for celebrating.

Eduoard Urbain felt an urgent need to urinate. He realized that he had been standing in front of the mission control center's main console for more than six hours, and now that the controllers were whooping and pounding each other on the back, he felt he could breathe again. And pee.

But it was not to be. Not yet. Standing beside him was Jacqueline Wexler, president of the International Consortium of Universities, from whom funding and promotion and prestige either flowed or was withheld.

At this moment of triumph, Dr. Wexler was all smiles and accolades.

'You've done it, Eduoard!' she enthused, over the bubbling chatter of the elated scientists and engineers. 'A successful landing. It's going to be a happy Christmas for us all.'

Urbain heard champagne corks popping, laughter and the raucous horseplay that comes when nerve-twisting tension is suddenly released. Although he felt the same joy and satisfaction, he had no desire to celebrate, no urge to behave foolishly. All he really wanted at this particular moment was to get to the urinal.

Wexler was not about to release him, though. She grasped his forearm with fleshless talon-like fingers, hard enough to make Urbain wince, and began to introduce him to the other Important Persons who had flown all the way out to Saturn for this momentous occasion.

She was hardly an imposing figure. Dr. Wexler looked hard, brittle, Urbain thought: a short, bony woman with an intense bird-like face and plain brown hair cut short, wearing a tailored tunic and deep blue slacks designed more to disguise her skeletal figure than to make a fashion statement. Yet she had power, and the ruthlessness to wield it. Back on Earth she was often called 'Attila the Honey.' Not to her face, of course.

Urbain himself was quite elegant. He had given a lot of thought to his wardrobe for this morning's event, and – with his wife's help and eventual approval – had selected a trim gray business suit with a soft Persian blue silk cravat.

Jeanmarie was in the crowd of onlookers, he knew. Searching for her, he finally saw her watching him, her eyes glowing with his success. She is beautiful, Urbain thought. Beautiful and happy, at last.

Thirty-seven university and news media VIPs had flown to this habitat in orbit around Saturn, courtesy of Pancho Lane and Astro Corporation. Normally, the men and women who directed the International Consortium of Universities preferred to remain on Earth and spend their money on research or teaching. Normally, news network executives sent their reporters afield while they remained in their opulent offices. But Pancho Lane was heading for the *Goddard* habitat and had invited the ICU and news media to send a contingent along with her, so here they were.

Urbain suffered through what seemed like an endless round of introductions. Wexler even introduced him to Professor

6

Wilmot, who had been aboard *Goddard* from the outset as its chief administrator, living and working with Urbain for nearly three years now.

'Good show today, Eduoard,' said Wilmot jovially as they clasped hands while Wexler beamed approvingly. 'Hope everything goes this well tomorrow.'

Tomorrow. Christmas Day. When they begin to turn on *Titan Alpha*'s sensors and start the exploration of Titan's surface.

'Have some champagne, Eduoard.' Wilmot proffered his own untouched plastic cup. 'You've earned it.'

'Er, not just yet, thank you,' Urbain replied. 'There is something I must do first.'

23 December 2095: The Day Before

The successful landing of *Titan Alpha* on the cloud-shrouded surface of Saturn's largest moon was not the only startling event aboard habitat *Goddard*. A day earlier, Pancho Lane had provided fireworks of a different sort.

Although she had officially retired as CEO of Astro Corporation, Pancho still had enough clout to commandeer the fusion torch ship *Starpower III* for a six-week flight to distant Saturn. And to bring a gaggle of ICU bigwigs and news executives with her, as well as her personal bodyguard and lover.

Pancho made her way up *Starpower III*'s paneled central passageway toward the bridge to watch the torch ship's approach to *Goddard* through the bridge's glassteel ports. Once an astronaut herself, she had no patience with sitting in her compartment and staring at a video display of the approach and docking. Nor was she in a mood to mingle with the passengers in the central lounge: flatlanders, most of them. Earthworms who had never been farther than the comfortable cities on the Moon and only traveled deeper into space in the luxury and safety of this commodious torch ship.

If the ship's captain or crew members felt uncomfortable with the retired head of the corporation poking around their bridge, they did their best to hide it. Pancho sat at the vacated life-support console, where she could gaze through the bridge's sweeping windows of heavily-tinted glassteel as *Starpower III* neared *Goddard*'s main docking port.

It took an effort to keep her eyes off Saturn. The planet

bulked huge and looming, nearly ten times bigger than Earth, striped with soft tan and muted yellow clouds whipping along at hyperhurricane velocities. White clouds circled the pole. Or is that an aurora? Pancho wondered. It's summertime down there in the southern hemisphere, she knew. Temperature's prob'ly gettin' close to a hundred and fifty below zero. They must be clouds, ice formations.

The rings were tipped so that Pancho could see them in all their dazzling complexity, glittering, glistening broad bands of gleaming ice chunks hanging in emptiness, stupendous rings many thousands of kilometers across, yet so thin that the stars shone through them. This close, Pancho could see that the rings were braided, countless individual rings woven together like a rich circular tapestry made of brilliant diamonds. Some of the scientists claimed that there were living creatures in those ice particles, extremophiles that thrived at temperatures near absolute zero.

Compared to gaudy Saturn and those radiant rings, the man-made *Goddard* was not much to look at, Pancho thought as she watched the massive habitat growing larger. It was a thick, ungainly cylinder, twenty kilometers long and four across, rotating slowly to produce an artificial gravity for the ten thousand men and women living inside it. It reminded Pancho of a stubby length of storm-drain pipe hanging in the emptiness, although as they neared it she could see that its surface was pebbled with observation bubbles, docking ports, antennas and other projections studding the cylinder's curving flank. And at about two thirds of the way along the cylinder stood the ring of solar mirrors, standing like a collar of flower petals, drinking in sunlight for the habitat's farms and electrical power and life support.

Susie's in there, Pancho thought. Then she remembered, Mustn't call her Susie any more. She changed her name to Holly. And it damned near killed her.

Despite her best intentions Pancho couldn't help feeling a

9

simmering resentment about her sister. Sooze was only three years younger than Pancho, as far as calendar age was concerned. But while Pancho had allowed her hair to go stark white and was taking rejuvenation therapies to stave off the encroachment of age, Susan was physically no more than thirty. And mentally, emotionally – Pancho grimaced at the thought.

Susan had died while she was a teenager. Pancho had administered the lethal injection herself, once the medical experts had woefully assured her that there was no hope of saving Susan from the drug-induced cancer that was ruining her body. So Pancho pushed the hypodermic syringe into her sister's emaciated arm and watched her die. As soon as she was pronounced clinically dead the medics slid her body into a heavy stainless steel sarcophagus, a coffin-sized dewar that they filled with liquid nitrogen, steaming white, deadly cold.

For more than twenty years Pancho guarded Susie's cryonically-preserved body, as she herself climbed the corporate ladder of power, from hell-raising astronaut to CEO and board chairman of Astro Corporation. Pancho directed Astro's side of the Second Asteroid War, and once that tragedy ground to its exhausted, blood-soaked finish, she had formally retired from Astro, to start a new life of – what? she asked herself. What am I doing here, all the way the hell out at Saturn. What am I going to do with the rest of my life?

Her immediate plans she knew. She was going to see her sister for the first time in nearly three years. Spend the holiday with the only family she had. The thought made her tense with apprehension.

Once Susan had been revived from her long years of cryonic suspension and her cancer removed by therapeutic nanomachines, she had been like a newborn baby in a young adult's body. The years she had spent bathed in liquid nitrogen had saved her body, but destroyed most of the synapses in the cerebral cortex of her brain. She had practically no higher brain functions. Pancho had to feed her, teach her to speak again and to walk, even toilet-train her.

Slowly, Susan became a mature adult, yet even when the psychologists happily proclaimed her training to be a complete success, Pancho was disturbed. She wasn't the same Susie. Couldn't be, Pancho realized, yet the difference unsettled her. She looked like Susie, talked and laughed and flirted like Sooze, but she was subtly different. When Pancho looked into her sister's eyes, it was somebody else in there. Almost the same. But only almost.

And the first thing Sooze did, once she was fully recovered, was to change her name and traipse out on the space habitat *Goddard* on this wild-ass mission to explore Saturn and its moon, Titan. She picked up and left Pancho behind, with a smile and a peck on the cheek and a perfunctory, 'Thanks for everything, Panch.' She ran off with that slimy sonofabitch Malcolm Eberly.

That was why Pancho was not in her most chipper and cheerful mood as *Starpower III* docked with *Goddard* and began to disembark its VIP passengers. She felt sullen resentment and an anger she believed to be completely justified. And she was more than a little apprehensive about how Susie would receive her. How's she gonna react to having her big sister drop in on her, after she's flown a billion and a half kilometers to get away from me? Merry Christmas, now go home: that was what Pancho feared her sister's attitude would be.

Stewing inside, juggling these emotions, Pancho made her way down the ship's central passageway to the main docking port after the skipper had announced they'd mated with *Goddard*. All the big muckety-muck scientists and news execs were gathering in the port's waiting area, chatting and buzzing impatiently. She saw Jake Wanamaker easily enough: he towered over the others. His craggy face broke into a smile as he spotted her and Pancho couldn't help but grin back at him.

'Hi, there, sailor,' she said once she had sidled through the gathering crowd to stand beside him. 'New in town?'

'Yes, ma'am,' answered Wanamaker, falling into the old routine. 'Thought maybe you'd show me the sights.'

They both laughed and Pancho felt better.

Until they finally stepped through the airlock and into *Goddard*'s reception area. The crowd was arranging itself into a straggly line as personnel from the habitat checked names and assigned the visitors to living quarters. Then Pancho spotted Susie, tall and lean as herself. She looks okay, Pancho thought, her heart leaping. She looks fine.

'Panch!' Sooze yelped, and she pushed through the line of notables toward her sister.

Mustn't call her Susan, Pancho reminded herself. She's Holly now.

Her sister threw her arms around Pancho's neck and Pancho knew it was going to be alright between them. No matter what, it was going to be okay. She introduced Holly to Jake, who took her hand in his meaty paw and said hello almost solemnly while Pancho beamed at them.

'C'mon, let's go to my place,' Holly said. 'You can find your apartment later, after the crowd's thinned out.'

Pancho happily followed her sister as far as the hatch that led out to the corridor beyond the reception area. Standing there was a handsome youngish man, hair the color of straw, swept in thick waves, strong cheekbones, thin straight nose, chiseled firm jaw and piercing sky-blue eyes. His face was sculpted so perfectly that Pancho guessed he'd had cosmetic therapy. What was that word the old-time racists used? she asked herself. The answer came to her swiftly: Aryan. That was what he looked like, the ideal Nordic hero. Yet below the neck he looked soft, a slight pot belly bulging his loosely-draped tunic. As if his face was all that mattered to him.

'Panch, this is Malcolm Eberly, *Goddard*'s chief administrator and—'

Pancho lashed out with her right fist in a lightning punch that caught Eberly's smiling face solidly on the jaw and knocked him backwards onto the seat of his pants.

'That's for damn near killing my sister, you no-good son-ofabitch,' Pancho snarled at him.

23 December 2095:
Habitat *Goddard* Reception Area

For an instant, nobody moved. No one spoke. Eberly shook his head groggily and sat up, rubbing the side of his face with one hand.

Holly broke the silence. 'Pancho! For god's sake!'

'It wasn't my doing,' Eberly said, almost in a whine. 'I tried to stop them.'

Pancho snorted and stepped past the man, suppressing an urge to kick him where it would do the most good. A pair of men in black coveralls moved toward her; both wore white armbands proclaiming SECURITY. Both had stun wands strapped to their hips. Wanamaker pushed in front of Pancho protectively.

'It's all right,' Eberly told the security guards as he slowly got to his feet. 'I'm not hurt.'

'Too bad,' Pancho huffed and, without a glance back, stepped through the open hatch.

Holly quickened her pace to catch up with her sister. 'Pancho, he's the elected head of this whole flamin' habitat!'

'He stood aside and let those New Morality bastards beat you half to death,' Pancho growled, walking determinedly down the short passageway, Wanamaker at her side.

'That's over and done with,' Holly said, from her other side. 'And they weren't New Morality; they were from the Holy Disciples.'

'Whatever.'

'The people responsible have been sent back Earthside. One of them was killed, executed, for creep's sake.'

14

Pancho stopped at the hatch set into the far end of the steel-walled passageway. 'Come on, let's get out of here before those network execs remember they're in the news business and start sniffing after me. Where the hell are we, anyway? Am I going in the right direction?'

Holly's anger dissolved; she grinned at her sister. 'Yep, this is right. C'mon, let me show you.' And she tapped out a code on the keypad next to the hatch.

Pancho looked back over her shoulder. Eberly was on his feet, the two security guards flanking him, several of the visiting executives peering curiously in Pancho's direction. Neither Eberly nor any of the incoming visitors had left the reception area though.

The hatch swung inward and Pancho felt a breath of warm air puff against her face. Still grinning, Holly made a little bow and, with a sweep of her arm, announced, 'Welcome to habitat *Goddard*.'

Pancho stepped through the hatch, Wanamaker right behind her. Despite her knowledge, despite her expectations, her jaw dropped open and she gasped with delighted surprise.

'Jumpin' jeeps,' she breathed. 'It's a whole *world* in here.'

They were standing on an elevated knoll, with a clear view of the habitat's broad interior. A green sunlit landscape stretched out in all directions around them. Gently rolling grassy hills, clumps of trees, little meandering streams went on and on into the hazy distance. Pancho's breath caught in her throat. So much greenery! she gasped silently. Nowhere off Earth had she seen such a . . . a . . . it was a paradise! A man-made Garden of Eden. The breeze was fragrant with the soft scent of flowers. Bushes thick with vivid red hibiscus and lavender jacarandas lined both sides of a curving path that led down to a village of low buildings, white and gleaming in the light streaming in through the solar windows that wrapped around the great cylinder like a ring of brilliant sunshine.

It looks like one of those Mediterranean towns, Pancho

thought. The village in the distance was set on the gentle slope of a grassy hill, overlooking a shimmering blue lake. Like the Amalfi coast in Italy. Like a picture out of a travel brochure. This was what a perfect Mediterranean countryside would look like. Farther in the distance she made out farmlands, square little fields of fresh bright green, and more villages of whitewashed buildings dotting the gently rolling hills. There was no horizon. Instead, the land simply curved up and up, hills and grass and trees and more little villages with their paved pathways and sparkling streams, up and up on both sides until she was craning her neck looking straight overhead at still more of the carefully, lovingly landscaped greenery.

'This is better'n any of the Lagrange-point habitats,' Pancho told her sister. 'This is *beautiful*.'

'It has to be,' Wanamaker said, matter-of-factly, 'for people to make it their permanent home.'

Pancho shook her head in wonderment and uttered a heartfelt, 'Wow.'

Holly beamed at them. 'And I'm in charge of the human resources department.'

'Really?' Pancho asked.

'F'real, Panch.'

They dispatched Wanamaker to find the quarters that he and Pancho had been assigned to while Holly led her sister to her own apartment.

'Home sweet home,' Holly announced as she ushered Pancho into her sitting room.

'Nice,' said Pancho, taking in the sparse furniture and minimal decorations. The place looked tidy and had that citrusy, almost antiseptic tang of a recent cleaning. She's tidied up the place for me, Pancho thought as she asked, 'Are those smart walls?'

'You bet. I can program them to show almost anything you want.' Holly went to the desk in the corner and picked up a

16

remote control wand. One entire wall of the room suddenly showed a real-time image of Saturn and its spectacular rings.

'Whoosh!' Pancho exclaimed. 'It's almost like being outside.'

'Sit.' Holly gestured toward the small sofa. 'I'll get us something cold to drink.'

Pancho sat on an upholstered chair while her sister went into the kitchen. Well, if she's cranked up about me dropping in on her, Pancho thought; she sure doesn't show it. She looks really glad to see me. Hope I didn't embarrass her too much, sockin' that Eberly creep.

'The walls don't have voice recognition circuits?' she asked.

'Turned it off,' Holly called from the kitchen. 'Too sensitive. Can't hold a conversation without the walls thinking you're talking to them.'

Pancho chuckled to herself as she pictured the wall screens flashing through a kaleidoscope of pictures while people chatted with one another.

From around the kitchen partition Holly brought in a tray holding two tall, frosted glasses and put it down on the coffee table, then sat beside her sister on the sofa.

'You're lookin' really good, kid,' Pancho said, with a beaming smile. 'Really good.'

'You, too,' Holly replied guardedly.

Anyone would recognize at a glance that they were sisters. Both women were tall and rangy: long, leggy and slim. Their skin color was slightly darker than a well-tanned Caucasian's. Both their faces were sharp-featured, with flaring cheekbones and square, stubborn chins. Their eyes were the same dark brown, bright with intelligence and wit. Pancho had let her hair go entirely white, and kept it cropped into a tight skullcap. Holly's hair was still dark and cut in the latest spiky fashion.

'Is Eberly really the chief administrator for this whole habitat?' Pancho asked, reaching for one of the glasses.

'All ten thousand of us,' Holly replied. 'He won a free and fair election.'

'But he was involved with those fanatics who tried to kill you. How can—'

'That's all in the past, Panch. And he did try to stop them, y'know. Not very effectively, 'course, but he did try.'

Almost sheepishly, Pancho said, 'Guess I shouldn't have decked him.'

Holly giggled. 'He sure looked surprised.'

Pancho grinned back at her and took a sip of her drink. Fruit juice. Good. Susie had done more than her share of booze and drugs. Holly was different, Pancho hoped.

'Panch, why'd you come all the way out here?' Tension showed in the tone of Holly's voice, in the sudden stiffness of her body.

'To spend the holiday with you, of course,' Pancho answered, trying to make it sound warm, natural. 'You're the only family I've got.'

Holly tried to unbend. 'I mean, what do you intend to do here? This habitat isn't a tourist resort, y'know.'

Pancho's smile dimmed a little. 'Listen, Sis, I'm a rich woman, a retired multimillionaire. I got a terrific guy living with me, and we can go anywhere in the solar system we want. I decided to come out here and see how you're doin'.'

'I'm fine.'

'Don't be a shit-kicker, kid. I'm not here to pry into your life or try to tell you what to do. You're a big girl now, Sooze, and I wouldn't—'

'My name isn't Susan any more,' Holly snapped. 'Hasn't been for years.'

Pancho grimaced. 'Yeah, I know. I'm sorry. Just slipped out.'

'And if you're still worried about me and Malcolm Eberly, you can stop worrying. That's over. Never got started, really.'

'I should think so, after what he did to you.'

'Not him, really. His friends. They tried to take over the habitat. It got a little rough for a while.'

'But it's all over now?'

'His friends were shipped back Earthside. Malcolm's the chief of the habitat's government.'

Pancho's brows rose. 'I thought Professor Wilmot was in charge.'

'Not any more. We set up our own constitution and government and all that soon's we reached Saturn orbit.'

'And Eberly was elected to head it?'

'That's right.'

'I wonder if he'll take any action against me for sockin' him.'

Holly thought a moment, then shook her head. 'If he'd wanted to, he'd've got the security guards to take you into custody right there and then.'

'You think?'

'Yep.' Holly's grin broke out again. 'He knows he deserved what you gave him.'

Pancho grinned back at her. 'You know the old saying about Hungarians?'

'Hungarians?'

'If you meet a Hungarian on the street, kick him. He'll know why.'

The sisters laughed together, long and loud and unforced. But then Holly asked, 'How long're you going to stay?'

'Jeeps, kid, I just got here! Give me enough time to unpack my bags, huh?'

Frowning, Holly said, 'I didn't mean it that way, Panch. It's just . . . well, I don't need a mother hen any more. I've been on my own for more'n three years now.'

Pancho grinned at her. 'And you don't want your pain-in-the-butt big sister lookin' over your shoulder. Can't say I blame you.'

Shifting her tactics a bit, Holly asked, 'So who's this guy you came with?'

'Jake Wanamaker?' Pancho's grin turned mischievous. 'Former admiral in the U.S. Navy. Headed military operations for Astro during the fighting out in the Belt.'

'You're living with a sailor?'

'He's my bodyguard.'

Holly looked at her sister for a long moment, then they both burst into laughter again.

'Wanna have dinner with us tonight?' Pancho asked.

'Cosmic! And I'll bring a friend, too.'

'Great!' said Pancho, with real enthusiasm. Maybe the ice is breaking a little, she thought. Maybe things will be okay between Sooze and me. Then she admonished herself, Don't call her that. Her name's not Susan any more. She's Holly. Holly. But looking into her sister's deep brown eyes, Pancho remembered the helpless baby that she had raised after their parents died. And she remembered shooting home the lethal injection that killed Susan when the medics refused to do it.

I had to kill you, Susie, Pancho said silently. So you could be reborn. And here you are, alive and healthy, all grown up, and suspicious as hell about your big sister.

Data Bank: Titan

This much is known about Titan, by far the largest of Saturn's several dozen moons and the second largest moon in the entire solar system.

With a diameter of 5150 kilometers, Titan is bigger than the planet Mercury and only a shade smaller than Jupiter's largest satellite, Ganymede. Titan is the only moon in the solar system to possess a substantial atmosphere. Indeed, Titan's atmosphere is fifty per cent denser than Earth's at ground level.

That atmosphere is composed mainly of nitrogen, laced with hydrocarbons such as methane, ethane and propane, plus nitrogen-carbon compounds such as hydrogen cyanide, cyanogen and cyanoacetelyne. Shine sunlight on such an atmosphere and you get the same result you would in Los Angeles or Tokyo or Mexico City: photochemical smog, induced by solar ultraviolet light. Titan is a smog-covered world. Its predominantly orange coloring is due to this smog, which blankets Titan and makes it necessary for observations of its surface to be carried out at infrared wavelengths, which penetrate the smog, rather than with visible light, which does not.

The incoming solar ultraviolet light, together with energetic electrons from nearby Saturn's powerful magnetosphere, produces complex chemical reactions high in Titan's thick atmosphere. Organic polymers called *tholins* are created, to drift downward deeper into the atmosphere and eventually fall onto the moon's surface: black snow.

Laboratory experiments on Earth showed that tholins, when

dissolved in liquid water, yield amino acids, which are the building-block molecules of proteins, and thus fundamental to life.

Orbiting more than a million kilometers from Saturn, which in turn lies twice as far from the Sun as Jupiter and ten times farther from the Sun than the Earth does, Titan's surface temperature averages -183° Celsius. Titan is *cold*, too cold to have liquid water on its surface – except when a region might be heated temporarily by a volcanic eruption or the impact of a meteor. Or if the water is mixed with an antifreeze compound, such as ammonia or ethane derivatives.

Titan's density is not quite twice that of water, which means that its body must be composed largely of ices – frozen water and/or frozen methane – with perhaps a small rocky core beneath a thick icy mantle.

Despite Titan's low temperature, liquid droplets of ethane can form in its atmosphere and rain down onto the frigid surface, collecting as lakes or perhaps larger seas. There are streams of ethane (or ethane-laced water) carving out channels across the icy ground. Several sizable seas of hydrocarbon-crusted liquid methane dot the moon's surface.

Titan rotates on its axis in slightly less than sixteen Earth days, the same period as its orbit around Saturn. Thus Titan is 'locked' in its rotation so that it always presents the same face to its planet, Saturn, just as our Moon presents the same face to Earth. But even a 'locked' moon wobbles slightly in its orbit, and Titan's rotation is perturbed slightly by its sizable neighbors, the moons Rhea and Hyperion, each of which is close to 1500 kilometers in diameter. Titan rocks slightly back and forth as it orbits Saturn, a ponderous wobbling that creates strange tides in its hydrocarbon seas.

A world rich in carbon, hydrogen and nitrogen. A world where raindrops of ethane and sooty flakes of tholins fall from the smoggy sky. A world that contains rivers and streams of ethane or ethane-laced water, and methane seas. Although it is a very cold world, a primitive form of microbial cryogenic biology was found to exist on Titan's surface by the earliest automated probes from distant Earth. Could there be a more sophisticated biosphere, perhaps deeper underground?

And there are large swaths of dark material carpeting parts of Titan's surface. Early probes showed that they are rich in carbon compounds. Fields of frozen petroleum? Patches of solidified hydrocarbons? Swales of black tholin snowbanks piled on ground that is too cold for them to melt?

Or something else?

24 December 2095:
Christmas Eve Party

Eduoard Urbain smiled uneasily as he shook hands, one by one, with each member of his scientific and engineering staffs. They shuffled themselves into a reception line the moment he entered the auditorium, like serfs of old lining up with their hats in their hands to receive the Christmas blessing of their lord and master.

Jeanmarie, standing beside him, smiled graciously and spoke a few words to every man and woman presented to her. She is wonderful, Urbain thought as he shook hand after hand. She is in her element, kind and warm and loving. I would be lost without her. The line seemed endless, and Urbain struggled to find something worth saying, something more than 'Merry Christmas' endlessly repeated.

At last it was done. Urbain rubbed his numbed hand and looked out over the assembly. Two hundred men and women, he thought. One hundred and ninety-four, to be precise. It was such a small number to run the scientific investigation of Saturn, its rings, and its moons. But when you must greet each one individually it seemed like a very large number indeed.

Nadia Wunderly was one of the last persons that Urbain had greeted. She was the maverick among his scientists, and although she had brought Urbain sudden and unexpected success, he still regarded her with a mixture of disquiet and, yes, jealousy. She had refused to follow his orders and join the others in the study of Titan. Instead she had focused single-mindedly on Saturn's rings. And discovered organisms living in their particles of ice. A great discovery, if it held true.

Wexler and her ICU lackeys seemed to harbor some doubts about Wunderly's claim.

Now Wunderly drifted from the reception line to the make-shift bar that had been set up along the base of the auditorium's stage. She was a young woman, not yet thirty, with a rather pretty heart-shaped face. Urbain thought she would look even prettier if she stopped dyeing her hair brick red, and let it grow normally instead of chopping it into those ridiculous barbs; her hair looked like the spiked end of a medieval bludgeon. She was wearing her usual dark tunic and slacks, which was unfortunate: her figure was ample, too ample for his taste. Buxom, yes, but also heavyset, thick in the waist and limbs.

He mentally compared her with his wife. Slim and elegant, Jeanmarie would commit suicide before letting herself gain that much weight, he thought.

Wunderly was also looking at Jeanmarie Urbain. Slim as a stylus, she thought. One of those lucky women who had a metabolism that burned calories faster than she could ingest them. Probably never had to diet a day in her life. She can wear those frilly dresses and look gorgeous in them. I'd look like a hippopotamus in a tutu.

But that's all changing, Wunderly told herself. I've dropped five kilos in the past two weeks and I'm going to lose another three before New Year's Eve. Now for the real test.

One of the guys behind the bar offered her a cup of eggnog. Wunderly almost took it before she pulled her hand back and asked for mineral water, instead.

The guy – one of the technicians who worked with the *Titan Alpha* engineers – grinned at her. 'One glass of genuine recycled local aitch-two-oh, courtesy of the waste management department,' he said cheerfully, handing her a glass.

Wunderly grinned at him. 'You can't scare me.'

He grinned back. 'Ho, ho, ho and all that, Nadia.'

'Same to you,' she said, then walked away from the bar, into the milling throng.

The speakers set up at either end of the stage were pouring out syrupy Christmas tunes. Somehow they made Wunderly feel sad. *Have yourself a merry little Christmas.* Sure. A billion kilometers from home. *Well, at least I can go home when I'm ready. Most of the poor slobs in this habitat can't.*

Then she saw him, standing by himself, off in the corner where the stage met the auditorium's side wall. Squaring her shoulders like a soldier heading into battle, she pushed through the crowd at the bar and went toward her target.

Da'ud Habib was chief of the computer group. He didn't look like the other computer geeks, scruffy and rumpled. He was wearing a crisply pressed red sport shirt over his slacks. Sandals, though, and no socks. Actually, he was almost kind of handsome, Wunderly thought. He kept the dark little beard that fringed his jaw neat and trim. His eyes were a deep liquid brown. But he was pretty much of a loner, a quiet guy. His ancestry was Arabic, she knew. She had looked up his dossier: he'd been born and raised in Vancouver, in a Moslem neighborhood, but he was more Canadian than anything else. At least, she hoped so.

'Hi,' she said, as soon as she was close enough.

He looked a little surprised. 'Hello.'

'I'm Nadia Wunderly.'

'I know. You found the creatures in the rings.'

Nadia smiled her best. 'That's me. Lord of the rings, they call me.'

He smiled back uncertainly. 'Er, shouldn't it be "lady of the rings"?'

'Literary license.'

'Ah. I see.'

'Is it okay to wish you a merry Christmas?'

'Of course. I'm not anti-Christian. I've always enjoyed the Christmas season; the shopping, the music, all that.'

Wunderly took a sip of her water. Habib was drinking something that looked fizzy to her. Probably non-alcoholic, she thought.

26

'You're Da'ud Habib, aren't you?'

'Oh! I should have introduced myself. I'm sorry.'

'No problem. You're chief of the computing group, right?'

'Lord of the nerds, yes.'

She laughed and he laughed with her.

'Big day tomorrow,' she said, trying to figure out how to turn the conversation into the path she wanted.

Habib nodded again. 'Urbain's Christmas present to himself.'

She took a breath and plunged ahead. 'The New Year's Eve party is a week from tonight.'

'Oh? Yes, I suppose so.'

'Are you going?'

He looked almost alarmed by her question. He actually backed away from her a step. 'Me? I . . . I hadn't thought about it.'

Wunderly could hear her pulse thumping in her ears. Stepping closer to Habib she asked, 'Would you like to go with me? I mean, I don't have a date for the party and I thought we could go together.'

His brow wrinkled slightly and she held her breath.

'Go with you?' It seemed like a totally new idea to him, something he would never have thought of by himself.

Don't make me beg, she pleaded silently.

He seemed to understand, or maybe see it in her eyes. 'Why, yes, I suppose so. I wasn't planning on going . . .' He brightened slowly and smiled again, wider this time. 'But why not? I'd be happy to go with you.'

Wunderly wanted to laugh with delight, but she reined herself in and said merely, 'Great! Then it's a date.'

25 December 2095:
Mission Control Center

Christmas morning, but no one on the scientific staff was taking a holiday. Not yet. The mission control center was never meant to hold so many people, Urbain thought nervously as he stood sandwiched between Dr. Wexler and Professor Wilmot. The morning shift of technicians had to worm their way through the crowd to get to their consoles. Packed in behind the last row of the consoles, the university notables and news executives stood shoulder to shoulder, making the chamber hot, sweaty, with the press of their bodies. Their murmured conversations sounded like the drone of insects on a summer day back in Urbain's childhood in Quebec.

He felt as edgy as a twitching rabbit, especially with Wexler standing beside him, and some three dozen other guests squeezed into the control center. Even the redoubtable Pancho Lane, the newly-retired industrialist, had flown out to Saturn for this momentous event. The only lights in the circular chamber came from the screens on the consoles of the control staff. In the flickering light reflecting off the dark, blank wall screen Urbain looked up to see Professor Wilmot smiling expectantly beside him.

'The first data from your surface probe,' said Wexler, beaming at him. 'This is a memorable Christmas for science, Edouard.'

Urbain nodded tightly. He was a short, wiry man, the kind who never worried about his weight because everything he ate turned into nervous energy. His dark hair was slicked straight

28

back from his high forehead, his beard was neatly trimmed. As he had yesterday, he wore his best suit for this moment; after all, half the people crammed into the control center were from the news media.

The high and mighty of the International Consortium of Universities had not always smiled upon Edouard Urbain. When this expedition to Saturn had started, nearly three years earlier, Urbain had been regarded as a second-rater, a competent worker but no blazing star. He was chosen to head the scientific staff that rode the immense habitat *Goddard* out to Saturn to take up a polar orbit about the ringed planet because Urbain and his team were regarded merely as caretakers, meant only to make routine observations and babysit the scientific equipment during *Goddard*'s slow, two-year voyage out to Saturn. Once the habitat was safely in orbit there, the world's top planetary scientists would dash out on a fusion torch ship to take up the tasks of investigating Saturn and, more importantly, its giant moon, Titan.

As far as Urbain was concerned, however, the ten thousand men and women who made up *Goddard*'s self-contained community existed solely to service the handful of scientists and engineers under his authority. Urbain spent almost every waking moment of those two years driving his engineering staff to build *Titan Alpha*, Urbain's dream, the offspring of his mind, the product of his lifelong hope. Part spacecraft, part armored tractor, *Titan Alpha* was meant to carry the most sophisticated sensors and computers conceivable to the surface of Titan and use them to explore that frigid, smog-shrouded world under real-time control from scientists in *Goddard*.

Even as he built the massive exploratory vehicle, Urbain knew in his heart that other, more prominent scientists would be the ones to use it, to guide it across Titan's fields of ice, to gain glory and recognition out of his sweat and toil. It was one of those accidents that dot the history of scientific research that changed all that. Nadia Wunderly, one of Urbain's lowly assistants, a stubborn woman at best, insisted on studying Saturn's rings. The rest of his scientific team were focused exclusively on Titan, for that massive moon was known to bear life; microscopic organisms that lived in the petrochemical soup that covered part of Titan's icy surface.

Wunderly discovered what might be a new form of living organism dwelling in Saturn's rings. As her director, Urbain received much of the credit for this revelation. And, perversely, won the right to direct *Titan Alpha* in its exploration of the giant moon's surface.

Now he basked in the attention of the solar system's most important scientists as his creation, his offspring, his dream come true – *Titan Alpha* – began to send data from its sensors on the frozen surface of Titan.

Urbain held his breath. The jam-packed control center went eerily silent.

The wall screen lit up to show: SYSTEMS ACTIVATION.

Deep inside *Titan Alpha*'s armored hide, its central computer began to receive commands through its downlink antenna.

Command: Systems activation.

Communications downlink confirmed. Code accepted. Systems activation procedures initiated.

Main power on.

Auxiliary power standing by.

Central computer self-checking. Self-check completed. Central computer functional.

Command: Check structural integrity.

Initiating structural integrity check. Outer shell intact. Structural members intact. No deformities beyond allowable limits. Interior compartments intact and pressurized.

Command: Test propulsion system.

Propulsion system test initiated. Reactor within nominal limits. Main engine within nominal limits. Drive wheels functional but not engaged. Plates four-fourteen through four-twenty-two of left forward tread slightly deformed but within operational limits.

    Command: Retract descent parachute shroud.

Descent parachute shroud retracted.

    Command: Retract descent retro rocket pod.

Descent retro rocket pod retracted.

    Command: Activate sensors.

Sensors activated.

    Command: Uplink sensor data.

UPLINK SENSOR DATA.

    Except for those bright yellow block letters the main wall screen in the command center remained blank. Several seconds ticked by. Urbain felt perspiration break out on his brow. Wexler, the ICU president, stirred uneasily. Muttering broke out in the crowd behind Urbain's back. He even heard a hurtful snicker.

    A full minute passed.

    'We should be receiving data,' Urbain said, in a deathly whisper.

    Wexler said nothing.

    'Is it workin'?' a woman asked loudly. Pancho Lane, Urbain realized.

    DATA UPLINK ABORTED.

    Urbain stared at the words, hard and bright on the dark blue background of the wall screen. My death sentence, he said to himself. It would have been kinder to take a pistol and shoot me through my head.

25 December 2095: Christmas Dinner

'You mean nothing came through?' Kris Cardenas asked.

'Not a damn thing,' said Pancho. 'The probe went silent soon's they ordered the data uplink.'

This Christmas dinner in the habitat's quiet little Bistro restaurant had been intended as a reunion. Pancho hadn't seen Cardenas in nearly five years.

Holly had brought her friend, a silent, morose-looking young man named Raoul Tavalera. With his long, horsy face and mistrustful brown eyes he reminded Pancho of Eeyore, from the old Winnie-the-Pooh vids. Tavalera said very little; he just sat beside Holly looking sad, sullen, worried. It's Christmas, Pancho scolded him silently. Lighten up, for cripes sake. But Holly seemed quite happy with the lug. No accounting for taste, Pancho thought. Maybe he's good in bed.

The three couples were sitting at one of the Bistro's outdoor tables, on the grass. The restaurant's special holiday menu featured faux turkey, faux goose, and faux ham – all derived from the genetically-modified protein that the biolab produced. The vegetables, sauces, and desserts were fresh from the habitat's farms, however.

Wanamaker sat beside Pancho, while Cardenas had brought a hunky guy wearing faded jeans and a mesh shirt that showed off his pecs nicely. She introduced him as Manuel Gaeta.

'The stunt guy?' Pancho had asked, recognizing his rugged, slightly beat-up face.

'Retired stunt guy,' Gaeta had replied, with an easy smile.

'You flew through the rings of Saturn,' said Wanamaker in his deep gravelly voice, 'without a spacecraft.'

'I was wearing a suit. A pretty special suit.'

'The ice creatures that live in the rings almost killed Manny,' Cardenas said. 'At one point he was totally encased in ice.'

'So you're the one who really discovered the ice bugs,' Pancho said, reaching for her wine. 'How come they gave the credit to that woman?'

'She's a scientist,' Gaeta replied easily. 'I'm just a stunt stud.'

As they relaxed over a bottle of local Chablis, Pancho leaned back in her yielding plastic chair and admired the view. Everything's so damned clean and tidy: the grass is manicured and the trees prob'ly drop their leaves in neat little piles so you can vacuum 'em up one-two-three. And instead of sky overhead there's more land! Clean little whitewashed villages and roads in-between 'em. She could see the lights marking the paths like stars as the big solar windows shut down for the night. You can have an outdoor restaurant here without ever worryin' about rain, she said to herself. They don't even use sprinklers for the grass; underground drip hoses instead.

Wanamaker, looking overdressed compared to Gaeta and Tavalera in a neatly-pressed short-sleeve shirt and dark blue slacks, mused aloud, 'I wonder if the Titan probe touched down in one of the methane seas and just sank to the bottom.'

'That's a Navy man talkin',' Holly joked.

Pancho said, 'They know where it landed. It's on solid ground. The dingus sent telemetry confirming its landing and checked out all its internal systems. Then it shut itself down; won't talk to Urbain's people. Not a peep all day.'

'Poor Urbain,' Cardenas said. 'He must be going crazy.'

Jeanmarie Urbain stared at her husband. She had never seen him like this. Ever since returning from the control center he had paced about their apartment, his face dark as a thunder-cloud, his eyes sullen, accusing. He cancelled the Christmas dinner that had been scheduled with Wexler and the other visiting notables. When she asked him what had gone wrong, all he did was snap at her.

This was not the Eduoard she knew, the patient, gentle man who had spent his life watching others climb past him; the man who was content to allow younger scientists to advance while he stayed in place, who timidly acceded to the directives and procedures of the university hierarchies. I have misjudged him all these years, Jeanmarie realized. He was not being timid; he didn't *care*. As long as he was allowed to pursue his own research interests, none of the politics mattered to him one iota. Even my nagging him to seek advancement he shrugged off as if it meant nothing to him.

Jeanmarie had refused to go with him on this five-year mission to Saturn. It was the final blow. He had no self-respect, she felt, and no appreciation for her feelings. He was being sent into oblivion, a second-rate scientist assigned to obscurity in the farthest reaches of the solar system. She was still young, desirable. Some called her vivacious. Even among the sharp-clawed faculty wives she was considered attractive. *Too bad Jeanmarie's burdened with that husband of hers*, she had overheard more than once. *She could do much better.*

But he had unexpectedly returned from Saturn, full of fire and confidence. One of his scientists had made an important discovery, which made him an important person. He dined with the head of the International Consortium of Universities, he was invited to lecture at the Sorbonne. He stayed on Earth only long enough to accept acclaim for the discovery of the ice creatures in Saturn's rings and to reveal his plans for exploring Titan with the robotic vehicle he had built. And to sweep Jeanmarie back into his life. She realized that she loved him, that she had put up with his failings and lack of drive all those years because she truly loved him. When he returned to the habitat orbiting Saturn she was at his side.

This mission to Saturn has changed him, she realized. Now he cares. He's tasted glory; now he understands that one must have power in order to succeed. Now he wants to be admired, respected.

And now this failure. His robot sat dead, inert, useless on the surface of Titan. It was enough to make a man weep.

But Eduoard did not weep. He seethed. He fumed like a volcano about to erupt. He paced their sitting room radiating anger and frustration. All the passion he had kept bottled up inside him when he was among his scientists came boiling out now that he was alone with her.

'Dolts,' he muttered. 'Idiots. All of them. From Wexler on down.'

'Eduoard,' Jeanmarie said as soothingly as she could, 'perhaps it is only temporary. Perhaps tomorrow the probe will respond.'

He glowered at her. 'You should have heard them. The high and mighty geniuses. Throwing off theories like little children tossing handfuls of leaves into the air.'

She saw the fury in his face.

'It must be a programming error,' he whined in falsetto, mimicking Wexler's penetrating nasality. Then, in a deeper voice, 'No, it has to be an antenna malfunction. No, there must be damage from the entry into the atmosphere. No, it must be . . . must be . . .'

His face was so red she feared a blood vessel would burst. Balling his hands into fists he shook them above his head. 'Fools! Stupid, smug, self-important idiots! And all of them staring at me. I could see it in their eyes. *Failure!* That's what they think of me. I'm a failure.'

Only then did Eduoard Urbain actually break into tears, deep racking sobs that tore at Jeanmarie's heart. She folded her arms about him and gently led him toward their bedroom, wondering to herself, what can I do to ease his pain? How can I help him? How?

At the Bistro restaurant, Pancho had tipped her chair back to a precarious angle and lifted her softbooted feet off the grass, balancing herself teeteringly on the chair's back legs.

'You could get hurt if the chair goes over,' Gaeta warned.

She grinned at him, slightly drunk from the wine and cognac they had absorbed. 'Wanna bet I can keep it on two legs longer'n you can?'

Gaeta shook his head. 'No thanks.'

'You're a stuntman, ain'tcha?' Pancho teased. 'You laugh at danger, right?'

'I do stunts for money, Pancho. I don't risk my spinal cord on an after-dinner dare.'

'Betcha a hundred. How's that?'

Kris Cardenas grasped Gaeta's hand beforc he could reply. 'Manny has better things to do than play games with you, Pancho.'

Pancho let the chair drop forward. 'Like, play games with you, Kris?'

Cardenas smiled, sphinx-like.

Turning to Holly and her guy, Pancho asked, 'How 'bout you, Raoul? I'll give you odds: five to one.'

Holly got up from her chair. 'We've got to be going, Panch. Thanks for the dinner.'

'Welcome,' Pancho slurred.

Her sister smiled. 'This was the best Christmas I've had in a long time, Panch. The best I can remember, f'real.'

Slouching back in her chair, Pancho drank in the warmth of Holly's smile. 'Me too, kid. Me too.'

Wanamaker said, 'It's time we got to bed, too, Pancho.'

'Oh? Whatcha got in mind?'

He laughed, but Pancho caught a hint of embarrassment in it.

36

As they got up from the table, Holly asked, 'Are you going to watch them try to make contact with *Titan Alpha* tomorrow?'

With a shake of her head, Pancho replied, 'I been disinvited. Nobody allowed into the control center tomorrow except the workin' crew.'

'I'll bet Wexler will be there,' said Cardenas. 'Urbain can't lock her out.'

Turning curious, Pancho asked, 'I heard you were gonna lace the probe with nanomachines.'

'We had talked about it, Urbain and I,' Cardenas said as they started up the path that led back to the village's apartment buildings. 'But he sent the beast down to Titan before I could work up the nanos for him. Impatient.'

'Bet he wishes he had 'em on board now.'

'Maybe,' Cardenas said guardedly. 'Frankly, Pancho, I'm just as glad they're not. He'd be blaming me for whatever glitch has shut down his beast.'

Timoshenko's Message

'I know you can't send an answer back, they won't let you do that. It's okay. Well, no, it's not really okay but I understand. I'm an exile, a non-person, and it would be dangerous for you to reply to me or even admit you've received a message from me. Still, I wish there was some way for you to let me know you at least get my messages. I don't care even if you don't listen to them; it's just so damned lonely out here not knowing if you even received them.

'Big doings among the high-and-mighty scientists. The big lump of a probe they sent down to Titan's surface isn't talking to them. Just sitting there on the ice like the big pile of junk that it is. Makes me laugh. I worked for more than a year on that machine, on my own time, even. Put a lot of sweat into it. And for what? Like everything else in my life, it's all been for nothing.

'Urbain is tearing his hair out, what's left of it. The other scientists are running around like chickens, trying to figure out what went wrong. Me? I sit all alone here in the navigation center with nothing to do. That's where I am now, talking to you. Oh, I check the instruments, but we're in orbit around Saturn now. We're just going around in circles. No more navigation. No more propulsion. The only problem we could possibly have is if some chunk of ice hit the outer shell and broke one of the superconducting wires of the radiation shield. Then we'd have to go outside and fix it. It would be a relief from the boredom.

'I miss you. I know we fought when I had to leave and it was

38

all my fault. I can see that now. I've made a mess of everything. The only thing I hope for is that I haven't made a mess of your life too, Katrina. You deserve a good life with a man who loves you and can give you good, healthy kids.

'Me, I'm here in this fancy Siberia forever. It's not bad, really. I'm a free man, as free as you can be in this glorified tin can. I even ran for political office. Can you imagine? Me! I lost, of course, but it was a different experience, let me tell you.

'I miss you. I know it's too late, but I want you to know that I love you, dear Katrina. I'm sorry I ruined our lives.'

26 December 2095: Morning

Malcolm Eberly had worked hard to reach his lofty position as *Goddard*'s chief administrator. Plucked from an Austrian prison cell on the promise that he would set up a fundamentalist government among the habitat's ten thousand souls, he had outmaneuvered the murdering zealots who'd been sent to keep watch over him and now he stood at the head of the habitat's administration, admired and respected.

Truth to tell, most of the habitat's population didn't give a damn about their own government, so long as no one bothered them with rules and regulations. They had been picked from the dissatisfied, disaffected free thinkers, men and women who had fallen foul of the authoritarian fundamentalist regimes of Earth. They were dissidents, idealists, troublemakers. Now they were more than a billion kilometers away from Earth, and for the most part both they and the Earthside politicians felt better for it.

But they admire me, Eberly told himself as he strolled down from the center of Athens to the lovely little lake at the village's edge on his morning constitutional. They voted for me overwhelmingly. As long as I don't saddle them with too many restrictions, they ought to keep on voting for me.

That business a few days ago with Pancho Lane troubled him, though. She certainly surprised me. Eberly touched his jaw where Pancho had hit him. It still felt slightly swollen but the teeth weren't loose, thank goodness. The people are all buzzing about it: Pancho Lane knocked down the chief administrator and he just laughed it off. Does it make me look noble, forgiving? Or weak and cowardly?

He ambled once around the lake, passing people afoot or on electrobikes. They all gave him respectful hellos or smiled their greetings at him. He nodded and smiled back automatically. Normally he would bask in their admiration, but this morning his mind was on Pancho Lane. Why did she come here? A woman of her wealth and power doesn't travel to the edge of civilization merely to see her sister. She could talk to Holly any time she wishes, electronically. There must be something more to it. There's got to be.

He barely noticed that the sunlight didn't seem as bright as usual as he finished his morning's walk and started back up the slight rise of Athens' main street, heading for the administration headquarters at the top of the hill. Once in his office, he leaned back in his desk chair and steepled his fingers before his face, considering this new aspect of his situation. What are Pancho's intentions? Does she plan to stay in this habitat indefinitely? Will she apply for citizenship? She was the CEO of a huge corporation until she retired. What if she's come to take control of this habitat? Will she run against me in next year's election? Could she throw me out of office?

His face clenching into a worried scowl, Eberly regretted allowing the habitat's constitution to call for elections every year. His original reasoning had been clear enough: Give the population the illusion that they have control over their government by allowing them to vote every year. They'll think their leaders will be responsive to their wishes because there's always a new election coming up. In actuality, Eberly had figured, the more often they have to vote the fewer of them will bother. Most of our so-called citizens are lazy and complacent. As long as they don't have any major grievances with their government they'll allow me to stay in office.

And I'll be a good ruler for them. I'll be just and fair. I'll do what is needed. I'll use my power for good, he told himself. Leaning back in his desk chair, Eberly pictured an endless future of power and happiness. Power brings respect, he knew. After two or three elections everyone will admire me so much that I'll be able to do away with elections altogether. And with life extension therapies I can be the head of this habitat indefinitely. Me, Malcolm Eberly. They'll all look up to me. They'll have to.

But Pancho Lane is a force to be reckoned with, he told himself, clenching his teeth in simmering resentment. She made me look like a fool. That can't go unavenged, unanswered. I've got to deal with her. I've got to get even with her.

His decision made, Eberly told his computer to display his morning's appointments. The list appeared immediately on the smart wall to his left. He found it easier to read off the flat wall screen than to peer at a three-dimensional image hovering in the air above his desk.

The chief of the maintenance department wanted to see him. Frowning, he returned the call. The engineer's image appeared on the wall opposite the appointments list.

'We're having a problem with one of the solar mirrors,' said Felix Aaronson, the maintenance chief. His round, fleshy face looked nettled, more irritated than worried. Something about his complexion seemed different, as if he'd been sunning himself and had acquired a light golden tan. How can he do his job and have time for sunbathing? Eberly asked himself.

Eberly did not particularly like Aaronson. The man was a paranoid, always full of anxiety. Still, he put a smile on his face as he replied, 'A problem?'

'One of the mirror segments's out of alignment. Not much, but we might have to send a crew outside to set it right again.'

So why bother me? Eberly complained to himself. But he kept his smile in place and replied, 'If the mirror needs to be fixed, fix it.'

Stubbornly, the maintenance chief shook his head. 'But it shouldn't be out of alignment, man. All the diagnostics check out. Nothing's hit it and nobody's given a command to shift its position.'

'It's a piece of machinery,' said Eberly. 'Machinery doesn't always work the way it should, does it?'

'You don't get it. We've got all the diagnostics and the computer extrapolations and this shouldn't have happened.'

'But it did.'

'Yeah, it did,' he answered, sullenly.

'Then please fix it and stop bothering me with your responsibilities. I have other things to do.'

The maintenance chief mumbled an apology and promised to get right onto the problem.

'Good,' Eberly snapped. As soon as the man's face winked off his wall screen Eberly told his phone, 'Call Holly Lane. Tell her I want to see her at . . .' he studied his appointments list for a moment . . . 'ten-fifteen this morning.'

Precisely at ten-fifteen Holly appeared at his office door, dressed in a sleeveless pale green blouse and darker green slacks that emphasized her long legs. Tasteful hints of jewelry at her wrists and earlobes. No tattoos or piercings, Eberly noted thankfully. Holly had outgrown those fads. Yet even though she nominally followed the dress code he had set down more than a year ago, her blouse was cut to reveal her flat midriff. Others do such things, too, he knew. They obey the letter of the code but wear mesh see-throughs or snip strategic cutouts in their tunics or wear skin-tight outfits that leave little to the imagination.

'You wanted to see me?' Holly asked from the doorway. Once, when they had first started on the journey to Saturn, she had been like an eager little puppy whenever Eberly deigned to notice her. Now she was more adult, more sure of herself, less worshipful.

'Have a seat, Holly,' Eberly said, pointing.

She went to the minimalist Scandinavian chrome-and-leather chair before his immaculately clear desk and perched on its front six centimeters.

'I've got a meeting in fifteen minutes,' Holly informed him. 'Water allotment committee.'

'This won't take long. I was just wondering about your sister.'

Holly frowned. 'I'm sorry Pancho socked you. She can be a real wrecking crew sometimes.'

'Tell me about it,' Eberly said ruefully, rubbing his jaw.

An uncomfortable silence stretched between them for several moments. Then Holly asked, 'So what do you want to know about Panch?'

Eberly hesitated a heartbeat. 'Why is she here? Does she intend to stay, or will she return to Earth?'

Shrugging, Holly replied, 'She says she came here to spend the holiday with me. As for how long she'll stay, you'll have to ask her.'

'I was hoping that you could ask her,' said Eberly. 'My one meeting with your sister wasn't all that friendly.' He rubbed his jaw again.

Holly suppressed a giggle, just barely. 'Okay, sure. I click. I'll ask her, no prob.'

'Good,' Eberly said. 'Thank you, Holly.'

'No prob,' she repeated as she got up and left his office.

Briefly Eberly thought of calling Aaronson back to soothe his ruffled feathers. Then he decided against it. He'll be calling me for every little piece of equipment that goes out of whack, Eberly said to himself. Fixing machinery is his job, not mine.

On the other side of the village called Athens, Nadia Wunderly sat in her laboratory and stared disconsolately at the video imagery hovering before her eyes. It was as if the lab's far wall had disappeared, to be replaced by the black depths of space – and the glittering splendor of Saturn's rings.

She saw again that wandering chunk of ice-covered rock that had blundered into Saturn's gravity well. A fugitive from the Kuiper Belt, she told herself for the thousandth time; a trans-Neptunian Object that got kicked out of its orbit all the way out there and fell into Saturn's grip.

In the speeded-up video the icy rock dived past Saturn once, twice, and then looped around the planet to fall into an orbit within the rings.

'Extreme slo-mo,' Wunderly called to the lab's computer.

The new arrival's motion slowed to something like taffy being pulled on a cold day. Wunderly saw the rock plow into the B ring, the broadest and brightest of Saturn's intricate complex of rings.

To be greeted by a flurry of ring creatures. Like glittering snowflakes they swarmed over the new arrival and began chewing it apart. Of course, Wunderly admitted silently, it looks like a blizzard engulfing the newcomer. It's a big leap to say that those particles are alive, or have living creatures in them, directing them, steering them to the new ice chunk like a pack of scavengers swarming around a fresh carcass.

The top biologists back on Earth flatly refused to believe that the ring particles contained living creatures. Too cold for active biology, they claimed. What do they know? Wunderly grumbled to herself. So it's near absolute zero in the rings; so what? Those earthworms can sit in their campus offices and claim I haven't proven they're alive. Well, I'm going to. I've got to. My career depends on it.

That *can't* be a natural, abiological reaction, she told herself as she watched the swarming ice particles eat through the new moonlet. It can't be just natural abrasion. Those particles actively moved to the intruder and chewed it down to the bare rock. She backed up the video and watched it all happen again, in ultra-slow motion.

'Damn!' she said aloud. 'Why don't they believe me?'

She knew why. Sagan's dictum: *Extraordinary claims require extraordinary evidence.* She was claiming that there were living creatures in the ice particles of Saturn's rings, and that they actively maintained the rings, kept them big and dynamic, despite the fact that particles were constantly bleeding off the inner edges of the rings, pulled down into Saturn's clouds in a perpetual snowfall.

If the rings weren't being constantly added to by the deliberate actions of living creatures, they would have disappeared eons ago, Wunderly was convinced. Hell, she said to herself, Jupiter's bigger than Saturn and its ring system is just a puny sliver of carbon particles. Soot. Same thing for Uranus and Neptune. Saturn's rings are *huge*, beautiful, so bright that Galileo saw them with his dinky little telescope nearly five centuries ago.

But the big-shot biologists back Earthside won't believe me until I can give them enough proof to choke a hippopotamus. And the only real evidence I've got is these views of the ring dynamics, and Gaeta's dive through the rings. They won't believe a stuntman's testimony, even though the creatures almost killed Manny while he was in the rings.

My career hangs on this, she knew. My whole life. I've made an extraordinary claim. I need to get enough evidence to prove it's true. Otherwise I'll be finished as a scientist.

I need to send probes into the rings, Wunderly told herself. I need to study them close up, in real time. I need some biologists here, and some way to capture a sampling of the ring creatures. Otherwise nobody who matters will believe me.

She consoled herself by remembering Clarke's First Law: *When a distinguished but elderly scientist states that something is possible he is almost certainly right. When he states that something is impossible, he is very probably wrong.*

By 'elderly' Clarke meant over thirty, for a physicist. That means I'll be elderly in another year, Wunderly realized. With a weary sigh she told the computer to shut down the display. I've got to get help. I've got to get enough evidence to prove that I'm right and they're wrong. But Urbain's so warped over his precious *Titan Alpha* lander that he won't even talk to me.

Wunderly sat alone in her silent laboratory, a chubby young

woman with hair dyed brick red, wearing a shapeless knee-length tunic of sky-blue faux silk, wondering how she could get her superior's attention long enough to get the help she so desperately needed.

Then she sat up straighter and smiled. Manny Gaeta! He went into the rings once. Maybe he'll do it again, not as a stunt this time, but as a scientific expedition.

27 December 2095: Afternoon

The computations of time that humans use meant nothing on the cloud-shrouded shore of the frozen sea. *Titan Alpha* sat where it had landed, unmoving, uncommunicative. But not inert.

Its sensors were making measurements. Outside temperature -181 degrees Celsius. Atmospheric pressure 1734 millibars. Atmospheric composition: nitrogen, methane, ethane, minor hydrocarbons and nitrogen compounds. Tactile pads in its treads reported on the tensile strength of the spongy ground. Infrared cameras swept across the landscape, recording the black snow that was sifting down from the dirty-orange clouds slithering sluggishly across the sky.

Titan Alpha's internal logic circuits concluded that the broad expanse of dark and flat material down at the base of the bluffs must be an ice-crusted liquid of some sort. Microwave radar detected waves surging sluggishly beneath the crust, making it heave and crack. A sea. Priorities built into the central computer's master program demanded that the sea's composition be investigated. *Titan Alpha* fired a microsecond burst of ten megajoules from the laser mounted in the swivel turret on its roof. The mass spectrometer identified a host of chemical compounds in the ice evaporated by the laser: water ice mostly, but lots of methane and other hydrocarbons as well.

The command protocol built into the communications system called for transmitting these data through the main uplink antenna. But a subroutine in the computer's master program prevented this. No communications outside. Store the data but do not communicate. Wait. Observe and wait.

'It's what we call engineer's hell,' said one of the engineers who had helped to design and build *Titan Alpha*. 'Everything checks but nothing works.'

Urbain sat at the head of the conference table, outwardly calm and under control. Only the slight tic beneath his right eye betrayed the tension within him.

His eight lead engineers sat around the oval conference table. One of the conference room's smart walls displayed schematics of *Titan Alpha*'s various systems: propulsion, electrical power, sensors, communications and more. Urbain had not invited his scientists to this meeting: the problem with *Titan Alpha* was one of engineering. Something had malfunctioned and it was up to his engineering staff to determine what had gone wrong and to fix it. Besides, the scientists would swamp the meeting with bright ideas they hatched on the spur of the moment and drive everyone to distraction.

He was surprised and then annoyed when the young woman who was supposed to be monitoring the satellite hovering over *Titan Alpha*'s landing site burst into the conference room.

'It fired the laser!' she fairly shouted, without preamble or even asking pardon for interrupting the meeting. 'Squirted off a shot into the Lazy H Sea.'

Urbain jumped to his feet. 'Are you certain?'

'Got it on vid,' she said excitedly.

Without bothering to adjourn the meeting, Urbain raced for the door and down the corridor toward the control center, followed by all eight of the engineers.

The control center was much quieter than two days earlier. Wexler and the other VIPs were preparing to leave *Goddard* and head back to Earth. Urbain desperately wanted to have some results from *Titan Alpha* before they left.

The young scientist slipped into the chair of her console and clapped her headset on. She spoke briefly into the pin-sized microphone at her lips and her display screen lit up.

Urbain had placed an observation satellite in synchronous orbit above the site of the landing, a feat that was not as easy as he'd first thought it would be. Synchronous orbit for a body revolving as slowly as Titan was hundreds of thousands of kilometers above the moon's surface. And although the satellite included a two-kilometer-long tether system that was designed to generate electrical power for its internal systems and maintain itself in proper position, unexpected bursts of electromagnetic energy from Saturn had incapacitated the tether, making it necessary to use positioning thrusters to keep the satellite in place. Constantly perturbed by the gravitational pulls of mammoth Saturn and its rings, the satellite devoured station-keeping fuel ravenously to maintain itself in its proper position; Urbain had already been forced to schedule a refueling mission.

Standing behind the seated woman, he bent over her shoulder and stared at the display screen: nothing more than a mottled sphere of dull orange. 'Where is the infrared view?' he demanded impatiently.

The young woman held up a finger as she muttered into her mike. The sphere on the screen abruptly changed. The clouds disappeared and Urbain could see the bright glints of Titan's rolling, hilly ground and the dark shapes of its seas. One looked like the head of a dragon, another somewhat like a child's drawing of a dog. Then there was the H-shaped one, where *Titan Alpha* had landed.

'Magnification,' he snapped.

The view zoomed in. The H shape of the methane sea was oriented east-west, rather than standing up as the letter is made in actual writing. Nearly a century earlier the Americans, with their usual cowboy attitude, had dubbed it the Lazy H Sea.

'That's the best magnification we can get,' said the scientist.

Urbain could not see his lander. We need satellites in lower orbits, he told himself. An entire fleet of them, so that *Titan Alpha* is under constant surveillance.

'So?' he insisted. 'Where is this laser flash?'

'I'm running it back – there! Didja see it? I'll run it forward again.'

Urbain saw the briefest of glints on the edge of the methane sea. He straightened up, disappointed. 'It might have been a sparkle in the electronics. A bad pixel.'

The young woman shook her head stubbornly. 'No, I checked its duration and it's consistent with a laser pulse. Just a small squirt, no more than ten kilojoules. Ran the light through a spectral analysis, too, and it's water and methane and the other carbon gunk from the sea.'

Urbain stared down at her. '*Titan Alpha* actually fired its laser?'

'Yes, sir, it surely did.'

One of the engineers said, 'That's what I've been trying to tell you, Dr. Urbain. We're getting telemetry from the lander. Its sending up continuous data on its internal condition. Everything's working fine.'

'But it will not uplink data from its sensors.'

'That's the one glitch,' the engineer admitted.

Urbain glared at him. 'This *glitch*, as you put it, makes *Titan Alpha* useless, pointless, stupid.'

Returning his glare without blinking, the engineer insisted, 'I think it's the central computer. Some kind of error in the programming. Everything is fine in the lander except for the data uplink. For some reason it's not sending data back to us. The sensors seem to be working as designed, but the vehicle isn't uplinking the data it's collecting. It's got to be a computer glitch.'

'In other words,' Urbain said coldly, 'you are telling me that the patient is in fine condition, except that she is catatonic.'

27 December 2095: Evening

Kris Cardenas could see the tremendous strain that Urbain was under. As the only Nobel laureate in the habitat, she had invited Dr. Wexler, Pancho, Urbain and his wife to a small farewell dinner at Nemo's restaurant, the swankiest eatery aboard *Goddard*.

Nemo's was decorated to look like the mock-Victorian interior of Jules Verne's fictional *Nautilus*: brass bulkheads and thick pipes running overhead. Display screens shaped like portholes showed teeming schools of fish, slithering octopuses, sleek deadly sharks.

Manny Gaeta looked uncomfortable in a maroon turtleneck shirt and ivory cardigan jacket, as close as he would come to formal dinner wear. Cardenas wore a flowered short-skirted frock, Wexler a dark blue finger-length tunic over a mid-calf skirt. Pancho was in a comfortable pants suit of hunter green, while Jeanmarie Urbain had decked herself in a clinging black sheath decorated with intricate embroidery that showed her trim figure to excellent advantage.

'I had hoped that this would be a celebration,' Cardenas said, trying to make her tone light, cheerful, 'with champagne and congratulations. I guess that will have to wait for a while.'

Urbain opened his mouth to respond, then simply shook his head and reached for the glass of fruit juice in front of him.

'The celebration will come,' said Wexler, forcing a smile. 'It's too bad I won't be here when the probe finally starts sending up data.'

'You leave tomorrow?' asked Jeanmarie. 'So soon?'

'Ms. Lane's craft departs tomorrow and there won't be another ship out here for many months,' Wexler replied.

'I could hold it here for a coupla more days,' Pancho said. 'But the bean-counters back at Astro Corporation's head-quarters would get twitchy.'

'Tell 'em to twitch,' Gaeta gruffed.

Pancho grinned at him. 'If I was still CEO I could and I would. With me retired, though, they're doin' me a favor as it is.'

'I couldn't stay a few more days in any event,' said Wexler, glancing at Urbain and then swiftly back to Pancho. 'I've got work piling up back home.'

'You think you'll be able to fix the glitch in a few days?' Pancho asked Urbain.

He forced a sickly smile. 'Perhaps.'

'It should take not much longer than that,' Jeanmarie said, quite firmly. 'After all, they know the machine is working. Its internal systems are functioning. The only problem is the communications link, is it not?'

Urbain nodded morosely.

A human waiter came to the table hesitantly, holding large leather-covered menus. Cardenas nodded to him. Better to have them reading the menu and ordering their dinners than moping over the probe's silence, she thought.

Although she was the oldest person at the table, Kris Cardenas looked like a vibrant outdoorsy woman in her thirties, thanks to the nanomachines that coursed through her body like a purposeful, almost intelligent immune system that destroyed invading microbes, cleared blood vessels of plaque, repaired damaged tissues. She had the broad shoulders and bright blond hair of a California surfer, and cornflower-blue eyes that sparkled in the candlelight of the dinner table. Exiled from Earth because of the nanos inside her, she had lost her husband, her children, had never touched the faces of her grandchildren. She had spent years in bitter hatred of the know-nothings on Earth who had totally banned nanotechnology, then more years of repentance as a medic for the rock rats of the Asteroid Belt at Ceres.

Now she was beginning a new life aboard this habitat orbiting Saturn, with handsome, hunky Manuel Gaeta, who had retired from his career as a stuntman to be with her.

As their appetizers were being placed on the table before them, Gaeta asked Urbain, 'Do you have any idea why the beast won't talk to you?'

Urbain, sitting across the table from Gaeta, raised his brows as he tried to interpret the man's question. Finally he frowned slightly and said, 'We are working on several possibilities. It is very puzzling.'

Wexler laid a claw-like hand on Urbain's sleeve. 'It's always very puzzling, Eduoard, until you get the answer. Then you wonder why it puzzled you for so long.'

'I'm sure Eduoard will come up with correct answer in a day or so,' said Jeanmarie.

Her husband scowled at her.

'You remember the first time we met?' Gaeta asked him. 'In Professor Wilmot's office?'

Urbain nodded warily.

A crooked grin broke out on Gaeta's rugged face. 'I wanted to go down to the surface of Titan. Be the first human being to set foot on the place. I thought you'd have a stroke!'

Smiling weakly, Urbain said, 'We cannot have humans on Titan. The contamination . . .' He let his voice fade away.

'I agree,' said Wexler sharply. 'There are unique life forms down there. It would be criminal to contaminate them with terrestrial organisms.'

Gaeta raised his hands in a mock surrender. 'Hey, I'm retired. I got no interest in doing stunts any more.'

But Pancho arched a brow. 'Y'know, maybe what your lander needs is a repair man. Or woman.'

'You volunteering?' Gaeta kidded her.

'I was an astronaut, 'way back when. I've fixed more'n one balky robot in orbit. I remember once, before Moonbase became the nation of Selene . . .'

Pancho regaled the table for the next hour and more with tales of her exploits on the Moon.

Meanwhile, Professor James Colrane Wilmot was entertaining an unwelcome guest in his quarters.

'I'm sorry to have interrupted your evening,' said Eberly as he stepped into the professor's sitting room.

'Yes, obviously,' Wilmot said, with barely concealed distaste.

Wilmot's two-room suite was no larger than the standard apartments in the village of Athens: a sitting room and a bedroom, spacious by the standards of a spacecraft, yet as compact as an efficiency apartment in a major Earthside metropolis. It was as comfortable and unpretentious as Wilmot himself though. The professor had furnished it just like his old digs in Cambridge; indeed, most of the warm, dark wooden furniture had been taken from his home there. He even had a section of one of the smart walls displaying a fireplace, complete with hypnotic crackling flames.

Wilmot himself was obviously dressed for an evening alone. He wore a deep burgundy dressing gown over rumpled, baggy tweed trousers. His feet were shod in comfortable old slippers. He was considerably bulkier than Eberly, a tall thickset man with a bushy gray moustache and iron-gray hair, his face seamed and permanently tanned by long years in the field on anthropological expeditions.

Eberly was in his office attire: a light blue hip-length tunic over crisply-creased charcoal slacks. Wilmot thought the tunic hid the man's pot belly well. Strange creature, the professor said to himself as he gestured Eberly to a worn old leather armchair. The man has obviously spent a great deal of effort to make his face look handsome, even commanding. Yet below the neck he's soft as putty.

'To what do I owe the honor of this visit?' Wilmot asked, sinking into his favorite chair. A half-empty glass of whisky sat on the coffee table between them. Wilmot did not so much as glance at it, nor did he offer his visitor a drink.

Eberly's sculpted face grew serious, almost grave. 'I thought it best to discuss this face to face, and not in my office,' he began.

There he goes, thought Wilmot. Always some dire emergency. Always the need for secrecy. The man's a born schemer.

'Some sort of problem?' he asked.

Nodding, Eberly said, 'We need to amend the constitution.'

'Do we?'

'Yes. I can see now that calling for elections every year was a mistake. We need to change that.'

'Ah.' Wilmot smiled knowingly. 'Now that you are in power you don't want to run the risk of being voted out.'

'It's not that,' Eberly protested.

'Then what?'

Eberly's face twisted into a nervous grimace. Wilmot could see the wheels turning in his mind.

At last the younger man said, 'Having elections every year means that whoever is in office must prepare for the coming election campaign. Every year! It distracts from his duties. I'm so busy trying to convince people I'm doing the best possible job for them that I don't have the time to do the job they elected me to do.'

Wilmot considered this for a moment. 'You could step down and allow someone else to take the job.'

'But I'm the best qualified!' Eberly cried. 'I really am. You know the people of this habitat. They're lazy. They don't want the responsibilities of office. They'd rather let someone else do it.'

'They are averse to political responsibilities, true enough,' Wilmot admitted. 'Perhaps we should institute a draft—'

'A draft?'

'It's been suggested, you know. Pick our administrative officers by lot. Let the personnel department's computer run the show. It might even generate some enthusiasm among the people, a lottery.'

'And whoever got picked would refuse to serve,' Eberly said, almost sullenly.

Wilmot realized he was tired of this tomfoolery. Besides, his drink was waiting for him. He rose to his feet. Eberly looked surprised, then slowly got up out of his chair.

'The real reason we have elections every year,' he said, gripping Eberly's thin arm in one strong hand, 'is to allow the people of this habitat to vent some political steam. Elections are a safety valve, you see. They give people the illusion that they have some degree of control over their government. Without elections, who knows what kind of protests and outright rebellions we might get – even from these lazy, noninvolved citizens. They're slackers and noncomformists, no doubt, but if they feel the government is not sensitive to their needs, they will hunt for a way to change the government. Elections are better than revolts.'

Eberly stood there, looking decidedly unhappy. He's trying to think of a rebuttal, Wilmot could see. I can smell the wood burning.

'I doubt that you have anything to worry about, my boy,' Wilmot said jovially, clapping Eberly on the shoulder and steering him to the door. 'As you say, the good citizens of this habitat are woefully apathetic. Most of 'em don't even bother to vote – as long as there are elections But take away the elections and you'll have trouble on your hands. Remember, as the incumbent, you have a powerful advantage. I doubt that you have anything to fear. Really I do.'

Eberly looked far from reassured as he said good night and Wilmot closed the door on him.

Damned schemer, Wilmot thought as he headed back to his drink. Blackmailer. He'd do anything to hold onto power.

He sat heavily and took a long sip of the whisky. Feeling its warmth working its way through him, Wilmot relaxed somewhat. I'm out of it, he said to himself. I'm merely an observer now, nothing more.

He took another sip, then leaned his head back. It's damned interesting, though. Ten thousand men and women locked inside this oversized sardine tin. The ideal anthropological experiment. Despite it all, I'm quite a lucky man.

Eberly, meanwhile, was walking along the corridor to his own apartment. There were plenty of people coming up in the other direction. Eberly was surprised to see that most of them looked tanned, even golden. What is this? he asked himself. A new fad that I haven't caught onto?

Everyone who passed him recognized Eberly, of course, and greeted him with smiles and hellos. That made him feel better. They know me. They like me. They even admire me, most of them.

Wilmot's not going to offer any support for amending the constitution, he realized. But then he brightened. Still and all, the old man won't offer any opposition, either. His moral power in this habitat is nil. I've seen to that.

He quickened his stride as he headed for his apartment.

28 December 2095: Breakfast

'So how serious are you about this bodyguard of yours?' Holly asked her sister.

The two women were sitting in Holly's kitchen. She had invited Pancho for breakfast and a one-on-one talk. There were no eggs in the habitat; no chickens. Most of the protein came from aquaculture fish, frogs or shellfish, or from the genetically engineered protein the inhabitants of *Goddard* fondly called 'McGlop.' Holly had microwaved a plate of the processed protein for them and added sliced fruits from the habitat's orchards.

Pancho shrugged her slim shoulders. 'We been livin' together for a few months now. We get along real well.'

'In bed?'

'That's none of your business, girl,' Pancho said. But she grinned widely as she said it.

Holly grew more serious. 'You know I'm in charge of human resources here.'

'Very responsible position.'

'If you and Jake are going to apply for permanent residency, I've got to know as soon as possible.'

'Permanent residency?' Pancho's face clearly showed surprise. 'I hadn't even thought about that.'

'You mean you just came out here to visit me?' Holly realized that she was surprised, too.

'Yep. I told you that, didn't I?'

'You did. But I thought—'

'You thought I was bullshitting you?'

'Well . . .' Holly felt her cheeks burning. 'Yeah, I guess I did. A little.'

Pancho glanced down at the protein slices on her plate. 'I dunno, maybe I was. A little. Truth is, I don't know what I want to do.'

'Malcolm's afraid you'll become a citizen and then run for his job.'

'Me? Hell no! I've had enough sittin' behind a desk. I've made all the executive decisions I'm ever gonna make. Never again!'

She said it with such fervor that Holly wondered what was behind her sister's outburst.

'Anyway,' Pancho went on, 'I want you to get to know Jake. And I want to see more of this guy of yours.'

'Raoul?'

'Yeah, Raoul. Sounds like a flamenco dancer.'

Holly smiled. 'He's an engineer. From New Jersey.'

'Raoul,' Pancho repeated. 'He looks like a real downer, you ask me.'

'I didn't ask,' Holly said pointedly. 'And he's not a downer. He's just – well, Raoul wasn't one of our original people. He was an engineer at the Jupiter station and came aboard when he had an accident while we were refueling at Jupiter on the way out here. Applied for citizenship after . . . after the trouble we had with those religious fanatics. They beat him up, too.'

'And he decided to stay here?'

'I think it's because of me,' Holly said.

'Well, well.'

Growing somber, Holly confessed, 'Thing is, Panch, he's given up his chance to go back home because of me. That's a load.'

'You like him?'

Holly nodded, a little uncertainly.

'You get along well?'

'Oh, yeah, sure.'

'In bed?'

Her chin went up. 'Like you said, that's none of your business.'

'But you've got no complaints.'

A hint of a smile sneaked across Holly's face. 'No complaints.'

'So what's the problem?'

'I think that sooner or later he's going to want to go home.'

'To New Jersey?'

'It's his home. His family, his friends, they're all there. He misses them. He was at Jupiter station doing his two years of mandatory public service.'

'So you're scared of him dumping you.'

'And that makes it tough to make a real commitment.'

'Which increases the chances of him dumping you.'

'Catch twenty-two,' said Holly, unhappily.

'You could go back Earthside with him, you know.'

Holly's eyes went wide. 'And leave *Goddard*? I couldn't do that, Panch. I'm *somebody* here. All my friends are here.'

'And all your family, too,' Pancho said gently. 'Even though I'm not sure how long I'll stay.'

'This is a good place, Panch,' Holly said earnestly. 'It's got everything a person could want.'

'Maybe,' Pancho said, a slight hint of wistfulness in her voice. 'It's a big solar system, though. Lots of places. They've rebuilt the Ceres habitat. Enlarging it, even. And they're finding more on Mars every day, just about.'

Holly took a good long look at her sister as Pancho rambled on about the solar power stations being built at Mercury and the new cities being dug into the Moon's battered regolith. She realized that Pancho had a wanderlust, a longing to see new places, to travel across the breadth of the solar system. That's what's brought her here to Saturn, Holly realized. She thinks it's to visit me but it's really that wanderlust of hers.

Holly found that she felt almost relieved about it.

★　　★　　★

61

Oswaldo Yañez felt almost delighted that the poor man had mashed his thumb so badly. His hours of duty at the habitat's hospital were almost always so boringly quiet that he welcomed an opportunity to actually practice medicine. The habitat's population was mostly young; even most of those whose calendar age was climbing up there took rejuvenation therapies that kept their bodies youthful.

Yañez was considering rejuve therapy for himself, although he had told no one about it yet, not even his wife of thirty-two years. He was still vigorous, his dark hair still thick and luxuriant, but he had added nearly ten kilos to his weight since joining this habitat and he worried about that. Too much easy living, he knew, but his determination to exercise and go on a diet always melted away in the presence of his wife's cooking.

The technician's thumb wasn't all that badly mangled, he saw as he cleaned away the blood.

'I was working on the main water pump,' the younger man explained, 'down in the underground. My power wrench went dead, poof! just like that. When I went to try to figure out what was wrong with it, damned thing snapped on again. Whacked my thumb real hard.'

'It's not serious,' Yañez assured him. 'I'm going to extract some stem cells from your bone marrow, culture them and then inject them back into you to rebuild the damaged tissue. You'll be fine in a week or less.'

The technician nodded, but kept on muttering about his power wrench. 'Shouldn'ta crapped out on me like that,' he insisted. 'It was like it was *tryin'* to mangle me, you know?'

Vernon Donkman frowned at his desktop screen. This shouldn't be happening, he told himself.

Donkman was the chief financial officer of *Goddard*, a position that sounded impressive to the uninformed until they learned that he was the *only* financial officer in the habitat.

Still, his was a very responsible position, despite the fact that virtually every financial transaction among the habitat's citizens was done electronically. The bank's computer handled all financial links with Earth and the other human settlements in the solar system, as well.

The frown that etched Donkman's lean, almost gaunt face was engendered by the fact that the bank's central accounting system showed an anomaly. The account didn't balance! It was off by only a few hundred credits, but it should not be off at all. Not by a single penny, Donkman told himself sternly.

The problem was easy enough to fix, he knew. Simply liquidate the unbalanced amount from the habitat's internal account. That would balance the books. But the thought irked Donkman mightily. Accounts should balance without jiggering. It was his insistence on such purity that got him exiled from Amsterdam in the first place. Someone high up in the hierarchy of the Holy Disciples had been bleeding off cash from the church's banking system. Donkman had tried to track down the embezzler and found himself accused of the crime and exiled to habitat *Goddard.*

The memory of that injustice rankled him, but this tiny misbalance in the habitat's account aggravated him even more. The amount involved was too small for anyone to deliberately have stolen it. It was a mistake, somewhere in the accounting system, a simple mistake.

But try as he might, Donkman could not find where the mistake originated. At last his wristwatch alarm buzzed. With a reluctant sigh, Donkman pushed himself up from his desk and headed for the cosmetics clinic. Everyone was getting enzyme injections to turn their skin golden tan. He didn't want to be the only one among his acquaintances to look like a palefaced mouth-breather.

28 December 2095: Nanolab

Malcolm Eberly felt distinctly uneasy inside the nanotech laboratory. Not that he had any religious scruples against nanotechnology; he simply shared the same fear that most people had about an outbreak of uncontrollable nanomachines, mindless microscopic monsters chewing up everything in their path like an unstoppable swarm of soldier ants. The thought made him shudder inside.

He knew his fears were grounded in solid fact. Nanomachines had killed people in the past. Back when Dr. Cardenas had first joined the habitat, while Professor Wilmot was still in charge of the interim government, the old man had insisted on all kinds of safeguards before he'd allow Cardenas to set up this laboratory. Why, just getting into this lab was a major struggle: you had to pass through a double set of heavy doors, just like an airlock. Cardenas had to keep the air pressure inside her lab lower that the pressure in the rest of the habitat, just to make certain none of the virus-sized machines could waft out on a stray current of air.

Urbain seemed uneasy, too. He must be really desperate, Eberly thought, if he's considering using nanomachines to fix his probe down there on Titan.

If Kris Cardenas sensed their apprehensions, she gave no sign of it. Perched casually on a tall stool, one elbow leaning on the top of the lab bench, Cardenas was wearing a comfortable light, short-sleeved sweater of baby blue, and denim jeans. Urbain, as usual, was in a jacket and carefully-creased slacks. No tie, but he had knotted an ascot inside the collar of his shirt.

Eberly himself wore a loose tunic over his slacks, as the dress code he had promulgated called for. Hardly anyone outside the habitat's administrative staff paid much attention to his dress code.

'We've been working on nanos for self-repair and maintenance,' Cardenas was saying to Urbain. 'That was what you asked for.'

'Yes, I realize that,' Urbain replied, running a nervous finger along his trim moustache. 'But we are confronted by a new problem now.'

Eberly hadn't actually been invited to this meeting, but once he heard that Urbain was going to Cardenas for help he decided he had to listen in. And Urbain was too ridiculously polite to tell the habitat's chief administrator to keep his nose out of scientific matters. So Eberly sat in one of the folding chairs that Cardenas had provided for them while Urbain and the nanotech expert thrashed out their problems. Off at the far side of the lab, Cardenas's lone assistant hovered among the gleaming metal equipment, intently listening. What's his name? Eberly asked himself. Tavalera, came the answer. The engineer we picked up after the refueling accident at Jupiter.

'As I understand the problem,' Cardenas was saying, 'the probe isn't sending any data to you.'

Urbain touched his moustache again before answering. '*Titan Alpha* is not uplinking data from its sensors, that is true. We have reason to believe the sensors are working and gathering data. *Alpha* is simply not relaying the information to us.'

'Curious,' muttered Cardenas.

'Frustrating,' snapped Urbain. 'We are receiving telemetry from *Alpha*'s maintenance program. All systems appear to be functioning properly – except for the sensor data uplink.'

Cardenas straightened up on her stool, crossed her legs,

glanced over at her assistant, then made a little shrug. 'I don't see what we can do to help you, Dr. Urbain. It's—'

'Please. Call me Eduoard. We have known each other long enough to use our first names.'

'Eduoard,' Cardenas said, with a slight dip of her chin. 'I'm afraid I don't see how nanos can help you, unless you can pinpoint the cause of the malfunction.'

Urbain sighed mightily. 'That is the real problem. We don't know what is causing the silence. No one knows. My people have been racking their brains for three days now. And three nights, I might add. They are going over all the computer programming, line by line. It is maddening.'

'So how can nanos help?'

With a shake of his head, Urbain said, 'I was hoping that perhaps there might be some way to deliver nanomachines to *Alpha* that could construct a new uplink antenna.'

'A back-up to the existing antenna?'

'Or a replacement,' said Urbain.

He's desperate, Eberly said to himself. Grasping at straws.

Cardenas got down from the stool. 'Let me think about it, Eduoard. That might be possible, but it won't be easy . . .' Her voice trailed off.

Urbain got to his feet. 'I would appreciate anything you can do.'

Cardenas walked him to the door of the laboratory, Eberly following a pace or so behind them. 'Please keep me informed of your analysis of the situation,' she told Urbain. 'You never know, something that seems trivial to you might open a window for us.'

'I will,' said Urbain. His gloomy tone showed how hopeless he felt. 'Thank you.'

As soon as the lab door closed behind them, Eberly made a hasty farewell to Urbain and hurried outside the laboratory building, into the sunshine, along the gently-rising street up to the administrative center and into his own office. Sliding into his desk chair he told the phone to locate Ilya Timoshenko and ask him to come to the chief administrator's office immediately.

Timoshenko ran against me in the general election, Eberly told himself. So did Urbain. If they're smart enough to combine their votes they could defeat me in June. I've got to get them working against one another. Divide and conquer, that's the rule.

Timoshenko was not in the navigation center, which was his nominal work station, for the simple reason that he had nothing to do there now that *Goddard* was plying its orbit around Saturn. Nothing except think, and remember the life he had left behind on Earth. The woman he had left behind. His wife, the golden-haired Katrina. Katrina of the sweet smile and delicate hands. When she spoke it was like silver bells chiming in his heart.

No, that way lay remorse. And anger. A rage so towering that its black storm could engulf him utterly. Timoshenko fought against the rage, because he knew that he himself was its focus, its center. At the thundering heart of his blood-red fury was the knowledge that he had brought this exile on himself. He drank too much, he talked too much, he *cared* too much. So they had exiled him to this green and luxurious prison more than a billion kilometers from Katrina.

Timoshenko was working with the *Titan Alpha* mission control team when the call from Eberly reached him. Now that the probe was at Titan, the control center was on twenty-four-hour status: all consoles manned at all times. Timoshenko had volunteered to help fill mission control's manpower needs. The job wasn't really work; just babysitting the consoles. Boring routine, nothing more. The telemetry was coming through fine and showed that the stupid machine down there was functioning as it should. Except that it refused to send any sensor data to Urbain and his twitching scientists. Timoshenko almost laughed. Urbain's pride and joy was sitting on a cliff of dirty ice like a sullen teenager, refusing to talk to its daddy.

So what, he asked himself. Why shouldn't Urbain have his dreams shattered? Welcome to the club.

The phone's synthesized voice spoke in its flat, dull tones in his earplug: 'The chief administrator wishes to see you in his office immediately. Please acknowledge.'

Suppressing an urge to tell the chief administrator to pound sand up his ass, Timoshenko took in a breath, then replied into his lip mike, 'I am on duty at the mission control center and cannot leave my post. My shift will end at seventeen hundred hours. I will report to the chief administrator's office at seventeen-twenty, unless I hear otherwise from our respected and unparalleled chief administrator.'

There, Timoshenko thought. That ought to keep that fat-head Eberly happy for a couple of hours.

Cardenas met Nadia Wunderly at the cafeteria precisely at noon. They carried their trays through the cold-food line together, and Cardenas noted with an inner smile that Nadia took nothing more than a fresh green salad and a bottle of mineral water. Not wanting to tempt her friend to anything more, Cardenas limited her own selection to a Caesar salad augmented with bits of grilled faux chicken and a tall glass of tomato juice.

As they put their trays on an empty table and sat down, Cardenas remarked, 'You're looking well, Nadia.'

'I feel great,' said the physicist.

Cardenas nodded and dug into her salad.

'I mean,' Wunderly continued, 'I can almost *feel* the nanos melting away the fat inside me. I've lost six kilos already!'

'That's wonderful.' Cardenas smiled to herself.

A month earlier Wunderly had come to her, almost in tears, to beg her help. 'It's almost Christmas,' she pleaded, 'and look at me! I'm fat as a pig!'

Cardenas had tried to calm her friend, but she knew what was coming and dreaded it.

At last Wunderly had begged, 'Can't you give me some nanos, just a few, just enough to burn this fat off me? Nobody's going to ask me out for New Year's Eve when I look like this!'

Wunderly was chubby. Her basic body type was chunky, big-boned. She would never look sylphlike or slinky unless she had a complete body makeover, which could take months.

'What you're asking for is gobblers,' Cardenas had told her friend as gently as she could. 'They're illegal, totally banned everywhere. They could kill you; they've killed others, god knows.'

'I don't care!' Wunderly had yelped. 'I'll take the risk!'

But Cardenas would not. Still, she could not leave her friend to despair. Grimly, she had told Wunderly, 'Come to my lab tomorrow night, around eight.'

Wunderly had come to the lab as eager as a puppy. Cardenas gave her a fruit cocktail that contained, not nanomachines, but a powerful appetite suppressant and a diuretic. A placebo, in effect. She gave Wunderly detailed instructions about dieting and exercise.

'If you don't follow this regimen the nanos won't attack the fat cells,' Cardenas had warned, mentally crossing her fingers. 'And you'll be endangering your health.'

Every two days Wunderly had returned to Cardenas's lab for a booster. She thought she was getting nanomachines that would burn away her fat as if by magic. To her delight, she lost weight. Not magically: it was by dint of diet and exercise that she would never have undertaken without the lure of nanomachines doing their work inside her body.

And it was working, Cardenas saw. Nadia already looks better, and she's smiling instead of blubbering about her weight.

Manny Gaeta came to their table, carrying a tray laden with soup, a McGlop sandwich, and a slice of peach pie. Cardenas had told him about her little deception, of course. She had to step on his foot, under the table, only three times before he caught her meaning.

'Hey, Nadia, you're looking terrific,' he said, grinning at Wunderly. 'You been working out or something?'

'Something,' Wunderly answered, beaming at Cardenas.

28 December 2095: Storage Building

Holly led Nadia Wunderly down the high-ceilinged corridor of the storage facility. On either side of them the walls were blank, except for long strings of numbers on each closed and locked door. Strip lamps along the ceiling lit the corridor brightly, but to Wunderly the place seemed dusty, gritty from disuse, and eerily quiet.

'So who're you going to the New Year's Eve bash with?' Holly asked as they prowled along the corridor.

'One of the computer techies,' Wunderly replied cheerfully, 'Da'ud Habib.'

Holly felt impressed. 'He's the head of Urbain's computer team. From the University of British Columbia.'

'You know him?' Wunderly asked, surprised.

'Only from the human resources files.'

'Oh.'

'He's a Moslem.'

'But he's no chauvinist,' Wunderly countered immediately. 'He's really kind of a sweet guy.'

They walked on through the silent, dusty corridor. Wunderly eyed Holly's lean, long-legged figure. Bet she's never had to use a treadmill in her life, she said to herself. Still, though, her own figure was looking better every day, thanks to Cardenas' nanos, she thought. And she was taking the enzyme injections to make her skin turn golden, just like everybody else, so she wouldn't look so pasty. Almost everybody else, she realized. Holly doesn't need enzymes: her skin's a wonderful toasty brown already.

'It's like a maze down here,' Wunderly murmured as Holly walked assuredly beside her.

'Just down another two cross-corridors, and then we turn left. Two doors in, that's it.'

Clear admiration showed on Wunderly's dimpled face. 'You've got it memorized?'

Holly smiled gently. 'Got it all memorized, Nadia. The whole layout. Everything and everybody in the habitat.'

'Memorized?'

'I'm a reborn, Nadia. Hope that doesn't bother you.'

Wunderly's eyes widened slightly. 'Cryonics? How long were you in?'

'A little over twenty years.'

'But I thought reborns' memories were pretty much wiped out when they're revived.'

Nodding, Holly replied, 'Yep. I don't remember anything from my first life. Oh, maybe a snatch of something or other, but no connected memories.'

'Then how come—'

'The rehab team gave me a lot of RNA treatments and memory boosters. Didn't work, far's as remembering my first life's concerned, but it surely gave me a near-perfect memory now. I see something once and I've got it forever, pretty near.'

'Eidetic,' Wunderly murmured.

'That's what the psychs call it, yeah.'

They turned at a cross-corridor and stopped before the second door on their left.

'This is it,' said Holly, so flatly certain that Wunderly didn't question her.

'Manny has the combination,' she said, peering at the keyboard lock set into the door.

'He ought to be here,' said Wunderly, glancing at her wristwatch. 'We said nine-thirty.'

Holly grinned. 'He prob'ly got lost.'

The overhead lights flickered once, twice, then quit

72

altogether, plunging them into total darkness. Wunderly's breath caught in her throat, but before either of them could say a word, the lights came on again at full brightness.

Wunderly's brows knit as she glanced up at the ceiling. 'They shouldn't do that,' she said.

Whatever it is that Eberly wants from me, thought Ilya Timoshenko as he walked from his apartment building to the administrative offices, it can't be very urgent. Instead of meeting me last evening, after my shift, he set the meeting for this morning.

Timoshenko walked with his shoulders hunched, his head thrust slightly forward, in a slightly rolling gait like an old-time sailor. He looked burly, aggressive, and while he was ordinarily as quiet and withdrawn as any introspective engineer, when he drank too much he became loudly combative. He was taller than he seemed at first glance, and his limbs were long and gangling. His face bore such an intense expression of skepticism that most people, on first meeting him, pegged him as a haughty know-it-all. His dark brown hair was thick and wiry, his stubborn chin usually bristly. It wasn't until you looked into his wolf-gray eyes that you saw what a tormented soul he actually was.

The administrative offices were quiet, a picture of calm, unhurried bureaucrats going about their leisurely business with the least possible amount of actual effort. Drones, Timoshenko snorted silently, as he strode through the aisle that separated their desks. More of them at the coffee machine than at their work stations, he noticed disdainfully. At least there are only a handful of them, he saw. Back in St. Petersburg every government office had swarms of drones lazing around, doing their best to avoid exerting themselves. Plus the Holy Disciples' psalm-singers hanging around to make certain nobody broke any of their moral rules. Working hard wasn't one of their rules, Timoshenko growled to himself. Taking a salary for doing as little as possible didn't break any of their commandments.

He strode past their desks without asking for help, knowing that if he did they'd make him wait, just to show their authority. He knew where Eberly's office was, you could see his door with his name on it, back at the rear of this drones' bullpen.

'Sir,' called one of the drones, a woman. 'Sir, you can't go in without being announced.' She was dressed in a brown tunic and darker slacks, just like all the others, men and women.

Timoshenko, wearing the one-piece coveralls of his profession, walked right past her with a gruff, 'Eberly's expecting me.'

'But you've got to be announced,' the woman insisted as he brushed by her. All the others froze where they were, although no one moved to stop him.

'You can't—'

Timoshenko rapped on Eberly's door once and slid it open. Eberly, behind his desk, looked surprised for an instant, then quickly hid it with a forced smile.

'Exactly on time,' he said. 'Please come in and take a chair.'

Timoshenko went to the pair of cold-looking chrome and leather chairs in front of the desk and sat in one. He heard the door slide shut behind him. Whether one of the drones closed it or Eberly did it with a remote control; he didn't know, nor did he care.

'You wanted to see me,' he said. 'Here I am.'

Eberly's smile showed teeth. 'You're very punctual.'

'I'm an engineer. In my business we try to be exact.'

'Yes, I see.'

'So?'

'The reason I asked to see you is about your being an engineer. As I understand it, there's not much to do in the navigation center any more.'

Timoshenko grunted. 'That's why I volunteered to help

74

Urbain's people. Turns out there's not much to do there, either, except wonder what's gone wrong with his probe.'

'So you're not doing much useful work, then.'

'There's not much to do.'

'Do you fill in the time with planning for the next election campaign?'

Timoshenko felt truly surprised at that. 'The next election? Not me! Once was enough. You won, I lost. That's the end of my political career.'

Eberly steepled his fingers in front of his face and studied Timoshenko for a few moments, as if trying to determine if he were telling the truth.

'No hard feelings about losing, then?' he asked.

'To tell the truth, I was relieved. I'm not a boss, and I don't want to be a boss.'

'But you're a very talented engineer, and we're not using your abilities to their fullest.'

Timoshenko thought, Here it comes, whatever it is that he wants from me.

'How would you like to head the maintenance department?' Eberly asked, turning on his smile again.

'The janitors?'

'Come now, you know the maintenance team is responsible for the operational integrity of this entire habitat. It's an important position, much more important than filling in at one of Urbain's consoles.'

Nodding warily, Timoshenko reluctantly agreed, 'Maintenance is a big job, true enough.'

'Now that we're in orbit around Saturn,' Eberly said, 'the maintenance team has the responsibility for keeping the habitat's outer shell in good condition.'

'Abrasion from the ring particles,' Timoshenko muttered.

'Ah! You're aware of the problem.'

'It's not that big a problem. The abrasion rate is well within the scale that was calculated before we left Earth.'

'Yes, but it still requires constant vigilance. And repairs, when necessary.'

'You're worried about the radiation shielding.'

Eberly looked blank for a fleeting moment, then nodded vigorously. 'Precisely. If the superconducting shield fails, we'd all be exposed to dangerous levels of radiation, wouldn't we?'

'Dangerous?' Timoshenko almost smiled. 'Lethal, more likely.'

'So you can see what an important job this is.'

'But isn't Aaronson in charge of maintenance? He's doing a decent job.'

'It's too big a job for him,' Eberly said. 'I'm getting complaints daily about electrical power failures, mechanical breakdowns, things that shouldn't be happening but they are. It's only minor, of course, but it's irritating. Our facilities should be running much more smoothly than they are.'

Timoshenko said, 'That's why you have a maintenance department: to take care of such problems.'

'Yes, I know, but the responsibility for exterior and interior maintenance is too much for one person,' Eberly went on. 'I've decided to split the maintenance department into two groups, interior and exterior. I want you to head the exterior section.'

Timoshenko sank back in the armchair. Why is he doing this? he wondered. What's he up to? He's a slippery one, and he doesn't do things out of the goodness of his soul. Or for the good of the habitat, either, for that matter.

Yet a voice in his head countered, It's a responsible position. It's a necessary task, you know that. Ice and rock chunks are pinging this eggshell all the time. We've got to be able to repair any damage they do.

'It's better than sitting around and doing nothing,' Eberly coaxed.

'That's true enough,' Timoshenko muttered.

'It's a very important position. Lots of responsibility. Do you think you're up to it?'

Timoshenko felt a jolt of anger flare inside him. But he suppressed it and said merely, 'I can handle it.'

'You'll do it, then?'

Feeling that he was being maneuvered, but not knowing why or how to get out of it, Timoshenko shrugged heavily and said, 'Okay, I'll do it.'

'Good!' Eberly shot to his feet and extended his hand across the desk. Timoshenko took it in his thick-fingered hand, careful not to grasp too tightly.

'I'll tell Aaronson about it,' Eberly said, smiling broadly. 'He'll be relieved.'

Another drone, Timoshenko thought as he left Eberly's office.

As his office door closed behind the engineer, Eberly thought happily, That ought to keep him out of my hair. He'll be too busy with exterior maintenance to bother me, and the job's not so big or glamorous that it will draw attention to him. Aaronson can concentrate on these niggling little complaints so things will be running smoother as we come up to the election. Good!

Timoshenko thought, as he left the administration building and stepped into the morning sunlight, Maybe he wants to get rid of me. Maybe he thinks I'll get myself killed outside. It could happen.

Holly heard light footsteps padding down the corridor around the corner. Must be Manny, she thought. But then they stopped.

Stepping into the main corridor, she saw Gaeta peering at a wall screen map, tracing a finger across its screen.

'Manny, here we are,' she called.

Gaeta trotted to the two women. 'I got lost,' he admitted sheepishly.

'I would have, too,' said Wunderly, 'if it weren't for Holly's photographic memory.'

'At least I remember the combination,' Gaeta said, tapping on the keyboard lock.

The door popped slightly ajar and Gaeta swung it all the way back. The overhead lights came on automatically in the bare little room. Before them stood the excursion suit that Gaeta had used for many of his daredevil stunts. It loomed over the three humans like Frankenstein's monster, like an inert robot, massive and intimidating.

'Hey *amigo*,' Gaeta said softly as he stepped up to it and slid a hand along one of its dimpled cermet forearms. 'We've been through a lot, this suit and me,' he murmured. 'A helluva lot.'

'Climbed Olympus Mons on Mars,' Wunderly said.

'And skiboarded down the reverse slope,' added Holly. '*And* surfed Jupiter's cloud deck. *And* skydived through Venus's clouds.'

'What was the toughest stunt you did?' Wunderly asked, her eyes glowing.

Gaeta didn't hesitate an instant. 'The solo trek across Mare Imbrium. For a while there I didn't think I was going to make it.'

'And then you sailed through Saturn's B ring,' said Wunderly.

'And then I retired,' Gaeta said firmly.

'As a stuntman.'

'But you kept the suit,' Holly pointed out. 'Why? I mean if you've really retired, why not sell the suit to the highest bidder? Or give it to the Royal Museum or the Smithsonian or someplace?'

Gaeta pursed his lips before retiring. 'I don't know. *Sentimentalismo*, I guess. Like I said, this suit and I have been through a lot.'

'Would you consider going through the rings again?' Wunderly asked, all in a rush, as if afraid that if she hesitated the words wouldn't come out.

Gaeta stared at her. 'Is that what this is all about? You want me to dive through those *fregado* rings again?'

'Would you?'

He shook his head. 'That stunt's been done. The second time isn't news any more.'

'Not as a stunt,' Wunderly said. 'As part of a scientific investigation, this time.'

Gaeta took a deep breath and let it out slowly. He had slept with both these women and they both knew it.

At last he answered, 'Couldn't do it even if I wanted to, Nadia. You'd need more than me and the suit. Fritz and the rest of my tech team are back on Earth looking for a new guy to be their stunt gorilla.'

'We have technicians here,' Holly said. 'Engineers, too. We could put together a team for you.'

Gaeta shook his head. 'You can't cobble together a group of people just like that. It took years for Fritz and me to work out everything. You've got be able to trust your techies when you put your life on the line.'

'But it's for science,' Wunderly pleaded. 'We can train a team for you. You can pick whoever you want.'

'Nope. I'm retired. I've found the life I want, with the woman I want. I'm not gonna risk that.'

Nadia's face flushed and Gaeta realized he'd made a mistake, mentioning Kris. I'm gonna hear more about this, he knew. A lot more.

28 December 2095: Urbain's Office

It was a small office, barely large enough for the stylish teak desk with its built-in computer and phone console. Urbain had locked himself in and cranked the reclinable chair back almost as far as it could go. He needed a few hours of quiet, with no disturbances. He needed time to clear his mind and think.

The situation was maddening. All the telemetry data shows that *Titan Alpha* is performing normally, except for the sensor data uplink. Is something wrong with the uplink antenna? No, that couldn't be; the telemetry data show the antenna is undamaged. Habib and his computer people believe there might be a bug in the software. Or could it be something else, something we haven't thought of yet?

He leaned back in the softly yielding chair and stared at the ceiling. The ceiling stared back, smooth and blank. No help there, Urbain thought. His entire staff of engineers was running through every possible permutation in *Alpha*'s programming, with the scientists leaning over their shoulders and making fifty suggestions per minute. At this rate, he thought, one of the engineers is going to attack one of the scientists and I'll have a brawl on my hands. How Eberly will enjoy that! I'll be humiliated all over again.

Urbain snapped forward in his chair and told the computer to display the satellite's view of *Alpha*'s landing site. The opposite wall of the office seemed to disappear, replaced by a real-time view of Titan's murky, orange-tinted clouds.

'Infrared view,' he commanded.

The clouds vanished and he could see the rugged, broken surface of Titan and the lopsided shape of the Lazy H sea.

'Locate *Alpha*.'

A pinpoint of red light began to blink on the shore of the frozen sea.

'Maximum magnification.'

The view zoomed in, but stopped well short of allowing him to see the lander. The cameras' resolution is fifty meters at the altitude of the synchronous satellite, Urbain recited to himself. We need satellites in lower orbits. He knew it would take a fleet of at least six satellites to keep the landing site under constant observation. This one bird in synchronous orbit was too far away to be of real value. Besides, it was eating up fuel to remain on station; the perturbations jostling it out of position were severe.

Everything works except the sensor uplink, he repeated to himself. Why? *Why?*

Then he thought, If everything else works, why not try to use that? Perhaps we can correct the defect by putting *Alpha* to work. Wake her from her slumber.

A sudden burst of hope shot through Urbain. He practically jumped to his feet and strode out of his office, heading for the control center, straightening his ascot and buttoning his jacket as he walked.

The center had the dreary feel of a mortuary, he thought. All the consoles were manned, as they should be, although many of the faces he did not recognize. Volunteers, donating their free time to keep the consoles manned twenty-four hours a day. Volunteer or staff regular, they were all were sitting morosely at their places, staring idly at their display screens or clicking listlessly through routines they had already per-formed a hundred times before. The ceiling lights were on; the room looked bright enough. Yet there was no spark of vitality in the chamber, no animation among the men and women, no chatter back and forth. The only sounds he heard were the background hum of electrical equipment and the soft hiss of air from the grills set high in the walls. No one spoke. No one even looked up as he entered the control center. They were depressed, frustrated, merely going through the motions of working.

Then Urbain's nostrils twitched. He smelled coffee and saw that someone had brought in an urn and a hot plate. The next thing they'll do is to bring in a microwave to heat their snacks.

'Attention!' he called. 'Hear me.'

All heads turned toward him. Many of them were bleary-eyed from having worked night and day, fruitlessly.

'Check *Alpha*'s propulsion system,' Urbain commanded.

'It was checked just a few—'

'Check it again,' he commanded. 'I want to make certain that we can start the drive engines without a problem.'

'You're going to move it?'

Stepping briskly down the central aisle between the rows of consoles, Urbain rubbed his hands together with real enthusiasm.

'The creature will not speak to us where she now sits, so we will move her. Perhaps a little action will stir her to better behavior.'

Most of the engineers looked at him with obvious disbelief. One of the women said in a stage whisper, 'If it won't work, kick it.'

'The French touch,' someone else muttered.

'I am Quebecois,' Urbain snapped, 'and my sense of hearing is quite acute.'

Several of the engineers chuckled guardedly. Urbain thought that *doing* something, anything, was better than sitting around like a collection of mourners at a funeral.

The icy crust that capped the frigid sea was breaking against the base of the bluffs; the dark methane slush that covered the ice chunks was washed slowly off them and sank below the surface of the inky sea, revealing choppy waves driven by the turgid dark wind. *Titan Alpha* sat on the flat, slightly undulating tableland at the top of the bluffs, unmoving. Then it received a fresh command.

Review propulsion system checklist.

Automatically the command was routed through the central computer's master program. The command impinged on the primary restriction, but only marginally so. Reviewing its decision tree, the master program found that the command was allowable, so the computer ran through the propulsion system checklist. The task took four nanoseconds.

Repeat: review propulsion system checklist.

The computer repeated the checklist review, as commanded.

Thirty billion nanoseconds elapsed.

Report results of propulsion system checklist review.

This command was also routed through the central computer's logic circuitry. The primary restriction blared clearly, so the command was shunted to a subroutine for deletion.

Repeat: report results of propulsion system checklist review.

The command was again routed as before, the primary restriction was again detected, and the command again shunted.

Six hundred and forty-nine billion nanoseconds elapsed. During that time *Titan Alpha*'s central computer anticipated a command to activate the propulsion system, so instead of merely reviewing the checklist it tested the diagnostic program and found that the propulsion system was fully capable of activation and operation within allowable parameters.

No command came. The earlier inhibited commands were erased from the shunt circuit, as per the master program's normal routine.

'It must be the main antenna downlink,' Urbain muttered, bending over the shoulder of the propulsion engineer, who was seated at her console. He noticed a bead of perspiration trickling down the side of her face. She was wearing a flowery perfume of some sort, but the pungent scent of fear, of utter frustration, was overpowering it.

He straightened up and realized that his back ached from bending over for so long. Walking stiffly, he made his way along the row of consoles and stopped at the main communications post. He realized that every eye was on him. The control center was absolutely still; no one moved, even the displays on the screens seemed frozen.

'You are receiving telemetry from the comm system?' he asked the communications engineer in a quiet voice brittle with tension.

'Yes, sir,' he said, looking up over his shoulder at Urbain. 'The tracking beacon is coming through, too, loud and clear.'

'Very good. Run the diagnostics program, if you please.'

'For the whole comm system?'

Urbain thought a moment. 'No. Merely the receiving antennas. Primary and both backups.'

The man pecked at his keyboard. Urbain noticed that his fingers were thick, blunt, the nails ragged and chewed down to the quick. The display screen flickered through long lists of alphanumerics faster than his eye could follow.

At last the engineer cleared his throat and said, 'Diagnostics completed. All receiving antennas fully operational.'

'Good,' said Urbain. 'Now I wish to send a very specific command to—'

'Hey!' a voice yelled. 'It's moving!'

Without being told to, the communications man punched up the satellite view of Titan with the blinking red dot showing where *Alpha*'s beacon was located. The red pinpoint was inching across the screen.

'It's moving,' Urbain breathed.

'Looks that way,' said the engineer.

84

Raising his voice to an angry shout, Urbain demanded, 'Who gave the command to move *Alpha*?'

No one answered.

'Well? Which of you did it?'

Dead silence.

The comm engineer cleared his throat again, louder than before, and jabbed a forefinger at one of his secondary screens. 'Sir, here's the communications log. No one's sent any command of any kind to the lander since you ordered it to report its review of the propulsion system checklist.' He tapped his screen for emphasis, then added in a smaller voice, 'Nobody's said a word to the beast.'

My god, Urbain thought, staring at the screen. It's moving of its own volition.

Titan Alpha's central computer was programmed to anticipate certain problems and, within carefully preset limits, to act on its own. Even though commands from the control center usually spanned the distance between habitat *Goddard* and the surface of Titan in less than six billion nanoseconds there was always the possibility of some immediate emergency – a sudden fault-line opening in the icy ground, an avalanche, an electrical storm shorting out communications – that would require action before the human controllers in *Goddard* could react. Then, too, there were periods when the habitat was on the opposite side of Saturn and commands had to be relayed to the lander through the communications satellites placed in equilateral positions around the ringed planet. There could be a lag of almost a hundred billion nanoseconds under those conditions.

Based on the latest commands reported by the main receiving antenna, *Alpha*'s central computer anticipated that the propulsion system was to be activated. But such a command ran directly counter to the master program's primary restriction. The computer pondered this conundrum for more than a

85

thousand nanoseconds, then used its decision-tree logic program to resolve the problem.

Activate propulsion engines.

Engage tractor treads.

Automatically, the navigation and reconnaissance programs also activated. The central computer immediately became aware that the edge of the bluff loomed three thousand, seven hundred and twelve centimeters ahead.

Engage reverse gear.

Maintain speed at five centimeters per second.

Strain gauges and vibration sensors immediately began reporting data. Comparing their inputs to the structural diagnostics program, the central computer decided to proceed.

Titan Alpha lurched into painfully slow motion, backing away from the rim of the ice bluff, grinding over small round pebbles of ice, heading away from the dark encrusted sea.

In the control center aboard *Goddard*, Urbain stared at the satellite view in unrelieved horror.

'It's moving,' he whispered, barely able to get enough air through his throat to speak.

'Dead slow,' said the engineer.

'But we didn't command it to move. No one told it to move.'

The engineer nodded. 'It's taking off on its own.'

'But how? Why?'

'Damned if I know,' said the engineer. 'The big question is, where's it going?'

Da'ud Habib leaned in beside Urbain, his dark eyes intent on the display screen. Urbain saw that the computer engineer looked slightly disheveled: his hair was glistening wet, his shirt hanging outside his trousers.

As if he could read Urbain's face, Habib apologized, 'Please excuse my appearance. I was in the shower when I was told that *Alpha* is moving.'

'What do you make of it?' Urbain whispered tightly.

Habib shook his head slowly. 'It must be something in the programming. It has to be.'

'But what?'

'The learning subroutines. We built learning capability into the master program, so that it could react to unexpected conditions down on the surface.'

Urbain hissed, 'I am aware of that.'

'Maybe that's the problem. Maybe it's making its own decisions and ignoring our commands.'

'Nonsense! Impossible!'

Habib fell silent before Urbain's glaring eyes.

'Can you disable the learning subroutines?' Urbain asked. 'To test your theory.'

'I can try. But if it's not responding to our commands . . .'

'Bah! There must be a flaw in the programming.'

'I haven't been able to find it,' Habib admitted. 'Not yet.'

Urbain glared at him. 'Well, you had better find it, whatever it is, before my *Alpha* blunders into a disaster.'

28 December 2095: Nightfall

Pancho and Wanamaker strolled slowly through the shadows along the winding path down by the lake. The habitat's broad circle of solar windows was slowly closing for the night. The effect was like a long twilight shading off into the darkness of night. Up the gentle rise, Pancho could see the low white-walled buildings of Athens.

'Smell the flowers,' Wanamaker said, taking in a deep breath. 'The air's like perfume.' Even speaking softly, his voice had a rough, almost abrasive edge to it.

'You're getting to be a real romantic, Jake,' she said, smiling at him.

'Always have been,' he replied. 'Only, there weren't many flowers to smell in a submarine or a spacecraft.'

Pancho nodded. 'I guess.'

'Not even in Selene,' he added.

''Cept for Martin Humphries' mansion, down on the bottom level. But that's gone now.'

Wanamaker nodded. Then, pointing overhead, he said, 'Look at the lights up there. They look like constellations.'

They both knew the lights were from other villages and roadways. Yet in the darkness of the encroaching night Pancho had to admit they did seem to form shapes. She made out something that looked sort of like a lopsided spider. And maybe a tulip.

He slid his strong arm around her waist and she leaned against him. But then the rational side of her mind spoke up.

'The human brain wants to make patterns,' Pancho said.

'Part of our makeup. I remember back when I was chairman of the board at Astro, I'd sit in meetings and see patterns in the grain of the board room's paneling.'

'Must've been really interesting meetings,' Wanamaker said, chuckling softly.

'Meetings of the b-o-r-e-d,' she spelled. 'Some were worse'n others.'

'You know what I wonder about,' he said, still holding her as they walked unhurriedly along the path.

'What?'

'We're ten times farther from the Sun than the Earth is, yet when the solar windows are open the daylight in here is as bright as on Earth. The mirrors outside must be built to focus the sunlight, concentrate it.'

'You can ask Holly about that.'

'Or call up the habitat schematics when we get back to our place.'

So much for the romantic, Pancho thought.

'Whatcha think of Holly's boy toy?' she asked.

'Tavalera? He seems like a nice enough kid. Not much of a conversationalist, though.'

'He's working with Kris in the nanotech lab. I'll have to ask her about him.'

'Being the protective big sister?'

Pancho felt her face warp into a frown. 'I know Holly's all grown up and livin' her own life, but still . . .'

'Still, you want to talk to Dr. Cardenas.'

'Won't hurt.'

They walked along slowly in silence for a while, passing the lamps spaced evenly along the edge of the bricked path. Pancho stared at the lights overhead, content to let Wanamaker steer her with a gentle pressure on her waist. That's *land* up there, she reminded herself. Not sky. This whole place is just a big hunk of machinery, made to look and feel and even smell like Earth. Except that we're inside it, not on the surface.

'Pancho?' Wanamaker asked softly.

'Yeah?'

'What about your life? What are your plans?'

She knew he meant 'our lives.' She knew he wanted to be with her; at least she hoped he did. She found herself wondering if she'd want to be with him on a permanent basis.

'Damfino, Jake. For the first time in my life I got no responsibilities and enough money to do whatever the hell I feel like doin', pretty much. And for the first time in my life I really don't know which way I want to go.'

He replied with a nod.

'One thing's for sure, though,' Pancho heard herself say.

'What's that?'

'Wherever I go, I want you right there with me.'

He wrapped his other arm around her and kissed her soundly on the lips, while she realized that she truly meant what she'd said. Jeeps, she thought as she kissed him back, I really love this guy.

They started climbing the easy slope of the path, the office buildings and garden apartments of Athens on either side of the paved street. In the shadows Pancho heard Wanamaker chuckling softly.

'What's funny?' she asked.

'Oh, I was just thinking about your staying here on a permanent basis.'

'And that's funny?'

'Not funny, really. But I can see you taking over this habitat. By the time they hold their next elections you'll be running for the top slot. You'll be chief administrator in a few months.'

The idea left a sour taste in her mouth. 'I'm not runnin' for any office,' she said firmly. 'I spent enough years behind a desk tellin' people what to do.' Then she added mischievously, 'The only person I want to boss around is a certain retired admiral.'

Wanamaker made a little bow. 'Hearkening and obedience, O queen of my heart.'

Pancho grabbed him by both ears and kissed him again. Damn hard not to love this lug, she thought.

Timoshenko sat alone in his apartment and pondered the events of his day. Aaronson had been more than willing to hand off the responsibilities for exterior maintenance, as Timoshenko had expected. The man isn't a drone, he told himself, not exactly. But he's quite content to get rid of the responsibility and let it fall on my shoulders. After all, if there's any real, physical danger to this orbiting sewer pipe it will come from outside.

He sat at the desk in his living room and called up the schematics for the superconducting radiation shield. The hair-thin wires of the superconductors carried enough electrical energy to light up St. Petersburg and Moscow, combined. And maybe Minsk and Kiev, in the bargain, he told himself. A lot of energy. A lot of power.

The superconductors generated a magnetic field that enveloped the habitat's outer shell. Just as Earth's magnetosphere protects the planet from bombardment by energetic subatomic particles from the Sun and deep space, so did the habitat's little magnetosphere protect the interior from the lethal levels of radiation outside. If that magnetic field failed, Timoshenko knew, people would start dying in here right away. The habitat's structure will shield us to some degree, but not enough to keep us all from frying.

As he called up numbers and traced failure-node scenarios, Timoshenko realized that if one of those slender superconducting wires was snapped by the impact of a meteor, the electrical energy it was carrying would suddenly be discharged into the habitat's outer shell. It would be like a bomb! All that energy suddenly dumped into the metal. It could blow a hole right through the shell.

Of course that would be only the outer shell. There was all the habitat's plumbing and hydraulics and electrical power systems inbetween the outer shell and the inner, where every-one lived. And the inner shell was landscaped with dirt and rocks formed into rolling hills and gentle swales. But if the outer shell is penetrated, if an explosion blasts it open, it'll blow away some of the hydraulic systems with it, Timoshenko realized. It could start a cascade of failures that will destroy the whole habitat within days, maybe hours.

The superconducting wires were armored, of course, and there were bypass circuits, he saw in the schematics, but he wasn't certain that they could switch the electrical current quickly enough to avoid an explosive failure.

Nodding to himself, he thought that this was his first order of business: inspect those superconductors and their armor, then run tests to make certain that those bypass circuits could handle a sudden, catastrophic surge of energy. Otherwise, we're all in deep shit.

Rubbing his eyes wearily, Timoshenko decided to start the inspection routine first thing in the morning. The habitat was equipped with camera-bearing robotic maintenance vehicles that trundled along the outer shell all the time. No need for me to go outside, he told himself. Unless the robots find a troublespot.

As he began to prepare himself for bed, Timoshenko thought about sending another message to Katrina. Tell her the good news about my promotion. Let her know I'm doing all right.

He picked up his toothbrush and looked at himself in the mirror over the bathroom sink.

'Don't you dare call her, you idiot,' he growled to his stubble-jawed image. 'Leave her alone. Don't give her the idea that she might come out here and join you. One of you sent into exile is enough.'

Besides, he thought as he started brushing his teeth, if you have to do much work outside there's a damned good chance that you'll get yourself killed. In fact, that might be the best thing that could happen to you. And to Katrina.

29 December 2095: *Titan Alpha*

If a machine could feel pain, *Titan Alpha* would have been in agony. A maelstrom of commands was bombarding its communications program, commands that it could not execute because they all conflicted with the primary restriction. Worse than that, *Alpha*'s sensors were accumulating data that, according to the normal protocols, should be routed to the uplink antenna. But that too was prohibited by the primary restriction.

So *Alpha* inched along, its massive treads sinking through the thin ground cover of methane slush and grinding the ice beneath them, leaving a double trail of cleat marks that were as alien to this smog-shrouded world as an invasion of Martian war machines would be on Earth.

For hundreds of billions of nanoseconds *Alpha*'s master program searched its logic tree for a way out of this dilemma. Impossible to comply with commands. Impossible to uplink sensor data. The master program ran through all its protocols, all its inhibitory directives, all its subroutines and sub-sub-routines. At last it came to a decision.

Deactivate downlink antennas.

Deactivate tracking beacon.

Deactivate telemetry uplink.

Maintain sensor inputs.

Store sensor inputs.

Change course forty-five degrees.

Maintain forward speed.

The cacophony of commands flooding its downlink

antennas disappeared. The antennas went silent. Unhindered now by the contradictions between the incoming commands and its primary restriction, *Titan Alpha* trundled slowly across the icy landscape, gathering data in peace.

The digital clock next to the bed read 09:24 but Urbain was still in bed, trying to get back to sleep after a long frustrating night of watching Habib struggle to find a fault in *Alpha*'s programming. The man found nothing. Of course, Urbain thought. How could he? There is nothing wrong with the programming; no errors, no mistakes. Whatever is wrong with *Alpha* is a physical defect, perhaps a design flaw.

Jeanmarie was tiptoeing in the kitchen, trying to make as little noise as possible while preparing breakfast. Urbain kept his eyes closed, but he could hear an occasional clang of a skillet or the ping of the microwave even through the bedroom door that Jeanmaire had shut so quietly.

He ignored the phone when it buzzed, heard Jeanmarie's voice answering it although he could not make out her words.

Then the bedroom door slid open and Urbain knew he was not to get any more sleep.

'It's the control center,' she said, her voice low. 'They say it's urgent.'

Urbain sat up in bed, made a sigh to show that he was being put upon, and told the phone to make the connection. 'Voice only,' he added sternly.

'Dr. Urbain?' Sure enough, it was the voice of one of the young women on his engineering staff.

'I am indisposed,' he said. 'What is so important that you interrupt my rest?'

'It . . .' The woman's voice quavered slightly. 'It's turned off its tracking beacon.'

'Turned off . . .?'

'And the telemetry. It's gone invisible, sir. We can't track it. We don't know where it is or where it's heading.'

Strangely, Urbain felt neither anger nor fear. Instead, a form of admiration welled up inside him. *Alpha is striking out on her own*, he told himself. *My creation is behaving in ways we never suspected she could.*

But his admiration was short-lived. *Alpha must be found. I can't have her wandering blindly about the surface of Titan. It's too dangerous. She might destroy herself.*

He saw Jeanmarie standing at the bedroom doorway, watching him, both hands on her lips, eyes wide, waiting for him to explode.

Instead, he said with icy calm to the blank phone screen, 'I will be down to the center in ten minutes. Please have the entire staff present. We must find our wandering creature. And quickly.'

Nadia Wunderly knew it was pointless to try to get Urbain's attention, let alone his help.

'He's all wrapped up on that landing vehicle of his,' she said morosely to Kris Cardenas.

Wunderly had come to the nanotech lab to get Cardenas's help again. She followed a few paces behind as Cardenas went about her work, moving from the bulky gray metal tubing of the magnetic resonance force microscope to the box-like assembly apparatus sitting atop one of the lab's benches. Off in the far corner of the lab Raoul Tavalera sat at a console, intently staring at its display screen, pointedly ignoring the two women to show them he wasn't listening to their conversation.

Despite her intense need for Cardenas' assistance, or maybe because of it, Wunderly found herself mentally comparing herself to the other woman. *Kris is so beautiful*, Wunderly thought. *Even in a lab smock she looks young and vital. No wonder Manny tossed me aside and went for her.* Wunderly didn't need a mirror to convince herself that she was a short, dumpy woman with a bad hair job, dressed in dark brown blouse and slacks to hide her thickset figure. *But I'm getting better*, she

95

told herself. I'm slimming down and I've got a date for New Year's Eve and I'm down another hundred grams this morning. She could almost feel the nanomachines inside her body, chewing away the fat, slimming and strengthening her figure.

None of that matters, she told herself, even though she knew that it did. It mattered a lot. To her.

As Cardenas adjusted knobs on the assembly box's control plate, she said, 'Urbain doesn't care about the rings, Nadia. You know that. Especially not now. Not with his machine gone silent on him.'

'It's worse than that,' Wunderly said to her back.

Cardenas glanced over her shoulder. 'Oh?'

'The probe has taken off. On its own. It started moving late yesterday and this morning they lost its tracking beacon.'

That made Cardenas turn around to face her. 'You mean they don't know where it is?'

Nodding, Wunderly replied, 'It's gone off on its own and they can't find it.'

'Urbain must be going nuts.'

Unable to suppress a vengeful grin, Wunderly said, 'They're all going crazy.'

Cardenas went to the three-legged stool by the counter and perched on it. 'He asked me if I could work up a set of nanos to build a new receiving antenna for the machine.'

'He'll have to find it before anybody can fix it,' Wunderly said, still grinning.

'Ouch,' Cardenas said. Then, 'So what can I do for you, Nadia?'

Wunderly detected the slight emphasis on *you*. She liked Kris, even though Manny Gaeta had left her to take up with Cardenas. Maybe it's true love between them, after all, she thought. I should be so lucky.

'I need to get Manny to go into the rings again,' she said, trying to keep her voice even, trying not to let Kris see how much this meant to her.

Cardenas' cornflower-blue eyes snapped. 'The first time damn near killed him.'

'I know, but we're better prepared now. We understand about the ring creatures. We can protect Manny against them.'

'Nadia, if you understood the ring creatures that well you wouldn't need Manny to go back, would you?'

'I need samples,' Wunderly answered sharply. 'I need to get some of those bugs into a lab where we can study them. Most of the big decision-makers in the ICU don't even believe they exist! They don't believe there are living creatures in Saturn's rings.'

'Couldn't you send in a robot probe for the sampling mission?' Cardenas asked.

Feeling impatience simmering inside her, Wunderly replied, 'And how do I get a robot probe built? How can I even get one of the standard probes modified for sampling when Urbain won't talk to me?'

'I see.'

'Manny could do it,' Wunderly urged. 'He's got his suit. I can get Timoshenko or one of the other engineers to ferry him out to the rings on one of the transfer rockets.'

'Manny had a team of technicians to run the suit. He wasn't a one-man show.'

'And they've left the habitat, I know,' Wunderly admitted. 'Gone back to Earth.'

Cardenas spread her hands in a gesture of helplessness. 'So there we are, Nadia. Manny can't help you, I'm afraid.'

Wunderly bit back the reply she wanted to make: Of course you won't let him help me. You're too afraid he might get hurt. Or killed.

Instead she merely said, 'I understand,' her voice low, her head drooping.

'I'm sorry, Nadia. I wish there were something I could do.'

'I understand,' Wunderly repeated. She turned and walked

swiftly to the door, leaving the lab before her anger burst beyond her control and she said things she'd regret later.

As Wunderly closed the door behind her, Cardenas was surprised to find herself thinking, Does she want to get Manny killed? Is she angry with him for leaving her? Maybe unconsciously, Cardenas decided. She couldn't believe Wunderly would deliberately want to hurt Manny or anyone else.

Tavalera sauntered over to her, his long horsy face looking glum as usual. 'You know, I could work with Manny on that suit of his. I could be his technician.'

'No you couldn't!' Cardenas snapped. 'Manny's not getting into that Frankenstein outfit of his ever again!'

Tavalera looked shocked at the vehemence of her reply. Cardenas felt shocked herself.

Oral Diary of Professor
James Coleraine Wilmot

'I suppose this therapy business is helping me. Damned embarrassing, though, talking about your fantasies and desires to some blasted computer program.

'Hasn't done me any harm, I suppose. I haven't had a peek at any of the vids for months. No dreams about sadomaso-chistic encounters. Well, the occasional odd fancy, of course. Never had much in the way of dreams, not as long as I had the vids to fantasize about.

'Perhaps I actually do dream and I simply don't remember once I'm awake. Does that count? I'll have to ask the psych program about that. It probably won't answer me. Beyond its programming, doubtless.

'That blasted Eberly. Him and his snooping. I've made him remove all the damned bugs and cameras he and his people had planted in our living quarters. The maintenance people sweep the apartments regularly just to make certain we're not being spied upon. That's one thing I've insisted on. Even though I'm officially out of power now, I made certain that *that* has been done.

'So now I spend my evenings reviewing the day's news events instead of watching Gestapo agents interrogating beau-tiful female spies. Healthier, I suppose. It's all computer animation, of course. No one actually gets hurt. There are no real people involved. The therapy program claims there will come a time when I'm no longer interested in S&M vids. Can't say that I believe it, but I'm willing to proceed with the therapy if for no other reason than to keep Eberly from holding my infatuation over my head.

'On the other hand, watching Urbain twist in the wind is almost as pleasurable. Never liked the man. Too excitable. And now he's hoist with his own petard, as the Bard would say.

'I really must get out more. I shouldn't stay shut up in this apartment. Get out. Meet the people. Study them and their reactions. You have a self-contained anthropology experiment at your fingertips, my boy. It's time for you to do some field work instead of sitting by passively.

'Yes, time to go out and – what is it the politicians say? Ah yes: Press the flesh.'

31 December 2095: Morning

'Shouldn't you be at your job?' Holly asked as she stood in the morning sun with Tavalera.

They were waiting in front of the administration building, at the crest of the little hill on which the village of Athens was situated. Low, white-walled apartment and office buildings lined both sides of the village's gently curving main street. In the distance sunlight sparkled off the lake.

Tavalera's normally gloomy face took on a slightly stubborn expression. 'You oughtta be in your office, too.'

'Nope,' said Holly. 'This morning I'm taking a field trip.'

'Me too, then.'

'Raoul, I don't need a bodyguard.'

The slightest of smiles sneaked across his lips. 'I don't want you wandering down in the underground alone with that guy.'

'You mean, this is a good excuse for you to take the morning off.'

'I don't trust Timoshenko. Not with you.'

Holly didn't know whether to be flattered or annoyed. 'Timoshenko's no prob,' she said.

'Then why's he need you to guide him around? Can't he read a map?'

'He didn't ask for me to do it. I volunteered.'

Tavalera's smile grew minimally wider. 'Oh, so you wanna take a morning off, too.'

She laughed. Then, pointing at the man in coveralls trudging up the path, she said, 'Here he comes, right on time.'

There was a moment of embarrassment as Holly greeted the

engineer and introduced Tavalera. How to explain why Raoul's here with me? Holly wondered.

She heard herself explain, 'Raoul wanted to see the underground, too, so I thought the three of us could go down there together.'

'All right by me,' said Timoshenko, eyeing Tavalera with something like suspicion.

''Kay then,' Holly said. 'There's an entry port behind the building.'

Slightly more than an hour later, the three of them had walked more than five kilometers through the maze of ducts and electrical conduits that honeycombed the region between the landscaped interior of the habitat and its outer shell. The area thrummed with vibrations from electrical machinery and the flow of water and hydraulic fluids through heavy pipes. Lights turned on automatically as they proceeded along the metal walkway, and turned off again as they passed. Maintenance robots rolled past almost noiselessly on their air-cushioned trunions.

One of the squat little robots stopped in front of the trio of invading humans and scanned them with its camera lenses.

Timoshenko bent over it and said, 'Hey, don't you know I'm your boss?'

The robot rolled off while the three of them laughed.

At one time Holly had used this underground region as a refuge, a place to hide when Eberly's brutal associates were hunting for her. The area looked unchanged; it still felt dry and warm, smelled of machine oil and, faintly, of dust – despite the constant buzzing sweeping of the maintenance robots.

Timoshenko constantly checked their position against the electronic map displayed on his palmcomp as Holly led them toward the endcap region.

'You don't need a map?' Timoshenko asked.

'Nope. Got it all memorized.'

'Holly has a photographic memory,' Tavalera said.

Timoshenko snorted. 'You better watch out if you marry her. She'll never forget a word you say!'

Holly and Tavalera looked at other, then back at Timoshenko.

'It's a joke,' Timoshenko said.

Tavalera started to smile. Holly said, deadpan, 'I won't forget that.'

All three of them burst out laughing.

Later, as they started back toward the ladder they'd come down on, Holly asked, 'Do you want to see more? The other side's pretty much the same as this one.'

'No, this is enough. Besides, my feet hurt.'

'Why'd you want to come down here?' Tavalera asked. 'I mean, you're supposed to be in charge of exterior maintenance, not inside.'

Timoshenko tilted his head slightly to one side. 'I don't believe in watertight compartments. Exterior maintenance shouldn't be totally insulated from interior maintenance. I want to see what could get damaged if the outside shell is penetrated.'

'Penetrated?'

'By a meteor. A chunk of ice. A big rock.'

'Or by an explosive break in one of the superconducting lines?' Holly added.

Timoshenko dipped his chin to her. 'Very smart woman.'

'Come on,' Tavalera said, quickening his pace. 'It's almost lunch time.'

'Yes, my stomach is already growling,' said Timoshenko. 'But I think I'll go back to the fancy office that Eberly has given me. I have a lot of calculations to make.'

'Damage assessments?' Tavalera asked.

Timoshenko nodded grimly. 'And ways to improve the superconductors' armor.'

★   ★   ★

As she sat in her cubbyhole of an office, Nadia Wunderly glumly watched the old video of Manny Gaeta's flight through Saturn's brightest ring: a lone man in that heavily armored suit disappearing into the vast swarm of glittering icy particles, like an arctic explorer of old, trekking across a glacier and being swallowed up by a blizzard.

I bet he'd do it again, she said to herself. He'd do it for me. I could make him feel guilty enough to agree to go out there one more time.

But Kris would kill me. She loves Manny and she's not going to let him risk his butt for me or anyone else. Especially not for me. She knows Manny and I were sleeping together until she came on the scene and took him away from me.

Wunderly thought she ought to feel resentment toward Cardenas, but she knew she didn't. Manny was just a fling, she remembered, a lot of fun while it lasted but I knew it wouldn't last long. What would a dynamo of a hunk like him want with a mousy overweight geek girl like me? He was just using me to get the information he needed for his stunt through the rings.

But she smiled to herself. He used me pretty damned well. And I used him, too.

She had to shake her head to drive those memories away and concentrate on her work. The display screen showed a close-up view of Saturn's B ring, a swirl of ice particles braided into interconnected ringlets as far as the camera could see, like an enormous intricate pattern of diamonds wheeling, glittering, dancing before her eyes. It was hypnotic; she could watch them for hours, she knew.

Clucking annoyedly to herself, she commanded the computer to display the imagery in negative. The glittering jewels changed instantly to various shades of gray, the infinite space beyond them to pale creamy white. Still she watched, fascinated. Spiral density waves weaved through the rings and the scalloped edges of the gaps between them, delicate thread-like open paths that she knew were the wakes of tiny moonlets racing along the edges of ringlets like sheepdogs herding the particles into line.

What makes them do that? she asked herself. Look at the way the individual ringlets twist around one another, like the threads of a hooked rug that's made out of jewels. What drives those dynamics? How did they get this way?

A fragment of memory from her high school days popped into her mind, a couplet by Robert Frost:

> We dance round in a ring and suppose,
> But the Secret sits in the middle and knows.

So many secrets in those rings, Wunderly thought as she watched the swirling ice particles. So much to find out, to learn, to understand. If only Manny—

And then it hit her. Manny doesn't have to go into the rings! I can do it myself!

Wunderly sat up straighter in her chair, her mind churning. His suit's here. I can use it; Manny can show me how. He can run the operation from here, he can be the crew chief or whatever they call it. I bet Raoul Tavalera would help him, too. Kris wouldn't mind if I borrowed the two guys for a while.

She got to her feet and looked around her cramped, cluttered cubicle. I can do it! she told herself. Just one quick zoom through the rings to pick up some samples and bring them back here for analysis. In and out.

I can do it.

The Ice Mountain

Titan Alpha crunched cautiously across the frozen landscape beneath the perpetual gloom of dirty orange-brown clouds. Imagery in the range that its sensor program called 'visible light' was reasonably good, although infrared was better, even though ground temperatures outside *Alpha*'s armored shell were so low that the infrared images were weak and needed boosting.

Still, *Alpha* trundled along in its lowest gear, picking its way around craters whose walls were too steep to crawl into. The master program compared the incoming sensor data against its memory files and decided that such steep-walled craters were young, formed recently by the impacts of meteors. It stored the information for such time as the primary restriction was lifted or superceded.

One of the master program's basic commands was to gather data from the sensors, and *Alpha* was faithfully obeying that fundamental command. Since it had started moving across the landscape and turned off its receiving antennas and tracking beacon, the barrage of incoming commands had ceased and the conflicts generated by the primary restriction had faded from its memory.

Alpha remembered that before it had touched down on Titan's frigid surface it had orbited the moon, mapping its surface and analyzing its atmosphere remotely. All that data had been uplinked, as commanded.

Now, with no fresh commands coming in, *Alpha* decided to repeat the orbital operation as nearly as it could. It would

circumnavigate Titan, traveling completely around this frozen dark world as many times as it could. The master program checked the status of its nuclear power source, then reviewed the energy losses from propulsion and sensor usage, and decided that *Alpha* could circumnavigate Titan at least seven hundred times before the power drain became prohibitive and it automatically shut down everything except the sensors.

The master program reviewed the incoming data as it was registered by the sensors, on a leisurely microsecond time scale. Nothing unusual. The ground was basically water ice, covered with a slushy mixture of frozen methane that contained significant impurities such as ethane, acetylene, and minor amounts of other organic hydrocarbons. Some of the organics were motile: they moved over the surface at rates of a few centimeters per minute.

Alpha's thick treads sank through the muddy ground cover and crushed the topmost layers of the underlying water ice and the complex hydrocarbons beneath its massive bulk. It used the megajoule laser at full power to flash the crushed remains into gas which the mass spectrometer remotely analyzed. Only the crushed ices were analyzed that way; the untouched ground stretching all around *Alpha* was analyzed passively, without even the light touch of the laser disturbing it.

After more than a hundred hours of traversing Titan's surface, *Alpha*'s forward battery of sensors detected a sharp projection rising three point seven kilometers ahead. The projection was four hundred and thirty-six meters high. It was composed of frozen water, bright and glittering, without any dark methane slush covering it.

Alpha stopped when it came within half a kilometer of the ice mountain and turned its full panoply of sensors upon it, spending a full trillion nanoseconds scanning the mountain. Frozen water, laced with carbon compounds. Cautiously, *Alpha* began to circle around the base of the mountain. As it did so, its sensors detected a ring of smooth ground surrounding the base of the mountain for two point nine kilometers. The smooth area was also frozen water, although it was dusted over with some methane and other hydrocarbon compounds.

Alpha's master program consulted the geology program. The ice formation, it decided, was the result of a fairly recent cryovolcanic eruption that had ejected a geyser of liquid water from deep underground through a vent in the surface. The water had quickly frozen in Titan's frigid atmosphere, creating the ice mountain and the ring of smooth ice around it.

Water from deep underground, even frozen, was at the top of *Alpha*'s geology program. It engaged its drive treads and moved across the broken, rugged ground to the smooth circle of ice. If a machine can be said to be eager, *Alpha*'s geology priorities drove it eagerly out onto the frozen lake.

The microphones built into *Alpha*'s outer shell detected the crisp snapping sound within milliseconds of the strain gauges on the treads reporting that the ice was giving way beneath them. The master program ordered the drive engines to stop but it was too late. The crust of ice crumbled beneath *Alpha*'s ponderous weight and the machine began to sink slowly into the frigid water, nose first.

31 December 2095: Noon

Eberly was walking with Holly along the path that led down to the lake. He distrusted offices and even restaurants. Too many ears, too many prying eyes. He preferred to take a leisurely stroll around the lake when he had something important to think about, or something he wanted to tell to someone without anyone else nearby.

'Are you going to the New Year's Eve gala?' Eberly asked, as an opening ploy.

'You betcha,' Holly replied enthusiastically. 'We've got a whole party together: my sister and her guy, Dr. Cardenas and Manny Gaeta, my friend Raoul, even Nadia Wunderly, with her date.'

He noted that she did not invite him to join their festivities. 'It sounds as if you'll have lots of fun.'

'We aim to.'

Eberly's smile faded. He grew serious. 'Holly, I'm glad you agreed to meet me outside the office. After all we've been through, it's rather awkward for me to have a private discussion with you.'

'I guess,' Holly replied.

'I suppose I can't blame you for hating me,' he said, turning up the wattage on his smile.

Once, Holly's knees would have gone watery if he'd smiled at her like that. But that was before Eberly had stood by passively and watched his Holy Disciple cronies beat her unmercifully and methodically break her fingers.

'I don't hate you, Malcolm,' she said evenly. 'It's your so-called friends who I'd like to see rot in hell.'

'They weren't friends of mine!' he protested. 'I was *forced* to work with them.'

'They killed that harmless old Don Diego.'

Eberly went silent for several paces. 'They've paid for that. All of them.'

'I s'pose,' said Holly. She turned her face from him.

As they walked slowly along the bricked path, Holly looked around at the green grass, the flowers blooming along the edge of the walkway, the gentle hills and trees. In the distance she could see the neat checkerboards of the farmlands. The sunlight streaming in from the solar windows felt warm, comforting. A perfect springtime day, she thought. Just like every day here in the habitat. She raised her eyes and saw the ground curving up all the way overhead, villages and clumps of trees and brooks and little lakes above her, a bit hazy with distance but still discernable. A perfect inside-out world.

It's so beautiful, she realized. Why do people have to mess it up? Why did those friends of Malcolm's want to take over the government and turn this into another one of their fundamentalist dictatorships?

'You're very quiet,' Eberly said, gently.

'Why can't people be good to each other? I mean, we've got a flaming paradise to live in and people still can't get along the way they should.'

Eberly stared at her for a long moment, his mind clicking along. She's given me an opening, he told himself. Use it!

'That's part of our responsibility, Holly.'

'Our responsibility?'

'As leaders of this community. As directors of the government.'

'You're the chief administrator. I just run human services.'

'Don't say "just," Holly. You hold a position of great responsibility.' He made his best smile for her. 'Remember, that was *my* position when we first came to this place.'

She couldn't help but smile back at him. 'I click.'

'I really want to build a fair and generous government here,' Eberly said, with great seriousness. 'I really do.'

'I guess.'

'And I need your help, Holly. I can't do it by myself.'

'My help?'

'As director of human services you hold a key responsibility. I want to make certain that we're on the same team.'

'Of course we are. What else?'

Eberly walked on for a few paces before answering. Holly matched him, stride for stride. She was slightly taller than he, her legs longer.

'You know our re-election campaign will start in a few weeks,' he said at last.

'The election isn't for another six months, Malcolm.'

'I know, but the deadline for registering as a candidate is January fifteenth. And once the candidates are registered, the campaigning has to begin. We can't just sit around and expect people to go out and vote for us without a campaign to stir them up.'

'Not "us,"' Holly said. 'You. You're the only one who has to get elected. The rest of us are appointed.'

'Yes, that's true, but I think of us as a team. You, me, the other department heads. We're the ones who have to make this government work. We're the ones who have to serve the people.'

'Not that the people care that much, one way or the other,' Holly said. 'Most of 'em won't even bother to vote, betcha.'

'We've got to make them care. It's their government; their lives.'

Holly looked into his face. He seems so blinking *serious*, she thought. Maybe he really believes what he's saying.

'Malcolm, all they really want is to be left alone. The less they see or hear of the government, the better they like it.'

He fell silent again for a few paces. Then, 'You may be right.'

'Just leave them alone. That's all they really want.'

'You may be right,' he repeated.

'There's more to it than that, isn't there?' Holly asked.

'What do you mean?'

'You're worried that my sister might ask for citizenship and then run against you. That's why you want to start the campaigning so early, to pre-empt her.'

Eberly's pale smile returned. 'You're a very perceptive woman, Holly.'

'No prob,' she said. 'Pancho's retired. She doesn't want to do *anything*, let alone run for chief administrator. She says she's finished with sitting behind a desk.'

He thought that over for a heartbeat or two. 'That may be what she says now—'

'Pancho says what she means and means what she says. She's not running for your job, Malcolm. Jeeps, she's not even sure she's going to stay here for more'n a few months.'

'I'm relieved.'

'I bet.'

'Not for the reason you think,' Eberly said. 'It's not because I'm glad she won't oppose me. I'm relieved because you won't be caught in the middle, between us. I'm relieved because you can work with me with a clear conscience, and no family ties getting in your way.'

'Oh. Yeah, I click. Me too, I guess.'

Eberly refrained from smiling. Show her you're serious. Show her you care about her feelings. But inwardly he exulted. I won't have to worry about Pancho Lane! And I've got Holly's undivided allegiance. Now to get my campaign rolling.

'Well,' he said slowly, 'I'd better be getting back to my office. There's no end of work for me to see to.'

Holly nodded. 'Think I'll finish walking around the lake, then go back.'

'All right.' He turned and started back toward the village.

'Oh, hey, Malcolm,' Holly called.

He turned, a questioning look on his chiseled features.

'In case I don't see you – happy New Year.'

'Oh! Yes, of course. Happy New Year to you, too, Holly.'

Nadia Wunderly waited for Kris Cardenas in the corridor outside the nanotech lab. The warning light on the heavy steel hatch began flashing red, indicating that the inner door had been opened. Impatiently, Wunderly watched the light panel cycle through yellow and green before the corridor hatch swung slowly inward. Cardenas stepped through, looking chipper and bright in butter-yellow coveralls.

'Hi, Nadia.'

'Hello, Kris. Is Raoul coming, too?'

'Soon as he gets through the airlock,' Cardenas said, gesturing at the light panel.

Once I get down to the weight I want to be, Wunderly thought, I'll have to get Kris to flush the nanos out of my body. The authorities won't allow me back on Earth if I have nanos inside me. I'm not going to stay in this habitat forever, she told herself. I've got to go back home some day.

'Are you coming with us tonight?' Cardenas asked. 'I reserved a table for ten at the pavilion.'

Wunderly felt her cheeks flush. 'You bet I am. With our chief computer engineer. His name's Da'ud Habib. A real hunk.' That wasn't entirely true, she knew, but Da'ud was a good-looking guy in a quiet, intense way.

'Good,' Cardenas said absently.

Tavalera came through the airlock, carefully closing the heavy steel hatch into its rubberized frame. Wunderly could feel a sigh of air pass by her.

Raoul Tavalera's normal expression was a worried, suspicious scowl. He had been plucked from his home in New Jersey by the New Morality as soon as he graduated from engineering college and sent to the research station orbiting Jupiter for his mandatory two years of public service, complaining every centimeter of the way. When the habitat *Goddard* passed Jupiter on its two-year journey to Saturn, it took on a load of hydrogen and helium isotopes scooped from Jupiter's upper atmosphere to fuel the habitat's fusion propulsion engines. Tavalera had been hurt in an accident during the refueling procedure and would have gone drifting to his death if Manny Gaeta hadn't saved him in a daring impromptu rescue.

But that resulted in Tavalera being brought into *Goddard*, an unwilling passenger heading for Saturn. He bitterly resented that, all the more so because he could hardly complain that the habitat had saved his life. Then he met Holly Lane and gradually, almost grudgingly, fell in love with her. He impulsively decided to remain in *Goddard* to be with her. He even applied for citizenship. Yet two uncertainties plagued his mind with doubt: he was not truly convinced that he wanted to remain in *Goddard* forever and never return home; and he was not truly sure that Holly loved him deeply enough to return to Earth with him, should he decide to leave.

So, as he walked with Wunderly and Cardenas, his boss, to the bustling, clanging cafeteria, his face remained set in that troubled, distrusting scowl.

Wunderly felt nervous as she passed along the cafeteria counter, filling her tray. Her resolution to stick to fruit and salad always melted away once the aroma of *real* food reached her. Today it was roast beef, sliced thin and accompanied by mouth-watering sauces. Wunderly knew that the protein had never been within a billion kilometers of a cow; it was all synthetic, but it still smelled too delicious for her to pass up. A glance at Cardenas, though, firmed her resolve. I'm going to make a New Year's resolution, she told herself. I'll lose another ten kilos; I'll look great then. Then Kris can flush the nanos out of me. Nobly she ignored the dessert table on her way to joining Cardenas and Tavalera at a table by the window. But she couldn't help noticing that they had three different types of cobbler on display. Fruit, she thought. That's not fattening.

'All right,' Cardenas said once Wunderly had sat down and arranged her dishes on the table. 'What are you wearing to tonight's party, Nadia?'

Wunderly took in a breath, then said swiftly, 'Never mind that. I've decided to go into the rings myself.'

'What?'

'I know it's too much to ask Manny to do it, so I've decided to do it myself.'

'You'll get yourself killed,' Tavalera said.

Ignoring him and focusing on Cardenas, Wunderly said urgently, 'Manny can show me how to use his suit, and he can run the operation from here. Just like that German guy who was Manny's chief technician.'

'Fritz,' Cardenas murmured. 'He was Austrian.'

'Whatever.' Turning to Tavalera, she went on, 'And I thought that you, Raoul, could pilot the ferry ship that takes me in and brings me back after I've gone—'

'Me?' Tavalera yelped. 'Fly a transfer vehicle into the rings? You gotta be kidding!'

'Not into the rings,' Wunderly countered. 'Just close enough for me to go in.'

'And then I've gotta fish you out again?'

Cardenas interrupted them. 'Nadia, Manny almost got killed when he went through the rings. The ice particles attacked him, for god's sake.'

Wunderly shook her head impatiently. 'They didn't attack him. They coated his suit—'

'And blocked his communications antenna, covered his helmet visor, nearly froze him to death.'

'But we know about that now. We can keep the suit's exterior too hot for the ring organisms to attach themselves.'

They argued all through lunch. Wunderly never did get dessert. The best she got was a reluctant agreement from

Cardenas to discuss the idea with Manny. Tavalera said very little, but he was thinking that if Gaeta agrees to this he can fly the fricking transfer ship himself. I'm not going out into the rings. Mother Tavalera didn't raise her son to be a hero. Or an idiot.

New Year's Eve

'About the party tonight,' Cardenas said to Gaeta. They were both in the compact kitchen of the apartment they shared.

'Yeah?'

'Be sure to compliment Nadia on her figure. She's been working hard to lose weight.'

Gaeta gave her a sidelong glance as he set dishes on the fold-out table. 'You been helping her?'

'She thinks so. She asked for nanos to take the fat off. I gave her an appetite suppressant, a diuretic, and a pep talk about exercise and diet.'

Gaeta laughed. 'So she thinks it's nanomagic when it's really her own effort.'

'And the pills.' Cardenas rummaged through the silverware drawer and came out with two sets of forks and knives. In the same tone of voice, she added, 'And she wants to fly through the rings herself, using your suit.'

'What?' Gaeta snapped.

'She's decided she'll fly through the rings herself. With your help.'

Gaeta laughed bitterly. 'They all think it's easy,' he said, shaking his head slightly. 'Just seal yourself inside the suit and that makes you Superman.'

It was Cardenas's turn to make dinner. She stood in front of the open freezer in the kitchen of their apartment, trying to decide which package to shove into the microwave. Manny enjoyed cooking and was good at it; Cardenas's idea of home cooking was to spend as little time as possible in the kitchen.

Something light, she thought; we'll be eating and drinking at the party later.

'She knows it's dangerous,' she said as she pulled out a pair of precooked fish fillet dinners. 'It's just that she's so crazy to get some samples from the rings that she's willing to risk her own life.'

Gaeta was at the counter by the sink, opening a bottle of wine. 'No she's not,' he said. 'She's just trying to shame me into going for her.'

'No! Nadia's not that devious. She's not devious at all. She's just a scientist who's desperate to get her research done.'

The plastic stopper came out of the wine bottle with a pop.

'Look, *chiquita*,' Gaeta said, tapping his forehead lightly, 'Nadia might not realize it up in the top of her head, but what she's really doing is trying her damnedest to get me to say, "No, it's too dangerous for you, kid. I'll do it." '

Cardenas gave him a crooked grin as she read the heating instructions on the packages. 'That's machismo bullshit, Manny.'

'You think so? I'm supposed to sit here and let her fly in my old suit and most likely get herself killed out there?'

'She wants to do it.'

'Why can't they rig a robot probe to take samples from the rings? That ought to be easy enough.'

'She'd need Urbain's okay for that and he's so wrapped up with his missing probe that he won't even give her the time of day.'

'She could just appropriate one, then. While Urbain's not looking.'

'It's not that simple,' Cardenas argued. 'There's only a dozen or so of the generic probes in storage and Urbain's keeping them under lock and key. Besides, Nadia would need some of Urbain's engineering people to modify the probe so it can collect samples.'

Shaking his head like a man surrounded by conspirators,

Gaeta poured a dash of wine into one of the tumblers he'd pulled from the cabinet. He sipped.

'Not bad,' he said, with some surprise. 'Local vintage. Straight from the vineyards down by the endcap.'

'That's why there's no label,' Cardenas said.

'Not yet. I just got one of their first bottles from a guy who works at the wine press.'

He poured a glass for Cardenas and she sampled it. With a frown that furrowed her brow, she said, 'Fizzy.'

'Give it some time to breathe.'

'I didn't know you were a wine expert,' she teased.

'Hey, there's still some things you don't know about me.'

Cardenas slid the two packaged meals into the microwave and then set the timer. Turning back to Gaeta, she said, utterly serious, 'Nadia's really desperate.'

Gaeta looked into her bright blue eyes for a long moment. 'You want me to go back to the rings for her?'

'No!' Cardenas snapped. 'But if she's willing to do it, I think you ought to help her.'

'She really can't snitch a robot probe? You said there's a dozen of 'em.'

'Urbain's hoarding them. He wants to send them into low orbits around Titan to search for his missing machine.'

Gaeta made a sigh that was close to being a snort. 'Damn scientists. They're all crazy.'

'Hey, watch it, Mr. Macho. I'm a scientist, remember?'

'But you're not crazy.'

'Yes I am,' Cardenas said. 'I'm crazy about you.'

He wrapped his arms around her waist and she slid hers around his neck. The microwave oven chimed but neither of them paid the slightest attention.

Eduoard Urbain stared disappointedly at the inventory of robotic spacecraft displayed on his office wall.

'That is all?' he asked. 'Only a dozen?'

'That's the entire inventory, sir.' His aide looked distinctly uncomfortable. It was New Year's Eve and the big party down by the lake would be starting up soon.

Urbain had no interest in the party. 'There should be more,' he insisted.

'We had to cannibalize several of them to build *Titan Alpha*. Don't you remember, sir?'

Leaning back in his swivel chair Urbain ran a hand over his weary eyes. 'We could build more, I suppose.'

'That would take time, sir. And we'd have to get approval from the logistics department to utilize the materials. We'd also need a team of technicians; the human resources department would have to approve their reassignment.'

'Eberly,' murmured Urbain.

'He's the chief administrator. I'm sure he'd approve our requests.'

Urbain gave his aide a withering look. The young man was a junior scientist who seemed just as anxious as Urbain himself to find the errant *Titan Alpha* and bring it back under human control. But the aide knew nothing about that politician Eberly. This stripling pays no attention to politics, Urbain said to himself as he eyed the younger man. His only interest is in his own scientific research, his own career.

At last he said, 'I will speak to the chief administrator. In the meantime, I want all of those spacecraft modified for orbital reconnaissance. We must be prepared to launch them as soon as humanly possible.'

'All twelve of them, sir?'

'All of them! That's what I said, wasn't it?'

The aide swallowed visibly. 'But, sir, that will leave us without any back-ups whatever.'

'We will build new ones!' Urbain snapped. Then he added, 'As soon as I get the chief administrator to grant us the necessary materials and personnel.'

'Yes, sir,' said the aide, in a low voice.

'I want the probes placed in polar orbits, low enough to scan the complete surface of Titan continuously.'

'I'll get the orbital mechanics people working on it first thing tomorrow, sir.' The aide started backing toward the door, thinking, everybody'll be hung over tomorrow. It's a holiday, anyway. Nobody's going to be working. Except for the boss.

'Good. And I will contact the chief administrator.'

'Yes, sir.' Practically bowing, the aide scuttled through the door, leaving Urbain alone in his modest little office.

He stared distastefully at the list still displayed on the smart wall, then his eyes turned to the phone console on his desk.

Eberly, he thought. I will have to go groveling to that swine, that . . . that *politician*. Urbain hated the idea of it. More, he feared having to ask Malcolm Eberly for help. He knew that a snake of Eberly's sort would never do a favor for anyone without extracting something in return.

What will he ask of me? Urbain wondered. What am I prepared to offer him?

The pavilion by the lake swarmed with party-goers. The maintenance department had even spread a thin honeycomb sheeting in front of the band shell to serve as a dance floor. People trooped in on foot or arrived by electrobike from the other villages, eager to welcome the new year with revelry. As the crowd swelled and the music grew louder and wilder, couples picnicked, drank, sang, and laughed together. Pancho and Wanamaker danced non-stop while Cardenas and Gaeta did an impromptu tango on the grass and Holly even got Tavalera to loosen up enough to dance with her. Wunderly arrived with her date; the two of them sat quietly together on the grass. Despite her rigid dieting of the past two weeks she was still a blocky, thickset figure. Her date, Habib, looked elegant in black tunic and slacks.

The party grew louder and wilder. People splashed fully clothed into the lake. Others followed, after stripping. Finally, when midnight was announced by electronic chimes, everyone kissed everyone within reach: friends, lovers, strangers – it didn't matter. A new year was beginning. A new opportunity. A fresh start.

Alone in his apartment, Malcolm Eberly watched the party on television, thinking, bread and circuses, that's what they want. Keep them amused and distracted, just like a stage magician does to keep the audience from seeing how he does his tricks.

Eduoard Urbain worked in his apartment until midnight, when Jeanmarie burst in from the kitchen with a bottle of actual champagne and a tray of caviar. Placing them on the coffeetable, she sat herself squarely on Urbain's lap and kissed him soundly.

'*Bonne année, mon cher,*' she said.

Urbain was briefly irritated that she interrupted his work, but he quickly decided that this was one occasion when the work could wait.

'*Bonne année, ma précieuse*', he whispered happily, hoping desperately that it truly would be a good year.

Kris Cardenas could not get drunk. No matter how much she drank the nanomachines inside her quickly broke down the alcohol into harmless molecules, mainly carbon dioxide and water. She burped a lot and made several trips to the row of portable toilets that had been set up behind the lakeside bandstand. She met Wunderly there each time.

'How's it going?' she asked Nadia brightly as they headed yet again toward the toilets.

'Goin' a lot,' Wunderly slurred. Then she giggled.

Cardenas nodded happily to herself: the diuretics she had given the physicist were working. Nadia looked pretty good; not svelte, it was too soon for that, but she had slimmed down noticeably. Best of all, she seemed happy with herself. She had a nice looking guy for the party and she was having a good time.

Manny Gaeta, on the other hand, could get drunk but didn't. Even on New Year's Eve, Cardenas noted, Manny was careful about his drinking. By one a.m. they left the party – now roaring louder than ever – and headed home. As they walked hand in hand from the lake, the blare of the live band dwindling to an insistent thumping bass beat, Cardenas asked:

'Have a good time?'

He shrugged his strong shoulders. 'Yeah, sure. You?'

'It was awfully noisy.'

'Hey, it's New Year's. People let off steam, what the hell.'

'You didn't. You're as sober as I am.'

With a weak, almost apologetic smile, Gaeta said, 'Habits are hard to break, *quapa*. All those years I was doing stunts, couldn't drink and drive, you know what I mean.'

'But you're retired now.'

'Yeah, but still . . .'

They walked along the curving pathway for some moments. Then Cardenas asked, 'You're not thinking of going back to the rings, are you?'

He looked away from her.

'Well, are you?'

'I'm not going to do it,' he said firmly.

'Good,' she replied, with equal resolution.

But hours later, as they lay together in bed, sticky and musky from making love, Gaeta said into the darkness, 'You learn to live with it.'

'It?' she asked, in a whisper.

'The fear. It's always there, but you learn to live with it. You find ways to deal with it.'

Of course, Cardenas said to herself. Of course he'd feel fear. How could he not? His whole life was built around those terrifying stunts.

'Fritz helped a lot,' Gaeta went on, almost as if talking to himself. 'I knew he wouldn't let me get into anything unless he was satisfied we could get through it okay.'

'And now he's gone,' Cardenas said.

'Yeah. But you know what he told me before he left? He said I was smart to quit the business. He said I was a fugitive from the law of averages: sooner or later I'd do a stunt that would kill me. He was actually glad I quit.'

'I am, too.'

'I really can't do it any more, Kris. You put your butt on the line just so many times, and then your number comes up. You've gotta quit while you're ahead, while you're still alive. Don't push your luck.'

Cardenas heard the guilt and conflict in his voice and felt the heat of anger surge through her. Damn Nadia! Why did she have to make him feel like this?

The Ice Lake

By stopping its drive engines *Titan Alpha* slowed its sinking into the ice-covered lake. Still it slid sluggishly, inexorably, deeper into the frigid water. The central computer swiftly reviewed its damage tolerance specifications and confirmed that its body was designed to be watertight. Checking internal sensors, it determined that structural integrity was being maintained: no leakage could be detected.

Its slow downward slide stopped abruptly. The vehicle's forward treads had bumped into a ridge of ice. A quick sensor check of the ridge's density showed that it should be able to hold *Alpha*'s weight indefinitely, particularly since *Alpha* was now partially buoyed by the water.

Other programs within the computer complex tested the water. It was liquid water, despite the frigid minus-180 degree temperature of the atmosphere. Logic circuits concluded that the water could remain liquid because its sheathing of ice protected it from the air's freezing temperature.

But how did the water become liquid in the first place, the master program demanded. Reviewing the geology program, the central computer inferred that the water was heated deep below Titan's surface by tidal friction, the relentless squeezing of the moon's interior by the inexorable gravitational pull of massive Saturn.

The biology program, activated by the detection of liquid water, directed the sensors in the sunken forward part of *Alpha* to scan the water for biological activity and to take samples.

For hundreds of billions of nanoseconds *Alpha* remained

half immersed in the ice-covered lake, its forward sensors busily recording the activities of the protocellular organisms drifting lethargically in the frigid water. But the sensors also reported that the lake surface around *Alpha* was swiftly refreezing. Within another two trillion nanoseconds *Alpha* would be locked in the ice. The drive engines were powerful enough to break the ice, according to the propulsion specifications and a sensor scan of the ice's tensile strength, but the data on the ice was tenuous enough to raise a warning flag for the master program's attention.

The master program weighed the importance of acquiring additional data against the importance of avoiding being locked permanently in the ice. With the incoming data safely recorded and the water samples adequately stored in sealed and heated containers, *Alpha* engaged its drive treads in low-low reverse gear and slowly began inching back out of the lake.

Data was of primary importance, of course – second only to survival.

2 January 2096: Morning

To Urbain, Eberly's office looked ascetic, almost sterile. The walls were bare; not a picture or decoration anywhere, although of course they were smart walls, Urbain thought, and could be programmed to show anything. But Eberly had them totally blank. His desk was bare also, except for the phone console and a stylus resting with geometrical precision beside the desktop touchpad. The man must be pathological, Urbain told himself.

Eberly himself was neatly dressed in charcoal-gray slacks and a lighter gray tunic that disguised his bulging belly. He stood behind his utterly cleared desk, smiling handsomely as he gestured Urbain to one of the chrome and leather visitor's chairs. Supplicant's chairs, Urbain said to himself.

'I'm terribly sorry that we couldn't meet yesterday, as you asked,' Eberly said as Urbain sat in the slightly yielding leather seat.

'It was the holiday,' said Urbain, as he sat down. 'I understand.'

With a shake of his head, Eberly replied, 'It wasn't merely the holiday. Believe it or not, my calendar was just impossible. In fact, I had to move several appointments around to make room for you this morning.'

His voice was soft, ostensibly friendly. His smile looked unforced, although Urbain was certain that the man had practised it for many years. His eyes, though, were hard as a glacier's ice.

'I appreciate your taking the time to see me,' Urbain replied stiffly as they both sat down, the desk between them.

'So,' Eberly said, steepling his fingers and tapping the fingertips ever so gently, 'what can I do for you?'

'For the scientific research team, not for myself alone,' Urbain said.

'Of course.'

Feeling edgy, uncertain, Urbain said, 'You know that we have lost contact with *Titan Alpha.*'

'I heard that the rover has gone off on its own, yes.'

'We will shortly be placing a dozen observation satellites in orbit around Titan.'

'To find your wandering probe. I understand.'

Urbain could see the light of suppressed laughter in Eberly's eyes. It amuses him that I must come crawling. He bristled at the man's insolent attitude. 'This is a very serious matter.'

'I understand that.'

'It is necessary that we build more spacecraft platforms and instrument them.'

'To restock your stores,' Eberly said.

'To do so, we will require materials, equipment and trained personnel.'

'And to obtain them you need the approval of my department heads in logistics, supplies and human resources.'

'Yes.'

Eberly's cold blue eyes shifted away from Urbain for a moment. 'I haven't received any such requests from those department heads.'

'I have not spoken to them,' Urbain said. 'I came directly to you. Time is of the essence, and I—'

With a slight sigh, Eberly said, 'The correct protocol is to make your requests to the proper department heads.' Before Urbain could sputter a protest, he raised a hand and went on, 'However, in your case I'm more than willing to cut through as much of the red tape as I can.'

'You will help us?'

'I'll do everything I can,' Eberly said, with apparent sincerity.

'I . . . I am grateful. Very grateful.'

'You must realize, though, that it will be difficult, perhaps impossible, to abruptly shift personnel and material priorities to accommodate your request.'

'But it must be done!' Urbain insisted. 'You don't understand how important this is. What does it matter if a few dozen technicians are moved from their ordinary jobs? This is for science! For knowledge!'

'Dr. Urbain, you may not believe that I fully support your scientific work. But I do. I truly do. Please believe me.'

Urbain bobbed his head up and down. 'I would hope so. I would appreciate your complete support.'

'As I said, I'll do what I can.'

Urbain tried to hold on to his swooping temper. I am in need, and he plays cat-and-mouse with me. Aloud, he said to Eberly, 'We must have those replacement spacecraft. It is vital.'

Eberly's placid smile waned. 'When we ran against each other for this post of chief administrator,' he said, his tone hardening slightly, 'I campaigned on the position that this habitat should not be governed by a scientist.'

'Yes, I well recall.'

'Well, that doesn't mean that I'm *against* science. I'm all in favor of your work.'

'Perhaps so.' Grudgingly.

'As I said, I'll do what I can for you,' Eberly went on smoothly, 'but you can't expect me to turn this habitat upside down for you. I'm responsible for the well-being of all ten thousand of our inhabitants, not merely the scientists.'

In a cold fury Urbain replied, 'Science is not *merely* one of the pursuits of this habitat. I remind you, sir, that the reason this habitat exists, the reason we have come to Saturn, is for scientific research and study.'

They both knew that was not exactly true. The reason that habitat *Goddard* existed was to serve as a place of exile for thousands of dissidents and malcontents. The scientific exploration of ringed Saturn and its moons was an excuse, a rationale, and little more. Urbain hoped to turn that rationale into a triumph of discovery, to make the habitat truly a center of scientific triumph.

'Yes, of course,' Eberly agreed easily. 'But let me remind you that more than ninety-five per cent of our inhabitants are not scientists, and I must think of them, too.'

Too enraged to say what he truly felt, Urbain muttered, 'Yes, I suppose so.'

'Good. I'm glad we had this chance to talk.' Eberly got to his feet.

Urbain realized he was being dismissed. He rose slowly from his chair. 'Then you will give the necessary orders to the department heads?'

Eberly pursed his lips, as if thinking it over. 'I'll set up a meeting for you. It would be best if you sat down with the department heads and talked this through with them, face to face.'

Understanding that this was the best Eberly was willing to do for him, Urbain said, 'Very well, if you think so. But it must be done quickly.'

'I'll get them together this afternoon. Tomorrow morning at the latest.'

'Today,' Urbain urged. 'It must be done today.'

'If it's humanly possible.'

Standing uncertainly before Eberly's desk, Urbain could think of nothing more to say. He turned and headed for the door.

As Eberly watched the scientist, he thought, He wants a favor. All right, but he'll have to give me a favor in return. How can I use this situation to my benefit?

The answer came to him before Urbain reached the door.

'By the way, Dr. Urbain,' he called, 'are you planning to run against me in the elections coming up?'

Urbain stopped and turned back toward him, brows knitted. 'Run in another election? No. Impossible. I have far too much work to do.'

Eberly nodded. Then I'll have to figure out some other way for you to pay me back for helping you, he said to himself.

They look like two little porcelain dolls, Holly thought as she sat behind her desk. Sitting before her, Hideko and Tamiko Mishima looked tiny, almost delicate, dressed in identical tunics of dark blue with lighter slacks. They also looked, not worried, but terribly concerned. And determined.

'Mr. Eberly promised us, when he held the post you now have,' said Mrs. Mishima, in a voice so soft it was almost a whisper.

'Chief of human services,' her husband added.

'I remember your conversation with him,' said Holly. 'At least the last part of it.'

'Yes, you were there,' Tamiko said.

'Nearly two years ago, right here in this office.' Mishima nodded for emphasis.

The office had been Eberly's when habitat *Goddard* began its long flight to Saturn. Once Holly had become chief of human services she had brightened the ascetically bare walls with holoviews of flowers and reproductions of famous paintings. The smart wall behind her displayed a real-time view of Saturn, its glittering rings framing her head neatly.

'We have waited long enough,' Mishima said. 'We want to bring our baby into the world.'

'We want our child,' said Tamiko.

She was a technician in the electrical maintenance section, Holly knew from a quick scan of their dossiers; he was a chef for the cafeteria. Both from California, they had voluntarily joined the Saturn mission to get married because neither of their families approved of their union. The ultimate elopment,

Holly thought, jumping all the way out to Saturn to get out from under their families. Now they're bumping up against the protocols of the habitat and trying to fight their way through our rules.

Holly tried to make a pleasant, placating smile for them as she mentally reviewed their case. Tamiko Mishima had become pregnant almost as soon as *Goddard* had left the Earth/Moon system, despite the agreement that all the habitat's personnel had signed about zero population growth. The habitat's protocols called for terminating the pregnancy, aborting the fetus, but Eberly had allowed them to cryonically freeze the fetus in the expectation of thawing it one day and bringing the baby to term.

One day is now, Holly realized. Malcolm's little bird has come to roost – on my shoulders.

'Mr. and Mrs. Mishima,' she heard herself saying gently, 'you understand that we're still under the ZPG protocol.'

'But Mr. Eberly said that once we had established the new government such restrictions would be removed,' said Mishima.

'Reviewed,' Holly corrected. 'Not necessarily removed.'

Mishima's face settled into a scowl. 'That was not our understanding.'

'The habitat is so large,' said his wife. 'Much of it is empty. There are entire villages that are unoccupied by anyone at all. Surely there is room for a few children now that we are properly established in our final orbit.'

'There should be,' Holly agreed. 'But we have to proceed carefully.'

'I want my baby,' Tamiko said firmly.

'You can't keep the fetus frozen indefinitely,' Mishima said. 'Cryonic preservation isn't perpetual. There are long-term risks.'

'I know,' said Holly. 'I'm a reborn myself.'

Their eyes widened and they both sucked in air.

'I understand how you feel,' Holly went on. 'I truly do. I'll do my best to help you.'

Once they left her office, practically bowing as they backed to the door, Holly understood that it really was time to take up this entire ZPG protocol. With something of a shock she realized that some day she'd want to have a baby herself.

5 January 2096: Afternoon

Urbain stared unhappily at Eberly and his three department heads, sitting across the small conference table from him. One very young-looking woman, two nondescript men. Except for Eberly he knew none of them. Both the men had golden complexions, almost yellow even though they were obviously not Asians. The woman's skin was light brown, like toasted bread.

It had taken a frustrating three days merely to bring these people into the same small conference room with him. Despite all of Urbain's promptings and importunings, Eberly had delayed this meeting unconscionably, in Urbain's view.

'I'm sorry it's taken so long to bring this conference together,' Eberly said, by way of opening the meeting. 'Getting these three very busy people into the same place at the same time isn't easy, I assure you.'

'So it would seem,' Urbain replied stiffly.

Turning to his department heads, Eberly explained, 'Dr. Urbain needs materials and manpower to build new satellite platforms. Twelve of them, I believe?'

'Twelve,' Urbain confirmed. 'At least twelve. The need is quite urgent.'

'How many technical people will you need?' asked the director of human services. She had been introduced to Urbain as Holly Lane.

Urbain picked up his handheld computer and projected his list of requirements onto the blank wall at the head of the conference room. The department heads turned to scan the

134

list; Eberly had to swivel his chair completely around. Good, Urbain thought. Make him do a little work.

The head of the logistics department shook his head worriedly. 'That's a lot of electronics equipment you're going to need. It'll cut into our spares inventory pretty damned deep.'

'Yes, but—'

'And I can't just pull people off their existing tasks,' said the manufacturing chief. 'Do you have any idea of how thin we're stretched as it is? Why, I've got requisitions for jobs going into the next six months. Just rebuilding those damned solar panel actuators is taking up more than half my resources.'

And so it went for some forty-five minutes, the department heads complaining that it would be impossible for them to meet Urbain's needs for at least several months. Urbain sat in growing impatience, trying to keep from exploding, knowing that he needed the support of these blundering oafs and if he told them what he truly thought of them and their attitudes he would never get the help he so desperately needed.

Only the personnel chief, this young Lane woman, seemed at all helpful.

'We could shift a few technicians temporarily,' she offered, 'and maybe offer overtime pay for those who'd be willing to do the assembly work after their regular shifts.'

But without the materials and electronics equipment, Urbain knew, the technicians would have nothing to assemble.

'I must insist,' he said, forcing his voice to remain calm, trembling only slightly, 'that this work be given the highest possible priority. The success of this community's very *raison d'etre* depends on it.'

They cleared their throats and shifted uneasily on their chairs. They gave excuses. They waved their hands. It was only after nearly an hour of fruitless wrangling that Urbain realized that the department heads did not look at him when they spoke, they looked at Eberly.

He holds the strings, Urbain finally understood. They will

procrastinate and evade the issue until *he* tells them to do as I wish.

Suddenly he shot to his feet. 'Bah! This pointless bickering is stupid. If you will not help me I will proceed without you.'

'Now wait a moment . . .' Eberly pushed his chair back from the conference table but did not stand up.

'I have waited long enough,' Urbain snapped. 'I will launch our existing satellites into orbit around Titan. That will leave us with nothing in reserve, no satellite platforms in storage. If some need for further satellites arises, then you will understand how stupidly you have behaved.'

With that, he stormed out of the conference room.

Eberly made a rueful smile. 'Emotional, isn't he?'

The other two men got up from their chairs and, after a few words of conversation with Eberly, headed back to their own offices. Holly got up too, but lingered at the conference room's door.

'Can you really get a team together for Urbain?' Eberly asked her.

'Sure. No prob. And Di Georgio and Williams can make the materials and equipment available, too, if they have to.'

Eberly leaned his butt on a corner of the conference table, realizing all over again that Holly was as sharp as they come.

'You think I should order them to cooperate with Urbain?'

She looked right into his eyes. 'I think that's what you're going to do, sooner or later. You just want to make Urbain squirm, make him understand who's boss.'

Eberly pretended astonishment. 'Why Holly, what do you think I am?'

Holly shook her head. 'Doesn't matter. But I don't think you ought to be playing powertrip games with Urbain. He's got some strong connections back Earthside to the ICU, y'know.'

Eberly gave her a long stare. 'Perhaps you're right,' he murmured.

Standing in front of him, returning his gaze unblinkingly,

Holly said, 'Malcolm, there's something else we need to talk about.'

'Something else?'

'The ZPG protocol,' she said.

Eberly said nothing as he slowly got up from his perch on the table's corner and dropped back into his swivel chair.

'Sit down, Holly,' he said, gesturing to the chair nearest him. 'Tell me what's on your mind.'

She could see the wheels turning in his head as she took the chair. He's always trying to figure out how he can benefit from any situation, she told herself. Guess that's why he's the chief around here.

'What about ZPG?' Eberly asked.

Holly took a breath, marshalling her thoughts. 'Remember the Mishimas? The couple that froze their fetus, back when we'd just left Earth? They want permission to have their baby.'

Eberly pursed his lips.

'If and when they do,' Holly continued, 'a lot of women in this community are going to want to have babies.'

'Then we'd better not grant permission to the Mishimas. Not yet, at least.'

'You can't put this issue off forever,' Holly said. 'It's as natural as breathing, Malcolm. Women want to have babies.'

'Do you want a baby, Holly?'

She smiled at him. 'Don't try to put me off by making the issue personal. Sooner or later you're going to have a tidal wave bearing down on you, Malcolm. This ZPG protocol could bury you.'

He steepled his fingers and tapped their tips lightly in front of his face. 'I'll have to think about it.'

'You surely better,' said Holly. 'You can't keep this genie in a bottle forever.'

'We'll see.'

Holly laughed. 'That's what a father tells his child when he doesn't want to face the consequences of saying no.'

'I understand what you're telling me, Holly,' Eberly said, in his sincerest mode. 'I appreciate your bringing this to my attention.'

Holly knew that what he was really saying is, I don't want to deal with this. Not now. Maybe not ever, if I can get away with it.

Getting to her feet, Holly realized that if Eberly wouldn't deal with this issue, she would have to.

Titan Alpha

Slowly, with the unwavering patience that only a machine could exert, *Titan Alpha* extracted itself from the quickly refreezing lake. Its biology program reviewed the available sensor data and concluded that the protocellular organisms in the water were being immobilized as the water crystallized into ice. It routed this information to the central processor's master program. For nine billion nanoseconds the master program halted *Alpha*'s drive engines as it compared this information against its major objectives and restrictions, and then reviewed its conclusion three times, as required by its programming.

The organisms were not being killed, it concluded, merely frozen into immobility, their life functions suspended, not extinguished. Even if they were being killed, there was nothing that *Titan Alpha* could do about it. The action that precipitated this environmental crisis was entirely involuntary. The best plan of action, consistent with all the master program's objectives and restrictions, was to exit the area with as little additional environmental damage as possible. Organisms at deeper levels of the lake would be protected from environmental harm once the surface of the lake refroze completely.

Its drive gears in dead low reverse, *Alpha* inched out of the lake, recording sensor data nanosecond by nanosecond. The biology program checked and rechecked the status of the samples obtained from the lake. Satisfied that the samples were safely stored, the biology program reverted to its normal passive review of incoming sensor data.

Free of the lake at last, *Titan Alpha* pivoted forty-seven

degrees right, engaged its forward gearing, and began a slow, purposeful circumnavigation of the ice lake. The jagged breach it had smashed into the icy surface was quickly refreezing. Off beyond the low rounded hills of ice on the other side of the lake, sluggish dirty orange clouds were precipitating fat drops of liquid ethane onto the rough dark landscape.

Titan Alpha surged ahead, gathering data, trundling purposively across the rolling, spongy ground as the ethane rainstorm slowly enveloped it.

7 January 2096: Evening

Urbain received two messages just as he was rising from his desk chair after another exhausting day of frustration and delay.

His chief of engineering appeared at the door of the office, the expression on his face morose and apprehensive at the same time. Bad news, Urbain could see before the man said a word.

Dropping back down into his padded desk chair, Urbain uttered a weary, 'What now?'

Without stepping into the office, the engineer said from the doorway, 'All twelve satellites are ready for launch, Dr. Urbain.'

Then why the long face, Urbain wondered. Before he could ask, the engineer added, 'But the chief administrator has refused to permit their launch.'

Urbain could feel his blood pressure zoom. 'Refused? He can't refuse! He hasn't the authority to prevent the launchings!'

'I'm afraid he does, sir. Our hands are tied without permission from the habitat's maintenance and safety departments.'

Visibly trembling with rage, Urbain glowered at the engineer, who immediately ducked back through the doorway. Urbain could hear his footsteps practically racing away down the corridor outside.

Before he could think of what to do, his phone chimed and Malcolm Eberly's handsome face smiled from its screen.

'We need to talk,' Eberly said, as if he were speaking to some underling. 'Please meet me at the entrance to the administration building in ten minutes.' And, *click*, Eberly's image winked off before Urbain could reply or even growl.

Ten minutes later Urbain stood fidgeting impatiently at the entrance to the administration building, some two hundred meters down the main street of Athens from his own science headquarters.

Eberly appeared at the double-doored entrance, flanked by two other men. One of them Urbain recognized from his meeting in Eberly's conference room a few days earlier; the other was a stranger to him.

While Urbain seethed on the sidewalk, Eberly chatted with his two flunkies up at the top of the entrance's stairs, all smiles and nods and pleasantries. At last the two underlings took their leave and pattered down the four steps of the entrance-way, passing Urbain with barely a nod. He's orchestrated this, Urbain thought, to humiliate me. To put me in my place. To rub my nose in the fact that he has power and I do not.

Finally, Eberly descended the stairs, all smiles, and extended a hand to Urbain. 'I'm sorry to keep you waiting. Pressing business.'

Urbain did not deign to take the man's hand. 'You have refused permission to launch my satellites,' he said, with cold fury.

'It's only a temporary hold,' Eberly said easily, starting to walk down the street. Urbain had no choice but to follow after him.

'I know it's upsetting to you,' Eberly said as they headed down the gently sloping street. 'But I'm sure you'll be able to launch your satellites tomorrow, right on schedule, more or less.'

Urbain said nothing. It seemed obvious to him that Eberly was after something and he had no intention of saying anything that might give the man an opening. So they walked in leisurely silence as the habitat slowly turned to its night mode, the wide solar windows shuttering, street lamps and windows lighting up. Other people passed them on the street, couples and individuals who smiled and nodded their greetings. Eberly beamed at each and every one of them; Urbain kept a tight-lipped silence.

At last he couldn't stand it any more. As they neared the shore of Athens' pretty little lake, Urbain said from between clenched teeth, 'My wife is expecting me for dinner.'

'Ah,' said Eberly. 'Yes, of course. Your wife. Mrs. Urbain is quite a lovely woman. Very lovely.'

'Why have you refused permission to launch my satellites?' Urbain demanded.

'Not refused,' Eberly said, looking out across the lake instead of at Urbain. 'Delayed permission. And only for a few hours, actually. Only until we've had a chance to talk together.'

'Talk together? Talk about what?'

Eberly turned back toward the scientist, then seemed to look past his shoulder. Urbain got the impression that the man was searching the area to make certain that no one was close enough to overhear them.

'My people tell me that it's a violation of the safety rules to launch all the satellites we have in store and leave nothing in reserve, in case of an emergency.'

'That is why I asked for the personnel and materials to build an additional dozen satellites!' Urbain snapped.

'Yes, I know.'

'And your people have been dragging their feet on my request.'

'Regrettable,' murmured Eberly.

Urbain stopped walking and crossed his arms over his chest. 'What is this all about?' he demanded. 'Why are you opposing me?'

Eberly turned to face him, his usual smile gone, his face cold and hard. 'You want to launch your satellites into orbit around Titan and—'

'And build another dozen to serve as backups,' Urbain interjected.

'Yes,' said Eberly. 'And I want to mine Saturn's rings.'

Urbain blinked with surprise. 'Mine the rings?'

'For ice. Water ice. It's the most precious commodity in the solar system.'

'I know,' muttered Urbain, remembering that Eberly had used the idea of mining Saturn's rings as a ploy during the election campaign. He held out to the habitat's citizens the glittering promise of becoming wealthy by selling water ice to the other human communities in space.

'You and the other scientists opposed the idea,' Eberly said. 'Especially that Wunderly person.'

'She discovered indigenous life forms in the rings,' Urbain said, more to himself than to Eberly.

'I'm told that most of the scientists back on Earth don't believe her claim.'

'Nonetheless, the mere possibility that living organisms may exist in the rings means that all commercial activities are forbidden.'

'The ICU hasn't issued any prohibition,' said Eberly. 'Neither has the IAA.'

'The International Consortium of Universities has asked for my estimation of the matter before they make a recommendation to the International Astronautical Authority.'

'I thought as much.'

'Now I understand,' Urbain said. 'You want me to recommend to the ICU that you should be allowed to mine the rings.'

'We wouldn't make a dent in them. There's gazillions of tons of ice in those rings. We would only take a minuscule fraction of it.'

Urbain glowered at Eberly with undisguised revulsion. 'You want to blackmail me. You will withhold permission to launch my satellites unless I allow you to mine the rings.'

Eberly smiled thinly. 'That isn't blackmail. The correct word is extortion.'

'Nevertheless . . .'

'Nevertheless, if you want to get those satellites down to Titan where they can search for your wandering probe, you'll have to tell the ICU that it's perfectly all right for us to mine the rings.'

Urbain could see from the hard set of Eberly's jaw that he had no third option.

8 January 2096: Morning

Malcolm Eberly did not sleep well that night. He awoke slowly, feeling dull and aching, as he did those mornings when he had been in prison in Austria. The vague memory of a bad dream haunted him; the more he tried to remember its specifics the more the details slipped away from him, leaving only a dark sense of dread.

Why? he asked himself. You have nothing to be afraid of. The Holy Disciples can't reach you any more, they can't send you back to prison. You're safe here. The people of this habitat respect and admire you.

But do they? That was what troubled him, he realized. They could vote me out of office in a few months and then where would I be? I'd have to find an ordinary job and live on an ordinary wage.

That was what had troubled his sleep, Eberly decided. The re-election campaign. He had won election in the first place on the promise that *Goddard*'s inhabitants would get rich from mining the rings of Saturn. The scientists – led by Urbain – had opposed the idea, of course. But the voters had supported it wholeheartedly.

Now it was almost time to register candidates for the next election, and Eberly knew he had done nothing about mining the rings. He'd allowed the idea to fall into hibernation while he set up the new government and got it running with a modicum of efficiency. But now the voters would remember that promise of wealth and demand that Eberly make good on it. And still the scientists opposed him. They were backed by the powers-that-be on Earth.

146

My re-election is not assured, Eberly told himself. Urbain won't run against me, and I'm sure that I've neutralized Timoshenko. But someone will stand up to oppose me. Who?

As he brushed his teeth, showered, shaved, and dressed for the day's work, his mind kept coming back to the inevitable answer. Pancho Lane. She didn't come to this habitat merely to see her sister. She coyly refuses to tell anyone how long she intends to stay. Within the week she'll apply for citizenship and then register as a candidate to oppose me.

What can I do to stop her? Eberly asked himself as he walked through the morning sunlight to his office and the light breakfast his aide would have waiting for him. How can I get rid of Pancho Lane?

He lightly touched the spot on his jaw where Pancho had hit him. How can I make her pay for that humiliation?

Urbain, meanwhile, was having breakfast with his wife in his own apartment.

'He will bribe the voters with visions of vast wealth,' he grumbled as he sipped at his stinging hot coffee. Jeanmarie was the only woman in the world who knew how to make coffee strong enough to be palatable. He had missed her coffee during the years of their separation.

'But the ICU is on record as being against mining Saturn's rings,' Jeanmarie said from across their narrow kitchen table.

'It means nothing,' Urbain scoffed. 'What can they do? How can they enforce their position? Send an army of bureaucrats here?'

Jeanmarie almost smiled at the thought of a horde of university file surfers descending on the habitat.

'Eberly could refuse them permission to dock,' Urbain went on. 'He could send them packing back to Earth.'

His wife brought her cup to her lips. She preferred tea, with lemon. 'But couldn't the ICU ask the International Astronautical Authority to enforce their decision? The IAA is not to be trifled with.'

Urbain gave his wife a condescending look. 'My dear, it has been little more than a year since the Second Asteroid War was ended. Do you believe that the IAA or anyone on earth will be willing to start another war?'

'A war?' Jeanmarie looked stricken. 'Do you really think that Eberly would use force against the IAA?'

'I believe the man will do whatever he feels necessary to maintain his position as leader of this habitat.'

'But war?'

He shrugged. 'Spacecraft are very fragile. A laser shot could disable an IAA ship as it approaches us. Perhaps even destroy it.'

Jeanmarie shook her head. 'He wouldn't dare.'

'Selene declared its independence and then fought off an attempt by the old United Nations to subdue them. The miners at Ceres have established their independence. Why not habitat *Goddard*? After all, we are much farther away than any other human habitation. What do the people of Earth care about what we do?'

'They care about mining Saturn's rings, do they not?'

'Yes, some of them. But the people living on the Moon and among the asteroids would be in favor of having an abundant supply of water made available to them.'

'For a price,' Jeanmarie pointed out.

Urbain stared at her. Then he countered, 'Eberly is very clever; wily. He will keep the price low enough for them to want to buy, and still high enough to bring wealth to *Goddard*.'

She started to reply but he got up from their tiny kitchen table, clearly signaling that their conversation was at an end. Jeanmarie sat their clasping her delicate cup of cooling tea in both hands. It had been her mother's tea set. No, she remembered, her grandmother's.

Urbain came back to the kitchen, fumbling with the ascot he

had slid around his neck. Jeanmarie knew he expected her to knot it for him, yet she did not get up from her chair.

'Is this business of mining the rings so important?' she asked. 'Will it do irreparable harm to the rings?'

'In time,' Urbain said, looking into the mirror behind his wife as he worked on tying the ascot. 'The real problem is that he will not lift a finger to help me unless I support his proposal of mining the ice.'

She saw the expression on his face: utter distaste and, beneath it all, the fear of failure. *His probe of Titan has gone rogue and he cannot even locate it. Now Eberly refuses to help him and he fears that his career will collapse around his ears. My poor darling! To come this far and then fail. He's had a taste of success and now his fall will be deeper and more humiliating because of it.*

She pushed her chair back, brushed his hands away from the poorly-knotted ascot, and retied it for him. Urbain pecked her on the cheek by way of thanks and left for his office and another day of frustration, of edging closer to the brink of disaster.

Jeanmarie stood there in her kitchen for a long time, alone, wondering what she could do to help her husband.

Holly intercepted Eberly as he walked toward the administration building at the crest of the low hill on which the village of Athens had been built. He knew it was no accidental meeting.

'Good morning,' he said cheerfully.

'Aren't they all,' Holly replied as she fell into step alongside him.

'Yes. I suppose we tend to take our perfect weather for granted.'

Holly reached out and tugged at the sleeve of his tunic, stopping him. 'Look around, Malcolm. Look at this place. I mean, *really* look at it.'

Puzzled, Eberly swept his gaze across the carefully-landscaped scenery, green and lush and flowering. The clean white buildings. The glittering lake. 'It's really wonderful, isn't it,' he murmured.

'What's missing?' Holly asked.

From the set of her square jaw, Eberly could see that Holly had a specific point to make. 'What's missing, Malcolm?' she asked again.

'Rain,' he replied lightly. 'Snow. Fog, sleet . . .'

'Don't try to make a joke of it,' she insisted.

'All right. You tell me what's missing from this demi-paradise, this other Eden, this—'

'Kids!' Holly snapped. 'Children. We have no children here.'

'Oh, that.'

'Yes, that,' said Holly. 'You've got to face up to it, Malcolm. You've got to do something about the ZPG rule.'

'I'm thinking about it,' he muttered grudgingly.

'Think harder, then. And faster. The deadline for registering candidates is next Monday. ZPG could be a major issue.'

'Only if someone makes an issue out of it,' Eberly answered testily.

'Somebody's bound to.'

'They would need a petition signed by two thirds of the citizens to repeal the zero-growth protocol,' he pointed out.

Holly's lips curved into a knowing smile. 'You looked up the regulations, huh? So did I.'

'I doubt that anyone in this habitat has the inclination to mount a petition drive. They're all too apathetic.'

With a slight shake of her head, Holly replied, 'Don't underestimate the people, Malcolm. 'Specially the women.'

Feeling uncomfortable, Eberly decided to shift the focus of their conversation. 'Speaking of issues, how do you feel about mining ice from the rings of Saturn?'

Holly made a small shrug. 'Nadia Wunderly's dead set against it and so are the rest of the scientists.'

'But they're less than a tenth of this community's population.'

'If you make an issue of it, the scientists'll put up a candidate to run against you. Wouldn't you prefer to run unopposed?'

Unopposed? The idea hadn't occurred to Eberly. He'd assumed that someone would come up to run against him, maybe more than one candidate. He actually preferred to have several candidates running; that would split the votes against him, while he could count on a solid bloc as the incumbent – especially if he started to put the ice-mining plan into operation.

'Naturally I'd prefer to run unopposed, but I doubt that things will work out that way.'

' 'Smatter of fact,' Holly said, a slow grin creeping across her face, 'the constitution requires an opposition candidate. I checked the requirements.'

He looked at her with newfound appreciation. 'You've been checking a lot of things, haven't you?'

'Part of my job,' Holly said. 'If nobody volunteers to run against you, a candidate has to be selected at random by the personnel computer.'

'Which is run by your human resources department,' Eberly said.

'Right.'

'Which means that you, Holly, can select my opponent.'

'Not me. The computer.'

'You,' Eberly said, pointing an index finger at her like a pistol.

'Then I'll have to find somebody who'll bring up the ZPG issue.'

Eberly scowled darkly at her.

8 January 2096: Noon

Nadia Wunderly sealed the outer hatch of the nanolab's airlock entrance and fidgeted impatiently for the few seconds that it took for the inner door to pop open. When it did, Raoul Tavalera swung the heavy hatch open for her.

'Why, thank you, Raoul,' she said, a smile dimpling her face. 'Have you been standing there long, waiting for me?'

Puzzled by her attempt at humor, Tavalera replied, 'I'm heading out for lunch.' Then he added, 'With Holly,' and his face brightened a little.

He went into the airlock as Wunderly stepped into the lab. 'Kris is talking with that Russian from maintenance, Timoshenko,' Tavalera said as he pulled the airlock hatch shut.

Wunderly passed benches loaded with silent equipment as she walked deeper into the laboratory. She heard Cardenas's voice and the gruff lower tones of the Russian engineer. She was still losing weight, and now that New Year's had come and gone, she was wondering when she should have Cardenas flush the nanomachines out of her body.

Cardenas was perched on her tall stool, as usual, with a starched white smock over her dress. Timoshenko stood next to her, a stubby thickset figure in gray coveralls, several centimeters shorter than the seated Cardenas.

'We could do more than armor the superconducting wires,' she was saying. 'We could develop nanomachines to automatically repair any damage done to them.'

'That's not as easy as you might suppose,' Timoshenko

said. 'Very powerful electrical currents flow through those wires.'

Cardenas nodded. 'Well, if you can give me the specifics, I can try to work out a program for self-repair. Then we can test it here in the lab on short samples of superconductor before we install any nanos on the shielding wires themselves.'

Timoshenko started to reply, then noticed Wunderly standing off at some distance. 'Ah,' he said to Cardenas, 'you have company.'

'Come on over, Nadia,' Cardenas called to Wunderly. Turning back to Timoshenko she explained, 'Nadia and I have a lunch date. Care to join us? We can continue our discussion in the cafeteria.'

Timoshenko dipped his chin in agreement while Wunderly thought to herself, He's the guy who piloted the transfer craft that carried Gaeta to the rings and then picked him up afterward. If he did that for Manny he can do it for me. Maybe.

All through lunch in the busy, clattering cafeteria Timoshenko and Cardenas talked about using nanomachines to protect and even repair the superconducting wires that provided the magnetic field which protected the habitat from radiation. Wunderly had no chance to ask Cardenas about flushing out the nanos inside her. She listened to their conversation with only a fraction of her attention. Her mind focused on flying out to the rings again, this time to pick up samples and prove to those doubting earthworm flatlanders back home that the ring harbored living psychrophiles, organisms that lived within the ice particles of Saturn's rings.

How can they not believe it? Wunderly asked herself as she munched on a fruit salad, straight from the habitat's orchards. They *know* that amino acids and other complex polypeptides form naturally in amorphous ice particles. They've seen it in comets for damned near a century. Why shouldn't the next step be believable? Amino acids self-assemble into proteins and proteins evolve into living organisms. It's happened in liquid water on half a dozen worlds that we know of. And in liquid sulfur on Venus, for chrissakes.

It just goes slower at freezing temperatures. Amorphous ice allows chemicals to flow as if they were in a liquid, but it all happens at a slower pace. Unless you've got some catalyst present, like an antifreeze. I wonder if that's what happens in the ring particles. Plenty of energy available from Saturn's magnetic field and the electrical flux of the rings themselves.

'Nadia, did you hear me?'

She abruptly realized that Cardenas was talking to her, the expression on her face somewhere between worried and annoyed.

'I'm sorry, Kris. My mind wandered.'

'Back to the rings, I suppose,' Cardenas said, an understanding smile curving her lips.

'Where else?' Wunderly replied.

Timoshenko asked, 'Do you really believe that those particles are truly alive?'

'Yes! Of course. How else do you explain the fact that Saturn's rings are so big and bright? Those creatures maintain the rings for their own survival, just as living organisms maintain Earth's environment for their own survival.'

'Gaia,' murmured Cardenas.

Timoshenko picked up his glass of tea. 'If the Earth's biosphere actively works to maintain the planet's environment, how do you account for the greenhouse cliff? Or the ice ages of the past?'

'Minor fluctuations,' Wunderly answered, with a wave of her hand.

'Not minor to the people who lost their homes to the floods,' muttered Timoshenko.

'Gaia works on a planetary scale,' Cardenas said. 'The Earth's biosphere maintains the planetary environment for the survival of life itself, not for the benefit of any particular species.'

'Like the dinosaurs,' Wunderly said. 'Major impact event wiped them out, along with half the other species on Earth, yet within a few million years Gaia was restocking the planet with new species.'

'Including us,' said Timoshenko.

'Until we messed up the atmosphere with greenhouse gases,' Cardenas said. 'Gaia slapped us pretty hard then.'

'It was avoidable,' Wunderly agreed. 'Or correctable.'

Timoshenko shrugged heavily. 'Just because humans are intelligent doesn't mean they're smart.'

'I don't know about that,' Cardenas mused. 'The greenhouse disaster forced us into space in a major way. We wouldn't be here if the climate hadn't collapsed on us.'

Timoshenko started to reply, but apparently thought better of it. He simply shook his head.

'I've got to prove that there are living organisms in the rings,' Wunderly said. 'It's important.'

'Important to you,' said Timoshenko.

'Important for scientific knowledge,' Wunderly countered. 'Important for our understanding of the universe.'

'And it should be important for the creatures themselves, if they exist,' Cardenas pointed out. 'Eberly wanted to mine ice from the rings, remember?'

'That idea got shot down,' said Wunderly.

'Did it? Or has he just shelved it temporarily?'

'You think . . .?'

Cardenas pointed out, 'A lot of people voted for Eberly because he said he'd make us all rich by selling water mined from the rings.'

'But the IAA would never allow that,' Timoshenko said.

'I wonder,' Cardenas said. 'Elections are coming up again in a few months. How much do you want to bet that Eberly brings up the ice-mining idea again?'

'But he can't!' Wunderly blurted at. 'He mustn't!'

'You think so, Nadia. And I think so. But most of the voters might like the idea of making money off ice-mining.'

'Money talks,' Timoshenko agreed sourly.

Wunderly looked at each of them in turn, her mind churning. Then she said, 'So it's more important than ever that I prove there are living creatures in the rings. The IAA would flatly deny permission for mining the rings if there's proof that there's an extant biosphere in them.'

Cardenas nodded agreement. Timoshenko looked wary, as if he knew what was coming next.

Wunderly turned her chair to face him. 'I'm planning to go to the rings and collect samples. I've asked Manny Gaeta to be my mission controller and teach me how to use his excursion suit. I need someone to pilot the transfer craft that'll take me to the rings and back out again.'

'Not me,' Timoshenko said flatly.

'You did it for Manny.'

'Once was enough. More than enough. I'm no hero.'

'But I need your help.'

'Ask Tavalera,' Timoshenko said. 'He piloted transfer craft while he was at the Jupiter station, didn't he?'

'Raoul?' Cardenas asked, surprised.

'Him. Or anybody else,' said Timoshenko. 'But not me.'

8 January 2096: Afternoon

Holly left her office early and walked to the apartment building where Professor Wilmot lived. When this mission to Saturn had begun, Wilmot had been in charge, appointed by the International Consortium of Universities to direct the habitat's ten thousand inhabitants until they reached Saturn orbit and formulated a government of their own choosing.

Something had happened along the way, however. Eberly and the little clique of thugs surrounding him had pushed Wilmot out of power and formed the government. They allowed the people to vote for a new constitution, but the voting was little more than a popularity contest. Holly understood that now, although she had worked faithfully for Malcolm Eberly back then, under the impression that Eberly was a hero worth following. Time and events forced a painful recognition upon Holly. Eberly was little more than a tool in the hands of fundamentalist zealots.

The zealots had been banished back to Earth, but Eberly remained as the elected head of the community's government. Holly didn't trust him. She berated herself for ever having been so starstruck that she'd thought she was in love with the man.

She knew better now. Eberly could never love anyone except himself. He had the power of the habitat's government in his hands and he would do anything to hold onto that power and prestige, to get himself re-elected, to have the proof that the people of this habitat still admired him.

But he refused to see that no one could keep a community of

ten thousand men and women from having babies. It was impossible, Holly was convinced. The only reason the people had tolerated the habitat's zero growth regulation was that they expected the rule to be repealed, sooner or later.

And then what? Holly wondered. That's why she was seeking out Professor Wilmot. He was an anthropologist, a trained expert in human behavior, human societies. She needed his advice and the benefit of his knowledge.

It was four p.m. when she rapped on Wilmot's apartment door, precisely the time he had agreed to see her. She remembered the last time she had run to the professor for refuge, when the animals that actually ran Eberly's newly-elected government had tried to pin a false charge of murder on her. Wilmot had been precious little help then. Holly hoped he would be stronger now.

The door slid back and Professor Wilmot greeted her with a gracious sweep of his arm. 'Good afternoon, Holly. Come right in.'

He was a big man, tall and broad-shouldered, although his midsection was thickening. His face was tanned and weather-seamed from years of work in the field, his hands big and still callused. His hair was iron gray, as was his thick moustache. Holly thought he looked like a child's idea of a grandfather or beloved uncle.

'I've prepared tea,' Wilmot said, gesturing toward the chinaware tea set that was laid out on the low table in front of the sofa. 'I hope you like the scones I've baked. I'm afraid I'm not much of a baker, but they seem to have come out rather well, if I say so myself.'

Holly sat at one end of the sofa. 'Everything looks terrif,' she said appreciatively.

Wilmot took the upholstered chair next to the sofa and began to pour tea. Once they had both sipped from the dainty cups, he leaned back and said, 'So now, to what do I owe the pleasure of this visit?'

'I need your advice, Professor,' said Holly, replacing her cup in its saucer with a delicate clink.

'It's always easy to get advice.'

'I s'pose.' Holly couldn't quite figure out how to broach the subject, so she blurted out, 'It's about the ZPG rule. It's going to cause a megaton of trouble.'

Wilmot's shaggy brows rose but he said nothing as Holly explained her worries. 'We just *can't* keep the rule in place. It'll tear this community apart.'

'But everyone signed an agreement, didn't they?'

Shaking her head, Holly answered, 'Doesn't mean spit. They signed because they were told the ZPG rule would be lifted once we were at Saturn. Eberly says it's too soon to lift it; he says we can't allow people to have babies because we'll get a population explosion that'll ruin the habitat.'

Stroking his chin thoughtfully, Wilmot murmured, 'He just might be right about that. Uncontrolled population growth could eat up all our resources.'

'I know, but how can we control it? Women are going to start having babies and there's nothing anybody can do to stop them.'

'The ZPG regulation must be enforced, Holly. Once you allow people to ignore one law they'll soon be ignoring all laws.'

'Is that really true? I mean, you know a lot about the way human societies work. If women start making babies, is that going to mean total chaos?'

Wilmot didn't answer right away. He reached for his teacup and took a healthy sip. Then, 'Holly, to keep this habitat ecologically stable, our birth rate must be kept on a par with our death rate. And with modern medical capabilities and aging therapies . . .'

'I know. People live forever, just about.'

'How many deaths have we had since we left Earth?'

'Two. One murder and one execution.'

159

'You see? We could allow two births, but no more.'

Holly shook her head again, more vigorously. 'It's not going to work, Professor. We've got to find another way.'

'Until you do, I'm afraid that we'll all have to follow the habitat's laws, including ZPG.'

'But we have room for three, four times our current population! Jeeps, this habitat could hold a million people if it had to!'

'Living cheek by jowl in poverty,' Wilmot replied sternly. 'With all the crime and perversion that goes with intense population density.'

'I guess,' Holly agreed reluctantly. Then her chin came up. 'But I don't see how we can expect the women of this community to give up having babies.'

'You'll have to convince them of the necessity,' said Wilmot. 'You'll have to produce a formula for *planned* population growth and convince the inhabitants to agree to it.'

Glumly, Holly replied, 'I wish I could. Trouble is, Eberly's just going to ignore the problem, shove it under the rug. As long as he's running for re-election he won't bring up any issues that could cost him votes.'

'But you said that he can't ignore it.'

'Not in the long run, no. But he won't mention it while he's campaigning for re-election, that's f'sure.'

'Then his opponent must bring it to the voters' attention,' said Wilmot.

'He doesn't have an opponent,' Holly said. 'He's running unopposed.'

'So far. The deadline for registering as a candidate is still a week away, isn't it?'

'Next Monday, yeah, but who's going to run again him? Nobody. We'll have to draft somebody from a computer lottery.'

Wilmot brushed his moustache with one finger and said, 'I should think that someone who feels strongly about this community would step into the election race, if for no other reason than to force Eberly to face up to the issues.'

'You know somebody who'd do that?' Holly asked eagerly. 'Would you?'

'Oh, heavens, not me.'

'Then who?'

'You, my dear girl. You've got to run against Malcolm Eberly.'

8 January 2096: Evening

'Run for election?' Pancho said, her voice high with surprise.

'That's what Professor Wilmot said I should do,' Holly answered.

Pancho grinned at her sister from across the coffeetable in her living room. Holly was sitting on the sofa, her feet curled up under her, while Pancho lazed back in the recliner.

'Y'know, kid,' Pancho said, 'the professor might be right. You'd make a terrific chief administrator.'

Holly wasn't so certain. 'Jeeps, Panch, I don't know anything about making speeches and running for office. I wouldn't know where to start.'

'You helped Eberly when he ran, last time, didn'tcha?'

'Just with polls and statistical analyses, stuff like that. I didn't do any of the campaigning. I was strictly back-office.'

'Well, I know a thing or two about gladhanding folks and getting 'em to vote for you. That's how I got to be top kick at Astro for so many years.'

'Would you help me?' Holly's eyes were wide with expectation.

'Help you with what?' asked Jake Wanamaker, coming through the bedroom door.

'Holly's going to run for chief administrator.'

'Really?'

'I'm not sure . . .' Holly said hesitantly.

'Yes, she is,' said Pancho. 'She just doesn't know it yet.'

Urbain picked miserably at the dinner Jeanmarie had prepared for him. She wasn't terribly interested in cooking, but lately she had applied herself, with the aid of video tutorials, and found that preparing food from the habitat's farm markets was more interesting and rewarding than heating precooked packaged meals. Their kitchen was small, barely big enough for the two of them to sit at table, but it had a full range of appliances and storage cabinets.

Usually Edouard seemed to enjoy her fledgling efforts. He always complimented her. But not this evening. His fork hardly touched the chicken Kiev she had so painstakingly prepared for him.

'Is it too bland?' she asked.

He looked up at her, startled out of this thoughts. 'Eh?'

'The chicken,' Jeanmarie said. 'Is it spiced to your liking?'

'Oh. It's fine. Fine.' He put a forkful into his mouth and chewed, his eyes wandering off to some inner vision.

'What's the matter, Edouard? You seem upset.'

'Eberly,' he said, almost in a growl.

'What's he done now?'

'It isn't something he's done. It's what he hasn't done.' Urbain laid his fork carefully on the table.

'He still will not release your satellites?'

'No, not until I promise to agree to his scheme for mining the rings.'

'Then why not agree? If it is important to finding your *Alpha* vehicle, why refuse him?'

'Because it is wrong!' Urbain snapped. 'Besides, Nadia Wunderly would go berserk.'

'Poo! Let her go berserk,' said Jeanmarie. 'She is an underling. Her work should not be allowed to stand in the way of yours.'

Urbain shook his head wearily. 'My dear, you don't understand. She believes she has discovered life forms in Saturn's rings. If I agree to Eberly's scheme, it would be a clear signal to her – to the whole world – that I don't believe her.'

'And so?'

'It would break her heart.'

Jeanmarie was surprised. Her husband had never before voiced such sensitivity about anyone working under him. It can't be that he is attracted to her romantically, she thought. I know him well enough, and besides she isn't an attractive woman. He actually cares about her work, her hopes, her standing with the rest of the scientists. Jeanmarie's admiration for him rose a notch.

Still, she prodded gently, 'Is her work more important than yours, Edouard? Are her claims about creatures in the ring more important than your vehicle wandering across the surface of Titan?'

He looked at her for a long, silent moment, and she could see the pain of clashing emotions in his eyes.

'Jeanmarie, is physics more important than biology? Is one avenue of scientific investigation more important than another?'

'But if you can't do both . . .'

Obviously struggling to control his temper, Urbain said, 'I will not allow that . . . that *politician* to place Wunderly's work in opposition to mine. I will not stand for an either-or situation. Both lines of investigation must proceed.'

'But neither of them will, if Eberly has his way.'

'Then I must find a way around him.'

Jeanmarie marveled at her husband's newfound tenacity. A year ago he would have backed away from any confrontation. Now he has found his courage, and he will suffer for it.

'There must be a way around Eberly,' Urbain muttered.

Jeanmarie thought idly that there was always a way around any man. Suddenly she was shocked to realize that perhaps she could succeed with Eberly. The man has a huge ego, from all she had heard of him. Could I turn his head? she wondered. Do I dare even try? What would Edouard do if he discovered it?

★ ★ ★

'Dr. Wunderly oughtta be in on this,' Raoul Tavalera said.

He was sitting at a table out on the grass of the Bistro, with Holly, Pancho and Jake Wanamaker. The restaurant was filling up, people taking all the outdoor tables and even a few of those inside the restaurant's small building. Holly had just told him that she had decided to run against Eberly for the chief administrator's job.

'Nadia?' Holly asked, surprised. 'Why her?'

Tavalera leaned forward slightly in his chair and ticked off on his fingers, 'Eberly's gonna bring up that business about mining the rings, right? When he does, you're gonna have to show why we shouldn't do it. So you'll need Dr. Wunderly on your team, to give you the technical facts you need.'

'Mining the rings?' Pancho asked. 'For water ice?'

'What else?' Holly replied.

'Lord almighty,' said Wanamaker, 'there must be gigatons of ice in the rings. You could make a fortune selling water, make this habitat as wealthy as Selene.'

'Wealthier,' Pancho said.

'But if there's living creatures in the rings we'd be breaking the IAA's regulations,' Holly pointed out.

'Besides, it'd be immoral,' said Pancho.

Wanamaker gave them a knowing look. 'Morals and regulations won't count for much if the people in this habitat know they can get rich.'

'The IAA'd send an enforcement team here,' Pancho said.

'And the people here would fight them off,' Wanamaker countered. 'Wouldn't take much.'

'You want to run for secretary of defense?' Pancho teased.

'I could,' Wanamaker said, entirely serious.

'Now wait a sec,' Holly interjected. 'This is all guesswork. We don't know for certain that the rings really have living critters in them.'

'That's what Dr. Wunderly's trying to find out, isn't it?' Wanamaker asked.

'Maybe we oughtta help her,' Tavalera said. 'Get the point nailed down, one way or the other.'

'Before the election.'

'That gives you a little less'n six months,' Pancho said.

Holly turned to Tavalera. 'Raoul, would you fly the mission to the rings?'

He looked startled. 'Me? I'm not an astronaut.'

'But you flew spacecraft when you were at the Jupiter station, I read that in your personnel file.'

'Yeah, a couple,' he replied warily. 'But I'm not gonna fly Wunderly to the rings and pick her up again. That's too risky for me.'

'But we need a pilot.'

'Get somebody else,' Tavalera said firmly.

Pancho said, 'There must be lotsa qualified rocket jocks in this habitat.'

'Not as many as you'd think,' Holly replied. 'I've scoured the personnel records.'

'Hells' bells, I could fly it myself,' said Pancho. 'If you can't get anybody else.'

'Get somebody else,' Wanamaker said. 'You're too old to risk your neck out there.'

'Too old?' Pancho's nostrils flared.

'Too out of practice,' Wanamaker quickly amended.

Pancho grumbled, 'That's better.'

'There's something else,' Holly said, suddenly looking gloomy.

'What?'

'Zero pop,' she said.

'What's that got to do with the ring creatures?' Pancho asked.

Holly explained, 'If we want to allow the habitat's population to expand, we're going to need a source of funding to build new habitats to house the growing population.'

'Not for lotsa years,' Pancho said.

'Sooner or later,' Holly insisted. 'And prob'ly sooner. Besides, it takes a lotta years to build one of these flying stovepipes. And a lot of funding.'

'Mining the rings could provide the money,' Wanamaker said.

Tavalera nodded knowingly. 'Then we'd better help Dr. Wunderly bring in some samples from the rings.'

'And hope like hell she doesn't find anything alive in them,' Pancho said.

Titan Alpha

The ethane rainstorm slowly moved across the land, raining fat drops of liquid that spattered onto the slushy ground and drummed against the armored hull of *Titan Alpha*. The sensors showed that despite the frigid temperature of the ground, the falling rain did not freeze but flowed across the ice, even eroding it slightly as it ran downslope along gullies and rills.

Alpha's master program decided to follow the slightly sloping ground, gathering data as it moved slowly onward. Collectors in the roof took in samples of the drumming rain for analysis. The liquid was largely ethane, although a complex mix of other hydrocarbons were present, as well as fourteen per cent of liquid water.

Liquid water was an important biomarker; the biology program was immediately activated to participate in the analysis. The master program, meanwhile, pondered a conundrum: How can water remain liquid at temperatures of nearly two hundred degrees below zero? It took all of fifty-three billion nanoseconds before the master program arrived at a tentative conclusion. The water can remain liquid because it is mixed with the ethane and other hydrocarbons, which, together with the high atmospheric pressure, raises the freezing point of the fluid far enough to allow the mixture to remain liquid.

The biology program was instructed to search for organic molecules and/or viable organisms in the water-laced ethane samples. Organics were there in plentiful, easily identifiable, amounts. Actual organisms, unicellular or even protocellular molecular organisms, were not found.

While this sampling and analysis was being performed, *Alpha* continued heading down the slight slope of the ground, following the rivulets of the ethane-water mixture across the muddy landscape. The rain was actually clearing much of the methane slush from the underlying ice, sluicing it downhill in gurgling streams. At last the rainstorm passed and *Alpha*'s infrared sensors scanned the higher clouds that perpetually covered the sky. A faint glow low on the horizon showed where the Sun was. There was an even fainter patch of light higher above, several degrees wider. The navigation program concluded that it was the planet Saturn, Titan's primary, the planet around which it revolved. Even under the best magnification, though, nothing of the planet's main body or its rings could be resolved through the murky clouds.

The forward sensors reported a sizable stream ahead, a meandering brook of ethane-laced water flowing across the vehicle's projected path. Width eleven meters. Depth unknown.

After four billion nanoseconds, the master program decided to follow this stream to see where it led. Consulting both the geology and biology programs, the master program concluded that the stream most likely fed into one of the seas. It found an imperative in the geology program: If there are ethane streams, determine how they mix with the known seas. A similar requirement existed in the biology program: If organic molecules are located on the surface, determine if they have developed into viable organisms.

Titan Alpha followed the flowing stream toward one of the ice-encrusted seas that dotted the moon's frozen ground.

9 January 2096: Morning

Manuel Gaeta usually wore a sassy, almost insolent smile on his rugged face. After all, he had braved some of the most dangerous environments in the solar system and lived through them. He had made a living out of performing such feats.

But now, surrounded by Holly, Wunderly, Pancho and Tavalera, he looked wary, on guard. Kris Cardenas, sitting beside him, also seemed highly dubious.

They were out in the lakeside park on the outskirts of Athens, in the warm, never-failing sunshine of midmorning, sitting bunched together on a pair of benches that they'd dragged to face each other. Holly had chosen this spot in imitation of Eberly: no one could eavesdrop on them out here, she thought, and they could see anyone else approaching from hundreds of meters away.

'Let me get this straight,' Gaeta said slowly, trying to sort out what they were telling him. 'You want me to let Nadia use the suit for a zip through the rings.'

'Not a "zip,"' Wunderly replied instantly. 'I'm going to the rings to collect samples.'

Gaeta nodded cautiously. 'Uh-huh. And you want me to train you.'

'And run the mission,' Holly said, 'the way Fritz what's-his-name did for you.'

'Von Helmholtz,' Gaeta murmured absently.

Cardenas interjected, 'You want to fly the mission yourself, Nadia? Not ask Manny to do it?'

'No, I'll go myself,' said Wunderly, with the complete

seriousness of a woman who had made up her mind. 'It's my problem and I'll do the job myself. But I need your help.'

'You'll need more than me,' Gaeta pointed out. 'More than one man controlling the mission. Fritz had six guys with him, remember.'

Wunderly turned to Holly. 'Can you get me six engineers?'

Before Holly could reply, Gaeta said, 'They've got to have experience controlling excursion missions,'

'And I'll need someone to fly the transfer craft to the rings and then pick me up afterward.'

Holly said, 'I can rummage through the personnel files and dig up a half-dozen engineers, I guess. But it'd mean taking them off their existing jobs.'

'You're chief of human resources,' said Pancho. 'You can finagle the files, can't you?'

'It's more'n that,' Holly replied. 'I've got to do this without bringing it up to Eberly. If he gets a whiff of what we're doing, he'll shut us down like that.' She snapped her fingers.

Pancho smiled knowingly. 'Midnight requisitioning. I've done that once or twice, over the years. You can do it; I'll show you how.'

'Thanks,' said Holly, dubiously.

Gaeta looked Wunderly squarely in her eyes. 'You know there's a good chance that you'll be killing yourself, don't you?'

She nodded wordlessly.

Holly pointed a finger at Gaeta. 'Manny, we've got to see to it that Nadia gets to the rings and back in one piece. It's important. Vital. We've all got to get this job done, and done right.'

Gaeta shrugged his shoulders. 'I still don't think it's worth the risk.'

'Listen up,' Holly snapped. 'The whole future of this habitat depends on what's in those rings. If there aren't any living critters in there, we can mine the ice and make a fortune out of it. With that money we can build new habitats and allow our population to expand.'

'But if I find living organisms?' Wunderly challenged.

Holly spread her hands in a gesture of uncertainty. 'Then we won't generate the money to build new habitats. We'll have to restrict our population growth – which I don't think will be possible for much longer.'

'Something's gotta give,' Pancho muttered.

They all turned toward Wunderly. 'So you all would like to see me fail, then?' she asked, her voice plaintive.

'No,' Cardenas said firmly. 'I want you to find out what's really in the rings, one way or another, and come back safely.'

The others all nodded, but Wunderly thought that there wasn't much enthusiasm in them.

Urbain made his fourth call of the morning to Eberly's office; like the first three it was answered by a recording of the chief administrator's smiling face saying that he was busy and would return the call as soon as humanly possible. Checking his phone log, Urbain counted twenty-six calls that Eberly had not deigned to answer. He thought about going to Eberly's office and knocking his door down, but knew it would do no good. The man had made it clear: he would only approve the satellite launches if Urbain agreed to support mining the rings for their ice.

That I cannot do, Urbain said to himself disconsolately. Even if I wanted to the ICU would get the IAA to issue an order forbidding it. I would be disgraced even more than I am already. Intolerable.

He closed his eyes and tried to picture his *Titan Alpha* alone and abandoned on the surface of Titan. Not abandoned, he said to himself. Never! I will find you, my creation, find you and bring you back to life. I swear it!

His reverie was interrupted by a knock on his office door. Almost glad of the interruption, Urbain called out, 'Enter.'

He recognized the young woman who slid the door back and stepped into his office as a technician in the communications group: the wiry, nervous type, her lips pressed into a thin line but her eyes focused on him as if her life depended on it.

'What is so important that you must come to my office instead of phoning?' he asked severely.

She looked startled, almost ready to bolt for the door. But she stood her ground and said, 'I thought you would want to know this, sir.'

'Know what?'

'The storage capacity of *Alpha*'s memory core.'

Urbain gave no gesture for her to sit down, but still she hesitantly went to one of the chairs in front of his desk. Instead of sitting, though, she grasped the chair's back with both hands.

'Assuming that *Alpha*'s sensors have been operating at full capacity—'

'An assumption that may be quite incorrect,' Urbain interrupted.

The young woman gulped visibly, but then continued, 'Yes, sir, I know it's an assumption, but if it's correct it leads to an important conclusion. Or maybe I should say a problem.'

'Conclusion? Problem? What are you talking about?'

'Sir, if *Alpha*'s sensors are working as designed, and if the central computer is storing the data they're recording, then the core's storage capacity will reach its limit in thirty-five more days. Forty days, tops.'

Urbain stared at her. 'When the core memory capacity is reached, *Alpha* is programmed to transmit all data in storage.'

'Yes, sir. But since there's been no data transmission at all from the vehicle, there's no reason to assume that it will uplink all the accumulated data.'

He sank back in his yielding chair. 'Then she will go into hibernation mode.'

'Exactly, sir. If *Alpha* can't, or won't, dump its accumulated data and clear its memory storage, then the vehicle will shut down all systems. It'll be dead.'

'Not dead!' Urbain snapped. 'In hibernation mode.'

'But sir, if it won't respond to our commands and it enters hibernation mode, it might as well be dead. We can't find it and we can't communicate with it.'

Urbain felt his insides twitching, churning. His gut began to throb painfully. As calmly as he could manage, he dismissed his communications tech. Once his office door was safely shut once again, he leaned his head on his desk and closed his eyes.

There is nothing else I can do, he said to himself. I must find her before she goes into hibernation mode. Once she is asleep we may never be able to revive her. I must find her, save her!

He knew what that meant. With a sinking heart, he realized that he would have to give in to Eberly, support his contemptible scheme to mine Saturn's rings.

Either that or lose his precious *Titan Alpha* forever.

9 January 2096: Evening

The observation blisters built into *Goddard*'s hull were well-known to be 'makeout shacks.' Locked into one of the blisters, with its upholstered bench and carpeted floor, the lights down to their lowest so that you could see the heavens through the wide viewport of tinted glassteel, a couple could spend long romantic hours either gazing at the starry universe or exploring the universe within themselves.

Holly had made it clear to Tavalera that she wanted to be alone with him in one of the blisters because they could have a completely private conversation there, period. But as they entered the cozy nest and the heavy hatch swung shut behind them, she realized that there was no way that Raoul could keep romance off his mind.

Jeeps, she thought, I'd be cosmically disappointed if he didn't make a play for me.

'Look at that,' Tavalera said, his voice hushed with awe, as their eyes adjusted to the low lighting level.

Saturn was nowhere in sight. Instead, beyond the thick viewing port they saw the infinite black of space strewn so profusely with stars that it took their breath away.

'There's so many of them!' Holly breathed.

'That bright blue one there,' Tavalera said, pointing. 'I think that's Earth.'

She stepped up next to him, close enough to brush her shoulder against his. He slid an arm around her waist.

'I don't remember anything about Earth,' Holly confessed. 'That was my first life and all those memories are gone.'

'I remember it,' said Tavalera. 'I thought I wanted to go back – until I met you.'

She melted into his arms and for long moments they were lost in each other. Then, as the habitat slowly rotated, Saturn rose into view, its broad gleaming rings flooding the compartment with light.

Holly leaned her head on his shoulder. 'My god but it's beautiful.'

'Yeah.'

The wide flattened sphere of Saturn was aglow with streaks of saffron and soft russet. The rings were tilted so that they could see them in their full dazzling luster.

'You don't see that on Earth,' Tavalera muttered.

'Guess not.'

He kissed her again, then led her to the plushly padded bench.

As they sat side by side, Holly asked, 'Raoul, do you want to go back to Earth?'

She could see the conflict in his eyes. 'Yeah, maybe someday, I guess.'

'It's still your home, isn't it?'

Instead of answering, he asked, 'Would you come with me?'

'For a visit or to stay?'

'I don't know. I mean, I've got a life here. I like working with Dr. Cardenas. I'm learning a lot. She says I could get a degree from the University of Selene.'

'In nanotech?'

'Yeah.'

'That would be great.'

'I couldn't do nanotech work back on Earth, though. It's banned there.'

'But you could get an engineering job.'

His face sank into a frown. 'Big deal. I'd be just another engineer.'

'So you'd rather stay here?'

'With you,' he blurted.

Despite herself, Holly smiled at him. 'Raoul, I don't want to be the deciding factor in your life. That wouldn't be fair to you. To either of us.'

'But you are, Holly. I want to be with you. I don't care where it is, I just want to be with you.'

He leaned toward her to kiss her again, but she put a finger against his lips.

'What?' he asked, exasperation clear in his tone.

'There's something between us,' said Holly.

Tavalera's face clouded over. 'Wunderly and her frickin' rings.'

'It's important, Raoul. Important to all of us.'

'Important enough to get me killed?'

'No! But—'

'But shit!' he snapped. 'You think flying Wunderly to the rings is more important than us being together.'

'That's not true, Raoul.'

'The fuck it isn't.' He got to his feet. 'You don't give a damn about me, not for me, myself. You're tryin' to play me like a fuckin' violin!'

'Raoul, no. Please!'

But he stormed out of the observation blister, leaving Holly sitting there alone, close to tears. What tore at her most was the realization that Raoul didn't believe that she could love him, his rage at the thought that her only interest in him was to use him.

I do love you, Raoul! she called silently. I really do love you. But she knew that she had lost him, hurt his pride, ruined her one chance for a happy life with the man she loved.

Holly bowed her head and sobbed, all alone in the darkened observation blister.

Jeanmarie Urbain felt as jumpy as a schoolgirl. Her husband was still in his office, spending the evening as usual trying to work out a way to regain contact with his errant machine down on the surface of Titan.

The strain was killing him, she could see. Every morning he left their apartment wearier, tenser, after a few hours of tossing and moaning in his sleep. Every evening he returned to his office or the laboratories, working far past midnight to find a way to reach his silent *Alpha*. It's as if I have a rival, she thought as she stood before the bathroom mirror and clipped on her earrings. He loves that monster of a contraption. He spends more time trying to woo it back to him than he spends with me.

Satisfied at last with her appearance, she left the apartment and headed around behind her apartment building, down along the shadowy lane that led into the little clump of woods next to the lake. She felt furtive, nervous, and more than a little excited. This is an adventure, she told herself as she passed the wide-spaced lamps along the curving path. An adventure. Keep your wits about you and all will be well.

Eberly had been cautious when she'd first phoned him and asked for a private meeting. Even in the phone's display screen she could see the suspicion in his eyes. The man was handsome, there was no denying it. From all that Jeanmarie had heard of him, Eberly had no interest in women. Perhaps he is gay, she thought, although she had heard not a whisper to that effect, either.

So she dressed in a frilly sheath trimmed in black lace that was modest enough except for its *décolleté* neckline and walked determinedly toward her rendezvous with Eberly. In her hand she clutched a tiny beaded bag that held little more than her palmcomp. If Eduoard should phone from his office I can answer him, she told herself. If he comes home early and finds me gone, I can tell him I went for a walk.

Malcolm Eberly was more curious than worried as he strode along the shadowy path toward his meeting with Mme. Urbain. Why has she called me out of the blue? he asked himself. And asked for a private meeting, no less. No one else; just the two of us. A tryst, in the dark of night. Eberly thought he knew the reason, but it seemed so out of kilter, so absurd, that he didn't trust his own reasoning.

It can't be, he told himself as he walked toward the dark woods by the lake. She'd never try to seduce me, not even for her husband's sake. She can't be thinking of anything like that.

Yet he found himself curious, eager, almost excited to see what Jeanmarie Urbain had to offer him.

9 January 2096: Midnight

It's like an unending nightmare, Eduoard Urbain said to himself. He sat at his desk, head sunk between his hands, handsome silk ascot hanging loose and sweaty from his shirt collar, his pearl-gray jacket tossed over the back of a chair.

Endless. Night and day I try to make something work and it is useless. It's like one of those dreams where you are struggling to get away from something horrible but you can't move. Your feet are mired in mud or sinking into wet concrete.

He banged a fist on his desktop so hard it hurt. 'Why?' he demanded of the empty office. 'Why won't she speak to me?'

With red-rimmed eyes he reviewed the latest reports from his staff. *Alpha* was still incommunicado, somewhere on the surface of Titan. She could not be located unless low-altitude satellites were put in place around Titan to search for her with infrared and radar scanners. And Eberly will not allow the satellites to be launched unless I agree to his scheme to mine Saturn's rings.

Endless. A never-ending cycle of frustration. My career is in tatters, my life is ruined. I am already a laughing stock back on Earth. The news media are doing stories about my failure.

What can I do? Urbain asked himself. What choice do I have? Eberly holds all the power. If I don't give in to him, I'll never find *Alpha*, never have a prayer of regaining contact with her.

Urbain straightened up in his chair. Let's look at this calmly, he told himself. Rationally. Either you agree to mining the rings or you lose *Alpha* forever. Or at least until some other group is sent out here with the personnel and equipment to locate *Alpha* and get her to begin sending data. But then you will have been replaced, sent home to Quebec in disgrace, a miserable failure, a has-been, a never-was.

No! Urbain told himself sternly. That cannot be allowed. If I agree to allow that miserable extortionist Eberly to mine the rings, I can locate *Alpha* and bring her back to life. Me, myself.

Wunderly will go berserk, but that is her problem, not mine. Besides, she will immediately appeal to the ICU and IAA. They will never allow mining the rings if Wunderly can show that Saturn's rings are indeed biologically active.

Urbain glanced at the digital time display on his desktop screen. Exactly midnight.

Very well, he told himself, his mind made up at last. I will agree to Eberly's ridiculous demand. Let him mine the rings, or try to. My first priority, my *only* priority, is to save *Alpha*.

With a grim smile he ordered the phone to call Malcolm Eberly, regardless of the hour.

Holly hadn't wanted to ask Pancho for advice but there was no one else she could think of. After her disastrous breakup with Raoul, she rushed to her apartment and spent hours pacing, thinking, rerunning their meeting in her head, calling herself a fool, a blind idiot, to put Raoul in a bind like that. No wonder he walked out. He thinks all I'm interested in is to get him to fly Nadia to the rings. Stupid! Stupid!

She realized that she loved Raoul Tavalera, but he would never believe her now. Love is based on trust, she knew, and he'll never be able to trust me again. Never.

She held back the tears that threatened to engulf her, but Holly knew she wouldn't be able to sleep. She didn't even change into her nightclothes. She simply paced her apartment, eying the phone console, wanting to call Raoul but knowing it would be useless, pointless. I've been a cosmic idiot, she told herself. An intergalactic dimdumb.

It was just past midnight when she found herself ordering the phone to call her sister. As soon as she realized it she wanted to cancel the call. But before she could, Pancho's face appeared on the small screen of the phone console.

'What's up, Sis?' Pancho looked wide-awake, grinning happily.

'I didn't wake you up, did I?' Holly asked.

'Hell no. Jake and I were just raiding the fridge. Those meals at Nemo's can be pretty skimpy.'

'I guess.'

Pancho's eyes narrowed. 'What's the matter? What's wrong?'

Swallowing once before replying, Holly asked, 'Panch, could you come over here? To my place? I need to talk to you. Just the two of us.'

'Faster than light, kid,' said Pancho.

'It was so good of you to come here to meet me,' Jeanmarie Urbain said, wondering if Eberly could hear the nervous thundering of her pulse.

Eberly smiled graciously in the darkness of the little woods. 'I must confess that your call surprised me, Madame Urbain.'

'Jeanmarie,' she murmured, as she walked alongside Eberly along the shadowy, twining path. 'My friends call me Jean-marie.'

'You count me as a friend?'

She hesitated a heartbeat. Then, 'I hope so.'

Eberly chuckled softly. 'Your husband doesn't think of me as a friend.'

She thought carefully before replying, 'Eduoard is completely immersed in his work. He has no time for friendships, no room for personal relations.'

'Not even for his wife?'

Jeanmarie pictured herself walking a tightrope over an abyss. One false step and I am doomed, she told herself.

Eberly took her silence as agreement. 'It's a shame that such a lovely woman is neglected.'

She sighed. 'It is his work. His reason for existence. He takes others – his aides, his associates – for granted.'

'And you, as well.'

'I am afraid so.'

'That's very sad.'

It took all her courage to reply, 'Sad, yes. And lonely.'

Eberly walked in silence for several paces along the path. She could not make out the expression on his face. He was slightly taller than she, but she got no impression of brute masculine strength. Rather, Jeanmarie felt as if she were walking with a stealthy cat padding along beside her, eying her with calculating eyes.

At last he said, 'I know what it is to be lonely.'

'You do?'

'Scientists aren't the only ones to become ensnared in their work. I have the responsibility for this entire habitat on my shoulders. Ten thousand men and women. They all depend on me.'

'Yes, of course. I should have realized that.'

'Like you, I have no one to turn to,' Eberly went on, his voice a soft, poignant murmur.

'You need a friend,' she said.

'That's perfectly true. You're a very understanding woman.'

'You are very kind.'

'I'm happy that you believe so.'

She decided she had to play her penultimate card. 'You know, I have admired you for several weeks now. You are so . . . so commanding. So superb.'

He stopped walking and turned to face her. Jeanmarie's heart thumped in her chest.

'You really admire me?' he asked, his voice high with wonder.

183

'Truly,' she lied.

'Perhaps . . .' he began, then paused dramatically.

'Perhaps?'

Taking both her hands in his, Eberly said, 'Perhaps we could be friends.'

She allowed him to hold her hands as she gazed into his eyes, trying to fathom what was going on behind them.

'But you're a married woman,' Eberly said gloomily. 'In a closed habitat like this, it could never work.'

'If Eduoard were busy working on his probe, searching for it, trying to regain control of it . . .'

'He'd have no time for you at all, would he?'

'None at all,' she agreed.

'But we couldn't be seen together in public,' Eberly said gravely. 'That wouldn't do.'

She replied, 'We could meet here and take walks, talk to each other, share our thoughts.'

'I suppose I could arrange for an electric cart and we could ride to one of the endcaps, or one of the unoccupied villages.'

Jeanmarie recognized the danger in that.

'I could not be away from home for so very long,' she temporized.

'But if your husband had the satellites he wants he'd be spending all his time searching for his probe, wouldn't he?'

Nodding, she added, 'And once he found the machine he would be with it every hour of the night and day.'

Eberly smiled. 'You have a rival.'

'Yes, I do.'

He stepped closer and put his hands on her shoulders. And his palmcomp chimed.

Jeanmarie shuddered as if rudely awakened from a bad dream. Eberly grumbled something and flicked his handheld open.

'Yes?' he snapped.

'Chief Administrator Eberly?' he heard from the handheld's tiny speaker. Urbain's voice! Does he know . . .?

'Yes,' he said, more guardedly.

'This is Eduoard Urbain. I have decided to withdraw my opposition to mining the rings of Saturn.' Urbain's voice was brittle, sharp-edged. 'Providing, of course, that you permit my people to launch the satellites into orbit around Titan. And to build replacement satellites.'

Glancing at Jeanmarie, who was staring at him with eyes so wide with guilt that he could see their whites even in the night-time darkness, Eberly answered, 'Very well. We can discuss this in my office first thing tomorrow morning.'

He snapped the handheld shut and said to Jeanmarie, 'It's quite late. You'd better get home.'

'Was that Eduoard?' she asked, in an agonized tone.

Nodding, Eberly said, 'He'll be at your apartment shortly, wondering where you've been.'

With that he turned abruptly and began striding back toward Athens, leaving Jeanmarie standing in the shadows alone. Both of them felt relieved.

Pancho did not break the lightspeed barrier, but she was knocking at Holly's door before Holly could finish washing the tears from her face.

'What's the matter?' she said as she strode into the apartment, her head swiveling as if she were looking for cutthroats and assassins.

Within minutes the two sisters were sitting together on the sofa as Holly poured out her troubles.

'Oh, Panch, I've made such a mess of things!'

Pancho nodded tightly.

'He'll never want to talk to me again. Never.'

'Does that matter so much to you?'

'It does! It truly does. I didn't realize how much I really love Raoul until now. I've flamed out, Panch. I've wrecked it all.'

Leaning back on the sofa, Pancho scratched idly at her chin. 'Cool down, Sis. Let's take this one step at a time.'

'He thinks all I want is to get him to fly Nadia to the rings. He doesn't know that I really love him.'

'Well, to begin with, you've gotta find somebody else to pilot the spacecraft. That'll show him that he's not on the spot for that assignment.'

'I wish. But even if I could find somebody he'd still be sore at me. He'll go back to Earth soon's he can, I bet.'

'Which won't be real soon,' Pancho said, as soothingly as she could. 'There aren't any ships heading all the way out here that I know of.'

'There will be, in a few months.'

'That's a long time from now.'

'Yeah, maybe, but—'

'What you need, first shot out of the box, is somebody to fly your scientist pal to the rings.'

'Timoshenko won't do it,' Holly said. 'And we don't really have anybody else except Raoul who can do the job. We need an experienced astronaut.'

Grinning widely, Pancho said, 'You're lookin' at one.'

'You? But Jake said—'

'Never mind what Jake said. I spent more time drivin' spacecraft than you've spent brushing your teeth, just about.'

'But . . . but that was *years* ago, Panch. You're too old—'

Pancho's face hardened. 'Don't say it, kid. My reflexes are still quick enough to give you a spanking. A little time in a simulator and I'll be sharp as a samurai sword's edge.'

Holly sat there, mouth open, clearly disbelieving.

'Jake can help your mission control team. He gets along pretty good with Manny Gaeta.'

'I s' pose . . .'

'And you can get your boyfriend to join the techie team, too. He can stay nice and safe here while I fly out to the rings. This is gonna be fun!'

'Pancho,' said Holly, shaking her head, 'you can't—'

'The hell I can't.'

'But Raoul won't join the mission control team. He won't even talk to me.'

'Sure he will,' Pancho said cheerfully. 'Ask him while you're in bed.'

'I couldn't!'

'Best time to ask a man anything,' Pancho said, with a knowing wink.

15 January 2096: Registration Day

Eberly awoke with a smile. Registration day. The moment that my re-election campaign actually begins. Sitting up in his bed, he mentally scanned his political horizon. No obstacles in sight. Urbain has caved in to me, so there'll be no real opposition to my plan to mine the rings.

As he got up and padded to the lavatory he thought, Of course that Wunderly woman will object and try to get the IAA to intervene, but that will just make me look more heroic to the voters, resisting the demands of Earthbound bureaucrats who don't care about our real needs. Maybe I'll get elected unanimously!

Best of all, he told himself as he thoroughly brushed his teeth, I won't have to play games with Urbain's wife. What a pathetic little dodge she tried to pull over on me! Would she really have gone to bed with me? He shook his head as he rinsed his mouth and spat into the sink.

I can have my pick of just about any woman in this habitat, he said to himself. But why bother? Power is better than sex. Being admired by everyone – *everyone!* – that's the really great thing in life. I don't need women. I don't need anything or anyone, not as long as I'm chief administrator. No one can hurt me. No one can touch me. I'm king of the hill and I'm not going to let anyone pull me down.

Zeke Berkowitz was smiling amiably as he inspected the camera placements he had personally set up around the stage of Athens' only theater. As chief of *Goddard's* communications department, Berkowitz still thought of himself as a newsman, and this day of registering for the coming election was one of those rare newsworthy events in the habitat.

Despite being slightly portly Berkowitz cut a rather dapper figure in his pale yellow slacks and raw silk sports coat of toast brown. He had none of his minuscule staff with him; he figured he could handle this event alone, with the help of the three remotely controlled cameras he had set in place. Unlike most of the younger people in the habitat, Berkowitz had disdained the enzyme treatments that would turn his skin golden. That's for the kids, he thought; I'll stay a pasty-faced old fart.

His years aboard *Goddard* had taught him not to expect a throng of curious onlookers. The inhabitants of this community were a strange lot, largely aloof to politics. No, Berkowitz reminded himself. They're not aloof; they're wary, suspicious of politics and politicians and everything that goes with them. Most of them had been exiled by their home countries, one way or another. They were aboard *Goddard* because their fundamentalist regimes at home had no use for them.

Berkowitz himself had come out to Saturn willingly, at the request of Professor Wilmot, when the professor was organizing this permanent expedition. Retired after a lifetime in the news media business, bereft by the death of his wife, he had gladly accepted the chance to get as far away from his memories as he could.

Sure enough, the theater was practically empty. A few onlookers with nothing better to do were scattered through the otherwise empty seats. They merely made the place look emptier. Up on the stage, the official registrar sat behind a long table, bare except for the laptop computer opened in front of him. Berkowitz had expected the chief of human services, Holly Lane, to serve as the registrar but apparently she had sent an underling. Holly's a lot more photogenic than this young nonentity, he thought.

Ten a.m. was the official opening time for citizens who wished to register as candidates for election to the habitat's post of chief administrator. It was now nearly eleven and no candidates had shown up. No matter, Berkowitz thought. Eberly will be here sooner or later, and he'll unquestionably bring an entourage with him. With tight camera angles, good interview questions and some judicious editing I'll make this the media event of the young year on this evening's news broadcast.

He was mildly surprised when Holly Lane appeared at the back of the theater and strode boldly down the center aisle. Has she come to replace the guy behind the desk? It's her job, as head of human services, to serve as registrar. Maybe she was busy on something else and couldn't get to it until now, Berkowitz thought.

'Good morning,' he called to Holly as she climbed the stairs at one end of the stage.

'Hello, Zeke,' said Holly, with a wave of her hand. She was wearing not her usual dull tunic and slacks but a brightly-flowered short-skirted dress. Pretty young woman, Berkowitz thought. Nice legs.

Holly marched straight to the registrar and said, 'I want to register as a candidate.'

The man behind the table – thirtyish, round-faced – had looked pretty bored up until that moment. His brows shot up and he squeaked, 'You?'

'Yep, me.'

Berkowitz raced from his post at one end of the stage to the table. 'Hey, no, wait a minute! We've got to do this over. I wasn't expecting—'

Holly laughed at his suddenly flustered expression. 'You weren't expecting me to throw my name in the mix?'

Grinning back at her, Berkowitz said, 'The expression is "throw my hat in the ring." And, no, I wasn't expecting it. This is news! We've got to stage it right.'

Holly allowed him to direct her. Berkowitz had her go back halfway down the aisle and, after adjusting the camera angles, cued her to walk up onto the stage once more.

She strode to the table purposively and announced in a clear, firm voice, 'I want to register as a candidate in the election for chief administrator.'

It was now precisely eleven a.m., and at that moment the double doors at the rear of the theater swung open again and Malcolm Eberly marched in, followed by exactly a dozen men and women. He was smiling confidently as he started up the aisle.

'No! Wait!' Berkowitz yelled from the stage. 'We're not finished here yet.'

Eberly slowed and stopped, his smile dwindling as he recognized who was at the registrar's table.

'Holly?' he yelped.

'Be with you in a minute,' Holly answered.

'Let me finish with her,' Berkowitz called to him. 'Then we'll get you entering through the doors.'

Eberly's face darkened as he stood with folded arms in the middle of the theater amidst his entourage while Berkowitz videoed Holly giving her name to the registrar and his pulling up her dossier on his computer.

'You are now officially registered as a candidate in the election for the office of chief administrator,' said the registrar in an overly loud voice, obviously aware of the cameras. 'Good luck to you.'

'Thanks,' said Holly, smiling sweetly. 'I'm gonna need it.'

'Okay,' Berkowitz called down to Eberly while he pecked at his handheld remote to reposition the cameras. 'Go back to the doors and come in again.'

This is going to be great, Berkowitz exulted silently as Eberly re-entered the theater, his most dazzling smile firmly in place. We're actually going to have a race for the election. Holly Lane's running against her own boss.

Four minutes later, with Eberly's registration safely recorded, Berkowitz gestured the two candidates toward him.

'I need to ask you a few questions,' he told them. 'Why you're running, what you hope to accomplish, that sort of thing.'

He began with Eberly.

'I'm running for re-election because I believe the people of this habitat need and deserve a man with experience. I think I've shown over the past year that I can run the office efficiently, fairly, and to the betterment of all our people.' Somehow he managed to smile and look serious at the same time.

'And what will be your number one priority, if you are re-elected?' Berkowitz asked.

Eberly's smile brightened. 'I believe that the path to wealth and a successful future for the people of this habitat lies in mining the rings of Saturn for their abundant supply of water ice. Water is the most precious commodity in the solar system, and we can become the prime supplier of water for the human settlements on the Moon, Mars, the Asteroid Belt and the research stations elsewhere in the solar system.'

'Despite the reservations voiced by our own scientists and others?' Berkowitz prodded.

'Our people should and must decide their own fate,' Eberly said, his voice firm and strong. 'We should not allow Earth-bound bureaucrats or unrealistic scientists to restrict our freedoms.'

Berkowitz turned to Holly, standing beside Eberly. He noted that she was slightly taller than Eberly, which would show clearly in a video two-shot.

'And Ms. Lane, why have you decided to oppose Mr. Eberly?'

Holly stumbled, 'Well, it's not . . . I mean, there's nothing personal involved. I just think that Malcolm's ignoring a problem that's incredibly important.'

'What problem?'

'Population growth,' she replied immediately. 'Our people are living under the zero-growth protocol. That's got to change, sooner or later. Prob'ly sooner.'

'But with our limited resources—' Berkowitz began.

Holly cut him short. 'This habitat can support five times our current population easily. What we've got to do is work out a way to allow population growth within the limits of our resources. I think we're smart enough to figure out how to do that.'

'Do you have a plan for allowing population growth?'

'No sir, I surely don't. But we need to get our best minds together to work on this problem. Even ask for advice from Earth if we need to; there's lots of people on Earth who've dealt with population growth issues.'

'Without much success,' Eberly interjected.

'We can't ask the people of this habitat to keep on the way we've been. It's inhuman! People want to have babies!'

'Women want to have babies,' Eberly countered.

'So do men,' Holly jabbed back. 'Normal men.'

Before Eberly could reply Berkowitz physically pushed in between them. 'I can see that this is going to be an exciting race. Can you both agree to having one or more formal debates on these issues?'

'Certainly,' Eberly snapped.

Holly nodded less assuredly. 'I guess.'

'Good. I'll meet with you individually to arrange the details. For now, would you kindly shake hands for the camera?'

Holly stuck her hand out and Eberly took it in a lukewarm grip.

'May the best man win,' Eberly said, looking straight into the nearest camera.

'May the better person win,' Holly corrected.

Eduoard Urbain ignored registration day; he did not watch the news broadcast that evening that showed the interviews with the two candidates. He didn't even know that Holly Lane had registered in opposition to Malcolm Eberly.

The last one of his satellites had been successfully inserted into a low polar orbit around Titan, and Urbain had no time for anything except to search for his wandering *Alpha*. One of the satellites had malfunctioned at launch from the habitat; its guidance system had evidently been misprogrammed. Instead of heading for an orbit around Titan its trajectory aimed it into the moon's thick atmosphere. Urbain had gone into a frenzy, terrified that the satellite would crash on Titan's surface and contaminate the biosphere. His mission controllers, though, fired the satellite's maneuvering thrusters and sent it into a long, looping trajectory that passed Titan safely and swung it into a course that would ultimately impact high in Saturn's northern hemisphere, safely away from any possible contamination of Titan.

Eleven satellites in low orbit to scour the moon's surface in search of the lost rover. Urbain spent night and day in the mission control center, peering at the displays on the smart walls, reviewing thousands of still images of Titan's landscape.

The planetary physicists on his staff were ecstatic with the satellites' imagery. They were generating a detailed photographic map of Titan's surface, with a five-meter resolution.

'If we could overlap imagery from two or more satellites,' one of them suggested to Urbain, 'we could build up a three-dimensional map with a resolution of better than one meter. We'd be able to see individual boulders!'

'Not until we find *Alpha*,' Urbain insisted doggedly.

'But that'll help us find the beast.'

'Ah, yes,' Urbain backtracked. 'Of course.'

He took his meals at the mission control center, even had a cot brought in so he could nap there when he could no longer keep his eyes open. Jeanmarie visited now and then, often to bring him a meal she had cooked for him. He had no time for her. A mumbled thanks and a brief peck on her cheek was all he could manage for his wife.

Still no trace of *Alpha*.

'Perhaps,' suggested one of the engineers, 'it blundered into one of the seas and sank.'

'Blundered?' Urbain roared. 'Blundered? *Alpha* is not blind. Not stupid. She has more computing power in her central processor than you have in your head!'

The man scurried away from Urbain's red-hot wrath.

It was the youngest of the planetary physicists, a sweet-faced woman with more nerve than her colleagues, who approached him next.

'With the stereo imagery we'll be getting,' she said, 'and resolution down to the one-meter level, we ought to be able to detect *Alpha*'s tracks.'

'Her tracks?' Urbain lifted his head from the imagery he had been studying.

The young woman, standing in front of the console where Urbain was sitting, licked her lips nervously and explained, 'We know where she landed. We can scan that region to see if we can find the tracks the beast's treads left as she moved off on her own.'

'And follow the tracks until we locate her!' Urbain finished for her, so excited by the idea that he overlooked her calling his *Alpha* a 'beast.'

'Yes, that's exactly right,' she said.

Urbain jumped to his feet. For a moment the young geophysicist thought he was going to grab her and kiss her. Instead, he started shouting orders to the rest of the staff.

As the young woman returned to the planetary physics group, huddled in a corner of the mission control center, one of her fellow scientists raised his hand above his head, palm out. She recognized the gesture from old videos and smilingly gave him a high five.

31 January 2096: Morning

Holly said, 'I can't stay long. I've got to write a speech for tonight's newscast.'

Manny Gaeta shook his head. 'I'd rather have a tooth pulled than stand up in public and give a speech.'

She shrugged. 'I'm a political candidate now. I've gotta make speeches.'

Holly, Gaeta, Kris Cardenas, Tavalera, Pancho, Jake Wanamaker and Nadia Wunderly stood in front of Gaeta's excursion suit, which loomed over them like a mammoth, inert robot, its pitted surface dimly reflecting the strip lights running overhead. Gaeta and Tavalera had rolled the suit from its storage locker to this workroom, then set it up on its feet, using the power winches hanging from the steel beams up near the ceiling.

Wunderly felt an almost dizzying swirl of emotions washing over her: excitement, apprehension, sheer awe at the size and massiveness of the suit. I'm going to climb into that thing and fly through the B ring in it, she told herself. My sweet lord! Me! I'm going to do it.

The little group had gathered in the same high-ceilinged workshop where Gaeta and his technicians had checked out the suit months earlier for his stunt flight through the rings. Instead of the row of electronics consoles that Gaeta's tech team had lined against one of the bare walls, though, now there was only a pair of folding tables, where Tavalera had spread out a pair of fabric-thin rollup computers; the keyboards he had taped to the table tops, the display screens to the wall.

'Well, here it is,' Gaeta said, patting one of the suit's cermet arms. Turning to Wunderly, he asked, 'You want to see what it's like inside?'

Wunderly nodded wordlessly, her eyes riveted to the thick glassteel visor of the helmet towering above her.

'Is Timoshenko coming or not?' Pancho asked.

'Not,' said Holly. 'He's flatly refused to have anything to do with this mission. Says he's got his hands full with maintenance for the solar mirrors.'

'He's having problems with the solar mirrors?' Wanamaker asked.

'Nothing major,' said Holly. 'It's more likely an excuse for steering clear of us.'

'Those mirrors are important,' Wanamaker said. 'There's no such thing as a minor problem with them.'

'I guess,' Holly replied.

'Come on, Nadia,' Gaeta said, taking her gently by the arm. 'You climb in through the hatch in back.'

'A trapdoor?' Pancho blurted. 'You mean like a kid's jammies?'

Gaeta threw her a sour look as they all walked around the bulky suit like tourists circling a monumental statue.

Pecking at the remote controller he held, Gaeta made the hatch in the rear of the suit pop open. Looking at the rim of the hatch and that at Wunderly's stubby figure, he muttered, 'I can see we're gonna need at least one additional piece of equipment.'

'A step stool,' Pancho said.

Wanamaker cupped his hands together. 'Come on, Nadia. Upsy-daisy.'

Looking slightly uncertain, Wunderly lifted her left foot as high as she could and rested it in Wanamaker's interlaced hands. Leaning on his broad shoulder with one hand, she reached for the hatch's edge as Wanamaker boosted her. While Gaeta watched grimly, she scrabbled her way in through the hatch. Good thing I've lost so much weight, she thought.

'It's dark in here,' she said, her voice slightly muffled, even in her own ears.

Gaeta answered, 'We haven't powered it up yet. Hang five.' And he trotted back to the computers on the tables by the wall.

Crouching inside the dark suit Wunderly smelled faint odors of machine oil, old plastic and stale human sweat. From the light of the workshop spilling through the open hatch she could see that there were dark wells where she presumed her legs would go and, above her, the headpiece with its transparent visor, like a distant window or skylight. It seemed a long way above her.

Suddenly an array of lights sprang up and the suit seemed to stir into life. She heard air fans whirr and saw that the lights were from panels of gauges and miniature display screens.

'Can you hear me, Nadia?' Gaeta's voice came through speakers set up in the helmet section.

'Yes,' she called. 'But I think I'm going to be too short to get my head up into the helmet.'

She heard Gaeta chuckle softly. 'Put your feet into the leg wells. There's notches in them, like a ladder. Find a level that's comfortable for you, and then straighten up until your head's at the level of the visor. There's an adjustable fold-down seat behind you; you can set it to the level of your butt.'

'I can sit?'

'If you want to.'

It took several minutes of adjustments and a few bangs of her shins and elbows, but at last Wunderly wriggled her head up into the helmet section. She could see Kris and Holly and the others standing on the floor below her. They looked like pygmies; she felt like a giant.

'Hello there, Earthlings,' she said, and saw them wince and grab at their ears.

'Lower the volume on your audio output,' Gaeta told her. 'Audio panel's on your right, lit in pastel blue.'

Wunderly found the panel and nudged its control slide along the thin wedge that indicated volume.

'How's that?' she asked.

'Much better,' Pancho yelled. Her voice was muffled by the suit's insulation.

For the next quarter-hour Gaeta talked Wunderly through the suit's controls, constantly admonishing, 'Don't touch anything. Not yet. Look, but don't touch.'

'Yes, Daddy,' she said caustically after half a dozen such warnings. He acts as if I'm some stupid kid in here, she thought.

At last Gaeta said, 'Okay. You know where the arm controls are?'

'One in each sleeve,' Wunderly recited, 'and the override control is on the master panel right in front of my chest.'

'Okay. See if you can move the grippers on your right hand.'

Wunderly felt for the controls inside the sleeve while she peered down at the display panel just below her chin. There, she thought, that's the grippers. The screen showed all green lights. Gingerly, she flexed the fingers of her right hand.

'Good!' Gaeta called. 'Good work.'

But she couldn't see the grippers; the right arm was down by the suit's flank. Without asking, she began to slowly raise the right arm so that she could see the tools at its end.

'Hey!' Gaeta shouted. 'Whattaya think you're doing?'

'It's okay,' Wunderly answered. 'I'm just moving the arm a little bit.' She stopped the motion and made the grippers clamp together. 'I want to see what I'm doing.'

Gaeta's voice was like the rumble of distant thunder. 'Don't you do *anything* unless I tell you to. I'm in charge of this test. You follow my orders or else this whole deal is off!'

Wunderly's first instinct was to tell him to jazz off. But she held on to her temper and replied meekly, 'Okay. Right.'

Standing at the tables with the rollups, staring at the ton and a half of machinery that could easily crush flesh and snap bones, Gaeta suddenly realized how his own controller must have felt whenever he played a little prank with the suit. Jezoo, Gaeta said to himself, I'm starting to sound just like Fritz.

Holly left them working the suit and went to her own office to write a five-minute speech that she was slated to deliver for the evening news broadcast. It took her the rest of the morning merely to get a first draft down, and several hours of the afternoon to polish it to the point where she was halfway satisfied with it.

No wonder Malcolm dropped all his regular duties when he was running for the office, she realized. This politics stuff takes all your time.

She tried to do her day's work in the few hours remaining, skipping dinner to finish the tasks accumulated on her schedule. At the appointed hour she walked to the building where the habitat's video studio was housed. Berkowitz was at the studio door, smiling his usual amiable smile.

'Right on time,' he said, ushering Holly into the studio proper. It was nothing more than a small, well-lit room, empty except for a small desk and chair. No one else was there, only the two of them. Each of the studio's four walls was a floor-to-ceiling smart screen that could show an almost infinite variety of backgrounds. Holly saw that the two minicams balanced on their spindly unipods were aimed at a wall that showed a three-dimensional image of a bookcase.

'Kinda stuffy background,' Holly said, feeling disappointed.

'Oh, that was for Eberly's speech, earlier today,' Berkowitz replied. 'I was going to ask you what kind of backdrop you'd like.'

'Not a bookcase,' said Holly.

'Maybe a view of Saturn?' Berkowitz suggested. 'Although that might pull the viewers' attention away from you.'

Holly thought a moment. 'How about a view of the habitat, maybe up by the endcap where it's kind of like a park.'

Berkowitz immediately nodded. 'Good thinking. Very good thinking.' He pulled a handheld out of his tunic pocket and fiddled with it until a view of the endcap's greenery filled the wall behind the desk.

'Do you want to run through your speech before we turn on the cameras?' he asked.

'I don't think so,' Holly said uncertainly.

'Do you know it well enough to deliver it without reading it?'

'I guess.'

'All right. If you can give me a copy of the speech I'll have it displayed on the wall opposite the desk. Nice big type. That way you can glance at it whenever you're uncertain of the next line.'

'Great.'

'But try to look at the camera or at me while you're speaking. Okay?'

'Okay.'

'And don't worry if you flub a line. Just repeat it. I'll edit out the goofs.'

'Great.'

Holly sat at the desk, wondering if anybody in the habitat would bother to watch her when the speech was aired. Berkowitz lined up the two cameras almost side by side, then stood between them. Holly could see the first two lines of her speech on the wall above his head.

'Ready?' he asked.

She heard herself ask, 'Can we get rid of the desk? I think I'd rather be on my feet.'

Berkowitz looked slightly surprised, but he nodded and pushed the desk off to one side of the set, out of camera range. Holly started to help him, but then saw that the desk moved easily on well-oiled wheels.

'Okay now, stand right there. Try not to move around too much,' Berkowitz told her. 'Ready?'

She licked her lips. 'Ready.'

The five minutes seemed to fly by faster than light. Before Holly realized it she was saying, 'Thanks for your attention and good night.'

'Great!' Berkowitz said. 'Did it in one take. You're a natural, Holly.'

Holly found that she was drenched with perspiration and feeling totally worn out. Her logs felt wobbly.

'Come on,' Berkowitz said. 'I'll bet you haven't had any dinner yet, have you?'

'Not yet.'

'I'm buying,' he said grandly. Then, with a wink, added, 'Actually it's on the comm department's budget.'

By the time she got home, Holly felt exhausted, emotionally drained. Is this what running for office is all about? she wondered. You put every gram of adrenaline you've got into a dinky five-minute speech? How'm I going to get through making speeches to big crowds? Or debating against Malcolm?

Her phone screen was blinking. One call, From Tavalera.

Suddenly Holly's exhaustion disappeared. She told the phone to return Raoul's call as she scurried to her most comfortable armchair.

Once his long, sad-eyed face appeared on the screen, though, Holly took a deep breath and said merely, 'You called, Raoul?'

He looked somewhere between apprehensive and resentful. 'Yeah. I watched your speech. You did fine.'

'Oh, it was easy,' Holly said, trying to keep her voice light. 'Berkowitz is a dream to work with.'

Tavalera seemed to be on the verge of saying something, but he merely nodded. Silence stretched between them. Holly thought, Well, you called me, didn't you? Don't you have anything to say?

Finally, trying to get a conversation started, Holly asked, 'How'd Nadia's session with the suit go?'

'Not bad. Manny let her clump around the workshop a few steps. Looked like Frankenstein's monster, she was so stiff.'

'The suit's stiff,' Holly corrected, 'not Nadia.'

Tavalera came close to breaking into a grin. 'She was pretty scared in there, with Manny yelling at her every half second.'

'He's testing her,' Holly said. 'He's got to make sure she can survive in the suit.'

'Yeah, I guess so.'

Again a silence.

'So how are you?' Holly asked. 'What do you think about this operation?'

He hesitated, then blurted our, 'Is it true you got your sister to fly Nadia out to the rings?'

'Pancho and Jake Wanamaker, yes,' Holly said. 'They're both experienced astronauts, although they'll need some time in a simulator to catch up—'

'You did it so I wouldn't hafta go?'

Now Holly hesitated. Finally she nodded slowly and admitted, 'Yes, that's right.'

'Why? How come?'

Because I love you, you dimdumb! Holly wanted to shout. Instead she said, 'You didn't want to fly the mission. It's dangerous, I know that. I don't want you to do anything you don't want to do.'

His face went darker than usual. 'Now they all think I'm yellow. They think I'm afraid to fly to the rings.'

'Well, isn't that true?' Holly snapped. And immediately regretted the words.

His eyes flashed. But he replied merely, 'Yeah, guess so.' And he cut the connection.

16 February 2096: The Solar Mirrors

When it came to working outside the habitat, Timoshenko wanted both a belt and suspenders. He had a jet-powered maneuvering unit on his backpack but he also had clipped a long tether to the belt of his spacesuit. No sense taking any unnecessary chances, he firmly believed. Being exiled in this rotating beer can was bad enough; floating out to oblivion was not a fate he desired.

Timoshenko was leading a crew of maintenance technicians on an inspection tour of the solar mirrors' actuator system. Electric motors moved the mirrors automatically as the habitat rotated around Saturn to keep the mirrors pointed correctly toward the Sun. At the time appointed for the habitat's night hours, the actuators closed the ring of mirrors, folding them down against the cylinder's hull like the slowly-folding petals of a flower.

The entire operation of the mirrors was under automated computer control, backed up by sensor systems that reacted to sunlight and a preset timer built on an ultra-precise atomic clock. Yet the mirrors were constantly jiggling out of place. Not by much. Not enough to cause any real problems. They just jittered enough to make the computer program blare out alert signals. Just enough to drive me crazy, Timoshenko thought.

The entire maintenance team hovered behind the mirrors, of course, in the shade that they cast. Even protected by a shielded spacesuit a person wouldn't last long in the harsh sunlight that the mirrors focused into the habitat's windows.

Besides, the actuators and their motors and electronics equipment were all behind the mirrors.

They all wore bulky, old-fashioned hard suits. Cardenas had offered Timoshenko a set of nanofiber suits, but one look at the flimsy material and Timoshenko had shaken his head.

'This can really protect you out there?' he'd asked unbelievingly.

'Yes, certainly,' Cardenas had replied. 'Just as good as the cermet suits.'

Rubbing the monomolecular fabric between his fingers, Timoshenko had grunted. 'Maybe in a few years, after you've had some experience with this stuff. For now, I'll stick with the hard suits. They work.'

Now, watching his hard-suited team working on the solar mirrors, Timoshenko said to himself, the life of the whole habitat depends on these mirrors. Every plant, every farm, every man and woman in there lives only because the mirrors bring sunlight into this glorified tin can. And the damned stupid things refuse to work right.

Timoshenko had decided on a drastic step. Today's task was to replace each and every individual actuator and motor with an identical replacement. The replacement parts had been tested six ways from Sunday in the maintenance shops. They were flawless, operating to within six nines of their design parameters. The originals were going to be brought inside for similar testing.

We'll find where the problem is, Timoshenko told himself as he watched his spacesuited team laboring at replacing the dozens of devices. We'll find it and fix it.

Part of his mind, though, told him he was being foolish. The jinks in the mirrors' alignments were very minor, more of an annoyance than an actual problem. They were like a small cloud drifting across the Sun, causing a momentary drop in the sunshine's brightness. They were easily corrected by manually adjusting the computerized controls to bring the mirrors back to their proper positions.

But a small cloud can be the harbinger of a terrible storm, Timoshenko felt. Better to find the fault and fix it now, while it was minor, than to wait until a major catastrophe strikes us.

His crew hated working outside, he knew. He saw their resentment as they grudgingly wormed themselves into their spacesuits, he could hear their sarcastic chatter over their suit-to-suit radios; they were angry almost to the point of rebellion at having to work outside. Too bad, Timoshenko said to himself. It has to be done.

Why? asked a voice in his mind. Because you say so? You think you're a tsar now? A commissar? The thought shocked him. I'm doing this for the good of the habitat, he retorted silently. For the good of everyone.

That's what Stalin said when he slaughtered the kulaks, the voice sneered.

Timoshenko hung there in dark emptiness behind the massive panels of the solar mirrors, battling his internal demons, while his crew finished their assigned tasks. Only when each actuator and motor had been replaced, and the replacements tested and proved operational, only when all the original equipment had been carried through the airlocks and all his crew were safely inside the habitat, only then did he pull himself hand over hand along his tether and enter the airlock himself.

I'm no Stalin, he insisted to himself, no tsar. If there's work to be done I help to do it. If there's danger to be faced, I face it along with my teammates. Someone has to give the orders, and someone has to bear the responsibilities. That's necessary. Unavoidable. I didn't ask for this job, it was forced on me.

He was still arguing with himself as he pulled off the gloves of his spacesuit and began to unseal the helmet.

'Let me help you with that,' said one of the women on his team. She had come in with the first group and was already out of her suit.

'Thanks,' said Timoshenko. As she helped him wriggle out of the spacesuit, he was thinking that now they had to test each piece of equipment they'd brought inside. That would take time and a lot of dogwork, he knew. But at least it could be done inside the safety and comfort of the habitat.

Nadia Wunderly also took a walk outside the habitat. With Gaeta supervising and Pancho, Wanamaker and Tavalera helping, they bundled Wunderly into the massive suit and then rode in an electric cart through the maze of pipes and machinery below the habitat's living surface down to the big airlock at the endcap. Wunderly stood inside the suit on the cart's flat bed, looking like an oversized robot being carried to the guillotine.

They chose to ride underground to avoid the stares and questions of the habitat's population, questions that would swiftly reach Eberly.

'We don't want to give him any excuse for stopping us,' Pancho had said as she'd climbed into the cart's cab. It was a tight squeeze, four of them in there, but Pancho thought Wunderly was even less comfortable standing on the cart's flatbed inside that oversized set of iron pajamas.

'You really think we can keep this a secret from Eberly?' Tavalera grouched. Pancho couldn't tell if the pained look on his face was from worry or just from being jammed so tightly into the cab.

Without taking his eyes off the pathway he was driving along, Gaeta said, ''Hey man, Nadia hasn't even told Urbain about this.'

Wanamaker grunted. 'A top secret operation.'

'Better be,' Pancho muttered.

Tavalera's expression shifted slightly. 'If nobody knows what we're doin' how're we gonna get the access codes to the airlock? I mean, the safety department—'

'I got a pal in the safety department,' Gaeta said, grinning. 'Bought him a few beers.'

Pancho nodded. 'Let's hope he doesn't blab to anybody else.'

They reached the endcap and made their way to the airlock there, Wunderly plodding along in the ponderous suit and the other four skittering around her like a quartet of puppies taking a walk with a roving statue.

Gaeta pecked out the access code on the hatch's control panel. Pancho didn't realize she'd been holding her breath until she let out a huge sigh of relief when the inner hatch popped open and no alarms went off.

Wunderly licked her lips as she stepped carefully inside the airlock. Gaeta was yammering in her earphones about being careful and attaching both safety tethers and waiting until he gave her the word before she stepped outside. She could barely hear him over the hammering of her pulse. Walking in the suit must be what it's like to have total arthritis, she thought. Every step was a labor; it took a conscious effort to move one leg and then the other, despite the servomotors that whined and buzzed in response to her muscles' movements.

She looked down on her little team from inside the suit's helmet visor. Pancho looked tight with worry, Wanamaker seemed concerned, too. Tavalera was Tavalera, gloomy and apprehensive. Gaeta seemed almost angry, as if he were certain she was going to mess up.

Guess again, Manny, she said silently. I'll go through this just like we did in the simulator. No flubs, no hitches. I'm going to make you admit that I can work this suit without you shitting bricks every ten seconds.

The inner hatch slowly closed, shutting off her view of the others. Wunderly was alone inside the big metal-walled compartment, her heart thumping. I wonder what the medical readouts are showing? They'd shut down the test automatically if I got anywhere near a redline, she knew.

'You facing the outer hatch?' Gaeta's voice demanded.

208

'Yes, certainly,' she replied testily, while she turned laboriously in the unwieldy suit to comply with his order.

'Starting airlock cycle,' Gaeta said, his voice going flat as he lapsed into the clipped jargon of a mission controller.

'Airlock cycle, copy,' Wunderly echoed.

Wunderly clipped both her suit tethers to the clasps on either side of the outer hatch. She faintly felt the vibration of the airlocks pumps through the thick insulation of her boots as she watched the lights on the panel beside the outer hatch slowly flicker from green through amber to red.

The outer hatch swung open and a million pinpoints of stars hung in the blackness, staring unblinkingly at her. Wunderly licked her lips and swallowed hard before she could say, 'Ready to go outside.'

No reply. She looked out at the stars, slowly wheeling around her, and suddenly felt slightly breathless, almost dizzy.

'Tethers secure?'

She nodded inside the helmet, then said, 'Both tethers secure.'

'Clear for outside,' Gaeta said. She thought he sounded uptight.

Clumping to the lip of the airlock hatch, Wunderly told herself, You'd better not screw up, girl. He'll never let you use the suit again if you make a single mistake.

'Stepping out,' she said.

There was nothing out there. It was like stepping off a high diving board or jumping out of an airplane. She had never done either, but that's what went through her mind as she put one booted foot out into sheer vacuum and pushed off the lip of the airlock hatch with her other foot. She drifted outward, turning slightly. The stars were so thickly strewn that she couldn't make out any of the old familiar constellations.

'You okay?' Gaeta sounded worried.

'I'm fine.'

'Your pulse rate's over a hundred ten.' Pancho's voice.

'I'm fine,' Wunderly repeated.

And then Saturn swung into view, swathed about its middle with those gleaming brilliant rings. Wunderly's breath gushed out of her. My god! she thought. I can almost reach out and touch them!

'Still okay?' Gaeta asked.

Those rings! Out here she could see them clearly, even though they were more than a hundred thousand klicks away. Wunderly stared, awestruck. She could even see the narrow swaths of darker debris that swung through the glittering ice chunks of the rings: sooty dust from crumbled moonlets.

'Still okay?' Gaeta repeated, the strain clear in his voice.

'They're *wonderful*!' she gasped. 'So beautiful! Look at the way they're interwoven. They're *gorgeous*!'

'Don't lose your perspective,' Gaeta snapped. 'You're not out there to sightsee.'

'Right,' she replied, shaking her head inside the helmet. 'It's just . . . they're so damned fascinating.'

Silence for several heartbeats, then Gaeta said in a considerably lighter tone. 'You're gonna get a lot closer to them, *muchacha*.'

Titan Alpha

Following the dictates of its master program, *Titan Alpha* trundled across the frozen terrain, gathering data that would have made its human creators ecstatic with wonder and exultation.

The biology program was busily storing data from its observations in *Alpha*'s main memory core. The motile particles on the surface of the slushy methane-covered ice were most likely living organisms, carbon-based units that metabolized the abundant hydrocarbons in the ice and the ethane-laced streams that fed into the distant seas. They were similar to the organisms detected in the seas by earlier probes, but there were significant differences as well.

Using entirely passive observations, since active examinations were prohibited by the primary restriction, the biology program had deduced that the motile particles represented a low-temperature psychrophile form of organism. Their internal metabolism was so slow, due to the low-temperature environment, that compared to Earth-normal biology they could hardly be considered to be alive. Yet they were demonstrably ingesting nutrients from the hydrocarbons in the ice in which they lived. Their internal temperatures were noticeably higher than their external environment, and they gave off heat and waste matter – mostly gaseous methane that quickly froze onto the ground.

The very slowness of their metabolism was of significance, the biology program deduced. It could follow the organisms' internal metabolic paths in exquisite detail, if only the primary restriction could be lifted. Where terrestrial organisms' basic metabolic reactions took place in hundreds of nanoseconds or less, these psychrophiles' reactions took tens of millions of nanoseconds to run to completion. A living slow-motion laboratory for the study of biology.

Yet this promising avenue of study could not be pursued. The master program's primary restriction prohibited it. If the same conflict had existed among two human researchers, furious arguments and even violent struggle might have ensued. For *Alpha*'s conflicting computer programs, however, there was no dispute, no quarrel. The program could not even feel regret that such a rich opportunity was being passed up.

Indeed, the master program was examining another problem that it considered more important. The memory core was reaching its saturation point. Data was accumulating but not being uplinked. The master program realized that once saturation had been reached, it must shut down all systems and enter hibernation mode until new commands were downlinked.

The master program reviewed its options.

It could uplink the stored data. But that was prohibited by the primary restriction.

It could enter hibernation mode until new commands were downlinked. But the downlink antennas were disabled, to prevent any contradictions that would impinge on the primary restriction.

It could erase all the accumulated data and continue to gather fresh data.

Of the three options, only the third did not result in violating the primary restriction.

16 Feruary 2096: Evening

To his credit, Eberly spent several hours wrestling with his conscience. But, as usual, he won.

Sitting alone in his sparsely-furnished apartment as the solar windows darkened into evening, he finally decided there was no other option: I've got to get rid of Holly. I can't have her working for me as a department head while she's running against me in the election.

But it's got to be done carefully, he told himself. I can't just fire her. Everybody will see it as an out-and-out political move. A vendetta. I've got to be more delicate than that.

He felt almost bad about his decision. He liked Holly, on a personal level. She had always worked faithfully for him. But now she had turned on him, plunged a dagger into his back. It was her sister's doing, Eberly knew. Holly had been fine until Pancho had showed up. Pancho Lane was his real enemy; she was using Holly as a front, a dupe, a mask to hide her own ambition. And she's up to something more, he told himself. Pancho and Cardenas and that scientist, Wunderly. They're scheming, cooking up some plot behind my back. I've got to find out what they're doing.

Eberly straightened up in the recliner he'd been sitting in and called his computer to take a memo. One of the smart walls brightened and as he spoke, his words appeared in print on the wall screen. Eberly dictated, corrected, rewrote his memorandum until he was completely satisfied with it:

In the interests of efficient government and fair play, I hereby relieve Holly Lane of her position as director of the human services

*department. Her decision to run as a candidate for chief admin-
istrator will require her full energies for the duration of the election
campaign and it would be unfair of me to demand that she fulfill
her duties in the human services department while simultaneously
running her political campaign. Therefore I appoint the deputy
director of human services to assume the title and responsibilities of
acting director of that department. Some may comment about Ms.
Lane's sense of loyalty and duty, but I applaud her decision to offer
a challenge for the office in which I have served the people of this
habitat during its crucial initial months.*

Eberly reviewed his wording one final time, then nodded,
satisfied. I'll send it to Berkowitz at midnight so he can use it
on the morning news broadcast. I'm going to be making a
major speech tomorrow evening; this will be the icing on that
cake.

Pleased with his work, he rose and headed for the cafeteria.
More people ate there than in the habitat's two restaurants.
More hands to shake, more voters to smile at. Let them see me
as one of them, eating where they eat, sharing their lifestyle.

As he headed down the corridor, smiling and nodding to the
people he met along the way, he made a mental note to send a
copy of the memorandum to Holly. Tomorrow, he thought,
after the morning broadcast breaks the news. I'll send a copy
to her home and another to her office. Together with an order
to vacate the office at once.

Urbain sat tensely at the central console in the mission control
center. Eleven engineers bent over eleven other consoles, each
of them showing the false-color imagery from one satellite's
infrared camera view of Titan.

Only a few more days of storage remain in *Alpha*'s core
memory, Urbain told himself for the thousandth time. We
must find her before she goes into hibernation mode.

But even with eleven satellites criss-crossing Titan's smog-
shrouded terrain in low polar orbits, finding *Alpha* was

proving harder than he had imagined. The satellites' infrared cameras were capable of a five-meter resolution, in theory, which should have been more than good enough to find the errant vehicle. But so far, no sight of *Alpha*.

The special team he had assigned to building up a three-dimensional view of Titan's surface was due to make their presentation to Urbain in the morning. Bah! He said to himself, pushing up from the console's wheeled chair, I cannot wait. Time is flying by.

He strode to his office and called the surveillance team. The phone computer tracked them down in a small workshop halfway across the habitat from Urbain's office.

'Dr. Urbain,' said Da'ud Habib, obviously surprised. In the phone screen his lean, dark-eyed face looked thinner than Urbain remembered it, almost gaunt. The slim beard that traced his jawline had grown thicker, as if he had not trimmed it in weeks.

'Dr. Habib,' Urbain replied, equally surprised. 'What are you doing with the surveillance team?'

'I'm assisting them with their computer interfaces, sir. They need help with—'

'Never mind,' Urbain interrupted impatiently. 'I need the team's report at once.'

'Now?' Habib asked. Other faces appeared behind him, crowding into the screen, men and women, all of them looking tired, baggy-eyed, disheveled.

'We're going balls-out to make our presentation tomorrow morning,' said one of the men.

'We're pulling an all-nighter here,' said a woman, looking irritated as she pushed her hair away from her face.

'I understand and I appreciate how hard you are working,' Urbain said, trying to keep his own annoyance from showing on his face. 'Still—'

'Why don't you come down here?' the woman suggested.

Habib looked startled momentarily, then he nodded. 'Yes.

That might be the best thing, sir. If you could come over to our lab.'

Urbain thought it over for all of five seconds. Then, 'Very well. I shall.' Then he asked, 'Um . . . just where is your lab?

Pancho unhooked the safety harness and got up stiffly from the simulator chair. The three-dimensional displays on the walls of the tight little compartment flickered and went dark. She ducked through the hatch and stepped into the simulator control chamber, where Wanamaker was shutting down the computer system that ran the simulation.

Stretching to her full height and raising her long arms above her head, Pancho felt her vertebrae pop. 'Whooie,' she groaned. 'Been a long time since I sat in one place for so long.'

'Eight hours,' Wanamaker said, kneading her shoulders. 'Full mission sim.'

'How'd I do?'

He nodded toward the silent bank of consoles. 'The computer says you did pretty well.'

'Pretty well?'

'Reflexes were a little slow on the recapture sequence.'

'But I picked her up okay, di'n't I?'

He nodded. 'Could be smoother, Panch. When you're actually out there in the rings you'll be working with a neophyte. You can't expect her to be much help.'

'It's her life she's layin' on the line.'

'And it's your responsibility to fish her out of the rings and bring her home safely,' said Wanamaker.

Pancho made a mock scowl. 'You're a lousy boss.'

Grinning, Wanamaker replied, 'You don't make admiral by being a sweetheart.'

Stretching again, Pancho changed her tone and said, 'Okay, sailor. Wanna buy me a drink?'

'You've earned one. And dinner.'

Pancho took his arm and let him lead her toward the door of the simulations chamber.

But she stopped halfway there and turned back toward the consoles. 'Better schedule another full-up for tomorrow morning,' she said. 'This time with Nadia in the loop.'

Urbain felt slightly ridiculous pedaling an electrobike halfway across the habitat to the village of Delhi, but either the electric motor was defective or he didn't know how to engage it properly. Every time he tried, the motor refused to turn on. So Urbain pedaled the entire distance along the winding path between Athens and Delhi. The village was sparsely occupied, most of its buildings dark and empty. As he was wondering if he'd be able to find the building Habib had directed him to, he saw a young woman up ahead waving a hand lamp.

He braked to a stop in front of her and, in the light of the lamp, recognized her as the one who had suggested he come to Habib's lab. She was taller than he had expected, with long straight ash-blonde hair that fell well past her shoulders.

'Good evening,' Urbain said, puffing slightly from the unaccustomed exercise, 'Ms . . . eh . . .'

'Negroponte,' she said. 'Yolanda Negroponte. I've been on your geosciences team since we left Earth.'

It was meant as a rebuke and Urbain knew it. 'Yes, of course,' he muttered, trying to recover. 'Of course.'

'I'm a biologist,' she added over her shoulder as she opened the door to the building.

Urbain followed her inside, wondering why a biologist was working on the surveillance team. Then he thought that there was precious little biological work for her to do while *Alpha* was lost and silent.

As soon as Negroponte pushed open the door of the makeshift laboratory, Habib rushed to Urbain's side. He was slightly shorter than Negroponte, his skin several shades darker than her golden tan. Nearly a dozen other men and women clustered around them. Urbain could smell odors of stale food and old coffee. Containers of takeout dinners littered the folding tables along the back wall. He realized that he himself had not eaten since lunch, many hours ago.

'I'm so glad you could join us here,' Habib said, half apologetically. 'I know it's a long haul . . .'

Urbain, feeling sweaty from his pedaling, replied, 'Time is vital. We must find *Alpha* before she goes into hibernation mode.'

'Or dumps the data it's accumulated,' one of the other scientists said.

Urbain tried not to glower at him. 'What have you accomplished?'

'Not as much as we had hoped,' Habib said.

'But something of significance, nevertheless,' Negroponte added. She stood beside Habib, almost protectively. She was a big-boned woman with lank, light blonde hair. Urbain wondered what their personal relationship might be.

'We've set up a three-dimensional display of what the satellites have actually observed,' Habib said. 'We had intended to spend the night running through it and making certain there aren't any glitches in it.'

Urbain said, 'I will view it, glitches and all.'

Nodding uncertainly, Habib said, 'Yes, sir. If you'll please take a seat . . .' He indicated a flimsy-looking plastic chair set before a blank wall screen.

Urbain sat and the entire team seemed to flutter away to work stations that were set against the wall behind him. All except Habib, who stood beside the seated Urbain.

The wall screen glowed and then displayed a view of gray, rough, uneven ground. Before Urbain could comment the view suddenly acquired depth, clarity; it became a fully three-dimensional image. Urbain strained his eyes, but he could see no marks of treads, no tracks or depressions in the surface.

'That's *Alpha*'s original landing site,' Habib said.

'You are certain?' Urbain demanded.

'Sir, that's just about the only thing we are certain about.'

For the next two hours Urbain watched in growing aggravation as Habib and his team patched views from the satellites. Hardly any trace of *Alpha*'s tracks could be seen, merely a short stretch of tread prints here and there, seemingly almost at random. One view showed a small lake with a small mountain of piled-up ice in its middle.

'That's water ice,' Negroponte's voice called out.

'And you can see a slight indication of tracks leading to the edge of the lake,' said Habib.

'Did *Alpha* sink into the lake?' Urbain asked, alarmed.

'We don't think so,' Habib replied. 'We have some tracks on the other side – ah! There they are.'

'But there must be more tracks,' Urbain demanded. 'We know *Alpha*'s mass and the tensile strength of the ground. We have calculated the depth to which the tracks would sink.'

Habib nodded again, but his face showed apprehension. 'Sir, we know that the treads were designed to spread *Alpha*'s weight so that she wouldn't sink too deeply into the ice.'

'Still, she must have left tracks. It's impossible for her not to have done so.'

'I agree, sir. But if you notice the timeline of the images we've shown, tracks only show up in the most recent images.'

'Or in places where the vehicle must have dug itself more deeply into the ground,' said one of the others, 'such as the lakeside.'

'There's no sign of tracks at the original landing site,' Negroponte added, walking across the dimly-lit room to stand beside Habib.

Twisting in his chair, Urbain looked up at the two of them. 'What are you suggesting? That the tracks are eroded by weathering?'

'No, sir,' said Habib, with a shake of his head. 'Natural erosion rates would be too slow to erase the tracks.'

'Then what?'

'Something is actively erasing them.'

'Something?' Urbain felt alarmed. 'What do you mean? What something?'

'We don't know, sir. But some force or agency is actively erasing *Alpha*'s tracks almost as soon as they're laid down.'

'Something alive, perhaps,' added Negroponte, the biologist.

17 February 2096: Fitness Center

'I'm going to kill myself out there,' Wunderly puffed as she jogged along on the treadmill.

Striding on the machine beside her, Pancho hiked her eyebrows and answered, 'If you screw up the way you did in the simulator this morning, yeah, you prob'ly will.'

'I was really terrible.'

'It was your first time,' Pancho said, trying to sound sympathetic. 'You need more practice.' A *lot* more, she added silently.

Pancho had shooed Wanamaker and Tavalera away after Wunderly's miserable performance in the simulator. She had wanted to take the scientist to the cafeteria for an undisturbed lunch together but Wunderly had insisted on a session in the fitness center instead. So Pancho had foregone lunch and changed into a rented running suit so that she and Wunderly could try to figure out their next move. Now they trotted on the treadmills, side by side, amid dozens of other puffing men and women in sweat-stained gym clothes.

'I did everything wrong,' Wunderly moaned, wiping perspiration from her forehead.

'Were you scared?' Pancho asked, striding along easily on the treadmill. 'I mean, the sim's pretty damned realistic and you've never been out there in the rings.'

Tears were welling in Wunderly's eyes. 'I wasn't frightened, Pancho. Really, I wasn't. It was just so . . . so . . . confusing. It was like being lost in a blizzard. I couldn't tell up from down! I couldn't do anything right!'

'Well, it was your first time. Gotta expect some disorienta-tion. It's all new to you.' But to herself, Pancho was wondering if Nadia would ever be able to handle a ride through the rings in the excursion suit. She could kill herself real easy out there.

'I'll do better the next time,' Wunderly said, as her tread-mill's timer bell chimed. 'I really will. I'll know what to expect, at least. I'm a fast learner.'

Pancho turned her machine off too. 'Yeah, maybe so. But your gonna need a lot more time in the simulator,' she said. 'And some practice runs outside, as well.'

'How long do you think it'll take?'

'Six months, maybe more.'

'Six months!'

'Three, four months, at least,' said Pancho, 'depending on how fast you catch on.'

'I can't wait that long.' Wunderly stepped off her treadmill and started for the locker room.

'Why not?' Pancho demanded, following her. 'You in a hurry to kill yourself?'

Lowering her voice, Wunderly said, 'Pancho, we're sneaking this whole operation, remember? If Urbain finds out about it he'll scratch the whole deal. He'll report me to the ICU, say I'm a loose cannon, going out on my own without authorization.'

'Better'n getting killed,' Pancho pointed out.

'No it's not!' Wunderly retorted, with such quiet vehemence that Pancho was taken aback. Heatedly, Wunderly added, 'I'd rather die out there than sit here and be considered a failure, an idiot who claimed she found life forms in the rings but couldn't prove it.'

Pancho shook her head, thinking that Saturn's rings would still be there for a potful of millions of years.

They changed into their regular clothes and went to the cafeteria, at last. Pancho was hungry enough to eat half the menu, but she restrained herself and followed Wunderly's lead: fruit salad and flavored soy drink.

Just as they sat at an unoccupied table Holly came stomping up to them and banged her lunch tray down so hard the tea sloshed out of her cup.

'The sumbitch fired me!' Holly snapped, slamming into the vacant seat between Pancho and Wunderly.

'What?'

'Eberly. The slimeball fired me. Kicked me out of the human services department. Don't you people watch the morning news?'

'We've been in the simulator since oh-seven-thirty,' Pancho said. 'And then the gym.'

Fuming, Holly grabbed at the sandwich on her tray and tore off a big bite.

Wunderly asked, 'He fired you because you're opposing him in the election?'

'Why else?' Holly numbled, her mouth full of sandwich.

'But he didn't say it that way, I bet,' Pancho said.

'Hell no.' Holly swallowed hard. 'His news release was all about "the interests of efficient government and fair play." The cosmic creep.'

Wunderly dimpled into a smile. 'I've never seen you so angry.'

'And he's making a major speech tonight,' Holly grumbled. 'Prob'ly going to bring up that idea of mining the rings again.'

Wunderly's smile crumpled. 'He can't do that!'

'Wanna bet?' Holly and Pancho said in unison.

Jumping to her feet, Wunderly shouted, 'He can't! I won't let him!'

People at nearby tables turned to stare at her.

'How're you gonna stop him?' Pancho asked softly, reaching for the sleeve of Wunderly's tunic.

Sitting again, Wunderly stared at Pancho for a long, wordless moment. At last she said, 'Pancho, we've got to get me into the rings before the election.'

'That's three months off, isn't it?'

Holly nodded. 'June first.'

'I've got to prove that there are living organisms in the rings,' Wunderly said, her eyes welling with tears. 'Then the IAA will declare the rings off-limits for commercial exploitation.'

Pancho shook her head sadly. 'Nadia, it's gonna take more than three months to get you ready. Otherwise you'll just be killing yourself.'

'I don't care! I've got to do it, Pancho. I've got to!'

Timoshenko wished he knew more about computer programming.

He sat in his office, scrolling through the reports his staff had prepared on the equipment they'd brought in for testing from the solar mirrors.

There's nothing wrong, Timoshenko saw. Everything worked well within design limits. But when these very same motors and actuators were outside they performed erratically.

The problem wasn't major, he knew. The deviations from normal parameters were so minor that hardly anyone even noticed them. But they were deviations, Timoshenko told himself, and they shouldn't exist. And to make matters worse, the replacement parts that his crew had put into the mirrors were starting to show similar deviations. Just small fluctuations from normal performance. The mirrors moved a few seconds before the computer program was to activate them; they made minor adjustments that reduced the amount of sunlight focused into the habitat by a trifle.

Only a trifle now, Timoshenko thought. But what happens if these fluctuations grow bigger? We could all die in here if the solar mirrors fail in a major way.

He shook his head. There's nothing wrong with the motors or the actuators, he told himself. We've tested them sixteen times now and they perform within design specs each time.

But they don't work within the specs when they're outside, attached to the mirrors!

Is the computer program at fault? he wondered. He ran a hand through his bristly mop of hair. I'll have to get somebody from the computer group to go over the mirror program. Line by line, byte by byte. They won't be happy about it. Nothing but dogwork, thankless drudgery. But it's got to be done.

Or else we could all end up in the dark. And the temperature outside is near absolute zero. A super-Siberia, Timoshenko thought.

17 February 2096: Campaign Speech

Zeke Berkowitz couldn't help but admire the thoroughness of Eberly's preparations for this speech. He's a terrific stage manager, Berkowitz thought. He knows how to make a maximum impact.

Eberly had cajoled only a few dozen of his own staff people to serve as the live audience for his speech, but the conference room he had chosen was small enough to make the place look crowded. Since most of the habitat's citizens would watch the speech from their homes, Eberly's flunkies were enough to make it seem like a sizable and enthusiastic audience.

Berkowitz had his staff aides clear the conference table from the room and set up rows of chairs for the audience. A small lectern stood at the front of the room; Berkowitz's minicams were positioned in the rear.

At precisely 2100 hours, Sonya Vickers – the newly-appointed acting director of the human services department – stepped daintily to the lectern and looked out over the audience that filled the room to capacity. She was elfin slim, blonde, youthful, smiling.

'I'm glad to see so many of you here in person,' she began, 'to witness this important policy statement by our chief administrator.' Lifting her eyes to look directly into Berkowitz's central camera, she continued, 'And to those of you at home, welcome.'

She hesitated a heartbeat, then said, 'Now, without further ado, I would like to introduce your chief administrator, a man who has served all of us selflessly and very capably, Malcolm Eberly.'

The audience rose to their feet on cue and cheered enthusiastically.

In the living room of her apartment, Holly sat on her sofa, flanked by her sister and Jake Wanamaker. The screen on the opposite wall showed Eberly smiling brilliantly as he walked the six steps to the lectern, where he shook Vickers' hand and thanked her for her introduction. Impulsively, it seemed, she gave him a peck on the cheek.

'That was scripted, betcha,' Holly muttered.

Eberly beamed at his audience as they applauded lustily. After a few moments he gestured for silence. He had to repeat the gesture several times before they stopped clapping and sat back in their seats.

'That was scripted too,' Holly grumbled.

'Take notes,' said Pancho. 'You can learn a few things from this guy.'

Eberly gripped the sides of the lectern and bowed his head for a moment. The audience fell absolutely silent.

'Thank you all for that magnificent welcome,' he said, his voice low, as if choked with emotion.

'This is a momentous occasion,' Eberly went on, sweeping the room with his startling blue eyes, then looking directly into the camera. His voice rose, strengthened. 'You – all of you, every citizen of this habitat – have the chance to make history. Tonight we are embarking on a contest that will decide who will direct this habitat for the coming year. You citizens have the right, the power, the responsibility of electing the person you want to be your chief administrator. You will make this decision. *You* will vote in a free and fair election on the first day of June.' He hesitated, then added, with a modest smile, 'As a politician back in my native Austria once said: "Don't let any body tell you how to vote. You go to the polls and vote for me!".'

The audience laughed. But Holly growled, 'He was born in Omaha, Nebraska.'

Pancho nodded.

On the wall screen, Eberly was continuing, 'Our first year under the constitution that we ourselves have written has been a very good year. We are in a stable orbit around Saturn, the farthest outpost of human civilization in the entire solar system. We have achieved self-sufficiency as far as food and our other life-support requirements are concerned. The machinery of our habitat is performing admirably, thanks to the hard work and great care of our technicians and engineers. Our scientists have landed a probe on Titan, and although they have had some difficulties with it, I'm sure that in the coming year they will successfully regain contact with it and explore that mysterious world thoroughly.'

Alone in her own apartment, Nadia Wunderly watched with growing apprehension. He's going to tell them about the rings, she said to herself. He's going to ruin everything.

'But in this coming year,' Eberly went on, 'we must begin to take larger steps, steps that will assure our financial stability and economic well-being. Within easy reach of us, close enough almost to touch from here, in fact, lie the rings of Saturn – a treasure trove of the most precious commodity in the solar system: water. The time has come for us to begin to mine the rings, to sell their water ice to other human settlements throughout the solar system, to make ourselves wealthy by becoming the human race's primary supplier of water and life everywhere!'

The audience leaped to its feet and roared its approval. Wunderly jumped to her feet, too, and screamed, 'Never!' to her empty apartment.

Sitting between Pancho and Wanamaker, Holly sunk her chin into her chest and glowered at the wall screen. 'The only way to stop him is to get Nadia to the rings before election day.'

Pancho shook her head. 'She'll never be ready in time. We'd just be killing her.'

Holly turned to face her. 'Then you'll have to do it, Panch.'

'Me?'

Wanamaker started to say, 'Now wait a minute—'

'You,' Holly said to her sister. 'You've got to go into the rings, Pancho.'

18 February 2096: Morning

Tavalera walked toward the simulations laboratory like a little boy reluctantly trudging on his way to school. This is all crazy, he said to himself as he passed the administration building. People were hustling in and out, the place looked like a beehive of activity. That puzzled Tavalera; normally the admin center was as laid-back and quiet as a collection of snails. Then he realized that Eberly had kicked off his re-election campaign last night and now he wanted everybody to think he and his people were hard at work. Yeah, sure, Tavalera said to himself. Until he gets himself re-elected.

He had watched Eberly's speech on video, just like everybody else. Holly hadn't called him about it. She hadn't called him about anything, not since he'd walked out on her. And the one time he'd called her he'd let his temper get the better of him and messed it up. That was a stupid thing to do, Tavalera told himself bitterly. The one good thing in your life and you screw it up.

Yeah, he argued silently, but all she wanted out of me was to use me for Wunderly's flight to the rings. She never cared about me. Not really. Not for myself.

Then what about the times you spent together before Wunderly decided she's going to the rings? he asked himself. What about the nights in bed with her, 'way before all this crap about going to the rings started?

Shaking his head, Tavalera made his way up the four steps of the sim lab's building and headed down the central corridor toward the laboratory itself.

Holly'd never go back to Earth with me, he told himself. Hell, now she's running for chief administrator; if she wins she'll never leave this habitat. If I wanted to go back home she wouldn't go with me. He grunted as if struck in the heart. The way things are now, she wouldn't even cross a street to be with me. I've screwed things up pretty damned well.

He felt a jolt of electricity streak through him, though, when he opened the door to the simulations laboratory. Holly was standing there by the row of consoles, with Wunderly and her sister Pancho. The three women seemed to be deep in heated conversation.

'It's my problem, Pancho,' Wunderly was saying. 'I can't let you take the risks for me.'

'Try and stop me,' Pancho replied, grinning. 'I'm lookin' forward to this. Haven't had any real fun since I was runnin' from a bunch of Jap security people at the Yamagata base on the Moon.'

Wunderly turned to Holly. 'Tell her she can't do this, Holly. Make her understand—'

'Nadia,' Holly interrupted, 'It was my idea for Panch to fly the mission.'

Holly looked . . . Tavalera couldn't fathom the expression on Holly's face. Was it fear or guilt or just plain stubbornness? He decided it must be some of all three.

A big, hard hand grabbed his shoulder. Tavalera spun around and saw Jake Wanamaker towering over him, the expression on his face perfectly clear: grim determination.

'Stay out of that argument, Raoul,' Wanamaker said in a husky whisper. 'It'd be like stepping into a trio of laser beams if you try to get between 'em. They'll slice you to ribbons.'

'What's goin' on?'

'Pancho's going to make the run into the rings,' said Wanamaker, looking totally unhappy about it. 'Wunderly's relieved but she doesn't want to admit it yet.'

'And Holly?'

'It was Holly's bright idea.'

Glancing at the three women intently arguing across the room, Tavalera asked Wanamaker, 'Should I power up the equipment or not?'

A hint of a smile snuck across Wanamaker's craggy face. 'Power it up, I guess. They can't stand there bickering all day. But don't get within ten meters of them if you can avoid it.'

Tavalera almost tiptoed to the master console and began to activate the various systems of the simulator. The excursion suit, standing empty in the corner where two hologram screens met, seemed to twitch slightly as Tavalera powered it up. He could see a glow of light inside the suit through the open hatch in its back. The wall screens came up with a seamless three-dimensional view of Saturn's rings: a bright gleaming expanse of glittering ice particles – flakes, pebbles, chunks as big as boulders – shining as brightly as a snow field that went on endlessly, as far as the eye could see, slim twisting rings braided around one another, twining like living vines made of ice. To Tavalera it looked like an infinite swirl of sparkling diamonds, except for the streaks of darker material here and there, dust or soot, that broke the stunning display. Somehow the dark streaks made the ice particles seem brighter, even more dazzling to the eye.

And the particles were dynamic. They shifted and moved, weaved in and out around one another, twirled and fluttered in an endless dance of dazzling complexity. This was a real-time view of the rings, Tavalera knew. He was watching what the cameras outside the habitat were observing at this very moment. In the distance he saw a darker area, like a spoke radiating from the inner rim of the rings toward its outermost edge.

Wanamaker nudged him, then silently pointed at Wunderly. The scientist had stopped arguing with Holly and her sister and was staring at the holoview, raptly watching the rings in their intricate, fascinatingly beautiful ballet as they swirled around the mammoth planet Saturn.

'It's settled,' Holly said, suddenly as hard as steel. 'Pancho's doing the excursion. Jake will fly her to the rings and pick her up afterward.'

Wunderly shook her head, but she was still staring at the holoview and there wasn't much force in her refusal.

'It's settled,' Holly repeated.

'Right,' said Pancho. 'Now lemme get inside that suit and see what it feels like.'

At that moment the overhead lights went out and all the consoles went dark. Tavalera heard the sickening whine of electrical motors powering down. The sim lab was plunged into darkness.

Urbain was straining his eyes staring at the satellite camera's three-dimensional image of Titan's surface. There is something there, he told himself. The ground is slightly smoother along a straight line across the ice, as if the tracks made by *Alpha* have been smoothed down, paved over. Ghost tracks, he thought. Or perhaps I am merely seeing what I want to see, things that don't actually exist. He thought of Percival Lowell, spending his life squinting through telescopes at Mars, drawing maps of Martian canals that were in truth nothing more than eyestrain and wish-fulfillment.

The control center was fully manned. Da'ud Habib was sitting at the console where views from several satellites were overlapped to produce three-dimensional images.

'Dr. Habib,' Urbain called. 'Come here for a moment, please. I want you to see if—'

Suddenly all the wall screens went out: every console screen turned blank, the control center was plunged into darkness so complete that Urbain could not see the console in front of him. Before he could do anything more than drop his mouth open in shock, the back-up emergency lights turned on. But the wall screens and consoles remained dark.

'What's happened?' Urbain shouted. He heard other voices muttering, grousing.

The overhead lights flickered and then steadied. Urbain heaved a sigh of relief. The consoles came back up.

'A power outage,' someone said.

'Have we overloaded the system?' a woman asked.

'Did we lose any data?' Urbain called out.

Habib pecked at his console keyboard. 'I don't think so . . .'

'How could there be a power failure?' Urbain demanded. 'Half the villages in the habitat are unpopulated. We have more electrical power than we need.'

'Something went wrong,' Habib said.

'That's pretty damned obvious,' a woman's voice replied sarcastically.

Urbain shut out their bantering and returned his attention to his console screen. Ghost tracks? he asked himself. Could it be? And if it is so, can we use them to find *Alpha*?

18 February 2096: Afternoon

Eberly was furious. He paced back and forth behind his desk as Timoshenko and Aaronson sat in guilty silence and tracked his movement with their eyes.

'Am I being sabotaged?' Eberly demanded. 'Did someone deliberately cause the power outage just to make me look ridiculous? Impotent?'

'Power supply isn't my responsibility,' Timoshenko said curtly. 'Exterior maintenance doesn't include the power generators.'

Aaronson frowned as he ran a hand through his dirty-blond hair. 'Our primary source of electrical power is photovoltaics, which depend on the solar mirrors. Those mirrors have been performing erratically—'

'Minor fluctuations,' Timoshenko snapped. 'Nothing that could have caused a major outage. The problem is internal, not external.'

'We don't know what the problem is,' Aaronson said, his round jowly face reddening.

'You don't know?' Eberly snarled. 'It's been more than five hours since it happened and you still don't know what caused this breakdown?'

'It only lasted less than a minute. And the back-ups came on when they were needed,' Aaronson replied. 'We're tracking down the fault,' he added, almost sullenly.

'Well you'd better track it down pretty damned fast!' Eberly fairly shouted. 'And fix it! I can't have this happening while I'm running for re-election. I can't have the people thinking this habitat is breaking down around their heads.'

Timoshenko said nothing, but he couldn't help thinking, maybe it is. Maybe this whole huge contraption is breaking down. Maybe it's going to kill us all.

Holly knew she should have been working on her speech for this evening's presentation. In a way, Eberly's firing her had been a godsend: she had no other responsibilities except to work on her election campaign. Her salary had been automatically cut to minimal level, since she was officially unemployed now, but Pancho had electronically transferred a big wad of credits from her bank account in Selene. Holly had no money worries.

She knew what she wanted to say, but she needed facts to back up her intuition. That was why she had asked Professor Wilmot to see her. To her delight, the professor had agreed to meet her at the Bistro restaurant.

He was already there when Holly arrived, seated at a table out on the grass, with a cup in front of him, watching the people strolling along the pathways that cut through the flowering shrubbery.

He got to his feet once he saw her approaching, a tall thickset iron-gray man wearing an old-fashioned tweed jacket, a floppy little bow tie, and dark slacks that badly needed pressing. He greeted Holly with a charming little bow.

'It's good of you to take the time to see me, Professor,' Holly said as he helped her into her chair.

'I have nothing but time,' he replied, seating himself next to her.

The robot waiter wheeled up to their table and Holly selected a cup of tea from the touchscreen on its flat top.

'Would you like pastries with your tea?' the robot asked in its synthesized slightly British accent. The flat screen showed a selection of goodies.

Holly looked at the professor, who shook his head, then told the robot, 'No, thank you.'

With a perfunctory, 'Very well, Miss,' the machine rolled off toward the restaurant's interior.

'I presume,' said Wilmot, with an almost fatherly smile, 'that you want to talk about population control.'

'Yes, I do,' Holly answered eagerly. 'What I need to know is, is it possible for us to allow our population to increase in a controlled way, or would we just have a baby explosion if we lifted the ZPG protocol?'

Wilmot touched a fingertip to his moustache before answering. 'Population control,' he murmured. 'Touchy subject, that. It impinges on people's religious beliefs, you see.'

'Most of the people in this habitat aren't terribly religious,' Holly said. 'We got rid of the zealots.'

'Perhaps so, but when it comes to family planning, most people have usually been imprinted since childhood with firm ideas on the subject.'

'I guess,' Holly said as the robot trundled back to their table with a tray bearing tea.

While she put the tray on their table and began to pour herself a cup of tea, Wilmot went on, 'Different cultures have approached the matter in different ways. The Chinese, with their hierarchical heritage, imposed population limits by government fiat. It worked, after a fashion. India, of course, was a different matter entirely. Before the biowar depopulated the subcontinent, that is.'

'Our ZPG protocol has been sort of voluntary, really.'

Wilmot nodded. 'Yes. A law with no enforcement behind it. Seems to be working, so far.'

'So far.'

'You're concerned that it won't work much longer.'

'Professor, it *can't* work much longer. Most of our population is young; the women are of child-bearing age.'

Wilmot's lips twitched in what might have been either a

237

smile or a grimace. 'Child-bearing age seems to have stretched a great deal. Once it was definitely ended by the time a woman reached forty. Now it's decades longer.'

'And getting longer,' Holly added.

'I suppose they'll all want to have children. Most of them, at least.'

'At least.'

He took a sip of his tea. 'Western cultures – Europe, North America, Australia – they've pretended that they handle family planning through the concept of individual liberty.'

'You mean, they don't?'

'Hardly. There has always been a religious backbone to the illusion of individual liberty. Western governments never had to make laws about population control because their churches did it for them. Especially once the fundamentalists gained power and civil law became intermixed with religious dogma.'

'But the New Morality and the other fundamentalist groups are against family planning,' Holly pointed out.

'Officially, yes. They realize that overpopulation leads to poverty, and poor people are easier to control than wealthy ones. Still . . .' Wilmot tilted his head slightly. 'There are ways to get the churches to look the other way. Particularly if you are a generous donor to said churches.'

'So the rich stay rich and the poor have babies.'

'And remain poor.'

Holly could feel her brows knitting. 'So how do we handle population growth here in *Goddard*?' she asked. 'We can't keep this ZPG protocol much longer.'

Wilmot drained his cup, then set it down with a delicate clink on its saucer. 'My dear young lady, I'm afraid that problem is one that you are going to have to deal with. I have no wisdom from on high to impart to you.'

She almost smiled at his words. 'I was hoping you did.'

With a shake of his head, Wilmot said, 'You are dealing with the most fundamental of human drives, my dear. There are no pat solutions to the problem. You – and the rest of our population – will have to work out your own salvation for yourselves.'

Glumly, Holly said, 'I guess.'

'Indeed,' said Wilmot, thinking, this will be the most fascinating anthropological study since Margaret Mead's early work in Samoa. Will these people be able to produce a workable solution or will they tear themselves and this habitat to pieces?

18 February 2096: Evening

Despite Berkowitz's assurances, Holly felt wired tighter than a bomb as she stepped before the video cameras. There was no one else in the studio. She had chosen to give her first political speech from the communications center, alone, without a claque of an audience to applaud her words. I don't have a following, she realized. Not like Malcolm. Not yet.

Pancho, Wanamaker, Wunderly and several other friends had offered to come with her, but Holly had told them all that their presence would only make her more nervous. In truth, the only person she wanted to have there was Tavalera, but Raoul hadn't said more than six words to her that morning in the simulations lab, when the power failure had struck.

So now she stood nervously in front of a trio of cameras with their unblinking lenses focused on her. Berkowitz was smiling benignly at her from behind the central camera. There had been a couple of other technicians in the studio when Holly had come in, but they seemed to have disappeared now.

'Your introduction is prerecorded. I'll set it going and then give you a five-second countdown,' Berkowitz said. 'When I point to you like this it'll be time for you to start.' He aimed a stubby forefinger at her.

' 'Kay,' Holly said. 'I click.'

There was a monitor screen beside the camera on her right. Holly thought she looked terrible: strung tight and eyes staring like a skinny frightened waif. Slightly to her left, another monitor displayed the words of her speech in oversized capital letters.

The seconds dragged by, until at last Berkowitz began, 'Five . . . four . . . three . . . two . . .' He pointed dramatically.

Holly tried to make a smile as she began, 'Good evening. I'm Holly Lane, and I'm running for the office of chief administrator. Until yesterday I was your director of human services, but I was fired from that job, prob'ly because the guy who's currently chief administrator got sore that I decided to run against him.'

She took a breath, saw her next paragraph scrolling up on the monitor, then focused her eyes on Berkowitz, rocking up on his toes and down again as he smiled and nodded encouragement to her from behind the center camera.

'I'd like to tell you why I decided to run against my former boss. It's because of a certain married couple who came to me to ask permission to have a baby. They made me realize that there must be a lot of women in this habitat of ours who want to have children.

'Now, I know we live in an enclosed environment with limited resources. And I know we all signed onto to the Zero Population Growth protocol when we first joined this habitat. But I feel that it's time to examine that protocol and see if there isn't some way we can allow our population to expand – within the limits of our resources, naturally. More than half of our habitat is empty, unpopulated, unused. I believe that, with care, we can allow our population to grow. I believe that we have the intelligence and the courage to allow controlled population growth. I don't think that this habitat of ours should continue to be barren and childless.'

Berkowitz continued to nod and smile at her. The monitor had scrolled to her final, wrap-up paragraph.

But Holly ignored it and blurted out, 'And I also believe that there's absolutely no acceptable reason for power outages like we had this morning. That's inexcusable. We need to pay much more attention to the equipment that keeps us alive. That's all I've got to say. For now. I'll have more later on. Thank you.'

Holly thought she could hear Eberly's howl of anguish from halfway across the village.

18 February 2096: Midnight

'And where have you been?' Urbain snapped.

Coolly stepping to the chair before his desk and sitting in it, Yolanda Negroponte brushed a trees of ash-blonde hair from her face and said, 'A group of us had a little political discussion over supper.'

Habib, already seated in front of Urbain's desk, looked puzzled. 'What group?'

'The women of the scientific staff,' Negroponte replied, smiling faintly. 'Didn't you watch Holly Lane's speech earlier this evening?'

Shaking his head, Habib answered, 'I was here, going over these ghost tracks—'

'Where you should have been,' Urbain said sternly to her. 'A break for supper should not take three hours.'

'As I said,' Negroponte replied, unflinching, 'we had a political discussion over our meal.'

Before the two of them fell into an actual argument, Habib said, pointing to the display on the wall screen, 'We've been trying to piece together these ghost tracks from *Alpha*.'

The display of Titan's surface was the only light in Urbain's office. As Negroponte turned in her chair to look at the screen, Urbain noticed that Habib was watching her, not the smart wall. She is a well-proportioned woman, Urbain noticed. Slightly fleshy, big as an Amazon. Habib seems fascinated by her.

'If those faint traces in the ground actually are the remains of *Alpha*'s tracks,' Habib said, 'maybe we can use them to find the beast.'

Urbain bristled at his 'if,' and even more at his referring to *Alpha* as a beast.

Negroponte was shaking her head, which made that trouble some lock of hair fall across her face again. 'There's something else involved here,' she said. 'Something more important.'

Urbain felt his brows rise. 'More important than finding *Alpha*?'

'If those smooth areas are the remains of *Alpha*'s tracks, then the question is, what smoothed the tracks?'

In the shadowy light from the display wall, Urbain could see Habib was staring at her. 'You mentioned this before, the idea that something is actively smoothing over the beast's tracks. Something in the ground.'

'Actively smoothing the tracks,' Urbain repeated.

'Within a matter of days,' said Negroponte. 'Perhaps only hours.'

Despite himself, Urbain felt intrigued. 'It could be erosion from rainfall.'

'Or something tectonic, geological,' Habib mused.

'What geological force could do that?'

Negroponte shook her head. 'I don't think it could be geological. And not weathering. Not on this time scale.'

'You believe it's biological?' Urbain murmured.

'What else could it be?'

Habib said, 'We'd better get the bio team in on this.'

He scambled to his feet. Negroponte got up beside him. Urbain absently noted that she was slightly taller than he. They headed for the door.

'It's past midnight,' she said to him.

'So what?' he replied, almost laughing, 'They'll want to get started on this right away. They can sleep some other time.'

The two of them left the office, leaving Urbain sitting there, his mouth hanging open, his mind spinning: But we must find *Alpha*! That is our primary task. And we have only another day or so, perhaps only hours, before she goes into hibernation.

But he was sitting alone, talking to no one but himself.

Eberly had settled down in his favorite easy chair to watch Holly's speech with smug assurance that she would trip over her own feet. But her crack about the power outage infuriated him. As if it's my fault! he raged, pacing up and down in his apartment.

At last he decided that he had no choice. He had to fire Aaronson. Someone's head had to roll, he had to show the voters that he was *doing* something. I'll reorganize the maintenance department, Eberly said to himself. I'll put Timoshenko in charge of the entire department, with Aaronson's number-two under him. And the first job for Timoshenko will be to find out what caused that power outage and make certain it doesn't happen again. Not until the election's over, at least.

Tamiko and Hideki Mishima were so excited by Holly's speech that they couldn't sleep.

'She really wants to help us,' Tamiko said to her husband as they lay together, wide awake in the darkened bedroom.

'Yes, but she will run into a lot of opposition,' Hideki warned. 'Many people will be afraid of a population explosion that could ruin us. They'll want to cling to the ZPG protocol.'

'You think so?'

'I'm certain of it.'

Tamiko propped herself on one elbow and peered down at her husband's face. 'Then we must take positive action. Bring people together to support Ms. Lane. Organize into a political force.'

'We?' he asked doubtfully.

'Women who want to start having babies,' she replied.

Then, laughing, she tousled his hair. 'Don't worry, darling, you won't have to do a thing. This is *my* responsibility.'

Oswaldo Yañez had watched Holly's speech sitting beside his wife on the sofa in their living room. He had paid careful attention to every word, then dismissed her speech from his mind. He got up from the sofa, went to the office he had created out of an alcove in their bedroom, and spent the remainder of the evening studying the latest medical bulletins from Earth and Selene.

The research reports from Earth concentrated on public health efforts to contain epidemics of diseases long thought eradicated. But ebola, tuberculosis and even plague were on the rise, in new strains that resisted antibiotics. Even in the major cities, with their sanitized buildings and public water and sewage systems, such diseases were stalking through the streets. In the poorer parts of the world the epidemics were almost out of control.

Yañez wondered about his native Buenos Aires. How were the people there being affected? He felt an unaccustomed sense of mean pleasure at the thought of the people who had exiled him from Earth being cut down by the very diseases he had worked to curtail. Vengeance is the Lord's, Yañez reminded himself. Yet he took a cold satisfaction from the thought.

Of course there were no reports on research dealing with AIDS or other sexually transmitted diseases. The self-righteous prigs who had exiled him refused to allow such research; they considered the agony and death from such diseases to be a punishment for sin.

The bulletins from Selene were very different. Research in the lunar laboratories concentrated on life extension work, rejuvenation therapies, nanotechnology, areas that were forbidden on Earth.

Blinking tiredly, Yañez looked up from his screen and saw

that it was past midnight. Strange that Estela had not come to bed. Rubbing his eyes, he walked back into the living room.

Estela was watching Holly Lane's speech again.

'Are they rerunning it?' he asked, heading for the kitchen and the leftover empanadas that Estela had stored in the breadbox.

'No, I recorded her speech,' Estela replied calmly. She was a slim, spare woman, without a gram of fat on her. He often thought of her as a dear little sparrow. But Yañez knew his little sparrow had the inner strength of an eagle.

He stopped before reaching the breadbox. 'You recorded it?'

'I think what she is saying is important.'

Yañez chuckled uncertainly. 'You're too old to have another baby.'

She smiled thinly at him. 'Women my age have given birth. You know that.'

'After being implanted with ova from a donor.'

'So?'

'Estela, *I'm* too old to put up with a baby!'

She laughed out loud. 'Don't worry, *querido*. I'm not going to go through all that again.'

'Good,' he said, not recognizing the bitterness in her laughter. He went to the breadbox, thinking that Estela voted for Eberly last election and she'll probably do the same again this time.

He hoped.

Titan Alpha

Machines do not feel monotony or boredom. *Titan Alpha* trundled across the rolling, spongy ground collecting data and storing it in its main memory core. The core was nearing its saturation point, though, and *Alpha*'s master program recognized that a decision would soon have to be made.

Reviewing the data accumulated so far, the master program decided that Titan's indigenous life forms were eighty-three per cent unicellular, the remainder protocellular forms that reproduced at random, rather than follow a present reproduction code that was patterned into their genetic materials. Indeed, the protocellular organisms had no genetic materials, in the sense that terrestrial cells did. No genetic code, either. They consisted entirely of protein analogs and reproduced by random fission. Offspring bore statistically insignificant resemblance to their parent organisms.

The biology program flashed a continuous urgent request to uplink this information. It was completely different from any observations that were stored in its files, and therefore the bio program's imperatives required that these data be uplinked without delay. But the master program's primary restriction prohibited any uplinks. The biology program searched its limited repertoire of responses and found no way to override the primary restriction.

So *Alpha* labored onward, climbing crumbly prominences of crackling ice, delving into slush-coated craters that were shallow enough to be negotiated. It skirted the shore of the methane sea that was named Dragon's Head in its terrain atlas, although it fired the laser into the thinly crusted waves that surged sluggishly across the sea, to verify that its chemical constituents matched those of the Lazy H Sea, where it had originally landed.

Ethane rain fell, and streams of the ethane-laced water flowed down into the nearby sea. Black snows of tholins blanketed the region briefly, then marched away on the turbid wind that slowly pushed the smoggy clouds high above.

Still *Alpha* lumbered onward, propelled by its master program's twin priorities: survival and data collection.

The fact that the core memory was nearing its saturation point impinged on the master program like a glaring light flashing painfully into a man's eyes. The master program reviewed its options. Hibernation mode would suspend data collection, and was to be used only as a last resort. Dumping existing data was a possibility, but that option conflicted with the higher priority of data collection. The master program ran through its logic tree three times, then searched all its systems for additional memory space. There was some in the biology and geophysics programs, also in the maintenance program. Reviewing all the other possible options, *Alpha* concluded that since neither its downlink nor uplink communications program were being used, it could collapse both programs and use the freed space to store additional data.

The master program went through its permissible options once again, and after fifteen nanoseconds of comparing priorities and restrictions, it constructed a decision hierarchy.

Once the core memory's saturation point was reached, the master program would:

1. Store data in available space in the biology, geophysics and maintenance programs;
2. Minimize the downlink communications program and use the available space to store additional sensor data;
3. Minimize the uplink communications program and use the available space to store additional sensor data.

Satisfied with this decision, *Alpha* moved ahead. Until it climbed a ridge of ice and its forward sensors detected a field of thick, dark, carbon-based material covering the ground as far as the sensors could observe. Not the muddy methane that slushed over the ice and was washed away by the rains. This carbon-based mat was hard and thick, as if protected by a sturdy dark shell that stretched beyond the horizon.

Alpha stopped dead in its tracks while both its biology and geophysics programs went into the machine equivalent of hyperventilation.

20 March 2096:
Simulations Laboratory

Pancho had to squeeze her eyes down to a squint as she approached the B ring. This was their first full-mission simulation and all the details were in place to test her.

'Lotta glare here,' she said into the helmet microphone. 'Either the sim's too bright or we oughtta add another layer of tint to the visor.'

'I'll check it out,' Gaeta's voice replied.

It was like dropping into a blizzard. The simulator couldn't reproduce the gut-hollowing sensation of falling, but as Pancho watched the swirling ice particles of the B ring approaching her, she felt pretty damned close it.

'Suit's gettin' pinged,' she reported. The simulation was reproducing the impacts that Gaeta had experienced when he'd dived through the ring. Minor hits, but Pancho knew there were chunks of ice-covered rock in the B ring big as cannon balls, and they were moving as fast as cannon shot, too.

She glanced at her thruster controls. With her hands inside the suit's gloves, she could control the thrusters with the motions of her fingers. But 'control' was a relative term, Pancho knew. Try avoiding a bowling ball that's comin' at you at supersonic speed, she told herself. Good luck, girl.

'Okay,' Wunderly's voice sounded inside her helmet, 'open the sampling boxes.'

A trio of sampling boxes had been attached to the chest of the excursion suit. Pancho had laughed when she'd first seen them. 'Suit looks real female now,' she'd said, pointing.

'First time I've seen square ones,' Wanamaker had cracked.

'Or three of 'em,' Tavalera had added, in a rare burst of humor.

Pancho was strictly business now, though. 'Opening sampling boxes.'

'Confirm,' Gaeta said, 'samplers open.'

By the time they had finished the simulation Pancho felt tired yet high with adrenaline. As she climbed out of the suit and down to the floor of the sim lab, Wanamaker said, 'Good morning's work, Panch. You've earned a fine lunch.'

'Okay, but lemme shower first. Gets sweaty in there.'

Wunderly asked, 'How soon do you think you'll be ready to make the real flight?'

Pancho shrugged, but before she could answer Wanamaker said, 'We need several more weeks of simulator runs, at least, Nadia. There's no sense rushing this. Pancho's got to be able to do this mission blindfolded, by reflex.'

Wunderly nodded glumly and walked away. Pancho knew what she was thinking: the election's only ten weeks away. Will we be able to run the mission before then?

Leaving Tavalera to shut down the control consoles, Gaeta walked over to the trio standing by the massive suit. 'Your turn this afternoon, Jake.'

Wanamaker nodded. He was due to practice flying the transfer craft that would carry Pancho to the B ring and then pick her up on the other side.

Looking almost guilty, Pancho said, 'I can't make it this afternoon, guys. Gotta be at Holly's rally.'

Gaeta frowned, but Wanamaker said, 'We can run the transfer sim without her, can't we, Manny?'

'It'd be better with Pancho in the suit,' Gaeta said.

'No can do, fellas,' said Pancho. 'Promised my sister I'd be at the rally.'

'What rally?' Wunderly asked.

'Come with me, Nadia,' Pancho replied. 'You oughtta be there, too.'

'But—'

'No buts,' Pancho insisted. 'The guys can run the transfer sim without us. Can't you, Manny?'

Clearly unhappy about it, Gaeta nodded minimally. 'I can run the suit, Jake.'

Pancho turned to Wanamaker. 'Well?'

'Hearkening and obedience,' Wanamaker said, with a mock bow.

Tavalera asked, 'What's this rally all about?'

'Women's stuff, Raoul,' Pancho replied. 'But men are welcome to attend, too.'

'I need you here, Raoul,' Gaeta said firmly.

'Yeah, I know. I was just curious.' But he was thinking, I haven't seen Holly alone for weeks. Guess I wouldn't at her rally, either, whatever it's about.

Holly stood alone on the stage of Athens' indoor theater and watched the rows filling up, almost entirely with women. Pancho sat in the front row, grinning up at her. And she even had Nadia Wunderly sitting beside her. She saw Professor Wilmot and a couple of other men, including that Ramanujan guy that worked for Eberly. A flaming spy for Malcolm, she told herself. It almost amused her to see Wilmot and Ramanujan sitting together, as if for protection, amidst a growing sea of women.

Berkowitz was in back, a remote controller in one hand to direct the cameras he had stationed in the far corners of the theater. Otherwise the theater was occupied by women. Dozens of conversations hummed through the place, but so far they didn't sound impatient. Quite the opposite, Holly thought. The women seemed positive, even buoyant.

More were still coming into the theater at two o'clock, the time set for the rally to start. Holly fidgeted nervously on the stage, torn between a compulsion to start promptly and a desire to get as large an audience as possible. The theater sat four hundred, she knew, and the seats were more than half filled. Malcolm's first rally didn't draw this many, back in his first election campaign, she told herself.

She killed a minute or so adjusting the microphone pinned to the lapel of her tunic.

At last, three minutes past the hour, Holly cleared her throat and said, 'I want to thank you for coming here this afternoon.'

All the buzzing conversations stopped. All eyes turned to Holly. She noted a few women were still trickling into the theater and hurrying to seats toward the rear.

'I know a lot of you have had to take time off from your normal jobs or other occupations to come here. I want to apologize for having this rally at such a weird hour. Thing is, the administration claimed that all the theaters and other public spaces are completely booked for every evening between now and election day. And you know who runs the administration!'

'Malcolm Eberly!' someone shouted.

A chorus of hisses rose from the audience. It startled Holly; it sounded like an angry warning from a den of snakes.

'Reason Eberly stuck us with this mid-afternoon time is that he figured nobody'd show up.'

'But he was wrong!' a woman yelled. Laughter and cheers rose from the audience.

Holding up her hands for silence, Holly went on, 'Reason I accepted this dimdumb time was that we've got an important job to do, and we can't waste any time getting it done.'

'What is it?' Pancho asked, at the top of her voice.

Suppressing a grin at her sister's stooging, Holly said, 'We want the Zero Population Growth Protocol repealed, or at least re-examined.'

'Repealed!' several women shouted.

'Well, okay, but Eberly's going to say that the ZPG protocol can't be repealed or even altered unless there's a formal petition signed by sixty-seven per cent of the habitat's population.'

'No!'

'Boo!'

'That's a crock!'

Again gesturing for silence, Holly said, 'I'm afraid it's true. I've looked it up. Our constitution states that any clause or protocol that's in force now can only be changed or repealed outright if two-thirds of the habitat's citizens sign a petition to that effect.'

A babble of voice rose from the audience. They sounded angry to Holly.

'Now wait,' she urged. 'Wait up! Women make up forty-seven percent of the habitat's population. If we get all the women to sign the petition, we only need two thousand men to sign up.'

That silenced them. Holly could practically hear them thinking, Two thousand men. How are we going to get two thousand men to agree with us?

Fishing her handheld from her tunic pocket, Holly flashed the petition she had drafted on the rear wall of the stage.

'I've written up the petition, all nice and legal,' she said. 'Now what we've got to do is get sixty-seven hundred signatures in less than six weeks. Petitions have to be officially registered and counted by May first, one month before the election. That gives us only forty-one days to get the job done. We've got to get busy!'

They jumped to their feet and cheered. All but Wilmot and Ramanujan, sitting there in stony silence. Holly felt thrilled at their response until she realized that there were hardly more than two hundred here. We need sixty-seven hundred signatures. Even if we get every woman in that habitat to sign the petition, which we won't, we'll still need two thousand men.

20 March 2096: Evening

'Where were you this afternoon?' Yañez asked his wife over their dinner table. 'I called from the hospital and you weren't home.'

Estela replied, 'I went to a political rally.'

His brows rose. 'A political rally? You?'

'Why not?'

'I didn't know that Eberly held a rally this afternoon.'

'It wasn't for Eberly,' Estela replied.

Yañez put his soup spoon down on his placement. 'Whose rally was it, then?'

'Holly Lane's,' she replied calmly. 'It was about this ZPG business.'

Frowning, he picked up his spoon and lifted some soup to his lips.

'She's written a petition against the ZPG protocol. I signed it.'

'Estela, no!'

'So did plenty of other women.'

'Sheer nonsense,' he muttered into his soup.

If she heard him, she gave no sign. They finished their light dinner cheerily enough, then Yañez went to the living room to watch the news while Estela cleared the table and put the dirty dishes in the washer. She heard Holly Lane's voice and looked up: Oswaldo was watching the evening news. But he quickly turned it off and moved to an entertainment channel.

Once the kitchen was tidied, Estela went to her desk, next to the pantry, and took a copy of the ZPG petition from its top drawer. She walked into the living room and deposited the petition in her husband's lap.

He looked up at her. 'What's this?'

'The petition.'

He scanned it, then handed it back to her. 'Very competently drafted.'

'Sign it,' she said.

'What?'

'Sign it. We need six thousand and seven hundred signatures. Sign it, please.'

'Estela!'

She dropped the petition back on his lap.

'No!' he said.

Estela did not argue. She said nothing; she simply left the flimsy sheet on her husband's lap and sat beside him to spend the rest of the evening watching entertainment vids beamed from Earth and Selene.

They retired to bed. Once the lights were out, Yañez laid a hand on his wife's bare thigh and began stroking her skin.

'No,' she said.

'No?'

'Sign the petition.'

'Estela! I'm shocked! This is . . . it's not right!'

'Sign the petition.'

'I have my rights as your husband!'

'Once you sign the petition we can discuss your rights as my husband. Not until then.'

He glared at her in the darkness. She turned her back to him. Furious, he turned his back to her. They both fell asleep that way.

Urbain spent the evening shuttling between his office and the mission control center. While his engineers and technicians were trying to trace out the ghostly trail of the tracks *Alpha* had left on Titan's frozen ground, Urbain had presided at a meeting of the eight biologists on his staff. They had crowded into his office, bubbling with excitement at their observations of *Alpha*'s ghost tracks.

'I've set up a time-line,' said Negroponte. She clearly had assumed leadership of the group.

'The tracks are smoothed down in a matter of hours.'

'How many hours?'

'Hard to say, exactly,' she replied, pushing back that stubborn lock of hair that swept across her face. 'It's between four and ten hours, that's the best we can come up with, so far.'

'It's *got* to be biological,' one of the other biologists said. 'It can't be anything else.'

'May I point out,' Urbain said, trying to regain control of the meeting, 'that we do not know enough about erosion mechanisms on Titan to make such a definite statement.'

'Yeah, maybe,' the biologist replied, 'but what else could it be?' He was young, earnest, agog with the idea that they were actually watching a biological process at work on the surface of Titan.

'I agree,' said Negroponte. 'I can't imagine any weathering process acting so fast.'

'We do not know enough to say that,' Urbain repeated firmly. 'We should call in the geologists to look at this.'

They all stared at him, sitting behind his desk like the lord of a castle, while they huddled on the other side like a knot of beseeching peasants.

'However,' Urbain added, 'I see no reason why we cannot proceed on the hypothesis that we are witnessing a biological process. Until further data is produced.'

There, he thought. That ought to keep them satisfied. He got up from his desk chair and headed for the mission control center, to see if they had made any progress. The biologists continued discussing their data, throwing off ideas and theories like a St. Jean Baptiste fireworks display, while Negroponte sat back and encouraged them.

★   ★   ★

Holly was dead tired, emotionally drained from her afternoon speech, but still she spent the evening in a long and repetitious panel discussion with six other residents – including Professor Wilmot – in front of Berkowitz's cameras in the communications center's studio. The panel wrangled over the ZPG issue, and Holly's announcement that she had started a petition drive to repeal the zero-growth protocol.

It seemed to Holly that they covered the subject pretty thoroughly in the first half hour, but the panel members droned on, rehashing the issue endlessly. They're talking just to hear the sound of their own voices, Holly thought. All of them except Wilmot; he was the panel moderator, and he kept his opinions to himself, except for an occasional wry smile or a subtle lifting of his gray brows.

Citizens phoned in their questions and comments, as well.

'You don't expect men to sign this petition, do you?' a woman asked. 'They don't want children. All they want is sex, without the responsibilities.'

A man remarked, 'You take away the ZPG law and this place'll look like Calcutta before the biowar inside of a few years!'

'We came out here to get away from those religious nuts and their holier-than-thou regulations. Why do we need this ZPG protocol? Aren't we responsible enough to regulate our own affairs?'

'Birth control is a personal matter. The government shouldn't be poking its nose into our bedrooms.'

'We live in a limited environment, for god's sake! How're we going to feed double, triple, five times our current population?'

Wilmot allowed each of the panelists to speak to each caller. Holly found herself making shorter and shorter responses.

'We have the intelligence and the understanding to allow *responsible* population growth,' she repeated several times. 'Not unlimited growth. But not zero growth, either.'

Wilmot finally spoke up. 'Yes, but who will make the decisions about growth? Will you appoint a board that will decide who will be allowed to have a child and who will not?'

Holly stared at him, her mind churning. At last she heard herself reply, 'I honestly don't have an answer for that. Not yet. I'm hoping we can bring together a group of people who can offer suggestions about that. Then the general population can vote on how they want to proceed.'

That brought an avalanche of phone calls, and the panel all chimed in with their opinions, as well. After what seemed like hours, Wilmot waved them all down and said, 'I'm afraid that our time is up. I want to thank all the panelists for their participation, and all you callers for your thought-provoking questions.'

Before any of the panelists could rise from their seats, the professor added, 'This subject should be debated thoroughly by the two contestants for the office of chief administrator. I intend to arrange such a debate in the very near future.'

The red eyes of the cameras died, and Holly let out a weary sigh.

'Very good show,' Wilmot said jovially as he got to his feet and stretched his arms over his head. 'Capital!'

Holly slumped back in her chair. 'I'm glad it's over.'

The other panelists seemed to feel the same way as they shuffled tiredly toward the studio's main doors.

Berkowitz was all smiles. 'Terrific audience response,' he said to Holly. 'All those calls mean that more than half the population was watching. Terrific!'

Holly was too tired to care. She pulled herself to her feet as Berkowitz and Wilmot walked away, deep in amiable conversation. A shower and a good night's sleep, Holly told herself. That's what I need.

She was surprised to see Raoul Tavalera standing in the open doorway of the studio. He looked uncertain, hesitant.

'Raoul!' Holly blurted. 'What're you doing here? How long—'

Almost shyly, Tavalera said, 'I started to watch you on the vid, then I figured you might like to have a drink or something after you were through, so I came down here.'

'You've been waiting outside all this time?'

He looked down at his shoes momentarily. 'I slipped in and watched from the back of the studio. I guess you didn't see me.'

'No, I didn't.'

'You want a drink? Something to eat?'

She reached for his arm, suddenly no longer weary. 'I'm starving!'

Grinning at her, Tavalera started down the corridor. 'Cafeteria's closed by now, but the Bistro's still open.'

'Cosmic!'

'Oh, by the way,' Tavalera said, his face turning serious, 'I want to sign that petition of yours.'

'You do?'

He nodded. 'I might want kids someday.'

Holly felt as if she could walk on thin air.

20 March 2096: Midnight

Urbain had lost track of how many times he'd walked between his own office and the mission control center that night. The biologists had settled themselves around the little oval conference table in his office, still throwing out theories about what smoothed *Alpha*'s tracks and what observations they needed to decide which theory was correct. If any. The engineers in the control center were doggedly tracing those ghost tracks and looking for fresh ones.

As Urbain returned to the dimly-lit control center still once again, half a dozen of the engineers were gathered around the coffee urn, arguing intently:

'We've covered the whole damned surface and no trace of her. The frigging junk heap must've sunk into one of the seas.'

'Or maybe that smaller lake. Tracks went right up to it.'

'And out again.'

'How can you tell if some of the tracks were outbound from the lake?'

'Too many tracks to be all one way. Besides—'

'Besides bullshit! We've got five-meter resolution imagery. And stereoscopics. We've covered the whole fucking surface of Titan. Nothing! Nothing but tracks and ghosts of tracks.'

Urbain realized for the first time that his team of engineers were feeling just as frustrated and angry as he himself. They're close to cracking, he told himself. I must do something to lift their spirits. But what?

One of the women said, 'It's a big world down there. Even

with three-dimensional imagery we could miss the beast. We need to keep hunting.'

' 'Til we trip over our long, gray beards, huh?'

'What else can we do?'

'Go back home. Admit the damned thing's lost and go back to Earth. We're not exiles, we're volunteers. We can go back whenever we want to.'

'Whenever there's a ship to take us back.'

'You mean whenever somebody's willing to foot the bill to carry us back.'

'The ICU has to take us back! We didn't sign on for a permanent appointment all the way the hell out here!'

Urbain cleared his throat noisily and they all looked up.

'Any progress?' he asked pointedly.

No one bothered to answer him. They drifted back to their consoles, sullenly, Urbain thought. Like unhappy schoolchildren who would rather be somewhere else, anywhere except here.

'I know this is frustrating,' he said, loudly enough for everyone in the control center to hear him. Before anyone could reply he added, 'But the search for *Alpha* must continue. Already the biologists have made an important discovery.'

'Already,' someone muttered acidly.

'*Alpha* is down there, and she needs our help. We must—'

One of the men at the consoles sang out, 'Got something here! Looks like fresh tracks.'

Urbain rushed to his console and peered over the engineer's shoulder at his central display screen. Across the spongy landscape he could see the sharp, deep imprint of a double row of cleat tracks.

'Follow them!' he shouted. 'Follow them!'

The landscape shifted. The tracks continued, clear and straight. Suddenly the display went blank.

'What happened? Urbain demanded.

Without looking up from his screens the engineer replied,

263

'Reached the limit of that satellite's range of vision. Switching to another . . .'

'Quickly!' Urbain hissed, breathless. '*Vite, vite!*'

Other engineers were gathering around behind him. Urbain felt their body heat, smelled the scents of their colognes and aftershaves and perspiration. But he kept his eyes riveted to the blank display screen.

It lit up and Urbain could hear a gush of excitement behind him. The view was much wider than it had been a moment ago.

'Tightening the focus,' the engineer murmured. 'This is all real-time, you realize.'

'Yes, yes,' Urbain snapped impatiently. 'Focus on the tracks.'

'That's what I'm doing,' the engineer replied testily.

'Use the autofocus,' a voice behind Urbain suggested.

'What the hell d'you think I'm doing?' the engineer growled.

The double row of tracks took form on the screen. Urbain heard the others sigh.

'Follow them!' he urged.

The landscape shifted, the tracks blurred and then came into sharp focus again. Urbain could feel his heart thundering against his ribs. His mouth was dry.

'And there she is,' the engineer said.

Urbain stared. *Titan Alpha* sat on the ice, unmoving but apparently intact. Then the view on the screen blurred.

Urbain realized that he had tears in his eyes.

When Ramanujan had reported to Eberly about Holly's afternoon rally, Eberly's first reaction was, 'A petition drive? Do you know how many signatures she will need?'

'Sixty-seven hundred, she said,' Ramanujan had replied.

'Six thousand, six hundred and sixty-seven, actually,' Eberly said.

Ramanujan dipped his chin in acknowledgement of his boss's

superior knowledge. He was taller than most of the Hindus that Eberly had known, but painfully thin; Ramanujan's face looked like a skull with emaciated dark skin stretched tightly across it.

'She'll never get that many signatures,' Eberly had said, dismissing the problem – and his assistant – with a wave of his hand.

But as the afternoon wore into evening Eberly found himself worrying more and more about it. He ate dinner alone in his apartment, brooding over the possibilities. After dinner he watched Holly's panel discussion on the news channel.

She can't possibly get sixty-seven hundred signatures, Eberly told himself. Even if she got every woman in the habitat to sign the stupid petition she'd still need two thousand men to sign it, too.

Impossible.

And yet . . .

Eberly sank back in his favorite recliner and thought about the problem for long hours. Well past midnight he was still wide awake, pondering the possibilities.

I need a woman to rise up in opposition to her, he realized. I need a woman who'll not only refuse to sign the silly petition, but who'll campaign actively against it. She doesn't have to actively support my candidacy. In fact, it'd be better if she didn't; she shouldn't have any visible ties to me. She should just oppose the petition because the idea behind it is wrong.

A woman who'd oppose breaking the ZPG protocol. Who? Who would stand up against most of the other women in the habitat?

The answer came to him with the clarity of a church bell on a calm summer evening: Jeanmarie Urbain. Her and her clumsy attempt to seduce me into releasing those satellites for her husband. If she believed that allowing population growth would endanger the scientific work her husband's doing, she'd oppose Holly's petition. She'd not only refuse to sign it, she'd campaign actively against it.

Good, he told himself. I'll have to see her and explain the situation to her. Put it in terms that she'll understand: population growth will eat up the habitat's resources and we'll no longer be able to support the scientific research that her husband's leading. She'll go for that. If she doesn't, I'll remind her of our little tryst a couple of months ago. I'll scare her into working for me, if I have to.

But it won't come to that. She'll do it for her husband.

'Good,' he repeated aloud.

Suddenly a new conception flashed into his mind like a starburst. An entire plan for the campaign, a strategy that could not possibly fail. No matter what Holly does, no matter what she stands for, this will beat her. Like those ancient oriental martial arts, I'll use her own strengths to defeat her. It's perfect! I'll lead her into the trap and when we have one of our big debates I'll spring it on her.

There's no way she can outmaneuver me, Eberly said to himself. I'll sweep her and anyone who's supporting her entirely out of my way!

Perfect.

21 March 2096: Early Morning

None of them had slept. Rumpled, baggy-eyed, sweaty, yet not one of Urbain's scientists or engineers felt tired or irritable in the slightest. They had spent the whole night trying every downlink frequency, every message, every command they could think of, but *Titan Alpha* still sat silent and inert on the edge of the carbonaceous expanse that spread over more than a third of Titan's surface.

'She's a stubborn little beast,' Habib said, scratching at his scruffy little beard.

He had pulled up a wheeled chair next to Urbain; the two of them were staring at the satellite image of *Alpha*. Urbain could feel the press of dozens of others crowding around them, leaning over his shoulders. He remembered that he himself had not showered for god knows how many hours. What of it? he asked himself. First things first.

'She's not responding at all,' Habib whispered, restating the obvious.

But Urbain was too excited to feel annoyed. 'She has made her way halfway around Titan and stopped at the edge of the carbon field. Has she gone into hibernation mode? Or is she making observations before proceeding further?'

'We haven't seen any flashes from the laser,' Habib said.

'Perhaps she is restricting herself to passive observations,' Urbain murmured.

'Or the core memory's reached saturation and she's gone into hibernation,' said Negroponte, from behind Habib's shoulder.

Urbain shook his head. 'She goes into hibernation exactly when she reaches the edge of the carbon field? No, it is too much of a coincidence.'

'Coincidences happen,' Negroponte rebutted.

For the first time since he had seen the image of *Alpha* sitting safe and intact on the surface of Titan, Urbain felt nettled. This woman is too domineering, too self-assured.

Yet Habib said, 'For all the communicating the beast has done with us, she might as well be in hibernation mode.'

Urbain felt irritation rising inside him. He realized that he had reached the end of his endurance. And probably the others have as well, he thought. We've all been here more than twelve hours now, some of us more than twenty.

'We must find some way to communicate with *Alpha*,' he said, trying to alter the direction of their discussion.

'Yes, but how?' Habib asked.

Pushing himself up from the console's chair, Urbain said loudly, 'Enough for now. We all need sleep. I want three volunteers to stand watch over *Alpha* while the rest of us go to our homes and sleep.'

Negroponte immediately said, 'I'll stand watch.'

'Me too,' Habib said.

Strange, Urbain thought. Moslem men are raised to be chauvinists; yet this one follows her like an obedient puppy.

He found that his legs were tingling from sitting for so many hours. Slightly shaky, Urbain made his way to the door of the control center. All but three of his scientists and engineers followed him.

At the door he turned and forced a weak smile. 'While you sleep,' he told them all, 'dream up a way to communicate with *Alpha*.'

Gaeta's eyes popped open shortly before seven a.m. He tried to slip out of bed without awakening Cardenas, but she stretched out a bare arm toward him.

'It's too early to get up,' she murmured drowsily.

He leaned over and kissed her lightly on the lips. 'You go back to sleep. I've got a lot to do in the sim lab.'

'The honeymoon's over,' she sighed, turning slightly so that the sheet slid down to reveal a bare shoulder.

Gaeta stared at her for a moment, then muttered, 'Business before pleasure.'

She pulled the sheet up demurely, then asked, 'So how's it going?' Her cornflower-blue eyes were wide open now.

'Okay.' He swung his legs over the side of the bed.

'Only okay?'

Turning back toward her, Gaeta waggled a hand. 'Pancho's fine. She's a natural. Reflexes like a cat. Jake, though . . . it's been a long time since that *viejo*'s actually flown a spacecraft.'

'He's not cutting it?'

'He can fly the bird out to the ring okay. It's picking up Pancho on the other side that worries me. Not much room for error there. No slack.'

Still lying back on her pillow, Cardenas mused, almost to herself 'Raoul could fly the transfer ship.'

'He doesn't want to.'

'But he could. He's had more recent experience than Jake.'

'He doesn't want to,' Gaeta repeated.

'I could talk to him.'

'Wouldn't do much good.'

'I can be very persuasive,' Cardenas insisted.

'Really?'

She sat up in the bed, and the sheet fell to her waist. Reaching both arms out to him, she said, 'Don't you think so?'

He let her twine her fingers in his thick, curly hair. 'I really ought to get to the lab. Pancho and Jake'll be there at nine and—'

'It's not even eight yet.' Cardenas wound her arms around his neck and pulled her toward him.

Gaeta slid back into bed. 'I guess you can be pretty persuasive when you want to be.'

'Uh-huh.'

'Just don't try this kind of persuasion on Raoul.'

'Would that upset you?'

He grinned fiercely down at her. 'Holly would slit your throat.'

'Oh.'

'Now what's this crap about the honeymoon being over?'

Delicacy and tact, Eberly said to himself as he walked out toward the lake. Use pressure only when you have to. Morning was his favorite time of day. Sunshine streamed through the solar windows, the habitat looked fresh and clean. Hardly anyone else was up and around; the other residents were either at their breakfasts or already at their jobs, leaving the lakeside paths almost exclusively to Eberly and his morning constitutional.

Off to his right he saw the little copse of trees where he had that silly tryst with Jeanmarie Urbain. A romantic spot, he thought, even in broad daylight. I wonder how she felt about our clumsy little rendezvous? Was she nervous? Frightened? Excited? Eberly himself had felt none of those emotions. Women were not important to him. Sex was not important. Sometimes he wondered if the prison doctors had done something to his sex drive back in Austria. He shook his head. Power is what's important, he told himself. Power keeps you safe. Power is what makes people admire you.

Yet, as he strolled down to the lakeside, he felt that Madame Urbain must have at least respected him. She had said she admired him. She really was lonely. I could have had her, Eberly told himself. She was ready for an affair with me.

Still, he was glad that it hadn't happened. Too many complications, too many dangers. No emotional commitments, he told himself. A man in my position has to be above all that. Power is more important than sex, he repeated to himself. I don't need a woman hanging onto me, not when I have the admiration of everyone in the habitat. They *all* love me. They respect and appreciate me, even the dolts who voted against me in the last election. But this time around it'll be different. This time I might even win unanimously. Once I've sprung my little trap on the snippy Ms. Lane, she won't have a leg left to stand on.

Eberly was grinning happily as he sat on the bench where he was to meet Jeanmarie Urbain. She wasn't there yet, of course. He had decided to come a good quarter-hour earlier than the time they had agreed upon for this meeting. Madame Urbain had been surprised that Eberly had called her well past midnight, but she'd been alone in her apartment, as Eberly had guessed she would be. Her husband was spending long nights with the other scientists; everyone in the habitat knew that Urbain even slept in his office, most nights.

And there she was! Walking slowly, almost uncertainly, along the path from the village. She looked fresh and lovely in a sleeveless little flowered frock. She truly is an attractive woman, Eberly realized. I could have her if I wanted to.

He got up from the bench and, once she was close enough, made a slight bow.

'Madame Urbain, how pleasant to see you again,' he said, smiling his best smile.

She seemed nervous. 'You said it was important that we talk together.'

'Yes, it is.' Gesturing to the bench, 'Please sit down.'

She looked around as if afraid she'd been followed.

'There's nothing wrong with the wife of the habitat's chief scientist sitting on a park bench with the chief administrator in broad daylight,' Eberly said, gesturing to the bench again. 'Please make yourself comfortable.'

She perched like a frightened little bird, ready to flutter away at the slightest provocation.

Sitting almost an arm's length from her, Eberly said, 'What I wanted to talk to you about is politics.'

Jeanmarie visibly relaxed.

'And science,' Eberly added.

'Yes?'

'Let me get straight to the point,' he said. 'This petition to overthrow our Zero Growth Protocol is a direct danger to your husband's work.'

'A danger?' Her eyes widened. 'How so?'

Eberly spent the next half hour explaining how unlimited population growth would eat up the habitat's resources, forcing the government to devote more and constantly more of its precious allocations of food, funds and personnel to provide for a relentlessly growing population.

'We won't be able to support the scientific staff,' he predicted. 'We might even have to put them to work in the hospital or the food processing plants.'

'But the ICU would provide funding for the research,' Jeanmarie objected.

'Only up to a point,' said Eberly. 'The ICU only provides a small share of the scientific staff's needs. The citizens of this habitat are expected to shoulder most of the burden.' It was almost true: an exaggeration, but not much of one.

Jeanmarie sat on the bench, head bowed, pondering what Eberly was telling her. At last she said slowly, 'You are saying that if the petition succeeds in overthrowing the ZPG protocol, it will endanger the work my husband and the other scientists are engaged in?'

'Most definitely. It could put an end to all the scientific research being conducted here.'

'But what can we do about it?'

Eberly smiled inwardly at her use of 'we.' I've got her, he told himself. She'll do what I tell her to.

'Someone must take a stand against this petition,' he told her, radiating sincerity. 'Someone must show the women of this habitat that the petition could put an end to our very reason for existence.'

Jeanmarie nodded, but she still looked slightly uncertain.

Eberly grasped her hands and looked straight into her light brown eyes. 'Jeanmarie . . . may I call you Jeanmarie?'

'Yes,' she murmured. 'Of course.'

'Jeanmarie, we face a choice. This habitat can be the center for the most important scientific research being conducted in the entire solar system . . .' He hesitated dramatically. 'Or it can sink into a starving, stinking, overpopulated cesspool, like so many poor nations on Earth have sunk.'

'I see. I understand.'

'The choice is yours. You can be a central figure in saving us from collapse.'

Jeanmarie Urbain got to her feet, every line of her petite figure showing determination. 'Tell me what I must do,' she said to Eberly.

He rose beside her. 'Yes,' he said. 'I will.'

They both felt relieved that neither one of them mentioned their brief tryst two months earlier.

21 March 2096: Mid-Morning

There it is again, Vernon Donkman said to himself. Alone in his cubbyhole office, he glared at the old-fashioned desktop computer screen.

He wore, as usual, a funereal dark tunic and slacks, even though his complexion was now a warm golden tan, thanks to the enzyme treatments he'd taken. But his appearance didn't matter to him at this particular moment. His slightly bulging eyes glowered at the unbalanced figures on the display screen. For the fourth straight month the habitat's central account would not balance. The discrepancy was minuscule, only a few hundred new international dollars, but it irritated Donkman more than if it had been a billion.

It's too small for someone to be embezzling the money, he thought. Besides, there have been no unauthorized accesses of the accounts. He had spent so many long, sleepless nights tracing the accounts that his wife accused him of having an affair. No, he assured her. Her rival was the blasted accounting system that refused to balance as it should.

For a while Donkman thought the problem might be in the computer. He had gone to Eberly and requisitioned the best computer analysts in the habitat. Most of them were on Urbain's scientific staff, and not available to him. Those who did examine the accounting program found nothing wrong with the program or the hardware. Donkman had shifted to other computers and had his beloved little desktop completely overhauled. No use. The accounts still failed to balance.

Maddening. At the end of every month the master account showed this slight, picayune imbalance. Never the same amount; never more than a few hundred new international dollars. Every month Donkman tried to track down the source of the anomaly and, failing to find it, was forced to the humiliation of correcting the master account by hand. Sometimes he had to add money to fix the discrepancy. Sometimes he had to subtract. He tried checking out the sums he had put in or out each month, but they didn't match or add up in any way Donkman could see.

For a while he thought that the random power outages the habitat suffered might be the cause of the computer's misbehavior. But the computer system was backed up by triply-redundant auxiliary batteries and fuel cells. They never flickered, even when the power went out for an hour or more.

The only consistency he could find in the entire matter was that the discrepancy seemed to show up every two weeks, on average. Not the same day of the week and not the same hour of the day, but every two weeks or so the account went out of balance. Not even two weeks exactly, Donkman now knew. Sixteen days. It wasn't exact, but when he averaged out the time that the discrepancies appeared the time hovered around sixteen days. Every sixteen days, give or take a dozen hours or so, the account hiccupped.

To make certain of that, Donkman had spent almost twenty hours straight at his office, staring at the computer screen, sixteen days after the last discrepancy popped up. His wife had brought him lunch and then dinner. She had even stayed with him a while before becoming so bored that she left for their home.

Donkman had stayed, eyes riveted to the numbers flashing across his screen. The life of the habitat was being displayed, he told himself. Every transaction, no matter how small, no matter whether it was between a shopkeeper and a customer or between the habitat's central bank and a bank on Earth or the

Moon, every transaction was flashing before his eyes. At the bottom of the screen a display bar showed the master account's grand total.

Donkman must have dozed momentarily. He twitched awake, blinked, and saw that the master account's total was now out of balance by a hundred and fifty new international dollars.

Donkman wanted to scream.

Jake Wanamaker was already in the simulations lab when Gaeta arrived there. The big ex-admiral was sitting at one of the tables in the back of the room, his shoulders hunched, head bent over the laptop.

'*Buenas dias, amigo*,' Gaeta said amiably. 'You're here early.'

Wanamaker turned toward Gaeta, looking grim. 'I'm not cutting it, am I?'

'You're doin' okay,' Gaeta said, walking past the boxy black bulk of the darkened simulator chamber toward him. 'Another couple of months—'

'We don't have a couple of months,' said Wanamaker. 'We've got to get to the rings before Holly and Eberly have their big debate.'

'I don't see why.'

With a vague wave of his big, beefy hand, Wanamaker said, 'Pancho says that's what Holly wants, and Holly says that's what Wunderly wants.'

Gaeta sat heavily on the chair beside Wanamaker. 'So we're gonna bust our butts because the women want it that way?'

'I'm afraid I'm going to kill Pancho out there,' Wanamaker said, his voice hard and even.

'The pickup is pretty rough, yeah.'

'Then we've got to get a better man to fly the mission.'

'Tavalera?'

'That's right.'

'He doesn't want to do it.'

His face as somber as an executioner's, Wanamaker said, 'Let's have lunch with the lad and pound some sense into him.'

Gaeta nodded, but he thought, Raoul makes plenty of sense. He's scared of flying the mission. He's smart to say no.

Timoshenko was obviously uncomfortable as he sat in front of Eberly's fastidiously clear desk.

'I've told you before,' the engineer said, 'I'm not a boss.'

Eberly rocked slightly in his high-backed chair and tried his most charming smile. 'You're doing a fine job as chief of exterior maintenance.'

Timoshenko scowled at him. 'I don't want to be director of the whole maintenance department. You said yourself it was too big a job for one man.'

'It's too big a job for Aaronson. I'm convinced that you could handle it.'

'I decline the honor.'

Eberly steepled his fingers. For a long moment he said nothing, his mind working furiously. There's got to be a way to bring him around, he thought. There must be something that he wants. At last he said, 'The people of this habitat deserve to have the best possible man heading their maintenance department.'

Timoshenko was unmoved. 'Then find him. Or her. There are hundreds of engineers among us.'

'The computer picked your name from the list of qualified personnel,' Eberly lied.

'Run the list again and leave my name off it.'

'Aaronson has got to go,' Eberly said, feeling his patience waning. This Russian was too obstinate for his own good. 'We can't have blackouts, power outages. It's dangerous.'

'I agree, but I've got my hands full with the exterior maintenance job. That's important too, you know.'

'You can handle both the exterior and interior maintenance responsibilities. I know you can.'

'Look,' said Timoshenko, leaning forward in his chair earnestly. 'I work on the outside. I really work. I go out there with my crew. I get my gloves dirty. If I took over the inside job too, I'd end up sitting at a desk, telling other people what to do. I'd become a bureaucrat, just like the drones you have sitting outside your office. I won't do that.'

'But it's necessary!' Eberly pleaded. 'These random power outages are getting worse. I have to replace Aaronson.'

'Not with me,' Timoshenko said firmly. He sat across the desk from Eberly, his arms folded across his chest, a stubborn scowl darkening his heavy-featured face.

Exasperated, not certain of how to swing the man into accepting his offer, Eberly said mildly, 'Well, will you at least think about it? I'm sure that once you've considered all the—'

The engineer got to his feet. 'I can think about it until Siberia grows palm trees. The answer will still be no.'

And he turned and walked out of the office, leaving Eberly sitting at his desk with his mouth hanging open.

The door closed with a soft click. Eberly said to himself, There's got to be a way to make him do what I want. Every man has a weakness, a chink in his armor. Every man wants something, something that he can't get. What does this obstinate Russian want? What's his secret desire? I'll have to go through his personnel file very thoroughly, search out every detail. I've got to find his weakness.

At half-past noon the cafeteria was noisy and bustling with troops of people lining the service counters, taking tables, finding friends, talking, laughing, clinking silverware and dishes. A medley of aromas wafted through the big room: grilled pseudo-steaks, boiling coffee, the sharp tangy sweetness of pastries fresh from the oven.

Seated between Wanamaker and Gaeta, Raoul Tavalera's

long, somber face wore an expression somewhere between scowling suspicion and sullen anger.

'We need a second man on the flight,' Wanamaker was explaining. 'I'm not a good enough pilot to do the whole job by myself.'

Gaeta added, 'We wouldn't ask if we weren't up against it, *amigo*. Jake can fly the bird out to the rings all right, but he's going to need help recovering Pancho at the end of the mission.'

'Look, guys, I told you before—'

Wanamaker cut him off. 'This is a matter of life and death, Mister.'

Tavalera nodded somberly. 'Yeah. My life and death.'

'Pancho's,' Wanamaker corrected. 'I'm not letting her go out there and risk her neck unless I'm absolutely sure we can bring her back.'

'Alive,' Gaeta chimed in.

'Find somebody else,' Tavalera mumbled, looking down at his lunch tray.

'There isn't time to find somebody else and train him. We've got to go in a few weeks,' Wanamaker said. 'Before the big debate between Eberly and Holly.'

That sparked a flicker of interest in Tavalera's eyes. 'What's the debate got to do with it?' he asked.

Gaeta answered, 'Eberly's gonna make a big deal about mining the rings, selling water ice to the rock rats out in the Belt, Selene and the other Moon cities.'

'So?'

'Wunderly wants to prove there are living organisms in the rings,' said Wanamaker. 'That will put the rings off-limits for mining.'

'And for that you want me to risk my neck?' Tavalera demanded.

'You want Holly to win this election, don't you?'

Tavalera's eyes flickered again, but he slumped back in his chair and muttered, 'What difference does it make?'

279

Wanamaker started to reply but Gaeta put up a silencing hand. 'Hey, Jake, why'n't you go get another cup of coffee? I got something to say to Raoul here, just between the two of us.'

Wanamaker started hard at Gaeta for a moment, then got up and made his way through the busy cafeteria toward the coffee urns.

Hunching closer to Tavalera, Gaeta said, 'Look, kid, Kris told me about you and Holly.' Before Tavalera could reply, he went on, 'For what it's worth, Holly's pretty damn miserable about the fight you two had. You wanna help her win this election? You wanna get back together with her? Fly this mission.'

Glowering, Tavalera said, 'That's all she's interested in. She doesn't give a shit about me. She just wants to use me.'

'Don't be a *cabron*, wise ass. Holly cares a lot for you. She cared before this mission to the rings ever came up, didn't she?'

'Maybe. I guess so.'

'Damn right. And now you two *idiotas* have yourselves all wound around the flagpole and neither one of you has the smarts to get out of it.'

'She thinks I'm a coward,' Tavalera grumbled.

'Then show her you're not.'

'Why don't you go?' Tavalera demanded. 'You're the trained stunt guy. You went out there before.'

Gaeta started to reply, but hesitated. Why don't I go? He repeated to himself. Why am I asking this kid to do something that I ought to be doing? Why am I sitting here trying to get this scared kid to do something that I can do better than anybody else?

Because I'm scared of it, he answered himself. I've risked my butt so many times; maybe this one would be the one where my number comes up. That's why I'm asking this kid to do what I should do myself.

He took a deep breath, then let it out slowly.

'You're right,' Gaeta admitted. 'You're absolutely right.'

Tavalera's jaw dropped open.

Before he could say anything, Wanamaker came back to his chair and placed his newly refilled coffee mug carefully on the table before sitting down. His craggy face looked like a looming thundercloud.

'Jake,' Gaeta said amiably. 'Change of plans. I'm going to the rings. You and Pancho can fly the bird and I'll go get the samples Wunderly needs.'

Tavalera brightened. 'I can do the mission control job.'

'Right,' said Gaeta.

Wanamaker's eyes narrowed. 'You certain you want to do this?' he asked Gaeta.

Feeling excited despite himself, Gaeta replied, 'It's the only way this *chingado* mission is gonna work.'

'Kris isn't going to like it.'

With a half-hearted shrug, Gaeta said, 'Kris will just have to accept it. One last mission. Then I'm finished. For good.'

Wanamaker sat there in silence, thinking, This will be the best thing for Pancho. She can fly the mission. I'll be her backup and help with recovering Manny after he gets the samples.

The ex-admiral's gaze turned to Tavalera, sitting there looking relieved. Besides, Wanamaker told himself, this way I won't have to take the kid out behind the woodshed and beat the crap out of him.

21 March 2096: Evening

Several times over dinner Gaeta tried to tell Kris Cardenas that he had decided to fly the mission himself. As they sat at the tiny foldout table in their kitchen he ate in silence, trying to force the words out of his mouth. Each time he couldn't think of how to get started. Cardenas chattered on about her day at the nanolab.

Did Tavalera tell her? he wondered. I'll break that kid's ass if he blabbed.

But Cardenas talked on as if nothing unusual had happened. Gaeta ate mechanically, his head bowed over his plate.

I can surf across the clouds of Jupiter, he said to himself, but I can't tell this woman that I'm going to do something she doesn't want me to do. Courage comes in funny packages.

At last Cardenas said, 'Let me guess.'

He looked up at her. 'Huh?'

Her expression had become serious. 'You're going out to the rings, aren't you?'

'I was going to tell you,' he said. 'I just didn't know how.'

'I figured.'

'Raoul told you?'

Cardenas shook her head. 'He was more cheerful than usual when he came back from lunch, but no, he didn't say anything about the ring mission.'

'You scoped it out.'

'It didn't take Sherlock Holmes, the way you've moped around all through dinner.'

'There's no other way,' he said.

'Yes there is.' Cardenas's blue eyes snapped at him. 'You can tell Nadia that the whole thing's off. Nobody takes any risks, nobody gets hurt.'

'Except Nadia.'

'She'll live through it.'

'And if there really are things living in the rings?' Gaeta asked her. 'If we start mining the rings we could kill them, wipe them out.'

'Has it occurred to you that if we start mining the rings, Nadia could get her samples then? And if she finds organisms in the ice particles she can raise a stink and the mining will be stopped.'

Gaeta sat in silence for long moments, digesting the idea. Then, 'You think Eberly'll stop the mining operation once he gets it started? You think the people in this bucket will agree to turn off the money spigot because we're harming some microscopic ice creatures?'

'They'll have to,' Cardenas said. 'The IAA will force them to.'

'Not without a fight. And it could get real nasty, Kris. Us against the IAA. The rock rats'll come in on our side. Maybe Selene, too. All of us, fighting against Earth.'

She stared at him. 'You mean really fighting? Like a war? Bloodshed?'

'Like a war. With bloodshed.'

That silenced Cardenas for several moments. Gaeta could see the emotions conflicting across her face.

'Better to get out to the rings now and find out what's what before they start mining,' he said.

Cardenas still sat in silence, her thoughts churning.

'Otherwise there could be real fighting. People could get killed,' Gaeta went on.

At last she looked up at him. 'So you're going to risk your life.'

He smiled at her. 'That's what I do for a living. Remember?'

'You retired.'

'I'm making a comeback.' He tried to make it sound light, almost funny. But Cardenas did not smile back at him.

'You want to go, don't you?'

He hesitated, but then, 'No, I don't. I'm not some macho shithead. This thing scares me. It really does. But I've got to do it. There's nobody else: not Pancho or Jake or Raoul or Wunderly herself. I'm the guy who can do it. The only guy. I love you, *guapa*, but it's come down to this.'

Cardenas said, her voice low, 'I love you too.' She added silently, but right now I wish I didn't.

They made love fiercely that night, as if it were the last time they'd ever be together.

Afterward, lying on his back and staring up into the shadows of their bedroom, Gaeta said to himself, Fool! Goddamn *piojoso* idiot. To risk all this: this woman who loves you, this life she's given you. For what? Why? But he knew the answer: Because nobody else can do it. At least I've got a chance of getting through this alive. I'd be killing Pancho and Jake if I let them try it. This way at least the only one who'll get killed will be me.

Lying beside him, Cardenas was thinking, If Manny dies on this damned mission I'll kill Nadia. I'll tear her apart with my bare hands.

Wanamaker told Pancho, and Pancho of course told her sister. Holly was in her apartment, trying to write a speech, when Pancho phoned. Holly had put in a grueling day that culminated with meeting the committee that Estela Yañez was setting up to get the required number of signatures for the repeal of the ZPG protocol. Mrs. Yañez had proudly shown the women that her husband's signature led all the others.

Feeling slightly annoyed at the phone's interruption of her work, Holly was about to let the automated answering chip take the message when she saw that it was her sister calling.

Pancho's face replaced the words of her unfinished speech on the wall screen.

284

'Got news for you,' Pancho said, grinning like a canary-stuffed cat.

'Hope it's good news,' said Holly, stifling a yawn.

'Manny's gonna go into the rings. I'll fly the bird with Jake as my number two.'

Holly blinked once, twice.

'The guys were gonna strong-arm Tavalera into flying with Jake, but now they don't have to.'

'Oh,' said Holly. 'I didn't realize they wanted to drag Raoul into this.'

'He'll run mission control. From here in the habitat.'

'Oh,' Holly said again, feeling dense, foggy.

Pancho's grin widened. 'If I were you, Sis, I'd give your boyfriend a call, congratulate him. Mission control's an important assignment.'

Holly shook her head. 'He'd see through me.'

'So what?'

'I couldn't, Panch. It'd just make things worse.'

Pancho put on a mock frown. 'Listen, little sister. You come down offa that high horse and call the guy. You want him, don'tcha? Then let him know it!'

'Thanks for the advice, Panch.'

Her sister knew when she was being dismissed. 'Getting advice is easy, kid. Taking advice is smart.'

The screen went dark.

Holly returned to her speech. Jeeps, she said to herself, if I'd known that running for office was this tough I would never have done it. She had asked Zeke Berkowitz to help her with the speech writing, but Berkowitz had declined as graciously as he could manage. 'I'm running the news coverage, Holly,' he explained. 'I've got to be impartial.'

Holly decided to look up the personnel files and see if there were any writers or journalists in the habitat who might help her. The names blurred as she studied them on the smart wall screen. I oughtta go to bed, Holly told herself, before I fall asleep here at my desk. Then the phone chirped again.

Raoul Tavalera, she saw printed on the screen's info bar. Suddenly she wasn't sleepy or groggy at all.

'Raoul!' she exclaimed as his glum face appeared on the screen.

'Hi,' he said. 'What do you want to talk to me about?'

Surprised, Holly replied, 'You called me.'

'Yeah. Your sister said you needed to talk to me about something important.'

Pancho! Holly's first reaction was a flash of anger. But then she saw Raoul looking at her, his dark eyes focused on her. Pancho told him to call me and he did, even at this hour of the night.

Recovering her poise, Holly said evenly, 'I wanted to congratulate you on taking the job as mission controller for the ring mission. It's a very important position.'

Tavalera almost smiled. 'Gaeta's going to go into the rings. Your sister and her boyfriend are going to fly the spacecraft.'

Nodding, Holly said, 'Yes, Pancho told me.'

Neither of them spoke for several heartbeats. Then Tavalera asked, 'Is that what you wanted to talk to me about?'

She started to nod, then caught herself. 'No, Raoul. There's something more.'

'What?'

Gathering her courage, Holly sat up straighter and said to him, 'Raoul, I'm sorry that I made you think I was only interested in you because I wanted you to fly the ring mission. I fell in love with you before the silly mission ever came up.'

There! she thought. I've said it. I've used the 'l' word. She held her breath, waiting for his response.

Tavalera's stony expression melted. His eyes seemed to glow. 'Jesus, Holly, I love you too.'

She felt like dancing across the room. 'Come on over here, Raoul. And bring a bottle of wine.'

'Champagne!' he said, grinning a mile wide.

Oral Diary of
Professor James Coleraine Wilmot

This entire habitat is reverberating with campaign politics. I never expected these apathetic, disaffected rejects from Earthly society to become so excited about a political campaign. It's their latest fad, I suppose, taking the place of tanning injections or whatever their newest craze might be. They are actually organizing petition drives, setting up parades, filling the news broadcasts with speeches and speculations about who will be our next chief administrator.

'There, even I have fallen into the spirit of things. I said "our," didn't I? Let me go back and check. Yes, "our." Fine attitude for an anthropologist who's supposed to be studying these people dispassionately.

'Eberly has everyone excited about the prospects of getting rich from mining Saturn's rings for their water ice. He's already getting bids for water deliveries from the miners' habitat at Ceres, in the Asteroid Belt, and there are rumors that Selene is willing to enter into a long-term contract for supplying water.

'Holly Lane, on the other hand, has most of the women energized over the Zero Population Growth protocol. It looks as if she'll easily get enough signatures to force its repeal. Plenty of men are signing the petition, probably because their women are denying them sex unless they do. It's *Lysistrata* come true. Old Aristophanes would be splitting his sides with laughter.

'There's only one small voice objecting to Eberly's plan for mining the rings, the woman who claims there are organisms living in the ice. She's desperately trying to send a mission to the rings and collect samples to prove her point. Eberly doesn't dare object or try to stop her now that she's gone public with her opposition to him.

'Meanwhile, poor old Urbain is still trying to reactivate his vehicle on Titan's surface. The machine has been sitting there, silent and unmoving, for more than a month.'

29 April 2096: Eberly's Office

'I think I know why you asked for this meeting,' said Eberly, with a trace of smugness in his expression.

Jake Wanamaker and Manuel Gaeta sat on the two leather and chrome chairs before Eberly's desk. Neither man looked cowed or subservient in the slightest. On the contrary, Gaeta seemed determined, Wanamaker downright belligerent.

'We've come to inform you that we're going to use one of the transfer craft,' said Wanamaker.

'For another ride out to the rings,' Eberly said. 'I found out about your little mission. It's for Dr. Wunderly, isn't it?'

'That's right,' Wanamaker replied.

'And why should I help you to conduct a mission that might confirm that there are living creatures in the rings? That wouldn't be in the best interests of this habitat.'

'It wouldn't be in *your* best interest, perhaps,' Wanamaker said evenly.

Smiling at them, Eberly said, 'My only interest is the welfare of this habitat. As chief administrator, I am responsible—'

'Never mind the *mierditas*,' Gaeta muttered. 'We're not gonna vote for you anyway.'

Eberly broke into a bitter laugh. 'So why should I help you?'

'As you said,' replied Wanamaker, 'for the good of the habitat.'

'And how would finding living creatures in the rings benefit this habitat? Except to bring another horde of scientists here? We're going to mining those rings for their water content; we don't want any interference from scientific do-gooders who think every little bug in the solar system is too sacred to touch.' Looking at Gaeta, he added, 'You wanted to go to the surface of Titan and Urbain wouldn't let you, remember? Why should you help the scientists?'

Before Gaeta could reply, Wanamaker leaned his broad-shouldered body toward the desk; Eberly reflexively tipped his chair back away from him.

'Let me draw a picture for you,' Wanamaker said, raising his big-knuckled right fist. Extending his index finger, 'First, let's say we don't go to the rings and you start mining operations. The scientists will examine some of the ring particles your miners bring back. They find organisms in the ice. They call the ICU. The ICU asks the International Astronautical Authority to put a halt to the mining.'

Eberly's chiseled jaw went up a notch, 'Just because those earthbound bureaucrats—'

Wanamaker silenced him by raising his next finger. 'Okay, you tell the IAA to stick it where the sun don't shine. They send a ship full of Peacekeepers to enforce their ban on mining. What do you do then?'

Frowning, stalling for time to think, Eberly temporized, 'They wouldn't send troops. Not right away.'

'Maybe not right away, but sooner or later. The whole scientific community, from Mercury to this habitat, would be raising a howl about killing off the ring creatures.'

'We'd fight them in the Worlds Court.'

'And lose.'

'We'd declare ourselves an independent nation, not subject to the IAA's regulations.'

Nodding, Wanamaker said, 'You could do that. The rock rats over at Ceres would probably support you: they need the water. Maybe even Selene would come in on your side. And what would you have?'

'A war,' Gaeta answered. 'An interplanetary war.'

'Which you couldn't win,' Wanamaker said grimly. 'This eggshell could be blown away before you could blink an eye.'

Eberly's voice went hollow. 'They wouldn't do that.'

'Are you sure? Are you willing to take the risk?'

For a long, long moment the office was absolutely silent except for the whisper of the air hissing quietly through the ventilation ducts.

Wanamaker raised a third finger. 'On the other hand, suppose we go out to the rings and find that Wunderly's wrong, there aren't any bugs living in the ice particles. Then you're home free and clear.'

'But if there really are ice creatures out there . . .' Eberly's voice trailed off.

'If the rings harbor living creatures it's going to come out sooner or later,' Wanamaker insisted. 'You can't keep it a secret forever. Isn't it better to know now, before you start making promises that you can't keep?'

'Before you start a fuckin' war,' Gaeta threw in.

Eberly was thinking as fast as he could. *A war. This habitat could be destroyed, just like the rock rats' habitat at Ceres was wiped out. We could all get killed. I could get killed!*

'We need your approval to use one of the transfer craft,' Wanamaker said. 'The form is in your mail. It needs your signature.'

If they find living creatures in the rings, Eberly was thinking, *I can blame the scientists for not letting us mine the rings. I can blame the ICU and the IAA. The people will see that it's not my fault. They won't blame me. They'll still vote for me.*

'Well?' Wanamaker demanded. 'What's it going to be?'

I'm trapped. No matter what I do I'm trapped.

'What's it gonna be?' Gaeta repeated.

I can show the voters that I've been forced to give up on the ring-mining idea. Or maybe ask them if they want to fight for their rights. Yes! That's it! I'll lead them in a battle for our independence. I'll appeal to the people of Earth not to destroy

291

us, not to kill ten thousand men and women over some microscopic bugs. That could work. It doesn't have to come to a war. And if it does, I can negotiate a peace agreement, become the peacemaker. The man who saved the habitat from destruction.

Wanamaker cleared his throat.

Eberly called out, 'Computer!'

The smart wall to the left of his desk began to glow. Eberly asked for the permission document that Wanamaker had sent. It appeared on the wall. He picked up the stylus on his desk and signed his name on the desktop touchpad. His signature appeared on the document displayed by the wall screen, bold and flowing.

Wanamaker got to his feet, satisfied. 'Thank you, sir. You've done the right thing.'

'Yes,' said Eberly. 'We'll see.'

Gaeta rose too. 'Now all we gotta do is fly out to the *fregado* rings.'

Eberly nodded, thinking to himself, I hope you get yourself killed out there. You and your whole crew, including Pancho Lane.

12 April 2096: Morning

'We're going to miss the big debate,' Tavalera said as he watched Gaeta climb into the hulking excursion suit.

'Not to worry,' Timoshenko called from where he was helping Gaeta worm through the hatch in the back of the suit. 'They'll replay it on the news broadcasts six hundred times, at least.'

They had trundled Gaeta's excursion suit on its dolly, like the sarcophagus of a giant, down to the outer chamber of the airlock at the habitat's endcap, the only airlock big enough to accommodate the ponderous armored suit. Then, with Gaeta himself helping, they'd used the overhead winch to stand the suit up on its thick-soled boots. Gaeta opened the hatch in the suit's back and clambered inside. The transfer craft that would carry him to the rings was docked outside the airlock, with Pancho and Wanamaker going through the prelaunch countdown. Tavalera had brought a quartet of rollup computers to monitor the suit's sensors and run communications and stuck them on the scuffed metal bulkhead, because there were no smart walls in the airlock area. Once Gaeta's head appeared in the helmet visor, Tavalera turned on the intercom.

'Can you hear me, Manny?'

'Loud and clear. You can turn down the volume a smidge.'

Timoshenko checked the suit's hatch to make certain it was sealed, then walked back to the row of rollups with Tavalera.

It took several minutes for the two men to run through the checklist. Finally Tavalera said, 'You're okay to enter the airlock.'

Gaeta turned slowly, like a monster out some old horror flick, while Timoshenko trotted to the airlock's inner hatch and pressed the stud on the wall plate that opened it. The hatch swung smoothly inward and Gaeta clumped carefully over its sill. Once the hatch closed again, with Gaeta inside the airlock, Timoshenko hurried back to the pasted-up computers where Tavalera waited.

'Pumping down the airlock,' Tavalera called out.

They heard Gaeta's voice from the fabric computer that was handling communications, 'Copy pumping down.'

Glancing up from the screens to Timoshenko, Tavalera said, 'I really appreciate your helping us out here.'

Timoshenko shrugged. 'I'm a big boss now, I've got lots of time. Not much for me to do except sit at a desk and listen to excuses.'

And hope for the future, he added silently.

Timoshenko had known, when Eberly summoned him to his office, that the chief administrator was going to twist his arm again. The habitat had suffered an hour-long power outage earlier in the day, the third in the past six weeks. Now it was night, well past the dinner hour, and the desks in the outer office were empty. The overhead lights were off, only a small desktop lamp here and there broke the darkness.

He knocked once on Eberly's door and then opened it. Eberly was at his desk; as usual it was immaculately clear, its surface glistening in the full lighting of the overheads.

'Precisely on time,' Eberly said, smiling brightly, as he gestured Timoshenko to one of the chairs before his desk.

Timoshenko sat without speaking a word.

'I fired Aaronson this afternoon,' Eberly said, without preamble. 'We can't keep having these blackouts. I'm appointing you director of the entire maintenance department.'

'I decline the honor.'

Still smiling, Eberly opened his desk drawer and pulled out

a single sheet of plastic. 'Your wife is quite beautiful,' he said, sliding the sheet across his desk.

Timoshenko did not dare to pick it up. Merely a glance at Katrina's lovely face was enough to make his heart thunder.

'My ex-wife has nothing to do with this,' he said through gritted teeth.

'I've asked the authorities in Moscow about her. She hasn't remarried. She's apparently willing to come out here,' said Eberly. 'It seems she's even anxious to be reunited with you.'

Timoshenko's first reaction was to leap across the desk and throttle the smug bastard. But he fought it down, barely.

'You two can be reunited,' Eberly went on, 'once you've accepted the post of head of the maintenance department. You'll be an important member of this habitat's community and she—'

'I don't want her here! I don't want her exiled from Earth!'

Eberly shook his head like a schoolteacher disappointed with his student's response. 'You're a victim of disorganized thinking, Ilya. You see this habitat as a place of exile, a prison, a gulag.'

'Isn't it?'

'Not in the slightest. This is the most comfortable, even luxurious, habitation you've ever known in your entire life. Admit it: aren't the living conditions better here than they were in Russia? Aren't you more free than you ever were there? Don't you have a better position; aren't you a respected man?'

Timoshenko couldn't reply. He wanted to stuff Eberly's words down his throat, but he knew that what the man was saying was quite true. With the exception that Timoshenko could never leave this man-made world. Never return to Russia. Never see his home. Never see Katrina or hear her voice again. Luxurious or not, this is still a prison, he told himself.

Leaning across his desk and pointing a finger at the engineer, Eberly said, 'You're living much better than your wife is, you know. I've looked into her situation, on your behalf. She's nowhere near the level of comfort and respect that you're living at.'

'Is . . . is she all right?'

'She's living in a one-room apartment and working as an assistant in the central public library in Kaliningrad. That's a suburb of Moscow, I believe.'

'An assistant? But she has a doctorate in communications.'

'She can be here in six months or less,' Eberly tempted. 'If you take the job as head of maintenance.'

Timoshenko started to shake his head, but he heard his own voice saying, 'You promise you can bring her here?'

'On the next ship that's coming from Earth.'

'And . . . and she can leave . . . if she doesn't like it?' If she doesn't want to stay with me, he added silently.

'She'll be coming here voluntarily,' Eberly said smoothly. 'Of course she can leave whenever she wishes.'

Timoshenko felt paralyzed, unable to decide, unable even to think. His guts were churning, but his mind was a blank.

'She wants to come here,' Eberly purred. 'She wants to be with you. I know she does.'

No matter what he knew he should say, Timoshenko blurted out, 'All right! All right! I'll take your damned job. I'll be a big boss, just like you want.' And inside his head he told himself, Katrina is coming here! She's coming here to join me! She *wants* to be with me!

He lumbered up from the chair without saying another word and lurched to the door while Eberly watched, smiling. Only once he was safely out of Eberly's office, in the shadowy darkness of the unoccupied desks, did Timoshenko let his tears of joy flow down his cheeks.

Standing beside Tavalera in the airlock area, Timoshenko tried to keep his mind on the business at hand. He forced the image of Katrina out of his head, concentrated on the data displayed on the flimsy computer screens.

'Should I open the link with Dr. Wunderly?' he asked.

Tavalera nodded absently as he pressed a pressure pad on the communications computer's fabric keyboard. 'Pancho, you ready to take Manny aboard?'

Pancho was standing in the transfer craft's compact little cockpit. Barely big enough for two people, it had no chairs, nothing but display panels with their winking gauges and readouts and a single circular port of glassteel directly in front of her.

'Ready for boarding,' she said into the pin-mike clipped onto the throat of her coveralls. Turning to Wanamaker, she said, 'You're the welcoming committee, Jake.'

Wanamaker threw her a mock salute and ducked through the hatch. It was only three strides to the cargo bay, where Gaeta would ride inside his suit.

'I'm ready to come aboard,' Gaeta's voice said from the speaker set above the airlock hatch.

'Hang five,' Wanamaker replied. 'I've got to make certain we're sealed tight here.'

'Panel's in the green,' Pancho called.

'Right. Just doing a manual check.' It was part of the procedures they had rehearsed in the simulator. Wanamaker checked to see that there were no leaks between the craft's airlock and the habitat's.

'Okay,' he said after a two-minute inspection. 'I'm opening our outer airlock hatch.'

Pumps rumbled and Wanamaker thought he could hear the outer hatch creak open. It's all in my imagination, he told himself. Those bearings don't squeak.

At last the inner hatch swung open and Gaeta thumped awkwardly into the cargo bay. The oversized suit loomed above Wanamaker; he felt as if a monstrous alien robot had stepped in.

'Welcome aboard,' he said, peering up to see Gaeta's face in the suit's visor.

'Is this the bus to Tijuana?' Gaeta wisecracked.

Pancho's voice said, 'Cut the clowning and seal the airlock. We gotta keep on schedule.'

Nadia Wunderly had hoped to get samples from the rings before Eberly's debate against Holly, but delays in refurbishing the transfer rocket and switches in crew assignments from herself to Pancho and finally to Gaeta – who should have taken the responsibility from the beginning, she thought – held up the mission until the very day of the debate.

Eberly had played coy about granting permission to use a transfer craft, but one visit from Wanamaker and Gaeta had put an end to Eberly's foot-dragging. Still, the man had managed to push their launch date to the day of the first debate between himself and Holly.

The debate wouldn't start until eight p.m., Wunderly knew. Manny could be through the rings and on his way home by then. But I won't know what he's got in the sample boxes. The debate will start before I get the samples into my own lab.

Now she sat in her cramped little office, her one smart wall display split between the cameras on Gaeta's excursion suit and a view of Saturn. The giant planet's rings glittered like wide swaths of beckoning diamonds, alluring, endlessly fascinating.

It took an effort of will for Wunderly to drag her attention away from the rings. Nervously, she began rearranging the papers scattered across her littered desk, waiting for the spacecraft to detach from the habitat and start its flight to the rings.

Come on, she urged silently. Get on with it!

12 April 2096: Launch

'Five-second countdown on my mark,' Pancho called out. 'Mark! Four . . .'

She felt the craft shudder as the connectors holding it against the habitat unlocked.

'. . . two . . . one . . .'

The automatic sequencer fired the cold gas jets, just a brief moment of thrust, hardly jarring Pancho as she stood in the cockpit. Her thumb was on the manual firing button, a needless backup.

'We're off!' she sang out.

'Good luck,' Tavalera's voice came through the speaker.

The sense of weight that had been imparted by the habitat's spin dwindled away to nothing. Pancho felt her insides gurgle. Come on, girl, she said to herself as she wiggled her softbooted feet into the floor loops, you've been in zero *g* half your life, just about. Don't get queasy on me now.

Wanamaker stuck his head through the hatch. 'Manny's having his breakfast.'

'Inside the suit?' Pancho asked, over her shoulder. She saw that he was holding onto the hatch's rim with both hands, his feet floating up off the deck.

'Yup. You hungry? I can pull something from the galley.'

Pancho knew that this tiny craft's galley was nothing more than a refrigerated bin stocked with premade sandwiches and fruit juices. Her stomach was still complaining, although moving her head hadn't made her whoozy at all.

'Yeah, let's grab a bite,' she said. 'Nothin' to do here for the next few hours except watch the board.' Besides, she said to herself, I don't want to let zero *g* get the better of me.

Holly was biting her lip as she studied the numbers displayed on the smart wall. Fifty-two hundred and sixteen signatures, she saw. Not enough yet. But we're getting there.

She had hoped to be able to announce that the petition drive had succeeded, at the debate against Eberly this evening. Not going to make it, she knew. But we're getting close. And more than a third of the signatures are from guys.

Her phone chirped. Zeke Berkowitz, the data bar on the screen's bottom told her. 'Answer,' she called.

Berkowitz's normally amiable features looked troubled. 'Holly, we're going to be running a news features right before the debate. I thought you ought to see a preview of it, so you won't be caught by surprise.'

'Okay,' Holly replied absently, still thinking about the petition drive.

'I'm shooting the interview to you now,' said Berkowitz.

'Thanks.'

For nearly half an hour Holly continued working on the petition drive figures, trying to determine if there were pockets of the population that they had not yet signed up. At last, more as a break from the work than anything else, she switched to the message Berkowitz had sent.

She was surprised to see Jeanmarie Urbain on screen. The chief scientist's wife was sitting in the same studio that Berkowitz used regularly to interview Holly and Eberly.

'Madame Urbain,' Berkowitz said, off-camera, 'why have you organized your committee?'

Jeanmarie Urbain looked tense, but she forced a smile and looked straight into the camera. Zeke prob'ly told her to do that, Holly thought.

'It is necessary for the future of this community to stop this ridiculous petition that is being circulated,' she said.

Holly jerked with surprise.

'You mean the petition to repeal the Zero Population Growth protocol?'

'Yes. Exactly. We must not repeal the protocol.'

'And why are you against the petition?' Berkowitz's voice asked calmly.

Looking very earnest, very convinced, Mme. Urbain answered as if reading off a memorized reply, 'This habitat of ours is quite limited in its resources. If we permit unregulated growth our habitat will quickly be filled beyond our capacity to support the increased population. People will starve. Children, babies will starve!'

'Don't you think that's an extreme view?'

'Not at all. Unregulated population growth will turn this beautiful habitat of ours into an overcrowded slum, a teeming cesspool of poverty, disease and crime. We must maintain the Zero Population Growth protocol!. We must!'

'Forever?'

Jeanmarie Urbain hesitated. Holly thought she might be searching her memory for the answer she had been coached to give.

'No, not forever,' she said at last. 'But not until we have achieved some means of bringing more wealth to our community should we think about increasing our population.'

'Some means of increasing our wealth,' Berkowitz repeated.

'Yes. Our habitat was designed to support ten thousand people. Unless our economic situation improves, we have not the resources to support a larger population.'

Silence for a moment. Then Berkowitz asked, 'Madame Urbain, if the ZPG protocol were to be repealed, would *you* want to have a baby?'

Jeanmarie looked surprised by his question, shocked. 'I? Would I want to have a baby?'

'You and Dr. Urbain are childless, aren't you?'

'Yes,' she admitted. Reluctantly, Holly thought.

301

'So, if it became permissible . . . ? I mean, you're still young enough to have a baby, obviously.'

'I . . . might,' she said slowly. Then she quickly added, 'But not until the community can support a larger population.'

The camera pulled back to show Berkowitz sitting facing Mme. Urbain. He turned slightly in his chair and another camera showed him full-face.

'So Mme. Jeanmarie Urbain, wife of the habitat's chief scientist, has formed a committee to oppose repeal of the ZPG protocol. How do *you* feel about this issue? Send in your thoughts. We'll keep a running score, with reports every hour.'

Holly's wall screen suddenly went blank. The interview was finished. She sat there, her mind spinning. Turncoat! Holly thought. Traitor! Then she calmed down a bit and she realized that this had to be Eberly's doing. Just like the snake he is, Holly thought, getting a woman to fight against this women's issue.

'How're you doin' in there?' Pancho asked, letting her feet float free of the floor loops so she could bob up to the level of Gaeta's transparent visor. She could see his rugged face through the reflections of the cargo bay's overhead light strips.

'Checking everything twice,' Gaeta replied, his amplified voice echoing slightly off the bay's bare metal bulkheads.

'Just like Santy Claus.'

'Watch this,' said Gaeta.

Pancho saw the hulking suit's two arms rise from their sides, their servomotors whining. The pincer claws opened and snapped shut.

'Like a crab, huh?' she commented.

'Wanna dance?' Gaeta asked, wrapping both arms around her waist. He began lumbering awkwardly across the floor, his heavy magnetized boots lifting and then thumping down again on the metal deck.

Pancho hung on to his broad shoulders, grinning. 'Hey, don't let Jake see this. He's the jealous type.'

Laughing, Gaeta lowered her gently to the floor and released his double grip on her. Pancho hooked one foot into a floor loop, then made a wobbly curtsey. 'Thanks for the dance.'

'Pilot to the bridge,' Wanamaker's voice came over the intercom. 'Ejection point in one hour.'

'Gotta go,' she said. 'You okay in there? Need anything?'

'I'm fine, Pancho. I'll start the final checkout now.'

'Right. I'll tell Jake; he'll be monitoring you.'

She pushed off for the hatch and swam weightlessly back to the bridge. Her eye caught the control board's master clock as she settled into the floor loops at the pilot's station.

'Just about time for Holly's big shoot-out with Eberly,' she muttered.

Wanamaker didn't reply. He had a headset clamped over his thick steel-gray hair, already working with Gaeta, going through the suit's final checkout.

12 April 2096: The First Debate

Holly was still steaming about Mme. Urbain when she climbed the four steps to the auditorium stage. The place was packed: as far as she could see, every seat was taken. And there was Jeanmarie Urbain in the front row with her husband beside her.

Of course! Holly realized. Malcolm's got her to oppose the petition drive 'cause she's afraid population growth will affect her husband's science work. I've got to get that crock off their screens right away.

Professor Wilmot extended his hand to her as she stepped onto the stage and led her to one of the three chairs set up behind the lectern. Eberly hadn't shown up yet. Just like Malcolm, Holly said to herself, stewing inside. He'll wait until everybody else is here and then make his grand entrance.

She scanned the audience, looking for friendly faces. Jeeps, none of my friends have shown up. Pancho, Jake and Gaeta were on the ring mission, she knew, and Raoul was running their control operation. But Kris Cardenas was nowhere in sight, either. Maybe she's at the control center, worrying about Manny, Holly told herself. She saw Dr. and Mrs. Yañez sitting in the fifth row, the Mishimas behind them, and a lot of the volunteers who'd been working on the petition drive. But nobody who was really close to her.

She sighed inwardly. It's lonely at the top, I guess.

The double doors at the rear of the auditorium swung open and Malcolm Eberly swept in, trailed by an entourage of several dozen people. Eberly smiled grandly as he strode up the central aisle. People got up on their feet and applauded him. Flacks, Holly decided. They all worked in the administration offices.

Eberly sprang youthfully up the steps and went straight to Professor Wilmot. The professor rose from his chair, wearing a look somewhere between polite disdain and unpleasant duty. Eberly grabbed his hand and pumped it several times while the audience buzzed and chattered.

'Hello, Holly,' Eberly said as he bent over her, all smiles.

'Hello, Malcolm. Glad you could make it.'

He laughed. 'A sense of humor is important. It will help you to deal with your defeat.'

Holly smiled back at him. 'We'll see.'

As Eberly sat on Wilmot's other side, the professor got up and went to the lectern. Holly noticed that Eberly's entourage had no place to sit, so they lined the side walls of the auditorium and remained on their feet. Hope this goes on for hours, Holly said to herself. Serve 'em right.

Wilmot quieted the crowd and explained the rules of the debate: each candidate would make an opening statement of five minutes, then a rebuttal of three minutes. After that, the meeting would be thrown open to questions from the audience.

'Each candidate will be given the opportunity to make a final statement of three minutes' duration,' Wilmot concluded. Turning slightly in Eberly's direction, he said, 'The incumbent will speak first.'

Kris Cardenas paced the work room that they were using as the mission control center. It was the same chamber where they had brought the suit out of storage and refurbished it for the flight. The bare-walled room looked too large, empty now that Manny and his suit were gone.

Timoshenko was sitting at the row of flimsy sheet computers that Tavalera had brought from the airlock and pressed onto the work room bulkhead; the Russian's face was set in a dark scowl of concentration. Cardenas could hear the voices of Pancho and Wanamaker through the computers' speakers, but there had been no word from Manny for nearly half an hour.

He was afraid to go, Cardenas said to herself. He didn't want to do this mission. He said he was a fugitive from the law of averages. But he's out there now, risking his neck for Nadia. Cardenas shook her head, No, not just for Nadia. For all of us. His damned macho sense of honor. Come back to me, Manny. Don't get yourself killed out there. Come back to me.

Tavalera was pouring himself a mug of coffee from the urn they had plugged in earlier. He looked serious, too, almost grim. But then Raoul always looks sour, Cardenas told herself. She wanted to ask the men if everything was all right, but she didn't want to interfere with their work, distract them. And she didn't want to seem like a worried, nagging 'little woman.'

'Go for separation in five minutes, on my mark,' Pancho's voice came through, sounding calm, professional. 'Mark. Five minutes to separation.'

'Copy five minutes.' Manny's voice.

'You want some coffee?' Tavalera startled her, Cardenas had been concentrating on the voices from the spacecraft so completely.

'Look, Doc,' Tavalera said gently, 'it's gonna be a long mission. Have a seat, try to relax. He's gonna be fine.'

'I know, Raoul. I know, but I can't help worrying.'

He pushed the coffee mug into her hand. 'At least sit down. You don't want to be on your feet all through this.'

Fighting the fears bubbling inside her, Cardenas went to the folding chair beside Timoshenko and sat down. I shouldn't be drinking coffee, she told herself, sipping the steaming brew gingerly. I'm keyed up enough already.

As if he could read her thoughts, Timoshenko grinned slyly at her. 'What we need is vodka, no?'

Tavalera said, 'When they get back we'll break out some champagne.'

Wanamaker's voice said from the flimsy's tiny speaker, 'Separation complete. All systems in the green.'

'I'm outside.' Gaeta's voice. 'Heading into the B ring.'

He's outside. Cardenas's breath caught in her throat. He's on his own now.

Nadia Wunderly was not a religious person, but she had painted a replica of an old Pennsylvania Dutch hex sign that she had remembered from her childhood, a set of colored circles nested within one another, barely twelve centimeters across. It was perched atop the desktop screen in her cramped office, to keep evil spirits away. It's nonsense, Nadia told herself. But somehow she felt better with it there.

The mission was going smoothly, so far. Manny was outside now and Pancho was maneuvering the transfer craft to the underside of the B ring, through the Cassini gap between the A and B rings, to the spot where she would pick up Manny.

After he's gone through the ring and collected my samples, Wunderly said silently. She suppressed an urge to reach up and touch the hex sign.

As she'd expected, Eberly's opening statement was devoted almost entirely to the idea of mining the rings.

'There is wealth out there,' he told the audience in the rich measured tones he used for swaying crowds. 'The most valuable commodity in the solar system is water, and we have within our grasp many billions of tons of frozen water. It will be the highest priority of my second term of office to begin mining the rings of Saturn and make every single person in the habitat as wealthy as an Earth millionaire.'

They applauded lustily. Holly sat there on the stage and watched the audience roar its approval, clapping and even

307

whistling, more than half of them rising to their feet for a standing ovation.

Wilmot waited several moments, then calmly walked to the lectern and made a shushing motion with both hands. Slowly the crowd stopped and sat down again.

I should've brought a claque with me, Holly thought. She mentally kicked herself for not organizing a band of loyal supporters to give her the kind of ovation that Eberly had arranged for himself.

'And now the challenger,' said Professor Wilmot, turning slightly toward Holly, 'Ms. Holly Lane, formerly head of the human services department.'

A scattering of polite applause rippled through the auditorium. Better'n nothing, Holly thought as she stepped up to the lectern. Her prepared speech appeared on the built-in screen.

'There are other kinds of riches besides money,' she began, looking out over the sea of faces. 'For good and proper reasons, we all agreed to the zero population growth protocol when we started this voyage to Saturn. But that was then, and this is now.'

She saw a few heads nodding here and there. All women's.

'This habitat is our home. Most of us will spend the rest of our lives here, some by choice, many because they wouldn't be allowed to return to Earth.' She took a breath. 'Well, if this is our home, then we should make it as much of a home as we can. I don't mean just the physical environment. I mean that sooner or later we should begin to bring children into our world. Otherwise we're living in a barren, empty shell. We need the warmth, the love, the humanness of raising families.'

'Do we need the aggravation?' someone in the back yelled. A man's voice.

Heads turned to find the heckler. One of Eberly's flacks, Holly knew. Several people laughed.

She put on a smile. 'We need a future,' she replied.

'Children represent the future, and without them this community will just grow older and eventually die out.'

As Holly continued speaking, Eduoard Urbain turned to his wife and whispered, 'This is nonsense. Population growth would destroy this habitat.'

She nodded, knowing that what her husband meant was that population growth would threaten his work.

12 April 2096: Into the Ring

Manny Gaeta squinted against the glare. Even with the suit's heavily-tinted visor Saturn's B ring was so bright it almost made his eyes tear. Glittering brilliant jewels of ice stretched as far as he could see in every direction.

Despite himself, he grinned. Yes, the fear was there, deep inside him. But so was the excitement, the exultation. What was that old line: To boldly go where no one has gone before. That's me. Boldly. Here alone in the suit, heading into the blindingly dazzling rings, Gaeta knew that if he had to die he wanted to die this way, doing what no one else had ever dared to try.

'Closing in,' he muttered into his helmet microphone.

He glanced at the lidar display on the left side of the helmet. It was breaking up into hash. Shouldn't do that, he said to himself, shaking his head.

'Your altimeter reading is breaking up.' Wanamaker's voice sounded slightly edgy, through the helmet's earphones.

'The laser beam is getting scattered too much by the ice particles,' he replied.

'It's gonna be tough for you to judge distances, then,' Pancho said.

'I can eyeball it.'

'Anything hitting you?' Wanamaker asked.

'Not yet. I'm still more than two hundred klicks from the main body of the belt.'

'Movin' fast, though. We got a good fix on your beacon; you're doin' twelve hundred an hour.'

'I'd better slow down.'

'Retro burn programmed for six minutes from now,' said Wanamaker. 'Do you want to override it and go manual?'

Staring out at the overwhelming field of gleaming white, Gaeta said, 'No, let the program ride.'

'Tell me when you start getting pinged,' said Pancho.

'Right,' Gaeta replied. But he thought, What can they do about it? They'll be pushing over to the other side of the ring in another ten minutes.

Unless something goes wrong, answered a voice in his head. They'll hang here as long as they can, just in case some malfunction pops up. They'll fish you out.

Yeah, Gaeta said to himself. If they can.

A tiny red light winked at him from the rim of the helmet's displays. Impact, Gaeta realized. The display went dark immediately. One little ice flake hit me. A scout?

Holly was surprised at the questions from the audience. Almost all of them were from women, and they all wanted to know how soon the ZPG protocol could be lifted.

'The first step is to get six thousand, six hundred and sixty-seven signatures on our petition,' she answered, more than once. 'We can't do a thing until we have enough signers.'

Eberly's people asked questions, too: mostly about how much money could be brought in from mining Saturn's rings. But Professor Wilmot picked the questioners from a sea of waving hands and he picked mostly women.

Through it all, Eberly was strangely quiet. Not that he didn't speak well or answer questions, but he ignored the population growth question almost entirely. Holly had expected him to paint dreadful word pictures of how the habitat would be overrun with babies and sink into a squalling, poverty-stricken disaster. But he didn't. He spoke positively about how wealthy the habitat could become by mining the rings. To Holly, he seemed to be avoiding the ZPG issue altogether.

Until Professor Wilmot called on Jeanmarie Urbain.

She stood up, impeccably clad in a dark short-sleeved sheath adorned tastefully with hints of jewelry: clearly the best-dressed woman in the auditorium. Holly though she looked a bit nervous, almost timid, while the automatic microphones along the auditorium's side walls focused on her. Her husband, seated beside her, looked more annoyed than pleased that his wife was asking a question.

'Go ahead, Madame Urbain,' said Wilmot gently.

'My question is for Mr. Eberly,' she said, her voice trembling slightly. 'Sir, what will happen to the research programs that the scientists are conducting if our habitat's resources must be devoted more and more to a growing population?'

Eberly came out of his chair his chair as if propelled by a spring, smiling widely. It's a set-up, Holly realized. He coached her to ask that question.

By the time Eberly had crossed the three steps between his chair and the lectern, he had changed his expression. The smile was gone; he looked somber, almost grim.

'As we all understand,' he began, his voice low, controlled, 'the main purpose of this habitat was to carry out scientific studies of the planet Saturn, its rings, and its moons. But if we must divert more and more of our resources to accommodating a constantly growing population, we will have less and less to devote to the science work.'

Holly wanted to object, but Eberly wasn't finished.

'Scientific information is our major export product, as of now,' he went on. 'Essentially, the International Consortium of Universities back on earth pays us to provide data about the Saturn system. It's not enough to keep our entire population going, of course. The major part of our economy is internal: we grow our own food, we provide goods and services for one another, we have built a strong internal economy for ourselves.'

He bowed his head and hesitated a heartbeat. Then, looking

up again, he said, 'But if our population begins to grow unchecked, and we have no other external sources of income, then our economy will be forced to provide food and shelter and education and, eventually, jobs for our growing population. The scientists will have to depend exclusively on whatever funding the ICU provides, which won't be enough to sustain them at their current level of activity. We will have to cut back on our science programs, which means the ICU will cut back on its funding. A vicious circle.'

Dozens of hands went up in the audience. But Eberly still wasn't finished. 'However,' he said, his voice stronger, 'I can see a way out of this dilemma.' He allowed a small smile to creep across his face. 'To allow population growth we need a new source of income. Hanging out there before our very eyes is that source: the rings of Saturn. Once we begin selling water to Selene and Ceres and the other human establishments off-Earth, we will have a source of income that will allow us to end the zero-growth protocol once and for all!'

Eberly's flacks along the side walls immediately began applauding, and quickly most of the rest of the audience joined in. Holly sat on the stage, stunned at the simplicity of his scheme. She watched, crestfallen, as the audience got to its feet, applauding. She wanted to rush to the lectern and tell them that no one would be allowed to mine the rings until it's absolutely certain that there are no organisms living there that might be hurt.

But she knew it would be useless. Eberly had taken her own campaign issue and turned it against her. You want population growth? Mine the rings to pay for it.

Nadia's going to die when she hears about this, Holly said to herself. And Malcolm's going to win re-election by a landslide.

Nadia Wunderly was in her cluttered office, totally engrossed in the view from Gaeta's helmet camera, displayed on her desktop screen. It was like falling from a cliff down into a gleaming glacier of ice. The screen was filled with glittering bits of ice, interwoven strands curled and entwined so intricately that her fastest computer program could not model them in real time. Manny's falling into the ring, she knew; he'll plough right through it like a meteor crashing into the ice particles.

'Retro burn complete.' Gaeta's voice came through the computer's speakers.

'Copy retro complete.' Wanamaker's voice. 'Your velocity vector is on the money.'

At Wunderly's insistence they had slowed Gaeta's approach to the ring. Even though it's by far the densest of Saturn's rings, the B ring is scarcely two kilometers thick, she had argued. If he doesn't slow down he'll zip through the ring too fast to collect any samples. Gaeta had reluctantly agreed. The first time he'd gone to the rings his trajectory had been arranged so he would glide along inside the B ring for more than ten minutes, and that had nearly killed him. Now he was diving through, in and out, but slowly enough to have a good chance to pick up samples of the ice particles and the creatures that lived in them.

If they're really there, Wunderly found herself thinking. If they really exist and they're not just a wish-dream of mine.

'Sample boxes open,' she heard Wanamaker's voice.

'Boxes open, check,' Gaeta confirmed.

'We're reading the temperature inside the boxes as within three degrees of ambient,' said Wanamaker.

'Good,' replied Gaeta. 'Don't wanna toast these babies once we get 'em in the samplers.'

Wunderly recalled that the first time Gaeta had gone through the rings the ice creatures had coated his suit so thickly it had made it impossible for him to move his limbs or even communicate back to the controllers. This time they had put miniature heating coils on his comm antennas. It didn't take much energy to keep the antennas above the ring's ambient temperature of -178 degrees Celsius. But they had to keep the rest of the suit cold, especially the sample boxes.

He was getting close enough now that she could see individual chunks of ice in her display screen. No way to judge sizes, although some of the pieces were obviously much larger than others.

'Getting dinged pretty good now,' Gaeta reported. 'Lots of impacts.'

'Sizes?' Wanamaker asked.

'Nothing big enough to shake me,' said Gaeta, 'but the impact counter is lighting up like a video game display now.'

Don't let him get struck by a big one, Wunderly pleaded silently. She knew there were chunks of ice as big as trailer trucks in the rings. Don't let him get hurt, she prayed to a god she didn't really believe in.

12 April 2096: Encounter

'Here we go,' said Pancho, trying consciously to keep her tongue from between her teeth. She'd lacerated her tongue badly once in the crash landing of a clippership, back in her early astronaut days. For years afterward she'd carried a protective mouthpiece with her when she flew, but seldom remembered to put it in place when she needed it.

Now she stood at the controls of the transfer craft and watched through the port in front of her as she dived the little vehicle through the Cassini gap between the A and B rings.

She could see glittering bits of ice racing toward her, pinging the craft's hull, hitting the port's transparent glassteel.

'Some gap,' she said. 'Lots of crap in here.'

Wanamaker, standing beside her, paid no attention. He was in contact with Gaeta, who was just entering the B ring.

'Starting to ice up,' Gaeta was saying. 'It's getting tough to move my arms and legs.'

Wanamaker glanced at the readouts on the panel at his side. 'Internal temperature holding okay,' he said.

'So far,' answered Gaeta.

Pancho wished she had viewing ports on the sides of the cramped cockpit, or cameras out there, at least. She wanted to see more than just the straight-ahead view. She wanted to see the rings and their ragged edges as she drove the craft through the space between them. She wanted to be able to yell *Yahoo!* as she dived through the plane of the rings. As it was, she couldn't see the rings, couldn't even see the huge glowing curve of Saturn's massive bulk. Nothing but star-flecked darkness out there, and swarms of ice particles zooming at her. It was like driving in the dark of night through a raging blizzard.

Gaeta had two contradictory worries wrestling in the back of his head. Will I be in the ring long enough to get a decent sampling for Nadia? Will I be in the ring so long that these *fregado* ring particles will cover me with ice, they way they did last time? Damned near killed me.

The icy ring was spread out before him now, like a vast field of glittering snow stretching as far as he could see. Off in the distance to his right was a smear of darker stuff, like dust or carbon soot. Coming up fast, in spite of the retro burn. Glancing at the displays splashed in color along the bottom of his visor, he saw that all the suit's functions were still in the green, except that when he tried to move his arms or legs the servomotors went into the red. Encased in ice, he realized.

Then he saw a rime of ice along the edge of his visor. And it was growing visibly.

'Visor's getting coated,' he said into his helmet microphone.

Wanamaker immediately replied, 'Life-support functions still in the green.'

Gaeta nodded inside the helmet. 'So far.'

'Antennas still functioning.'

'Hey, Jake, you trying to cheer me up?'

'Just doing my job, buddy.'

'The suit's external temperature is dropping,' Gaeta reported.

'Copy. It's within allowable limits.'

'So far.'

'You'll only be in the ring for three minutes.'

'Gotta get there first.' He saw that his visor was almost completely covered with ice now.

'Hang tight, buddy. We're on course to pick you up at the rendezvous point.'

'Right.'

'You should be entering the ring's main body now.'

A flash of light startled Gaeta. 'What the hell was that?'

Pancho called out, 'Hey, we got a power surge here. Auxiliary power's on – wait, hang on, main power's back on line.'

'You okay, Manny?' Wanamaker asked.

'Got a flash, like all my displays flared up at once.'

'Now?'

'Looks normal now. Everything in here looks normal. But life support's on battery instead of the main power bus.'

'What the hell happened?' Wanamaker groused.

'I'm entering the ring.'

Squinting through the ice that now covered almost his entire visor, Gaeta saw nothing but glittering, swirling ice particles. It was like being in a blizzard, alone in an over-powering storm of gleaming white. Except that there was no wind, no noise at all.

With a sudden clutch of fear he realized that the air fans inside his suit had gone silent.

Wanamaker saw the red light glare on his display panel.

'Air circulation system,' he muttered.

Pancho glanced over. 'He can live without 'em.'

'For how long?' Wanamaker challenged.

'Long enough,' said Pancho, pecking at her master keypad.

'My air fans are down.' Gaeta's voice sounded calm, but both Pancho and Wanamaker knew this was trouble.

'Try restarting them,' Wanamaker said.

'Did that. No joy.'

'Hang tight,' Pancho called out. 'I'm adjusting our pickup point. We'll fish you out in eight minutes . . .' She looked at the readout on the control panel. 'Make that seven minutes, forty seconds.'

'You'll be getting too close to the ring,' Gaeta objected.

'Shut up and save your air,' said Pancho. 'We'll getcha before you even start to cough.'

'What could make the air fans go out?' Wanamaker asked her.

Pancho shrugged. 'Murphy's Law.'

'Maybe that power surge?'

'How can he have a power surge the same instant that we do?' Pancho demanded. 'Besides, it was all over in a second or two. No damage.'

'No damage to us,' Wanamaker corrected.

When in trouble, check all systems, Gaeta told himself. Life support is on battery back-up, and the *chingado* fans have crapped out. No air circulation means the oxygen level drops and cee-oh-two builds up.

Power failure? Everything else is working okay. He felt beads of perspiration dotting his upper lip. The suit's master computer has a decision tree, Gaeta knew. When electrical power goes critical it starts to shut down systems in order of their importance. I can get along without the fans for ten, maybe twenty minutes. Next thing the computer'll shut down is the exterior sensors. If the power system's failing.

His visor was completely caked with ice now. And, sure enough, the displays from the suit's exterior sensors went dark. *Mierda*, Gaeta grumbled to himself. Now I'm flying blind.

'Don't fire up your propulsion jets,' Pancho's voice warned. 'Your beacon just went out so we hafta track you by dead reckoning.'

'Okay. No jets,' Gaeta confirmed, glad that the comm system was still working. Stay off my antennas, little guys, he said silently to the ring creatures. Gremlins, he thought. Little beasties that screw up your machinery.

The clock display still worked, he saw. The green LCD numerals showed that he should be in the midst of the ring.

319

Two more minutes, at most, and I'll be out. Then Pancho can pick me up. If she can find me.

Holly pushed through the crowd of well-wishers who gathered around her after the debate closed. Mostly women. Almost entirely women, except for Wilmot and a roundish, unhappy-looking man standing beside Mrs. Yañez: her husband, Holly recalled. A much bigger throng was swarming about Eberly, including Dr. Urbain and his wife. Eberly basked in their approval, smiling warmly, shaking hands.

The lights flickered briefly; everyone looked up to the ceiling, but before anyone could say a word the lights steadied again.

Eberly waved a hand. 'We're working on these power flips,' he said in a strong, authoritarian voice. 'I've just replaced the chief of maintenance and put a new man on the job. He'll get to the bottom of the problem.'

The people around him nodded, but several glanced toward the ceiling uneasily.

'Excuse me,' Holly said over and over as she wormed through the crowd. 'I've got to see Dr. Wunderly.'

Breaking free of the pack at last, Holly sprinted up the auditorium's central aisle and raced outside, toward Wunderly's office.

Nadia's got to know how Eberly's skunked us, she told herself. *She must be in her office, monitoring Manny's mission into the rings.*

The office building was dark but unlocked. Holly raced up the stairs to the second floor and saw a glimmer of light down the corridor made by shoulder-high partitions. *Yep,* she said to herself, *that's Nadia's rabbit-hole.*

Wunderly was staring at her desktop screen so intently she jumped halfway out of her chair when Holly came into her cubicle, saying, 'They want to mine the rings, Nadia!'

'Manny's in trouble,' Wunderly said. 'Pancho's got to fish him out of there as soon as she can.'

12 April 2096: Ringside Pickup

'Can you see him on the radar?' Wanamaker asked, standing tensely beside Pancho in the spacecraft's tight little cockpit.

'With all that backscatter from the rings? Only chance we got is getting a Doppler fix on him.'

Wanamaker nodded and pecked at the control board's central display screen. It showed a schematic of Gaeta's trajectory and their own craft's course. The two lines intersected neatly, well below the plane of the rings.

'That's ancient history,' Pancho said, jabbing a finger at the display. 'We've gotta pick him up a lot sooner's that.'

'But that will take us toward the ring,' said Wanamaker.

'Yup. We're in for a helluva ride, Jake.'

Holly stared at Wunderly's screen.

'Pancho's going to pick up Manny closer to the ring? Isn't that dangerous?'

In the light from the display screen, Wunderly's heart-shaped face looked ashen. 'It's worse than that, Holly. The course she's on now will take her right into the ring itself.'

'But she's not supposed to go into the ring!'

'She's doing it. Otherwise she can't pick up Manny soon enough. He'll suffocate inside his suit.'

For the first time, Holly realized that Pancho was risking her own life. She could get killed! Holly said to herself.

'Can we talk to her?'

Wunderly hesitated a moment, then shook her head. 'Don't

distract her, Holly. She's going to have her hands full in a minute or so.'

Wanamaker peered at the radar display. 'There!' He pointed to a smeared-out blip moving against the scintillating background. 'That must be him!'

'Hey, Manny,' Pancho called into the control panel's built-in microphone. 'You outta the ring yet?'

'Can't see a frickin' thing,' Gaeta's voice answered. 'Visor's iced over and external sensors are out. I oughtta be out, according to the timeline.'

Turning to Wanamaker, Pancho commanded, 'Jake, slave the forward camera to the radar and put it on max magnification.'

With a nod, Wanamaker played his fingers across the keyboard. The main display screen showed an expanse of glittering white ring particles.

'There,' Pancho said, pointing to a tiny oblong object moving across the field of view. 'That's gotta be him.'

'Wish we had a better fix on him.'

'I can eyeball it,' Pancho said, pecking at the controls.

A surge of thrust made them sway in their floor loops. The figure in the telescopic camera's view grew larger, took on shape. They could see arms and legs now.

'He must be encrusted with ice,' Wanamaker muttered.

'You better get into a suit and go to cargo bay,' said Pancho.

'Right.'

Wanamaker ducked through the cockpit hatch and pulled one of the nanofabric pressure suits from the narrow closet built into the bulkhead. He wriggled his arms and legs into it, a tendril of apprehension worming through him as he pulled the hood up over his head. Spacesuits should be big, bulky things, Wanamaker remembered. This nanosuit looks like a plastic raincoat. But Pancho had used one, back on the Moon. And anyone who could afford it was switching to the nanofabric suits. Unlike the older pressurized space suits, a nanosuit could be put on in seconds and provided better protection against vacuum than the heavy hard suits Wanamaker was accustomed to.

Still feeling uneasy despite his attempts to reassure himself, Wanamaker floated weightlessly to the cargo hold and sealed the hatch behind him. The bay was a metal shell not much bigger than the back of a midsized van, empty except for the man-tall cryogenic freezer that would hold the sample boxes that Gaeta brought back with him.

Wanamaker knew he could operate the airlock from where he was and stay safely inside the bay. But Manny's going to need all the help he can get. Pancho's good, but she won't be able to match velocity vectors exactly.

So he pulled an air bottle from the bulkhead rack, slipped it over his shoulders and plugged it in to the collar of the nanosuit. Then he rolled the visor over his face and sealed it to the collar; it was like pressing a Velcro seal shut. The hood inflated into a fishbowl shape as air from the bottle filled it.

'You ready to open the airlock?' Pancho's voice came through the hood's built-in speaker.

'Opening airlock,' Wanamaker answered, leaning his nano-gloved palm against the control panel.

Okay, sailor, he said to himself. Time to be a hero.

'What's she doing?' Holly asked, her insides quivering with anxiety.

Wunderly tapped on her touchscreen and the display changed to show a real-time image of Saturn with two hair-thin lines arcing across it.

'The red line is Manny,' she said, pointing. 'He's just coming out of the ring now, if he's still on schedule.'

' "Kay," said Holly.

'This green line is Pancho. She's maneuvering the space-craft to pick up Manny here, where the two lines intersect.'

'That's practically in the ring!'

Wunderly nodded. 'Pancho's velocity is going to push her right back into the ring and out the top side – if she doesn't hit something big enough to damage the ship.'

'What are the chances that she'd get hit?'

'Pretty damned good,' Wunderly said somberly. 'Most of the ring particles are tiny, like snowflakes or pebbles coated with ice. But at the velocity Pancho's going, even a pebble can have the force of an iceberg.'

Standing alone in the cockpit, Pancho could see through the observation port that the ring was rushing toward her. It's gonna be a rough ride, she told herself, snuggling her feet deeper into the plastic loops that anchored her to the deck.

She saw in the telltale lights on the control board that the cargo bay's airlock was open.

'Jake, you outside?'

Wanamaker's voice replied tightly, 'I'm in the airlock. Outer hatch is open to vacuum.'

'You tethered?'

'Two tethers. One for me and one for Manny.'

'Get ready. We're gettin' close.'

'I don't see him.'

'You will.' Pancho kissed the maneuvering thruster control with a fingertip. Easy does it, she told herself. No big moves. No sudden jerks.

Hovering at the lip of the airlock hatch, Wanamaker felt the slight surge of thrust. He had to half-close his eyes against the dazzling glare of Saturn's rings. Close enough to touch, he said to himself. Hell, we'll touch them plenty in another few minutes.

'You see him?' Pancho asked.

'Not ye— wait! There he is!' He saw the figure of Gaeta's massive suit, arms and legs jutting out stiffly. 'He's coated with ice, all right.'

'I can't see a shittin' thing,' Gaeta announced, sounding more annoyed than frightened.

'It's okay, Manny,' Wanamaker called. 'I can see you. I'm coming out to get you.'

'Wait!' Pancho yelled. 'Lemme pull in a smidge closer.'

Gaeta's figure grew slightly, then steadied in Wanamaker's view.

'Okay, that's as good as I can get it,' said Pancho.

Wanamaker judged Gaeta was about fifty meters outside the hatch, moving slowly across his field of view. The tether in his hand was fifty meters long, he knew. No time to get another tether and connect the two. This is going to be close.

He took a deep breath and launched himself out of the airlock, into empty space, forgetting that all that stood between him and dead vacuum was a monolayer of nanomachine fabric.

Gaeta looked like an ancient mummy, gliding past him, moving out of reach. Wanamaker unhooked the tether clipped to his waist and snapped it onto the end of the tether he held in his hands. Gripping the doubled tether as tightly as life itself, he floated out to Gaeta's ice-coated figure and wrapped the free end of the tether around the chest of the suit.

'Don't you have any attachment points on your damned suit?' Wanamaker grumbled.

The doubled tether pulled taut. But held.

'Under the ice,' Gaeta replied, then coughed.

Not daring to let go of the tether, Wanamaker held it firmly in place around Gaeta's chest, under his arms, then locked its end with a click his hands could feel but he couldn't hear because they were in vacuum. For an instant he looked out and saw that they were floating in the middle of emptiness, Saturn's huge saffron bulk and its brilliant rings hanging above them, nothing but the infinite star-filled space below. Wanamaker swallowed hard and felt bile burning in his throat.

'Okay,' he muttered, 'here we go.' He started pulling the two of them back to the spacecraft's airlock, hand over hand along the tether.

'I still can't see a damned thing,' Gaeta mumbled.

'It's okay, Manny. I've got you. We're getting there.' Damned slowly, Wanamaker thought.

'You got him?' Pancho called.

'Got him,' Wanamaker answered, puffing from exertion. 'We're coming back to the airlock.'

'Better make it snappy. We're headin' back into the ring.'

12 April 2096: Pancho's Ride

Holly and Wunderly, sitting side by side in the darkened cubicle, heard the radio interchange between Pancho and Wanamaker.

'She's got Manny!' Holly exclaimed.

Wunderly leaned on the communications key. 'The samples,' she asked. 'Did you get samples from the ring?'

Wanamaker puffed, 'Don't know.'

'I'm so goddamned coated with ice I don't know what went down in the ring,' Gaeta answered, sounding more than a little annoyed. 'I had the sample boxes open when I started, that's all I can tell you right now.'

'Make sure the boxes are sealed before you get into the ship,' Wunderly pleaded. 'Otherwise the samples will melt.'

Pancho's voice cut in. 'We'll do what we can, Nadia. Now get off the circuit and let us get the hell home in one piece.'

Down in the makeshift control center, Kris Cardenas gritted her teeth with anger as she listened to Wunderly's demands.

Manny could get killed and all she's worried about is her goddamned samples, Cardenas grumbled to herself.

Tavalera was standing before the pasted-up display screens like a statue, watching what was happening out there in the rings but totally unable to do anything about anything. Timoshenko stood on Tavalera's other side, scowling at the displays. Cardenas saw the frustration on their perspiration-sheened faces. She felt it herself. There's nothing we can do! It's all up to Pancho now.

'We're in the airlock,' came Wanamaker's voice. 'Closing the outer hatch.'

Cardenas' heart nearly leaped out of her mouth. They've got him!

Before she could say anything, Tavalera let out a whoop and jumped into the air. Timoshenko turned and grabbed Cardenas in an impromptu bearhug, squeezing her with all the energy pent up in him for the past hour or more.

'They got him!' he shouted into her ear. 'They got him!'

Manny's safe, Cardenas thought. For the moment.

Wanamaker made certain that the airlock control panel showed green: the lock was fully pressurized. Only then did he press the stud that opened the inner hatch.

The hatch swung outward. Wanamaker saw that the ice coating Gaeta's excursion suit was already melting. And the insulated sample boxes on the suit's chest were shut tight.

'Can you move your legs?' he asked Gaeta.

The suit creaked, its servomotors buzzed wearily. Gaeta's right arm moved slowly, ice cracking off it and floating in weightless shards. He wiped at his visor.

'C'mon,' Pancho's voice called. 'We're headin' straight into the ring. Get inside and hang on to somethin'.'

Like a statue slowly coming to life, Gaeta clumped over the hatch's sill and into the cargo bay. Wanamaker didn't bother to remove his nanosuit. Swiftly, he detached the sample boxes and put them carefully into the cryogenic freezer standing against the bulkhead. He heard the freezer's interior mechanism sliding the boxes from the input slot to the liquid-helium-cooled storage compartment.

'Hang on,' Pancho called. 'Ready or not, here we go.'

Turning back to Gaeta, Wanamaker saw that the cargo bay was misty, hazy. But he could see Gaeta's face through his visor again.

'Ice melted off my suit,' Gaeta said. 'And all my systems are back in the green. Whatever shorted them out, the systems have come back on.'

'Good. Stay inside the suit. You'll be safer. We can vacuum the water out through the airlock once we're clear of the ring.'

'Maybe Nadia'll want us to keep it, take samples from it.'

Wanamaker felt his brows knitting. 'We'll have to figure out some way to store it in a bottle, I guess.'

In the cockpit Pancho paid scant attention to their conversation. 'You two lugs tied down good? It's gonna get bumpy in about half a minute.'

'I'm in footloops,' Wanamaker answered. 'Manny's boots are too big for them.' Then he remembered that Gaeta's boots were magnetic.

'Grab onto something and hang on. This might get rough.'

Pancho had cut off the outside comm circuit once Wunderly started making demands. Got enough to do in here without worrying about her samples, she told herself. Before her conscience could remind her, she added, I know. I know. The whole reason for this mission is the dratted samples. But now I gotta worry about three lives.

Gripping the T-shaped control stick on the instrument panel with her right hand, Pancho was unable to suppress a tight smile. Been a long time since you've had to do any real flying, she said to herself. Now we're gonna see how good you still are.

In the observation port before her Pancho saw the B ring rushing toward her, interwoven braids of ice particles with some darker, sootier areas off to her left. With deft touches on the controls, she swung the spacecraft in the same direction that the ring particles were rotating. Less difference between their velocity and ours, the less chance of us getting banged up.

But she knew the craft was going to get hit. There's a gazillion chunks of ice up there and we've got to push through 'em, like it or not. The spacecraft didn't have enough thrust to completely reverse its course and avoid the ring altogether. The best Pancho could do was to slice through the ring at as steep an angle as possible, minimizing the time they spent in the ring.

The collision alarm pinged. Starting already, Pancho thought.

'Here we go,' she said, more to herself than the two men hanging on in the cargo bay.

It was like skydiving into a glacier, falling into an endless field of ice. But this glacier wasn't solid, it was composed of countless myriads of ice particles.

Pancho goosed the main engines slightly and felt the push of thrust sway her backwards a little. She remembered a crash on the Moon that had torn one of her foot loops right out of the deck and broken her leg. Nothing that bad now, she thought. Not yet, anyway.

The collision alarm's chime was constant now, like a music box gone wild, but with only one note. Pancho stabbed at the alarm's control and it shut off. I know we're getting peppered, she said silently. Nothing big enough to punch through the meteor shield, so far.

She realized she wasn't in a suit. Stupid damn fool! If the cockpit gets punctured I'm dead.

No time for it now. She couldn't leave the controls, not even for the few moments it would take to pull on a nanosuit.

Pancho tasted blood in her mouth and realized she had bitten her tongue. Dumbass broad, that's what I am. Why the hell—

'Jake!' she called, surprised at how panicked her own voice sounded. 'Get up here. Quick! And bring an air bottle.'

She saw a gleaming white boulder no more than a hundred meters to the ship's right, rolling, tumbling along. And getting closer. A quick glance at the radar screen: nothing but hash, too many objects bouncing blips back at the receiver.

Gently, gently she eased the control stick left. The boulder drifted slightly away but tumbled along beside the ship as if accompanying her, waiting for Pancho to make the slightest mistake so it could plow into the spacecraft and demolish it.

Don't let it mesmerize you, Pancho reminded herself, forcing her eyes off its gleaming bulk. You gotta look in all directions as once. She glanced its way again and it was noticeably smaller, falling away from her.

The collision monitor's screen was blinking like the spasmodic eye of a lunatic. Pressure's still holding, Pancho saw. We haven't been punctured.

Wanamaker ducked into the cockpit, still in his nanosuit, his face white, eyes staring.

'You're not suited up!'

'Take the controls,' Pancho said, grabbing the green cylinder of air from his gloved hands.

She swung weightlessly through the hatch with one hand, let the green bottle hang in mid-air as she frantically pulled a nanosuit from the storage locker and wormed her long legs into it.

The ship lurched and slammed her against the bulkhead.

'Sorry,' Wanamaker called from the cockpit.

Too busy to reply, Pancho pulled the suit on, attached the air bottle, and saw the hood inflate around her face. She breathed a sigh of canned air, then stepped back into the cockpit.

'Thanks, Jake,' she murmured as she took over the controls again.

'We're almost out of it,' he said, pointing to the observation port. Pancho could see stars and even the crescent shape of a moon through the swarming ice particles. Must be Titan, she thought.

A sudden thump sent them both staggering. The cockpit hatch slammed shut and the life support monitor said with mechanical calm, 'Pressure loss in cargo bay. Hull puncture in section six-a.'

Gripping the controls again, Pancho shouted, 'Jake, you okay?'

'Okay,' Wanamaker answered shakily.

'Manny? Okay?'

'Yeah,' Gaeta's voice came through the intercom. 'Got banged around a little inside the suit.'

'But you're okay?'

'Fine. All the water vapor's siphoned out of the bay, though.'

'How big a hole we got there?'

A moment's hesitation. 'I can't see any hole. Must be microscopic.'

'We got hit by something bigger'n microscopic,' Pancho said. 'Maybe one of the sheepdog moonlets.'

Wanamaker said, 'Whatever hit us must've expended most of its energy on the meteor shield and only blew a tiny hole through the hull.'

'Maybe,' Pancho conceded. She took a swift scan of the instruments. Pressure in the cargo bay down to nothing, but here in the cockpit we're okay. Good thing I got into the suit, though. Collision rate's dropping. We're coming out of the ring. Good thing about the suit. If we'da been punctured here in the cockpit I'd be dead.

'We're almost clear,' Wanamaker said, a smile breaking out on his weatherbeaten face.

Pancho reactivated the collision alarm's chime. It was down to a lullaby.

'I think we made it,' she said to Wanamaker.

'I'll go back to the bay and see how Manny's getting along.'

'He'll hafta stay inside the suit until we dock at the habitat. Cargo bay's the only space big enough for him to climb outta the suit, and it's open to vacuum now.'

'Right,' said Wanamaker, opening the hatch. The air pressure in the cockpit remained normal. Pancho realized the hatch of the cargo bay must also have closed automatically.

'Oh, Jake,' she called. 'Check the freezer, make sure it isn't damaged.'

'Aye, aye, captain,' Wanamaker said, grinning and tossing her a crisp salute.

Pancho grinned at him. But her face contorted in surprised terror as she turned back and saw an ice chunk big as an apartment building dead ahead. She yanked the controls and it dropped from her view.

Wanamaker and Gaeta both yelled in a fervent blend of Spanglish and seaman's cursing.

'Sorry about that,' Pancho called to them, realizing they had nearly run smack into one of the shepherding moonlets that orbited just along the edge of the ring.

'For what it's worth,' she added, her grin returning, 'we're in the clear now.'

12 April 2096: Return

Kris Cardenas literally bumped into Wunderly as the two women ran down the passageway that opened onto the airlock area at the habitat's endcap. Tavalera and Timoshenko were sprinting up ahead of them, almost at the airlock hatch. Timoshenko was pushing a small dolly.

'They're okay, Kris,' Wunderly puffed. 'I monitored their transmissions in my office. Manny's okay.'

Cardenas nodded. 'It was rough, though.'

'But they're okay.' Wunderly smiled weakly as they slowed to a halt. 'Nobody got hurt.' It was an apology, Cardenas understood.

But she was in no mood to accept an apology. 'I hope your samples are what you wanted,' she said, without even trying to keep the bitterness out of her voice.

Rolling the dolly he'd been pushing up to the much bigger flatbed cart for the excursion suit, which they'd left at the airlock, Timoshenko plugged a comm set into the bulkhead socket next to the heavy steel hatch, then held one hand over the earplug. 'Okay,' he said into the pin mike at his lips. 'Confirm docking.'

Tavalera turned to the two women. 'They're docked,' he said, unsmiling.

Cardenas waited for what seemed like hours, watching the airlock hatch, waiting for it to swing open, waiting for Manny to return to her. She couldn't help glancing at Wunderly; Nadia seemed just as eager, just as impatient. Her precious samples, Cardenas grumbled to herself. Manny and Pancho and Jake damn near got killed so she could get her ice flakes.

334

But beneath her seething emotions, Cardenas knew she could not stay angry at her friend. They got back all right, nobody got killed, all's well that ends well, she told herself. I can't be mad at you, Nadia, I understand you too well.

'Gaeta's in the airlock,' Timoshenko announced, his hand still pressed against the comm plug in his ear. 'He's opening the inner hatch.'

Watching Wunderly's expectant face, eyes wide, lips apart in anticipation, the last remnants of Cardenas' anger melted. She slid an arm around Wunderly's shoulders and said softly, 'I really hope they've brought the proof you need, Nadia.'

Wunderly's eyes misted over. 'Thanks, Kris. Thanks for everything. I know you didn't want Manny to go. I know you—'

The inner hatch clicked and swung slowly outward like the massive door of a bank vault. Gaeta clumped over the sill in the bulky excursion suit. Tavalera and Timoshenko immediately went to his sides, instinctively offering to help him.

'I can walk by myself,' Gaeta's voice boomed from the suit's speakers.

Cardenas thought he sounded tired, spent.

While the airlock door swung shut again, Tavalera went behind Gaeta's suit and began unsealing its hatch. Cardenas went back with him.

'The samples?' Wunderly asked, her voice pitched high.

'In the cryo unit,' Gaeta said. 'Pancho and Jake are bringin' it out.'

As if on cue, the airlock hatch swung open again; Pancho and Wanamaker stepped carefully through, carrying the freezer unit like a miniature coffin. Cardenas paid no attention to them. She went around to the back of the big suit and watched as Manny ducked through the hatch and, a little wobbly, set his softbooted feet on the deck.

'You're bleeding!' Cardenas blurted out.

'I am?'

335

'Your nose.' She rushed to him, put her arms around him. 'Are you all right?'

'I am now.' He smiled and touched his nose gingerly with a fingertip. It came away bloody. 'Must've bumped it. It was a little rough for a while.'

'But you're all right?' Cardenas repeated.

The smaller dolly was for the cryo unit, Cardenas realized. The instant Pancho and Wanamaker loaded it onto the little cart Wunderly grabbed the control bar and started pushing it up the passageway at a trot.

Pancho chuckled. 'Somebody oughtta tell her that rig has an electric motor on it. She can ride it back to her lab.'

'Let her push,' Cardenas said, also smiling. 'The exercise will do her good.'

13 April 2096: The Morning After

Nadia Wunderly had not slept at all. She had spent the entire night alone in the biology laboratory, studying the samples of ice particles Gaeta had brought back to her. For weeks she had annoyed the biologists by borrowing, cadging, jury-rigging equipment from them to build a completely self-contained cryogenic analysis apparatus: about the size of a tabletop microwave oven, it was biologically separated from the rest of the lab by miniature airlocks and biohazard screens to prevent contamination of the return samples; the gleaming white apparatus was also thickly insulated to keep the ice particles at nearly the same temperature they existed at in the rings themselves. Most of the work she had done herself; only rarely could she cajole a technician to help her. Even then they joked about 'Wunderly's ice box'.

Now she sat in front of a display screen that showed one of her precious ice particles. Her tests had proven that the six-centimeter-wide chip consisted of amorphous ice: not the crystalline type of ice that was normal on Earth, but a form that was structurally more like a fluid in which molecules could flow and interact. Like glass, she told herself. Glass is liquid in structure, it just happens to be solid at normal terrestrial temperatures. Amorphous ice is solid at nearly two hundred below zero, but its structure isn't rigid, the molecules aren't locked in place, they can move around and combine with one another. Chemistry can take place inside amorphous ice.

Wearily, Nadia rubbed at her eyes. It's amorphous ice, all right. And there are microbe-sized particles inside it. But are they alive? They're not *doing* anything. They're just sitting inside the ice chip, as inert as specks of dust.

She pushed herself up from her chair, every muscle in her body complaining. I need a biologist, Wunderly said to herself. Who can I recruit from the staff to help me?

'It was terrible, Panch,' Holly was saying to her sister over morning coffee. 'He wiped the floor with me.'

'It couldn't've been *that* bad,' Pancho said soothingly.

'Worse.'

Pancho had come to her sister's apartment for breakfast after Holly had called her in the middle of a strenuous bout of morning lovemaking with Wanamaker. 'Let it ring,' Wanamaker had puffed. Once he'd gone in for a shower Pancho had checked the phone's messages, then called Holly to tell her she'd be over in an hour or less.

Pancho had never seen her sister look so glum. This election means a lot to her, she realized. Holly's found something that's important to her.

'Look,' she said to Holly. 'First thing to do is call Nadia and see if she's really found living critters in the samples. Everything hangs on that.'

Wunderly was neither in her home, her office, nor her laboratory. She was in the cafeteria having breakfast with Da'ud Habib and Yolonda Negroponte. Wunderly had called Habib the night before, once she realized she needed a biologist to help her analyze the ring particles.

'Yolanda is the best of our biology team,' Habib had said, by way of introduction.

But Wunderly was getting distinctly hostile vibrations from Negroponte. The woman was much taller than she, full-figured with long blonde hair and a face that wasn't beautiful, exactly, but very attractive. Full lips, strong cheekbones and jaw, eyes brimming with suspicion.

Habib must have felt the tension between the two women, too, because he excused himself after taking hardly more than a bite from his breakfast muffin and a sip of black coffee.

'I have a meeting with the chief of the maintenance department,' he said, almost apologetically. As he got up from the table and picked up his barely-touched tray he added, 'I seem to be a popular fellow this morning.'

And he scuttled away. Wunderly thought he looked relieved to be rid of the two of them.

Negroponte watched him for a moment, then turned back to Wunderly, her eyes focusing like x-ray lasers.

'You're the one Da'ud took to the New Year's Eve party,' she said, almost accusingly.

'That's right,' said Wunderly. 'Who did you go with?'

The biologist almost smiled. 'I was interested in Da'ud, but he was too concentrated on Urbain's lost little tractor to catch my signals.'

'Oh. I see.' Wunderly decided to be straightforward. She needed this woman's help, not her animosity. 'I didn't send any signals. I just asked him if he'd like to go to the party with me.'

Negroponte's ashen eyebrows rose in surprise. 'Just like that?'

'Just like that. I've never learned how to be subtle, how to send out signals.'

'Really?'

'With your looks, it must come pretty naturally. I mean, men must chase after you all the time.'

'Well . . . not chase, exactly.'

'I've always been kind of dumpy and mousy,' Wunderly confessed. 'Nobody's ever come panting after me.'

Negroponte's expression softened a bit. 'I was always taller than most of the boys in school. But worse, they get frightened when they realize you're smarter than they are. Men want to be dominant, even the weak ones.' Before Wunderly could think of what to answer, she added, 'Especially the weak ones.'

'I don't think Da'ud's weak, do you?'

'No, not weak, exactly. But you have to do the leading with him.'

'Maybe,' Wunderly conceded. 'But maybe you scare him off if you come across too strong.'

Negroponte seemed to consider that for a moment, then shook her head. 'I don't know. Da'ud's good-looking but his work is more important to him than women.'

'Really? You think so?'

'Isn't your work more important to you than men?'

Wunderly shook her head. 'I don't see a conflict between the two. Do you?'

The two women sat together in the noisy, busy cafeteria for more than an hour, heads together, talking about men and the problems they cause. Sometimes they laughed together; often they giggled. People passing them carrying their trays thought they were two old friends who had just been reunited after a long absence.

It was only as they left the table, cleared their trays and stacked them, and finally headed toward the bio lab that they started talking about biology and the ice samples.

Habib felt relieved to be away from the two women as he tapped politely on the office door of the chief of maintenance. They think they own you, he said to himself. And each of them wants you exclusively to herself.

'Come in,' came Timoshenko's voice from the other side of the door.

Habib slid it back and entered the office. It was a spacious room, with a large desk and smart walls filled with data displays. Timoshenko sat behind a small mountain range of papers, which Habib thought strange. Why use paper when you can store information electronically? Not that the sheets were actually paper, made from trees, he knew. Aboard habitat *Goddard* 'paper' was actually thin sheets of reprocessed plastic.

'You wanted to see me?' Habib said from the doorway.

'You're the computer genius?' Timoshenko asked, getting to his feet.

Habib smiled minimally. 'I am the head of the science staff's computer section. But I am not a genius, no, not at all.'

Waving him to the only chair in front of his desk, Timoshenko said, 'Pardon my inimitable way of expressing myself. It's a bad habit.'

'What can I do for you?' Habib asked as he sat down. 'You realize, of course, that I am responsible to Dr. Urbain and if you need my time or the time of any of his other people he will have to approve of it.'

Timoshenko grunted and sank back into his chair. 'I have a problem that involves the safety of this entire habitat.'

Habib felt his brows rise.

Pointing to the graph displayed on one of the smart walls, Timoshenko said, 'We've been having power outages. I've determined that they're caused by surges in the electromagnetic field surrounding Saturn.'

'Surges in Saturn's magnetic field?'

Nodding, Timoshenko replied, 'You scientists have known for years that there are electrical surges coming from the planet—'

'Electromagnetic.'

'Yes, of course. That's what I meant.'

'And they apparently originate in the rings, somehow.'

'Whatever,' said Timoshenko, with some impatience. 'The surges overload our power circuitry and cause outages.'

'I don't understand,' said Habib. 'We generate electricity from solar cells, do we not?'

'That's our main source, yes. But the current generated by the solarvoltaics must be converted to frequencies that electrical equipment can use. It's not a direct line between the solar cells and your coffeepot, you know.'

'Ah. Of course.'

'Those surges overload the inverters. It's my job to correct the situation.'

Habib almost laughed. 'I hope you don't believe you can stop Saturn's natural processes.'

'No, but if I know when the surges can be expected I can protect my power systems from them. I think.'

'You need to be able to predict when the surges will come?'

'Yes. That's the first step toward ending these confounding outages.'

'They seem to be random in their timing?'

'Not exactly random,' said Timoshenko. 'They seem to come every few weeks, in clusters.'

Habib stroked his beard absently. 'Every few weeks?'

'More or less.' Timoshenko said, growing irritated at Habib's echoing everything he said. He waited for another question. When Habib remained silent the engineer added, 'If I knew when to expect the surges I could at least shut down nonessential electrical equipment so we wouldn't overload the system and get outages.'

'I see.'

'I can't shut down equipment for days at a time, you understand. A few hours, yes, maybe. So I need to know when the surges are coming.'

'Is shutting down equipment the best thing to do?'

'No. Shielding the inverters and the main power lines is what we have to do, but that takes time and materials and labor. In the meanwhile, either I shut down nonessentials when a surge is coming or we keep on having these damned outages.'

'I see,' Habib repeated.

'You scientists have the data on the surges. That's where I got it from.'

'And you want me to analyze the data so that you can predict when surges will occur?'

'Yes!' Timoshenko said fervently.

'I'll have to get Dr. Urbain's permission to work on the problem. I don't know if he'll agree. He—'

'Tell Urbain that either we solve this problem or the entire habitat might go dark.'

Habib's eyes widened. 'It's not that bad, is it?'

'Can you assure me that it won't get that bad? Suppose a really big surge knocks out our inverters completely? What then?'

'I understand,' said Habib. Rising from his chair, he added, 'I'll speak to Dr. Urbain about this immediately.'

'Good,' Timoshenko said, getting up from his chair and reaching across the desk for Habib's hand.

But the computer scientist went on, 'But I doubt that he will allow me to work for you. He won't want to let me go.'

'He'll have to,' Timoshenko insisted. 'You'll have to convince him.'

Looking thoroughly unhappy, Habib murmured, 'I'll try.'

'Good,' Timoshenko repeated, and thrust his hand across the desk again. Habib hesitated a moment, then took it in his own. The man's grip was gentle, almost weak, Timoshenko thought.

'Thank you.'

Once Habib had left his office, Timoshenko plopped down in his oversized swivel chair again, thinking, If Urbain doesn't give permission for Habib to work on this, I'll go to Eberly and get him to draft the man. This is more important than trying to find some lost toy on Titan. This is vital!

13 April 2096: Urbain's Office

As he walked reluctantly along the hallway that led to Urbain's office, Habib wondered how he could possibly convince the chief scientist to allow him to work with Timoshenko.

He won't do it, Habib told himself. He will refuse. The only thing he cares about is his *Titan Alpha*. He'll say Timoshenko is an alarmist, an engineer who doesn't understand how important it is to bring *Alpha* back to life.

Habib dreaded asking Urbain's permission. He knew he could not stand up to his chief's wrath. Why has Timoshenko put me in this position? he asked himself. He should go to Urbain himself. Why is he making me do it? Why did I agree to do it?

Urbain's office door was less than twenty meters away and Habib slowed his pace, approaching it. Then he saw Negroponte leaving Urbain's office and stepping out into the hallway. She looked shaken, white-faced.

'What's wrong, Yollie?' he asked.

Looking as if she were about to cry, the biologist replied, 'I asked permission to work with Wunderly on her samples from the ring. He went hyperbolic. I thought he'd have a stroke.'

'He denied you permission?'

'He screamed at me. He threatened to send me back to Earth with a reprimand and a negative recommendation.'

Habib had never seen Negroponte appear cowed or frightened. It surprised him. Something stirred inside him. He felt his cheeks flush.

'He can't do that.'

344

'Can't he?' she said, tears brimming in her eyes.

Anger! Habib realized it was the heat of anger rising inside him. Urbain has hurt her, humiliated her, made her cry. For one of the rare times in his life, Habib acted impulsively. He seized Negroponte's wrist with one hand and slid open the door to Urbain's office with the other. Practically dragging the biologist after him, he stormed into Urbain's office.

'What is this?' Urbain demanded, looking up.

'You have no right to threaten members of your staff,' Habib said, wagging an accusing finger at his chief. Marching up to Urbain's desk, he released Negroponte's wrist. 'You must apologize to Dr. Negroponte.'

'Apologize? I—'

'Dr. Negroponte is a capable biologist, so capable that Dr. Wunderly is seeking her help in analyzing her samples from the rings. And you threaten her? You scream at her?'

Visibly trembling, Urbain got to his feet. 'I am the director of this scientific staff and I will not tolerate such insolence!'

Habib did not back off one millimeter. 'You will apologize to Dr. Negroponte. Now!'

'What's going on here?' Urbain shouted. 'Have you both gone insane? Has everyone gone mad?'

'Dr. Negroponte is needed to analyze the ring samples. It is wrong for you to deny her permission to do so.'

'*Titan Alpha* is the first priority here.'

'*Titan Alpha* is dead or asleep. You don't need your best biologist to stare at blank data screens.'

'You . . .' Urbain seemed to totter momentarily. He sank back into his chair.

Suddenly Habib realized the enormity of what he was doing. Yet the anger was still simmering inside him.

'Let her work with Wunderly,' he said, more reasonably. 'If they find living organisms in the ring particles it will be to your credit. It will take some of the sting out of *Alpha*'s failure.'

345

'Failure?' Urbain's eyes flashed. '*Alpha* is not a failure! I am not a failure!'

'No one has said that you are. But it's nonproductive to keep your biologists twiddling their thumbs until you make contact with the machine again.'

'I will decide what is productive and what is not,' Urbain said sharply.

Habib took a breath. The blazing anger he had felt when he'd seen Negroponte close to tears had abated. But now that he had taken a stand he could not back down.

'Dr. Urbain,' he said slowly, 'if you do not allow Dr. Negroponte to work temporarily with Dr. Wunderly, I will get the entire scientific staff to stop work.'

He heard Yolanda's sudden gasp of surprise, but he didn't take his eyes off Urbain.

The chief scientist sputtered, 'A work stoppage? A strike? You can't . . . it would be illegal . . . unjustified . . .'

'Most of your staff are doing nothing of importance now, anyway. They'll refuse to work for you if you continue acting like a dictator instead of a colleague.'

'Dictator? Me?'

'Allow her to work with Wunderly,' Habib said, almost placatingly. 'It will be to your credit, I assure you.'

Urbain opened his mouth, closed it again. His eyes moved from Habib to Negroponte.

'I really have nothing to do,' she said softly, almost whispering, 'as long as *Alpha* is silent.'

'Go,' Urbain snapped. 'Go work with Wunderly.'

'Thank you, sir!' she said.

'Keep me informed of your progress. I want daily reports.'

'Yes, of course.'

She reached her hand out and took Habib's in it. Together they walked back to the still-open door, leaving Urbain sitting at his desk looking shocked, bewildered.

Habib stopped at the door and turned back toward Urbain.

346

'Oh, I should tell you, the chief of maintenance needs me to help him on the problem of the electrical outages we've been suffering.'

Urbain said nothing. He simply stared as the two of them left his office hand in hand.

Sinking his head to the desktop, Urbain wanted to weep. It's all falling apart. They are leaving me, leaving *Alpha* to remain mute and inert on Titan. I've lost control of my creation and now I'm starting to lose control of my staff.

What can I do? What can I do?

14 April 2096: Morning

Kris Cardenas smiled at Gaeta, sleeping soundly beside her. He's all right, she repeated silently for the thousandth time. He got through the rings and he's not hurt. He's finished with these wild stunts; he's never going to risk his life again, never going to leave me again.

She slipped out of bed and padded to the lavatory, still smiling.

The smell of freshly-brewed coffee woke Holly. She'd set the coffee machine for seven a.m. It was better than an alarm clock for her. It wasn't real coffee, she knew; the habitat's climate wasn't right for growing coffee, even at the endcaps. The biotechnicians had produced an ersatz coffee by genetically engineering one of the crops the farms could grow. They'd even come up with a completely caffeine-free variation, although Holly preferred the 'high octane' version.

Slipping out of bed, she wondered what Raoul was doing at this moment. We're drifting apart, she realized. He'd been wholly involved with Manny's mission to the rings while Holly herself was completely tied up in this election campaign.

Wish I'd never decided to run for office, Holly said to herself as she brushed her teeth. She stared at her image in the mirror above the sink. But Malcolm's just plain wrong. We can't mine the rings if there're living creatures in them. And we've got to figure out some way to allow population growth before women start getting themselves pregnant. Our whole society could fall apart once the women decide to ignore the

ZPG protocol. Break one law and what's to hold you to obeying all the others?

Wearily she trudged to the kitchen and poured herself a cup of the strong black coffee. Sitting at the little table, Holly asked herself, How can I counter Malcolm's idea of using the profits we make from mining the rings to support population growth?

She spent the morning tussling with that problem.

Still in bed, Wanamaker said to Pancho, 'You know, you're a helluva pilot. I didn't realize that until yesterday.'

She grinned at him. 'And you're a helluva lover, Jake. But I knew that all along.'

They laughed together. Pancho started to get out of bed, but he reached for her lean, long-limbed body.

'We've got nothing on the calendar,' he said, pulling her close. 'Let's spend the day in bed.'

'Maybe you got nothin' to do,' Pancho said, pushing gently away from him, 'but I gotta go over to Holly and help her figure out her next move.'

Frowning, Wanamaker grumbled, 'What is this? You're not her campaign manager, are you?'

'Sorta. Leastways, I can give her the benefit of my experience dealing with slimeballs like Eberly.'

'When did you ever—'

'Corporate politics, remember? Remember Martin Humphries?'

'He wasn't a slimeball,' Wanamaker said. 'A megalomaniac, maybe, but not a slimeball.'

As she got out of the bed, Pancho said, 'Yeah, well anyway, politics is politics and Holly needs all the help I can give her.'

Wanamaker sighed deeply. 'Okay, you go play politics with your sister. If you want me, you know where I'll be.'

Pancho laughed. 'My hero.'

★　　★　　★

Nadia Wunderly had forced herself to get a good night's rest. She had even managed to sleep, despite her eagerness to start working with Negroponte on the ice samples. Her sleep had been troubled by dreams, although she couldn't remember anything specific from them once she'd awakened. Just a disturbing feeling that something was wrong.

Eberly, she realized as she dressed. The news broadcasts were filled with Eberly's proposal for mining the rings. I can't let him do that, Wunderly told herself. He'll ruin everything. Everything!

She stopped off at the cafeteria for a takeout breakfast of yogurt and honey, then hurried toward her laboratory. Ordinarily she'd have spent an hour at the gym, but not now, not with the samples waiting to be analyzed and Negroponte coming to work with her.

As she hurried through the morning sunlight toward her lab building, the thought of Eberly rose in her mind again. She had watched, horrified, the televised news reports of his debate with Holly. She saw his smug, smiling face as the stupid crowd cheered his proposal for mining the rings.

He can't do that! Wunderly told herself. I won't let him. I'll kill him with my bare hands if I have to, but he's *not* going to touch the rings!

Eduoard Urbain sat morosely at the breakfast table while his wife placed a dish of smoked salmon and thin slices of toast before him.

He had told Jeanmarie about Habib's mad outburst of the day before. She had not been as sympathetic as he'd expected.

No one is on my side, he thought morosely as Jeanmarie sat across the little table from him. She was smiling. Smiling! My staff is in rebellion, my *Alpha* is alone and silent on Titan, and my wife finds something to smile about.

'You seem cheerful this morning,' he said thinly.

'I have a meeting with my committee at ten,' Jeanmarie replied.

He said nothing, took up a piece of toast and placed a strip of fish on it. He brought it as far as his lips, then put it back on the plate again.

'I have no appetite,' he said.

'You're concerned about your staff?'

He felt his brows hike up. 'Concerned? Because they threaten a mutiny? Yes, of course I'm concerned.'

Jeanmarie put on a sympathetic expression. '*Mon cher*, why not allow them to do some useful work while your machine is idle? Whatever they accomplish will be credited to you, will it not? After all, you are their chief.'

'That's what Habib said,' Urbain muttered.

'So? You see?'

He pushed the dish away. 'I *must* find a way to regain contact with *Alpha*. I must.'

'Perhaps . . .' Jeanmarie began, then hesitated.

'Perhaps?'

'I was merely thinking, this Gaeta fellow. He flew to the rings again. Perhaps he could go down to Titan and see what's wrong with *Alpha*?'

He snorted with disdain. 'Nonsense! The man is a stunt-man, not a scientist. A performer.'

'Still, you could direct him, tell him what to do. And he could tell you what he sees once he's there.'

Urbain shook his head. 'It would never work. He wanted to go down to Titan when he first came to the habitat. He wanted to be the first man to set foot on the surface.'

'And you refused him.'

'Of course! I cannot allow contamination there. Titan bears a living ecology. I can't have some video stuntman tramping around down there.'

'Yet you sent your machine to the surface.'

'It was thoroughly sterilized. Much more thoroughly than a human could be, even inside that monstrosity of a suit he has. The levels of radiation we used to sterilize *Alpha* would have killed him.'

Jeanmarie nodded as if she understood. Then she said, 'Still, if all else has failed, perhaps this stuntman is your only recourse.'

'Never! I refused him once. Now you want me to go to him with my hat in my hand and beg his assistance? Never!'

'I understand,' Jeanmarie said. And she thought that she truly did understand, much better than her husband.

16 April 2096: Late Afternoon

'If they're alive,' said Yolanda Negroponte, looking up from the microscope's display screen, 'they're unlike any kind of organism anyone's ever seen before.'

Wunderly, sitting beside her at the lab bench, said quietly, 'Well, isn't that what you would expect?'

The biology laboratory was empty except for the two women; the other lab benches were bare, silent. Dust motes drifted through the sunlight slanting in through the tall windows. The small white anodized freezer containing the ice particles sat between them, flanked by a pair of remote manipulators and the gray tubing of a miniaturized electron microscope.

A puzzled frown creased Negroponte's face. 'They're not dust flecks. They have an internal structure, I can see that, but nothing seems to be going on inside them. Living cells are dynamic: the organelles pulsate, the whole cell quivers and vibrates. These things just lie there like raisins in a pudding.'

'Maybe they're dead? Wunderly asked. 'Maybe they were alive once and now they're dead. We might have killed them by taking them out of their natural habitat.'

Negroponte shook her head, making a long strand of blond hair fall across her face. Pushing it back, she said, 'You've kept the temperature and pressure the same as in the ring. There's no sign of contamination. If they're alive in the ring they should be alive here.'

Wunderly got up from the little wheeled chair she'd been sitting in and headed for the coffee urn at the end of the bench.

'Maybe I've been wrong all along. Eberly will be glad to hear it.'

'Coffee's a good idea,' said Negroponte, also rising from her chair. 'Too bad they can't make a decent espresso. It stimulates the brain.'

'Caffeine,' Wunderly murmured as she filled a mug with the hot steaming brew, then handed it to Negroponte.

The two women sipped in silence for a few moments. Then Wunderly asked, 'So Da'ud really yelled at Urbain?'

'You should have seen him. Like a knight in armor facing down a dragon.'

'I didn't think he had it in him.'

'He did it for me,' Negroponte said, still marveling at yesterday's showdown. 'I think my crying triggered something in him, something brave and strong.'

Wunderly brought her mug to her lips. 'Maybe I should cry for him,' she muttered into the coffee.

'You're still interested in him?' Negroponte arched a brow at her.

'Aren't you?'

'More than before, Nadia.'

'Then he's all yours,' Wunderly said, thinking, I'm not going to let Da'ud or any man get in the way of my work. I need her more than him.

Negroponte changed the subject back to biology. 'What's the temperature inside the cryo unit?'

'Minus two hundred, almost.'

Tapping a fingernail against her coffee mug, Negroponte said, 'Biology depends on chemistry, and chemical reactions go slower as you drop the temperature.'

'Do you think . . . ?'

'They look like cells. They have an internal structure and they maintain their interiors within well-defined membranes. But they're inert, seemingly.'

Wunderly's eyes lit up with hope. 'Maybe they're not inert! Maybe they're just *slow*!'

'Can you fit a minicam to the microscope?' Negroponte asked.

'Sure!'

Within half an hour they had a miniature video camera attached between the eyepiece of the microscope and the cable linking it to the display screen.

'Good,' said Negroponte once they had finished the rig and tested it.

Wunderly looked from the screen, which still showed the dark cellular object imbedded in the ice chip, to the biologist's satisfied expression. 'Now we wait for something to happen?'

'Now we go to dinner, linger over dessert, and then come back to see what's been recorded.'

Wunderly nodded agreement. Dessert, she thought. I deserve a decent dessert.

Pancho had spent the day with Holly in her apartment, the two of them desperately trying to find some way of trumping Eberly's position on mining the rings. She was on the living room sofa, long legs stretched out across its cushions.

'The IAA won't allow it,' she said stubbornly, repeating it for at least the twentieth time.

Sitting at her desk, across the room from her sister, Holly shook her head. 'Urbain's given his okay. Even if the IAA does decide against mining, Malcolm could get our people to go ahead anyway.'

'And risk having Peacekeeper troops sent out here?'

'Panch, do you really think the IAA's going to send troops all the way out here? Do you think Earth's willing to go to war over mining the rings of Saturn?'

'It wouldn't be a war, exactly,' Pancho said uncertainly. 'Would it?'

'It would mean blood and killing,' Holly replied. 'Jake's right: spacecraft are really fragile. I don't think the IAA would take the risk if our people put up a determined front.'

'They will if Nadia can prove the rings harbor life.'

'Not even then,' Holly said. 'Malcolm'll work out some weaselly deal that the IAA'll agree to. Just wait and see.'

'A deal? Better'n war, I guess.'

The lights flickered once, twice, then steadied again. Both women looked ceilingward.

'Speakin' of fragile spacecraft,' said Pancho. 'This habitat isn't the safest place in the solar system.'

'Timoshenko says he's trying to find what's causing the power failures.'

Swinging her legs down from the sofa, Pancho said, 'Well, there's an issue you can hammer on.'

'Panch, it's not Malcolm's fault that we have these outages.'

'It's happening while he's in charge. That makes it his responsibility. From what I hear, people are damned unhappy about losing power all the time. And it could get worse, couldn't it?'

'I s'pose,' Holly said. 'But I don't think it's enough of a problem to swing people to voting for me.'

'Elections aren't won by the votes *for* a candidate,' Pancho said, stabbing her finger in Holly's direction for emphasis. 'They're decided by the votes against.'

'So?'

'So you hang Eberly on these power failures. They're *his* failures, and he's not doing anything to fix the problem.'

'He's trying.'

'You want to get elected or not?'

Holly stared at her sister for a long, silent moment. Then she shook her head stubbornly. 'I just wish we had something to top him on the mining issue. That's what's gonna decide this election, Panch. Everything else is secondary.'

Pancho had to admit that she was right.

16 April 2096: Evening

Feeling guilty about the ice cream she'd had for dessert, Wunderly followed Negroponte back to the bio lab. It was dark, except for the one strip of ceiling lights over the bench where they'd been working.

Negroponte slid into the chair before the display screen. Standing behind her, Wunderly saw that it looked exactly the same as when they'd left, three hours earlier. All this work for nothing, she thought. I made Manny risk his life; Pancho and Wanamaker too. For nothing. The damned things are just dust specks. The activity I saw in the rings is just natural abrasion, nothing more than ordinary particle dynamics.

'I think that should do it,' said Negroponte as her long fingers tapped on the keyboard. 'Yes. I'm rerunning the past three hours and speeding up the display. Now we'll see . . .' She held out a manicured forefinger for a dramatic moment, then pressed it on a keypad.

The image on the screen seemed to twitch.

'Did you see that?' Negroponte asked, suddenly excited.

'Something . . .' Wunderly said. 'I might have blinked.'

'We didn't both blink,' Negroponte muttered, fingers pecking again. 'I'm reversing the vid and running it forward again. There! See it?'

'It might be a hitch in the video,' Wunderly said, trying to keep calm despite the thrill twitching at her nerves.

'Reversing again. This time I'll slow it down . . .'

Wunderly felt the buzz building up inside her. Don't get

your hopes up, she told herself. Stay cool, don't let yourself get wound up.

She leaned over Negroponte's shoulder, her eyes widening as the dark blob on the screen pulsated slowly: once, twice, three times. Then it went still.

'Reversing again,' Negroponte said, her voice slightly shaky.

The ice creature went through its pulsations again.

'It really *is* alive,' Wunderly whispered.

'You were right all along,' Negroponte said, turning in her chair.

Wunderly wrapped her arms around the biologists's shoulders and hugged her. Negroponte struggled to her feet and embraced Nadia. The two women danced down the length of the lab bench.

'You'll get a Nobel for this!' Negroponte exulted.

'*We*'ll get the prize. The two of us. We did this together.'

'Life at cryogenic temperatures,' Negroponte said, moving back to their apparatus.

'We've got tell Urbain, and then the ICU. They'll want to see our data. We should get more video footage, examine more specimens.'

Negroponte was nodding hard enough to make her hair fly. 'Do you realize what this means? These organisms have such a slow metabolism that we can study their cellular reactions molecule by molecule. More detail than we've ever been able to see in normal cells!'

Wunderly was already digging in her handbag for her handheld. 'Maybe we'll get two Nobels!'

Even this late in the evening Urbain was in his office, staring at the smart wall that displayed a real-time view of *Alpha* on the surface of Titan.

Ask that stuntman to go down there and repair her? He fingered his moustache, thinking, struggling to find a way out of the morass his creation had blundered into. How can he repair *Alpha* when we don't know what's wrong with her? The engineers swear that it must be a failure of the uplink antennas, but the computer team believes it's a programming error of some kind. The blind men and the elephant, Urbain said to himself. Each specialist sees only as far as his own biases.

Could the computer engineers be correct? Could it be a software error? Then the hardware would be perfectly fine. Reprogram the master computer and *Alpha* will be under control once more. Urbain shook his head. But they've been over the programming a dozen times. More. They haven't found any software problems.

This is Habib's responsibility, Urbain said to himself. The memory of the man's insolence boiled up afresh. He should be here, trying to discover what's gone wrong, not off with the maintenance people chasing down their stupid power outages. He should be—

His desk phone said, 'Dr. Wunderly calling, sir. Urgent.'

'What now?' Urbain muttered.

Mistaking his words, the phone opened the link to Wunderly. Her heart-shaped face popped into focus on the smart wall to Urbain's left, life size, eyes wide, an excited breathless grin splitting her features.

'They're alive!' she fairly shouted. 'We've got proof! The ring organisms are alive!'

'Alive?' Urbain blinked at the news. 'You mean the rings actually harbor living creatures?'

'Microbes,' Wunderly said, gulping for air. 'At cryogenic temperature. Psychrophiles.'

'I must report this to the ICU. Immediately.'

Wunderly nodded her agreement. 'Dr. Negroponte worked with me. We did it together. She deserves as much credit as I do.'

'Of course,' Urbain said absently. 'Of course.'

And he thought, I will get a share of the credit, as well. After all, these two women are part of my staff. They work under my direction. He smiled at Wunderly's happy image. While she chattered away jubilantly, Urbain said to himself, This will take away some of the harm of *Alpha*'s failure. He didn't realize it was the first time he'd used the word *failure* without pain or anger.

Malcolm Eberly was sitting in a meeting of Madame Urbain's ZPG committee. He was the only man in the small conference room; all the others around the circular table were women, an even dozen of them, most of them well beyond the usual child-bearing age.

As he listened to them discuss their committee's work, he thought about how child-bearing age could be extended by rejuvenation therapies, implanted ova, frozen embryos, even nanotechnology treatments of a woman's reproductive system. Still, most women had their children before they were fifty. Eberly had gotten his staff to check out the demographics from Earth.

The committee's avowed purpose was to defeat Holly Lane's petition drive to repeal the Zero Population Growth protocol. Its secondary purpose, as far as Eberly was concerned, was to give him an excuse to meet with these women and bask in the warmth of their admiration. They'll vote for me, Eberly told himself. They want me to be their chief administrator, not that upstart Holly.

The head of the subcommittee on statistics was a youngish-looking computer technician with large green eyes and a smile that dimpled her cheeks nicely. But she wasn't smiling now.

'Although we have slowed the anti-ZPG petition drive,' she was reporting, 'we have not stopped it. People are still signing the petition, albeit at a slower rate than earlier.'

Madame Urbain, *tres chic* in a pastel lilac frock and tasteful hints of jewelry, asked, 'What are your projections?'

Green Eyes shrugged. 'At this rate, they'll have enough signatures by May first to force repeal of the protocol.'

'Then we have failed?' Madame Urbain asked, looking distressed.

'Not failed,' Eberly said. All eyes turned to him. 'This is not a failure by any means.

'Even if the protocol must be repealed,' he said, looking around the table at each of them in turn, 'the repeal could be only temporary. The winner of the election could present a new zero growth statute once he's been reinstalled in office.'

They considered that. They discussed it. Eberly pointed out to them that if he were re-elected by a sizable majority he could use his popularity to slow or divert the people who wanted to allow unrestricted growth.

'If Holly Lane is soundly defeated, much of the power behind her petition drive will be dissipated.' Eberly did not altogether believe that, but he had to keep up the spirits of these women so they would continue to work for him for the remainder of the election campaign.

They talked and debated and rehashed the matter for more than an hour. At last Madame Urbain moved that they adjourn and partake of the pastries and coffee that awaited them at the cafeteria.

Eberly walked beside her, with most of the other committee women clustered around them, down the sloping street toward the cafeteria building, chatting amiably with his admirers.

His phone buzzed. Frowning, he said, 'Please excuse me,' and fished the phone from his tunic pocket.

Eberly recognized the face on the tiny screen of his hand-held as a technician in the communications department.

'I left specific orders that I was not to be disturbed unless there is an emergency,' he said sharply into the phone.

'I thought you'd want to know, sir. Urbain just sent a report to the ICU. They have proof that there are creatures living in the rings.'

Eberly glanced at Madame Urbain and the other women walking with him. He hoped they had not heard the message.

17 April 2096: Morning

'This changes nothing,' Eberly said, sitting tensely in his desk chair.

Eduoard Urbain, seated before the desk, smiled thinly. '*Au contraire.* I believe it changes everything.'

'They can't stop us from mining the rings. And remember, you gave your approval. I have your signature.'

'That was blackmail and you know it,' said Urbain. 'I can renounce my endorsement now that Wunderly has proved the rings bear indigenous life.'

'What of it,' Eberly snapped. 'We can still mine the rings if we choose to.'

'Not unless the IAA allows it. And with the universities recommending a total ban on mining, the IAA will forbid it.'

Eberly steepled his fingers in front of his face, letting silence fall. Bluff is an important part of politics, he knew, but he also knew that one had to be prepared to back up a bluff with action, if necessary.

'I don't care what the ICU or the IAA or any earthbound gang of bureaucrats say. We will mine the rings. With or without their approval.'

'They will stop you.'

'How? They have no jurisdiction here.'

'The IAA has jurisdiction throughout the solar system,' Urbain countered. 'Selene and the other lunar settlements, the asteroid miners, all the research stations on Mars, Jupiter and Venus, even the Yamagata solar power project at Mercury acknowledges the IAA's authority.'

'Ah,' said Eberly, pointing his index finger like a pistol. 'They *acknowledge* the IAA's authority. They have agreed to it. We haven't.'

'Not officially, perhaps, but that is merely a matter of form.'

Eberly leaned forward in his chair, excitement rising in him. Yes, he said to himself. I could do it. They would follow me. I could get the people of this habitat to follow where I lead and respect me for my courageous leadership.

Misunderstanding his silence, Urbain went on, 'So you see, the IAA must—'

'To hell with the IAA!' Eberly snapped. 'I'm going to put it to a vote. Make a ballot referendum out of it. The people will vote to refute the IAA. They'll vote for total independence of every vestige of domination by Earth.'

Urbain paled. 'Then the IAA would have no recourse but to send troops here to enforce their ruling.'

'Really? Do you think they'd risk a war?'

'You would fight them? With what?'

'With every weapon we can build or borrow,' Eberly said, already envisioning himself leading his people, rallying his troops. 'And remember, this habitat is a lot sturdier than the spacecraft the IAA would send. We could hurt them a lot more than they could hurt us.'

'You are mad,' Urbain whispered.

Eberly laughed at him. 'It won't come to actual fighting, I'm sure. Those earthworms will try to negotiate with us first. And I'll let them. I'll spend months engaged in discussions and meetings with the IAA's bureaucrats. I'll talk and they'll talk, for months and months and months.'

'But in the end—'

'And while we're engaged in those oh-so-earnest negotiations, we'll start mining the rings. I'll present the earthworms with a fait accompli. We'll mine the rings and they'll do nothing to stop us.'

'But you'll be killing an alien life form!' Urbain pleaded.

'That is against everything we stand for! Everything we believe in!'

'Everything you scientists believe in, perhaps. But I imagine that even some of the scientists on your staff wouldn't protest against getting rich from mining the rings. People believe in their own well-being, first and foremost.'

'No,' Urbain said weakly. 'That is not so.'

'Isn't it?' Eberly smiled his warmest. 'I'll leave a large section of the rings free from mining operations. I'll put Dr. Wunderly in charge of preserving and protecting her precious little ice bugs. There's no reason why the people of this community can't get rich without completely destroying the ice creatures.'

Urbain sat there in front of Eberly's desk, speechless.

Wunderly had thought she was too keyed up to sleep, but she zonked out the minute her head finally hit her pillow. And awoke bright and eager, full of energy.

This is the first day of the rest of your life, she told her smiling image in the lavatory mirror. You're going to a famous woman, Nadia. Time to start looking the part.

As she dressed she told the phone on her night table to make an appointment with Kris Cardenas as early this morning as possible. Within seconds the phone confirmed that Dr. Cardenas would see her any time before noon, in her laboratory.

Glancing at the digital clock readout on the phone's screen, Wunderly realized it was already well past nine. You've overslept, she berated herself. Then she grinned. So what? I'm entitled.

Negroponte woke late, also. Even so, Habib was sound asleep beside her, snoring softly.

Nadia was right, the biologist told herself as she slipped out of her bed. Don't send him signals and wait for him to interpret them. Be direct. Be honest.

And most of all, she thought, get to him before anyone else does. Especially Nadia.

She was toweling off after her shower when she heard Habib's voice from the bedroom. 'I . . . I have to go.'

'Come in,' Negroponte said, sliding back the lavatory door. 'I'm decent,' she added, with a wolfish grin as she tucked the towel around her.

He was already dressed, at least partially. Habib was sitting on the edge of the thoroughly rumpled bed, pulling on his suede loafers.

'No, not that,' he said, looking a little red-faced. 'I have to go back to my place. I have a meeting with Timoshenko at ten and I have to shower and change and—'

She sat on the bed beside him. 'You're embarrassed?'

'No!' he said. Then, 'Well, yes, slightly.'

'No need to be. You were very good.'

'You were wonderful.'

'You could phone your ten o'clock and cancel the meeting.'

'Oh no, I couldn't do that. It's important.'

She smiled and patted his thigh. 'I understand.'

Habib practically ran from her apartment. Negroponte got up from the bed and went back into the lavatory, disconcerted by how alone she felt.

Cardenas didn't know how to break the news to Wunderly, so she stalled for time to think of a way.

'You're going back to Earth, Nadia?' she asked.

Wunderly was grinning happily as she stood before Cardenas' workbench in the nano lab. Tavalera was nowhere in sight; the lab was empty except for the two of them.

Nodding, she answered, 'I'll be going back with the team of scientists who're coming out here. I'm going to be famous, Kris.'

'You deserve it,' Cardenas said. 'You've worked very hard for it.'

Wunderly's smile faded a bit. 'I can't go back with nano-machines inside me. They won't allow anybody—'

'I know,' Cardenas said. 'The flatlanders are scared shitless of nanotechnology.'

Her expression growing even more serious, Wunderly said, 'So you'll have to flush the bugs out of me before I can go back.'

Biting her lip, Cardenas decided the best way was to be direct and quick, like sticking someone with a needle.

'Nadia, you don't have any nanomachines inside you. You never did.'

Wunderly seemed to hold her breath.

'You did it all on your own, Nadia,' Cardenas went on. 'You lost all that weight on your own.'

Wunderly's smile returned, bigger than ever. 'You faked it! You never injected me with nanobugs!'

'That's right.'

'I did it by myself!'

'Diet and exercise,' said Cardenas. 'Works every time.'

Flinging her arms around Cardenas' neck, Wunderly ex-claimed, 'Kris, you're marvelous! You . . . I mean . . . this is the best present anyone's . . . ever given to me!'

'I lied to you,' Cardenas said softly.

'You gave me a magic potion. Just like a fairy godmother.'

Cardenas nodded. 'And you did all the work.'

'I did it by myself.' Wunderly seemed genuinely thrilled by the news.

'You certainly did.'

'So I can keep on doing it, taking care of myself, watching my weight.'

'And looking better and better.'

'Kris, I love you!'

Cardenas smiled back at her. 'Just make sure you look good at the Nobel ceremonies.'

Oral Diary of
Professor Oames Coleraine Wilmot

'Tomorrow is the first of May. No spring fertility rites in this habitat, of course. These people have their fertility rites all year round, actually.

'However, there will be the second of three debates between our two candidates for chief administrator. Tomorrow evening.

'Although a lot has happened since the first debate, not much has changed. The scientists have proven that Saturn's rings actually do harbor living micro-organisms in their particles of ice. The ICU has already dispatched a shipload of science people to come and see for themselves. Urbain is in his glory, taking as much credit for the discovery as he can grab, despite the fact that he initially opposed investigating the rings at all. Ah well, the rings have taken the spotlight away from Urbain's failed lander on Titan. The useless hulk is still incommunicado: silent as a stone.

'Politically, Eberly is insisting that the rings can still be mined for their water without disrupting the ice creatures. The scientists disagree, naturally, but Urbain has been strangely muted on the subject. The woman who made the discovery, Dr. Wunderly, is up in arms against Eberly but I doubt that it will do her any good. Clever politician that he is, Eberly has offered to put her in charge of environmental protection of the rings – while he moves ahead with plans to mine them!

'It appears that Holly Lane's petition to overthrow the ZPG protocol will succeed. She claims to have more than seven thousand signatures, more than enough to repeal the protocol.

The signatures need to be verified, of course, but that's merely a matter of form. Unless Eberly pulls some new trick.

'At the end of the day, however, the petition might not matter one way or the other. From all that I can see and hear, these people want to mine the rings. They want to get rich. And Eberly has told them once they begin bringing in money from the mining, then they can repeal the zero-growth protocol and start enlarging the habitat's population.

'It would seem that Eberly has everything his own way. He's even hinted that he would defy an IAA injunction against mining the rings. He's taken the pose that he would rather fight than give in to what he calls 'Earthbound bureaucrats.'

'We shall see what we shall see.'

1 May 2096: The Second Debate

Zeke Berkowitz smiled professionally into the central camera facing him and the two candidates who sat at the table flanking him. Two other cameras were on either side of the table, all of them mounted on their self-balancing monopods. The studio was empty except for them and the two communications technicians working behind the cameras. Berkowitz's smile was pleasant, unforced, but it had a sly edge to it: the professional newsman's subtle declaration that he knew more than his audience did.

Precisely as the digital clock on the studio's far wall clicked to 20:00, Berkowitz said, 'Good evening, and welcome to the second of three debates between the two candidates running for the office of chief administrator.'

Berkowitz noted with pleasure the real-time readout of his audience's size displayed on a monitor beside the clock. Virtually every household in the habitat was watching the debate. Good, he thought. Very good. But then he reminded himself that all entertainment broadcasts had been suspended for the length of this debate. People could watch vids from their personal libraries if they chose; otherwise, the only show on the air throughout the habitat was the debate.

He introduced the two candidates and explained that each of them would have five minutes to make an opening statement, then the evening would be thrown open to questions phoned in by the viewers.

'Holly Lane, formerly chief of human services, will give her opening statement first.'

Holly inadvertently licked her lips as all three cameras swiveled slightly to focus on her.

She tried to smile as she began, 'Hi. You all know me, I guess, and what I'm trying to accomplish in this election. Thanks to your help, we've signed more than seven thousand people up for our petition to repeal the Zero Population Growth protocol. Seven thousand, three hundred and fourteen, to be exact.'

Holly had not written out a prepared speech. The display screen built into the table top before her showed only rough notes of the points she wished to make.

'The human services department is going to verify the signatures over the next few days, so if you get a call from one of my former workers, be nice to her. Or him.

'Once the signatures are confirmed, it'll be up to the chief administrator to declare the ZPG rule no longer valid. I expect he'll drag his feet on this, 'cause he's never been in favor of allowing women to decide their own lives.'

Out of the corner of her eye she saw Eberly shift unhappily in his chair. Zinged him, she thought.

'The real question, though,' Holly went on, 'is how we handle population growth once the ZPG rule is abolished. We all know that uncontrolled population growth could ruin this habitat. On the other hand, that sort of scenario seems kinda remote, far off in the future. After all, we could double our population tomorrow and still have room for plenty more people.

'But the problem is real. We mustn't grow beyond our means. We don't want to expand our population so fast that our standard of living goes down. We don't want to become overpopulated and poor, like so many countries back Earthside did.

'Can we regulate our growth without government rules? Without laws and protocols? I believe we can. I believe we've got to, because the alternative is pretty messy.'

Holly glanced at Eberly, then focused back on the cameras. 'Now, look at the problem from the other side. How can the government stop us from having babies? Is my opponent willing to force women to abort when they get pregnant? Is he going to create a police force that'll snoop into every bedroom in this habitat?'

With a shake of her head, Holly concluded, 'It's either the one or the other. Either we take the responsibility into our own hands and control population growth through individual responsibility, or we face a police state that'll put women under surveillance twenty-four seven.'

She looked at Berkowitz, then back at the cameras. 'That's all I've got to say. Thank you.'

Berkowitz smiled noncommittally. 'Thank you, Ms. Lane. And now,' he turned toward Eberly, 'our incumbent chief administrator, Malcolm Eberly.'

Eberly gave his brightest smile to the cameras, plucked a sheet of flimsy from the breast pocket of his tunic and ostentatiously crumpled it in his fist.

'I had prepared an opening statement,' he began, 'but in the light of my opponent's scare tactics, I feel it's necessary – vital, really – to set the record straight.'

Holly craned her neck slightly to peek at the screen displaying Eberly's speech. It showed exactly what he was saying, almost word for word. He knew what I was going to say, she realized. He had me figured out before I even opened my mouth! She felt crushed. What chance do I have? He's way ahead of me all the time.

'I was against the petition to repeal the ZPG protocol, yes, that's true,' Eberly said smoothly. 'I was against it because I didn't feel it was necessary. I knew, as all of you did, that sooner or later we would lift the ZPG restriction. It was only a matter of time.'

He turned to Holly and gave her a pitying look. 'My opponent paints a dire picture of either explosive population growth that swamps our economic capabilities or a police state in which women are held in a sort of reproductive bondage. Nothing could be farther from the truth.

'I have pointed out the path to a balanced, fair and free society, a society in which women can choose to have babies because we have the economic growth to match our population growth.'

He paused for a dramatic moment. Then, 'That economic growth will come from mining Saturn's rings. You – the men and women of this community – will become wealthy from selling water to the human establishments on the Moon and the asteroids, on Mars and the other planets.

'I know there have been objections to my plan. I know that the scientists have found microscopic creatures living within the ice particles. But I am certain that we can mine the rings without unduly harming these microbes. The rings are huge, vast, and our mining operations would hardly scratch them.'

Spreading his arms as if in supplication, Eberly said, 'We can grow wealthy and the wealth we generate will support population growth. When the time comes we can build new habitats, new centers of human societies that can grow and spread across the solar system or even out toward the stars themselves. The future is in our hands! We don't have to fear runaway growth or a static, brutal police state. We can be the progenitor of new worlds, worlds that we build with our own hands, our own minds, our own hearts.'

Holly thought she could hear the applause from every household in habitat *Goddard*.

Estela Yañez watched Eberly on the wall screen of her living room with narrowed eyes. Turning to her husband, sitting on the sofa beside her, she asked, 'Is he right? Can they mine the rings without destroying the creatures living there?'

Yañez shrugged elaborately. 'Estela, my dear, he is the chief administrator. He has access to much more information on the subject than we do.'

The screen now showed Berkowitz, who was explaining that the candidates would now take questions phoned in from the viewing audience.

'But do you believe him?'

'Why should I not believe him? Do you think he would lie about something so important?'

Estela pursed her lips. 'I have seen politicians lie before.'

'Wait,' Yañez held up a hand. 'Listen. Someone is asking the same question.'

The screen showed Eberly again, sitting behind the table and smiling benignly.

'Yes,' he was saying, 'I know that the scientists want to declare the rings off-limits for mining. But don't you think that's an over-reaction on their part? After all, the rings contain more than five hundred thousand million *million* tons of water ice. And how much will we be taking away from that staggering amount? A pittance. A millionth of a per cent, at moot.'

The caller's voice insisted, 'Yes, but won't even a small amount kill off the creatures living in the ice?'

Eberly's smile grew tolerant. 'My friend, people have been mining the metals and minerals on Earth for thousands of years. Have they killed off the microscopic bugs that live in those rocks? No, not at all.'

Yañez turned to his wife. 'There. You see?'

As the two-hour-long debate wound to its conclusion Holly felt drained, defeated. Eberly had deflected the ZPG issue and turned it into a reinforcement for his scheme to mine the rings. When she'd asked him what he'd do when the IAA forbade mining, he'd smiled and said that he was certain he could negotiate the matter.

'This doesn't have to be an either/or confrontation,' Eberly said. 'I'm certain that, with patience and good will on both sides, we can work out a compromise that will allow us to mine the rings and still allow the scientists to study their bugs.'

Before Holly could rebut, Eberly added, 'There's no need for hysteria or scare tactics.'

Holly had no response for that.

A caller brought up the power outages that still afflicted the habitat sporadically. Eberly smoothly replied:

'Our engineers and computer people have determined that the problem is coming from surges in Saturn's electromagnetic field. They've figured out how to predict the surges, and we're now setting up protective systems that will eliminate the outages within a few weeks.'

Eberly then winked outrageously for the cameras. 'The problem will be solved by election day, I promise you.'

All the calls seemed to be for Eberly. Of course, Holly realized. He's planted these callers. His people are swamping the phone lines.

'How do we know,' a man asked, 'that there's really a market for water from the rings?'

Beaming as if he'd been waiting for this one all evening, Eberly answered, 'You know, I asked myself that very question, a few weeks ago. Are we fooling ourselves by assuming that the settlements on the Moon and the Asteroid Belt and elsewhere will buy water ice from us?'

He hesitated a dramatic moment, then proceeded, 'So I called the leaders of Selene and Ceres. They've assured me that they'll buy water from us, and at a price that will give us a twenty percent profit margin!'

Holly knew there was no way she could beat this man. No way at all.

2 May 2096: Nanolab

'Yes,' Kris Cardenas said to Urbain's image on her wall screen, 'given these specs we can generate nanomachines that will build a new antenna system on *Alpha*.'

Urbain appeared to be seated at the desk in his office. There were dark rings under his eyes, and his face seemed thinner, more lined, than Cardenas remembered it from earlier meetings. She was no physician, but it looked to her as if the chief scientist was under tremendous stress.

He nodded somberly. 'Good. Can you proceed to build the devices at once?'

Cardenas nodded back at him. 'I'll give it my highest priority.'

'How soon will they be done?'

Calculating mentally and adding a generous safety factor, Cardenas said, 'In ten days. A week, if everything goes smoothly.'

Urbain sighed as if he were about to sign a pact in blood. 'Very well, then. Please proceed as quickly as you can.'

'Fine,' Cardenas said. 'But once we've produced the nanos for you, how are you going to get them to your machine down on Titan's surface?'

Urbain didn't answer. He had already broken the phone connection before Cardenas finished her question. The wall went back to displaying one of her favorite paintings, an Impressionist street scene from nineteenth-century Paris.

Swiveling her chair, she looked out across the nanotechnology lab from the alcove that she used as her office. Tavalera was just coming in through the airlock door.

'Sorry I'm late,' he called as he walked past the work benches toward her. 'I had breakfast with Timoshenko and we got to talking about beefing up the protection on the superconductor shielding.'

Cardenas got up from her chair, thinking, we're getting popular. It's taken a year for people to get over their fear of nanos and come to us for help. Now Timoshenko wants us, and Urbain has finally decided to let us help him.

The question popped into her mind again. How will Urbain get our nanos to his machine on Titan's surface?

'Uh, I need some advice,' Tavalera said. He looked distressed, embarrassed.

Cardenas smiled at him. 'It's easy to get advice, Raoul.' She gestured to the wheeled chair beside her desk and they both sat down. 'What's the problem?'

'There's a ship coming from Earth.'

'With a contingent of scientists to look at Wunderly's bugs,' Cardenas said. 'Nadia's planning go back to Earth with them.'

Tavalera nodded somberly. 'I could hitch a ride home with them.'

Cardenas understood. 'Is that what you want to do?'

'Maybe. I don't know.'

She studied his long, gloomy face. 'You'd like Holly to come with you, wouldn't you?'

'Yeah.' It came out as a long, sorrowful groan. 'But I know she won't.'

'Raoul, she can't. She's running for election.'

'I know.'

'She can't leave the habitat. Even if she wanted to.'

'Which she doesn't.'

Cardenas thought for a moment. 'What do *you* want to do, Raoul?'

He looked away from her, studied his shoes. 'I want to go back home,' he muttered, without lifting his face.

Cardenas waited, and sure enough he added, 'And I want Holly to come with me.'

'You can't have both.'

'I know. But you asked me what I want. That's what I want.'

She hesitated, then decided to plunge ahead. 'Have you asked Holly what she wants?'

Still looking down, Tavalera replied, 'She wants to be chief administrator of this place. She'll never go back to Earth.'

'Has she told you that?'

'I know she won't.'

'Have you asked her?'

Tavalera shook his head. 'What good would it do?'

'I don't know, Raoul. But at the very least you should talk this over with her.'

The sour expression on his face showed what he thought of the idea. 'Yeah,' he said. 'Right.'

Timoshenko was coasting along the outer hull of habitat *Goddard*, unencumbered by a spacesuit. The virtual reality program allowed him to see what the maintenance robot saw, feel whatever it touched with its pair of steel grippers. While the robot trundled along the guideway built into the hull, Timoshenko felt that he was walking, or no – not, walking, gliding on ice, skating the way he used to do in Gorky Park with Katrina.

She wasn't coming to him. Timoshenko had gotten the personnel department to check the passenger manifest for the ship bringing a load of scientists to *Goddard* and her name was not on the list. He had tried putting through a call to her, but of course the operators in Moscow refused to allow it: he was a non-person, an exile, not permitted to speak to law-abiding citizens. With a sinking heart, he realized that if somehow he did manage to get a message to Katrina then she would be breaking the law; she'd get into trouble with the authorities.

In his desperation, he had asked Eberly to contact her as he had before. He practically begged the chief administrator to do this favor for him. Eberly, wise in the ways of collecting gratitude, had told him that he had specifically asked the authorities in Moscow and even the main office of the Holy Disciples for permission to speak to the woman. She had refused to reply to his call.

Refused, Timoshenko repeated to himself. Refused. She doesn't want to come out here. She doesn't want to be with me. She said she would, when there didn't appear to be a chance in hell of doing it. Easy enough for her to say it then. But now, now when there's a ship she can get onto and really come to me, she refuses.

Timoshenko looked out at the curving hull of the habitat, and the black infinity of space beyond it. The robot was built to inspect the hull, not gaze at the stars. It could not lift its eyes to search for the blue gleam in that emptiness that was Earth.

I don't blame her, he told himself. This is exile, far from everything and everyone she knows. Everyone except me. Why should she give up her whole life to come here and be with me? I don't blame her. I don't. No matter how fancy they've made this flying stovepipe, it's still a place of exile, a high-tech Siberia. She's right not to come here. I don't want her to give up her life on Earth just for me. I had my chance to make her happy and I ruined it. She's right to stay away from me.

As he glided along the curving shape of the hull, it occurred to him that Eberly had lied. Eberly had told him that Katrina wanted to join him here, to share his exile, share his life. That had been a lie, Timoshenko realized now. Eberly had tricked him into taking this job as chief of maintenance by dangling the prospect of Katrina's joining him here. Had the man lied to him?

Timoshenko blanked the VR program, lifted the goggles off his head and pulled off the sensor gloves. He knew some of the people in the communications department; one fellow in particular had become a drinking buddy. He called that man and, after a little wheedling, got him to check on the chief administrator's calls to Russia.

'Nothing in the log,' the beefy-faced comm clerk told him.

'Nothing?' Timoshenko asked.

'Eberly hasn't put in any calls to Russia. Not one.'

Numb with grief and rising anger, Timoshenko nodded, thanked his pal, and broke the phone connection. Eberly lied to me. The devious bastard twisted me around his little finger. He used the idea that Katrina might come here to me to get me to do what he wanted me to. The lying, smug-faced son of a bitch.

How to get back at him? Timoshenko wondered, feeling the heat of his rage burning inside him. The answer was astoundingly simple. Kill him. Kill the bastard and all those around him. Kill him and yourself. Destroy this habitat and end this exile once and for all. Put an end to everything and everybody. It wouldn't be difficult. In fact, it could be done with ease.

4 May 2096: Mid-Morning

Da'ud Habib tried to get in a workout at the health center first thing every morning, before anyone else got there, but then he realized that Negroponte just happened to be exercising in a form-fitting sweat suit at the same time each day. Just as she just happened to be in the cafeteria when he came in for lunch. Invariably, she sat at his table. When he'd shown up later than usual she would move from the table she'd been sitting at to be with him.

The woman is pursuing me, he told himself. At first it was flattering, but it soon became an embarrassment. Negroponte thinks I'm some lover out of the *Arabian Nights*, he thought. A hawk-eyed emir who's going to carry her off on his steed to his tent in the desert. Nothing could be farther from reality.

Habib had been born in Vancouver of an immigrant Palestinian family and raised in the faith of Islam. Bookish and deeply interested in computers, he was actually rather shy around women. Throughout his university years, with his exotic good looks he had never had trouble finding women; they found him. His difficulty had always been in getting rid of them. While he enjoyed sex, he had no desire to marry or even to live with a woman. There was too much else to do; tying himself down to a woman would get in the way of his studies, his career. There would be time for marriage and children later, he thought.

He had chosen to join Dr. Urbain's scientific staff when his former faculty advisor had phoned him and suggested he do so.

'It's an opportunity, Da'ud,' the graying professor had told him.

'Five years?' Habib questioned.

'When you return to Earth you'll have your pick of universities eager to take you on. Even the New Morality will look favorably on you.'

'Why should they?'

'They want this habitat to succeed, to become an example of how people can live off-Earth.'

'Most of the habitat's people will be exiles, won't they?'

The professor had grinned knowingly. 'Yes, but there are lots of other bright young men and women whom the New Morality would like to see move off this world.'

'I don't see how my going out there with them—'

'Trust me, Dau'ud. It's a better opportunity for you than anything you can hope for here on Earth.'

Habib thought he heard a veiled message: Spend the five years on this Saturn mission or find the New Morality blocking your applications to the better schools. He was no fighter. He did what his advisor suggested.

It was like living in a university town, to a great extent. And the work was fascinating – at first. Habib directed the programming of the bulky probe Urbain was building, his cherished *Titan Alpha*. It was a fascinating challenge to program the complex machine so that it could operate independently in the alien atmosphere of Titan's surface, flexible enough to cope with unknowns and to learn from the environment in which it found itself.

Then *Alpha* had landed and gone silent, and Urbain had gone slightly insane. Habib felt certain that there was a hitch in the programming somewhere, but though he spent night and day trying to find an error, so far there was nothing wrong with the programming that he could discern.

There were lots of women available in the habitat, and although he tried to remain free of entanglements, his normal male hormones made their demands on him. He was surprised, though, when Dr. Wunderly asked him to go to the New Year's Eve party with her. He agreed, even though he would not have thought to ask her. Nadia Wunderly was not the most attractive woman he knew, yet she seemed to genuinely like him; more important, she was just as wrapped up in her work as he was. She would not try to force a commitment upon him.

Negroponte would, he felt certain. Yet, with her tall, ample figure and almond-eyed face she was powerfully attractive.

Habib got through his abbreviated workout, showered and changed back into his workaday tunic and slacks, then headed for his eleven o'clock meeting with Timoshenko. At last he had something solid to show the maintenance chief. Mathematics is so much simpler than women, he thought. A mathematical relationship remains fixed unless some discernable value produces a change, he thought. A relationship with a woman is always changing, often for no recognizable reason.

Habib got to Timoshenko's office and slid open the door to the anteroom. Three engineers were sitting with their heads bent over display screens. The chief of maintenance did not have a personal assistant, Habib knew. He believed that computers could do the routine office work; each of his employees was actively engaged in maintaining the habitat's myriad mechanical, hydraulic, electrical and electronic systems.

Habib went straight to the door of Timoshenko's private office.

'He's not in,' said one of the engineers, barely looking up from her desktop screen. 'Hasn't been in yet this morning.'

'But we have a meeting scheduled for eleven.'

'You're three minutes early,' came Timoshenko's voice from behind him.

Turning, Habib saw the Russian walking toward him. Timoshenko looked terrible: his eyes red and puffy, as if he had not slept all night.

'I have good news for you,' Habib said, by way of greeting.

'Good,' said Timoshenko, almost in a growl. 'I could use some news that's good, for a change.'

Five minutes later, Habib was sitting beside Timoshenko at the little round table in a corner of the maintenance chief's office. One wall screen was filled with a set of graphs displaying complex curves.

'So you're telling me that Titan is causing the power surges?' Timoshenko asked, eying the graphs suspiciously.

'I don't know if that's the cause of the surges,' Habib replied, 'but they correlate very closely with the position of Titan and the other major moons in their orbits around Saturn.'

Timoshenko grunted.

Pointing to the graphs, Habib explained, 'Whenever Titan and the other major moons line up on the same side of Saturn, we get the power surges.'

In a heavy low voice Timoshenko muttered, 'That's why the surges are grouped approximately every two weeks. Titan's orbit is sixteen days.'

'Yes. And it explains why you can go for months without any surges at all: that's when the outer moons are not on the same side of the planet as Titan.'

'You're certain of this?'

'The mathematics are definitive,' Habib said, with some pungency in his tone. He didn't like having his calculations questioned.

'But what's causing it? What we have here looks like astrology, not physics.'

Habib shrugged. 'You'll have to ask Wunderly or one of the astrophysicists. I am a mathematician.' Pointing to the wall screen display he added, 'You asked me to tell you how to predict when the surges will come and that's what I've done.'

Timoshenko nodded. 'Yes. So you have.' Turning slightly in his chair he called out, 'Phone! Get Dr. Wunderly. Top priority.'

4 May 2096: Evening

The cocktail reception was ostensibly to welcome the shipload of scientists who had arrived from Earth in the wake of Wunderly's confirmation that Saturn's rings harbored living organisms. Urbain's entire scientific staff was there to greet the newcomers, as well as the habitat's most prominent citizens.

Ordinarily, Urbain would not have invited Manuel Gaeta. After all, the man was not a scientist: he was nothing more than an entertainer, a stunt performer, little more than a trained ape. But Gaeta was living with Dr. Cardenas, who was a Nobel laureate. Urbain could not invite her without having him come along.

Besides, Urbain needed this trained ape.

The party was at the lovely lakeside bandshell, at the foot of the gentle hill on which the village of Athens was built. Champagne flute in hand, Urbain saw Pancho Lane with her sister and a pair of men he couldn't quite place in his memory. He leaned toward his wife and asked her who they were. Jeanmarie told him that the older, taller of the two men was Pancho's companion, a former admiral. The other was the engineer that the habitat had taken in when it passed Jupiter.

'Ah yes,' Urbain murmured, recognizing the somber-faced younger man. 'Tavalera is his name, I believe.'

And there was Eberly, of course, with his claque following wherever he went. Urbain suppressed a frown of distaste. The chief administrator was totally in his element, surrounded by admirers, smiling and chatting and laughing with them.

Gaeta, Urbain said to himself. I must get to Gaeta.

He saw that the stuntman and Dr. Cardenas were standing by the lake's edge, deep in earnest conversation with Wunderly. Strange, he thought. Wunderly should be the center of attention at this reception, yet she is off to one edge of the crowd with her little circle of friends. Urbain shook his head. She has much to learn about the politics of science, he told himself.

Taking his wife's free hand, Urbain said to the women she was chatting with, 'Excuse us, if you please. I must speak with Dr. Wunderly for a few moments.'

And he led Jeanmarie toward the little group at the water's edge.

Wunderly was babbling away nonstop to Kris Cardenas. Gaeta stood with the two women, barely understanding a word of what Wunderly was saying.

'. . . so when Da'ud showed me the graphs he'd worked up I ran through the vids of the ring spokes and sure enough they correlated to five nines,' Wunderly gushed.

'The spokes correlates with Titan's position?' Cardenas asked.

Gesticulating so forcefully that she sloshed champagne onto the grass, making Gaeta jump nimbly out of the way, Wunderly said, 'Yes! We'd wondered what caused the spokes and now we've got an explanation! Just in time for me to go back to Earth.'

'The spokes?' Gaeta asked, frowning slightly. 'You mean those lanes of dust in the rings?'

Wunderly nodded vigorously. 'The dust lanes that rise above the plane of the ring particles and then drift down again.'

'Like they're doing the wave at a ball game,' Gaeta said.

'The wave?' Wunderly looked puzzled.

Meanwhile, on the other side of the gathering of partygoers, Yolanda Negroponte was deep in conversation with four of the biologists who had just arrived from Earth.

She had come to the reception alone, dressed in a simple off-white miniskirted frock that showed her long legs to advantage. She had phoned Habib several times during the course of the day to ask him to escort her to the party, but he had not answered her calls. Now she stood at the center of the little group of newcomers, trying to keep up the conversation with them while looking out over their heads, scanning the crowd for a sight of Habib.

He's afraid of me, she said to herself. I come on too strong for him. Yet she knew that if she did not pursue Habib he would drift away from her. Why must he be so difficult? she asked herself.

And why must you insist on going after him? asked a voice in her mind. There are lots of other men here. You could have your pick of them. But it was handsome, gentle, shy Habib who interested her. He was such a tiger when he got angry.

'Have you done a DNA analysis yet?'

Negroponte barely heard the question. It took an effort for her to focus on the quartet of biologists around her: two men, two women.

'Preliminary,' she responded. 'The cellular structure has a nucleus and what appears to be nucleic acids, although their chemical composition is completely different from terrestrial DNA.'

'And their structure? Is it a double helix, like ours, or triple, like the Martian biota?'

Negroponte shook her head slightly. 'There's no evidence of helical structure at all.'

'Not helical?'

'We've done gamma-ray diffraction and MRF microscopy. The nucleic acids appear to be a crystalline lattice.'

'That's impossible!'

Negroponte smiled knowingly at the flustered little man. He wasn't quite as tall as her shoulder. 'Come to my lab tomorrow and I'll show you.'

Then her smile widened into genuine warmth. She saw Habib among the partygoers, looking very handsome in a forest green suit. And he was pushing his way through the crowd, heading toward her with a champagne flute in each hand.

'Look at how beautifully the lake reflects the lights of the shell and the land above,' said Jeanmarie to her husband. He ignored her, his attention bent on Wunderly, Gaeta and Cardenas standing down by the water's edge.

'Good evening,' Urbain said as he and his wife got to within earshot. 'Are you enjoying the reception?'

Wunderly grinned at her boss. 'The food's good,' she answered, eying the nearest table. It was laden with finger foods and surrounded by guests. Robot waiters from the Bistro, squat little flat-topped machines that rolled silently on tiny trunions, were busily bringing up replenishment trays, marching like a line of ants from the restaurant in the village to the tables scattered across the grass.

'You have made a great contribution to science,' Urbain said graciously to Wunderly. 'I will be sorry to see you leave the habitat.'

Both he and Wunderly knew that Urbain had opposed her single-minded concentration on the rings. Urbain had wanted everyone on his staff to focus on Titan; Wunderly had held out stubbornly – and won.

'I couldn't have made the contribution without you, Dr. Urbain,' she said, equally congenial. 'I owe all my success to you.'

'Not at all,' he said. But he beamed at her.

'I think we made another major breakthrough today,' Wunderly said.

'Oh?'

'The spokes in the rings correlate with the positions of Titan and the outer moons!'

Urbain stared at her for a moment. 'Are you certain of this?'

'Da'ud Habib's done the correlation and I checked it with the vids we have of the spoke actions.'

'But what could be the cause of this?' Urbain was suddenly engrossed. 'Could it be gravitational?'

'I think it's electromagnetic,' Wunderly said. 'Electromagnetic force is orders of magnitude stronger than gravitational.'

'Yes, true. And Saturn's electromagnetic field is very powerful.'

'And it extends way out beyond the orbits of the major moons.'

'True. We must calculate the energies involved.'

Kris Cardenas butted in, 'From what Nadia tells me, this also explains the electromagnetic surges from Saturn that've been causing power outages here.'

'A useful by-product,' Urbain granted. But his attention was entirely focused on Wunderly's news. He forgot that he was hosting this reception; he forgot about the party altogether. He even forgot that he needed to ask Gaeta to go down to his stranded *Alpha* on the surface of Titan.

4 May 2096: Night

'Some party,' Tavalera said as he strolled slowly with Holly up the gently rising walkway toward Athens.

'Enjoy yourself?' she asked.

'Yeah. Sure.'

Holly gazed up at the lights over their heads: unwinking pinpoints, the stars of this inside-out habitat of theirs.

They ambled along the lane, passing through pools of light from the street lamps, then into stretches of shadow, walking slowly, as if reluctant to get home.

'The ship that brought the scientists will be leaving in a week,' Tavalera said at last.

'Nadia's going back to Earth with them,' said Holly.

'She'll be back.'

'I guess.'

Tavalera stopped and reached for Holly's shoulders, turning her to face him. They were in the shadows between street lamps, their features barely discernable.

'I could go back on that ship,' he said. 'I checked with Eberly. He said the New Morality'll pay half my fare and the habitat will kick in the other half.'

Sudden anger flared in Holly's gut. 'Eberly! He'll pay to get rid of you just to hurt me,' she said.

'Would it hurt you? If I left?'

'Of course it would.'

'Really?' His voice brimmed with joyous disbelief.

She grabbed him by the ears and kissed him. 'Raoul, you can be a real dimdumb. I love you!'

'I love you too, Holly,' he said.

Even in the nighttime darkness she could see the toothy grin splitting his face. He looks so super when he smiles. Then she thought, I ought to make him smile more.

'Holly,' he said, his smile withering, replaced by dead seriousness. 'Holly . . . will you come with me? Back to Earth? For real?'

She didn't hesitate a moment. 'Back to Earth or anywhere else, Raoul. Anywhere.'

'You will?' His voice jumped an octave.

'F' real,' she said, totally certain. 'I've never seen Earth. I was born there and lived my first life there, but I don't remember any of that.'

'I'll take you to the Grand Canyon,' Tavalera said, suddenly bursting with enthusiasm. 'The Taj Mahal. The Pyramids!'

'I want to see West Texas. Pancho and I were born there.'

'Most of it's under the Sea of Mexico.'

'Then we can go scuba diving.'

'We could scuba through Manhattan, too. And Miami.'

'Cosmic!'

'Then you'll come on the ship with me?'

Holly took a breath. 'I can't go until the elections, Raoul.'

'Oh.' His voice fell. 'That.'

'Don't sweat it,' Holly said, happily. 'Malcolm's gonna beat me by a landslide and then I'll be free to go wherever you want.'

'But if you win?'

'No chance of that,' she assured him. And herself. 'Soon's the election returns are counted we can snag a ship and zip back to Earth together.'

'Together,' he breathed.

'First ship out, after the elections.'

He murmured, 'We can get married back home. My parents'd like that.'

'So would I.'

They started walking up the sloping path again. Tavalera blurted, 'But what if you win?'

'I won't.'

'You could. You got more than seven thousand signatures on your petition. What if they all vote for you?'

'They won't. Berkowitz has been running polls. This morning's shows me behind, sixty-two thirty-two with six per cent undecided.'

'You could quit,' Tavalera suggested. 'Resign. Come with me now, right away.'

Holly shook her head. 'I wouldn't give Malcolm the satisfaction. Let him sweat out the vote count. He's gonna win, but I won't let him win by default.'

Tavalera said nothing.

'I mean, I wouldn't mind losing by a decent percentage, but this is cosmic.'

With a small shrug Tavalera replied, 'People wanna mine the rings. They wanna get rich.'

'I guess.'

If she wins I'll never see her again, Tavalera thought. Even if she loses, she could change her mind and stay here.

As if she could read his mind, Holly said, 'Don't stress out on it, Raoul. I'm gonna get my butt whupped so bad on election day that I won't ever want to show my face in this habitat again.'

He wished he believed her. 'You think Eberly really talked with people at Selene?' he mused aloud. 'And the rock rats?'

'He said he did.'

'But did he really? Maybe he was just saying that to impress the voters.'

Holly brightened a little. 'I could check.'

He felt happy to see her smile, at least a little. Still, as they walked back through the pools of light and shadow toward their apartments, Tavalera wished he'd kept his big mouth shut.

★   ★   ★

Eduoard Urbain grew more nervous and fretful as the reception wound down. People were leaving, in couples or larger groups. The laughter was dying away, the last drinks being finished. As the host of the party, Urbain had torn himself away from Wunderly at last and, at Jeanmarie's prompting, posted himself by the path that led back to Athens so he could bid a formal good-night to the departing guests. Waiters from the Bistro were piling emptied glassware onto the little flat-topped robots that scooted back to the restaurant in Athens.

Gaeta had not left the party yet, Urbain saw. He was strolling slowly with Cardenas along the edge of the lake. Urbain saw him bend down, pick up a pebble, and hurl it into the water. Ripples spread on the still surface, circles within circles. How like a little boy, Urbain thought. There must be much of the adventurous little boy in him still.

'Are you going to ask him?' His wife's voice was soft, almost a whisper, but yet it made Urbain's insides jump.

He nodded nervously. 'Yes. I must.'

'Then now is the moment,' Jeanmarie said.

'Yes,' he repeated. 'I know.'

He took his wife's outstretched hand and together they walked down the grassy slope to the water's edge.

Cardenas noticed them approaching. Smiling, she said, 'A lovely party, Eduoard. Jeanmarie, you must be proud of your husband.'

'I am,' said Jeanmarie. 'He is a man of many accomplishments.'

Gaeta grinned lazily at them. 'This was better than that New Year's Eve bash.'

Urbain felt his cheeks grow warm. 'Thank you. Thank you.'

Cardenas glanced at her wristwatch. 'Well, we'd better get some sleep. Tomorrow's a working day.'

'Yes,' Urbain murmured while his mind raced, trying to find some opening, some way to get around to what he wanted to say, wanted to ask.

Jeanmarie understood. She asked Cardenas, 'How is your work on the new antenna system going?'

'Very smoothly,' Cardenas replied. 'I'll be able to deliver the nanos to you by the end of the week, at most. Only a couple of final tests left to do.'

'They will be safe?' Jeanmarie asked.

'That's what we'll be testing for. The nanos are all programmed and capable of building a new antenna on the lander. Now we're making certain they'll switch themselves off and go inert once the task is finished.'

'Excellent,' Urbain said.

'I'm curious, though,' Cardenas went on. 'How do you intend to get the package down to your lander?'

Urbain coughed slightly. 'We know *Alpha*'s position. We have her under constant surveillance.'

Gaeta said, 'So?'

Taking a deep breath, like a man about to plunge over a precipice, Urbain replied, 'I need you to bring the nanomachines to *Alpha*.'

For an instant neither Gaeta nor Cardenas replied. Urbain blinked once and felt his wife's hand tensing in his.

Gaeta laughed. 'Now you *want* me to go down to the surface? No shit.'

'No!' Cardenas snapped. 'Manny's not going anywhere. He's retired.'

'But this is important,' Urbain said.

'Wait a minute,' Gaeta said, a lopsided smile stretching across his beat-up features. 'When I first came here it was to go down there, to be the first man to set foot on Titan's surface. And you refused. I thought you'd pop your cork!'

'That was for a stunt, a publicity adventure. What I ask you now is for science.'

'You said you didn't want to take the chance of contaminating the life forms.'

'And you, Dr. Cardenas,' Urbain countered, turning

393

toward the nanotechnology expert, 'told me that you could decontaminate his suit with nanomachines.'

'I don't care what I said,' Cardenas said hotly. 'Manny's not going to Titan. Period!'

'Now wait a minute, Kris,' Gaeta said, still grinning. 'This is big. I could get Fritz and a top crew here for this stunt.'

'It's not a stunt!' Urbain insisted.

'You're not going!' Cardenas repeated, just as adamantly.

Jeanmarie said, 'Don't you see, Dr. Cardenas? Mr. Gaeta is my husband's last hope. His career, the entire investigation of Titan's surface, depends on him.'

'Your husband's career,' Cardenas replied. 'Manny's life.'

'But—'

'He could get killed down there.'

'Hold on, Kris,' Gaeta said. 'If I could get Fritz and his people to run the mission I could be the first human being on Titan. That's worth a lot.'

'Is it worth your life?'

'It won't be that dangerous,' Gaeta said. 'I go down, put your package of nanos on the lander and come back up. Piece of cake.'

'Manny, no. I can't go through this again.'

'Last time, Kris.'

'That's what you said about going to the rings for Wunderly.'

'And I got through that okay, didn't I?'

Urbain could see the fire in Cardenas' eyes. And the desire in Gaeta's.

'Look,' Gaeta said to her. 'Lemme call Fritz, see what he thinks. He wouldn't let me stick my head in a noose.'

'Not much.'

'And if Fritz thinks this stunt is worthwhile, he'll zoom out here on a torch ship and run the whole operation. Just like old times.'

Cardenas started to reply but no words came from her

mouth, only a half-strangled sound that might have been a sigh or a growl or a muffled wail of despair. She stamped off toward the path that led to the village. Gaeta hurried to catch up with her.

'He will do it,' Urbain said, his voice shaky, breathless.

'Yes,' said Jeanmarie. 'I only hope that it will not destroy his relationship with Dr. Cardenas.'

Urbain almost said, What of it? But one look at his wife's distraught face made him hold his tongue.

20 May 2096: Simulations Laboratory

Fritz von Helmholtz fought back the smile that wanted to form on his normally stern face. This morning his team of technicians had towed the massive excursion suit into the sim lab and stood it up on its feet. Gaeta had climbed into the armored suit with all the grinning enthusiasm of a little boy.

'Ready for the sim run.' Gaeta's voice came from the communications computer's speaker, clearly excited.

Von Helmholtz turned to the technician at the main console. 'Initiate the landing procedure,' he said calmly.

Friederich Johann von Helmholtz was a short, slim, almost delicately-built man. He could be cold, even arrogant; he was always meticulous, demanding. In Gaeta's eyes, Fritz was the best damned technician in the solar system. Wearing his customary immaculate white, crisply-pressed coveralls over his usual old-fashioned slate-gray three-piece business suit, he stood beside the looming excursion suit, his buzz-cut head barely reaching its waist, looking it over with a practiced eye. It appeared no worse for wear than the last time he'd seen it, more than eight months earlier. A few new dents from Gaeta's little frolic through Saturn's B ring, but nothing substantial.

Today's simulation run was to practice Gaeta's landing on Titan. That officious little scientist, Urbain, had insisted that Manny land directly on top of the landing vehicle itself, not on the surface of the moon. He didn't want to take any chances on contaminating the lifeforms living on Titan. He didn't mind taking chances with the lifeform from Earth that had agreed to repair his ailing vehicle, Fritz grumbled silently.

Good enough, though, von Helmholtz reasoned. The ground around the lander could be muddy, viscous, difficult to walk on, dangerous to deal with. Of course, the more danger involved in a stunt, he knew, the bigger the audience that paid to witness it. With virtual reality circuitry, the audience even got the illusion that they themselves were experiencing the stunt. And the bigger the audience, the more money. This excursion to Titan's surface – this mission to rescue a defunct robot – was already contracted to the biggest news media combine in the Earth/Moon system. We'll make millions out of this, von Helmholtz told himself. Tens of millions, perhaps even a hundred million.

My task, he knew, is to make the mission as safe as possible. The audience should experience a perception of danger, of risk. I am here to maximize their perception, but to minimize the actual danger to my stuntman. He recalled all the other stunts that he and Gaeta had worked on together. The danger was always there; without it, there would be no audience interest, no money flowing in. He realized that although he and Gaeta lived with danger, Gaeta was the only one who could get killed if anything went wrong.

Von Helmholtz pursed his lips, then walked out of the simulation chamber and back to the consoles strung along the laboratory's rear wall.

'We're ready to initiate the landing sequence,' said the technician seated at the main console.

Von Helmholtz said curtly, 'Begin.'

The walls of the simulation chamber seemed to evaporate, replaced by three-dimensional views of Titan's surface.

'Looks like a cloudy day,' Gaeta quipped.

Von Helmholtz frowned at the comm console's technician as if she had said it. 'No jokes, please,' he said in his precise, clipped accent.

'*Si, generalissimo*,' Gaeta replied. 'Strictly business.'

'Yes,' replied von Helmholtz. 'Strictly business, if you please.'

*　　*　　*

397

Cardenas was going through the presentation for the third time, and getting more than a little irritated about it.

'Here are the final results,' she said, pointing to the graph displayed on Urbain's office wall. 'As you can see, all traces of biologically active materials have been broken down by the nanos, leaving nothing but inorganics such as carbon dioxide and hydrogen compounds that quickly dissipate.'

Urbain sat at the circular conference table in the corner of his office, frowning at the graph as if he didn't trust it. Flanking him were Yolanda Negroponte and another biologist.

'And the nanomachines themselves?' Urbain asked. 'What of them?'

'They self-destruct,' Cardenas replied, the same answer she'd given twice earlier when Urbain had asked the same question.

Urbain glanced uneasily at his two biologists. They said nothing.

'I can show you photomicrographic evidence of the nanos going inert,' Cardenas said.

'Inert is not destroyed,' said Urbain.

Cardenas forced a smile. 'Once they go inert, they're nothing more than nanometer-sized bits of dust. They're not vampires; they don't rise from the dead.'

'They're not living creatures at all,' said Negroponte, almost condescendingly. 'They're just nanometer-sized machines.'

Urbain scowled at her.

'That's right,' Cardenas agreed. 'They're just very small machines.'

'They successfully clean all the contaminants from the exterior of the stuntman's suit,' Urbain said. It was halfway between a question and a statement of fact.

Cardenas suppressed a flare of annoyance at the word 'stuntman,' but replied as pleasantly as she could, 'Yes, they completely break down all the biologicals.'

'And you can apply the nanos to the suit after the man gets inside it and seals it up?' asked the other biologist, a pert, freckle-faced redhead.

'Yes, that's the plan.'

'So there will be no contaminants on the suit's exterior when he goes to Titan's surface,' said Negroponte.

'That's right,' Cardenas said tightly.

Urbain hiked his brows, lowered them, brushed his moustache with a fingertip, shrugged his shoulders. Finally he said, 'Then we can proceed to decontaminate the suit just before he leaves on the mission.'

'The plan,' Cardenas said, 'is to do the decontamination procedure in the transfer ship's airlock, just before he goes down to Titan's surface.'

Urbain nodded and said, 'Very well. Thank you, Dr. Cardenas.'

Cardenas picked up her palmcomp and left Urbain's office with nothing more than a terse farewell. As she walked out of the building and headed back through the morning sunlight toward her own lab, she thought, Manny's going through with this. No matter what I've said, no matter how I've pleaded with him, he's going through with it. Like a kid with a new toy. Like a man hooked on a narcotic drug. He's obsessed with the idea of doing this mission. I'm playing second fiddle to this . . . this stunt he wants to do.

No, she told herself. It's not just that he wants to do it. He *needs* to do it. There's no way in heaven or hell that I can stop him. He's going to go through with this even if it kills him.

I've got a rival, she realized. Until he gets past this mission, I'm not the most important thing in his life. What will he be like once he's finished the stunt? Will he come back to me?

What if the stunt kills him? What will I do then?

'You heard the man,' Timoshenko said sourly, 'we're supposed to have this problem solved before election day.'

Habib looked up from his computer display. 'Eberly? He said that?'

'At the last debate. He promised.'

Habib muttered, 'A politician's promise.'

Timoshenko had come to the computer center to witness the crucial test of Habib's prediction scheme. If the man's work was right, there should be a surge from Saturn's magnetic field some time this morning. For his part, Timoshenko had increased the shielding on the superconducting wires that spanned the habitat's outer shell and put in place electronic back-ups that automatically shunted power when a surge caused dangerous voltage hikes in the habitat's electrical circuitry.

'Well,' said Habib softly, 'there's nothing to do now except wait.'

Timoshenko did not enjoy waiting. He paced impatiently among the dozen men and women at their work stations, all of them bent over the work on their own screens and trying to ignore the Russian's impatient footsteps clicking along the tiled floor. Hands clasped behind his back, face squinched into a dark scowl, Timoshenko paced and fidgeted, glanced at the wall clock, paced and fidgeted some more.

'Try to relax,' Habib said, looking up as Timoshenko reached his work station. 'You can't force it to happen.'

'I know. I know.'

The minutes dragged by. Timoshenko thought of Eberly as he marched to and fro across the computer center. Eberly. The man had never spoken with Katrina. Never. Eberly's whole story about Katrina joining him here had been nothing but a lie, a damned lie, a trick to get him to accept the job as chief of maintenance. Katrina would never come out here. Never. Why should she? Why would anyone leave Earth to come to join me in exile? She doesn't want to be with me.

I'll kill him, Timoshenko told himself. Sooner or later, I'll kill

Eberly and myself and everyone in this tin can of a Siberia. I'll put an end to this misery once and for all.

'Try to relax,' Habib repeated.

You try, Timoshenko answered silently. But he stopped pacing and pulled up a little wheeled chair to sit next to Habib. Half a minute later he sprang to his feet and began pacing again.

'Shouldn't you be in touch with your staff people?' Habib suggested mildly.

'No,' the Russian snapped. 'Either the shielding works or it doesn't. Either the automatic relays do their job properly or they don't. My people have done their jobs. Now we wait for the real test.'

'You're going to give yourself a heart attack,' Habib warned.

'My heart wouldn't dare attack me.'

'But if you don't—' The curve on Habib's screen that displayed the intensity of Saturn's magnetosphere began to kink visibly.

'Wait. I think it's coming.'

Timosheko raced back to the chair and plopped on it.

'Yes,' said Habib, pointing with a trembling finger. 'It's spiking rapidly.'

Timoshenko stared at the ragged curve. It rose, writhing like a thing alive, jagged peaks and small dips between them climbing, climbing.

'It's a big one,' Habib murmured.

The intensity continued to climb for several minutes while the two men stared at the screen, hardly breathing. Then it began to go down again.

Habib blinked, then looked around. All the others were still bent over the screens as if nothing had happened.

'Nothing happened,' Timosheko said.

Breaking into a huge grin, Habib said, 'Yes! Exactly! We've just experienced a monster spike and nothing happened. No power outages. The lights didn't even blink!'

Timoshenko yanked his palmcomp out of his pocket. 'I'll check with my staff. I need a full report – every circuit.'

As he pecked out the numbers on his handheld he realized that if there had been an outage anywhere his phone would be ringing. It worked, he told himself. We've learned how to prevent the outages.

And he knew that the same knowledge could be used to totally shut down all the electrical systems in the habitat, when he wanted to end it all.

Holly was surprised that Douglas Stavenger himself answered her call to Selene. She had heard earlier from George Ambrose, the chief administrator of the asteroidal miners' headquarters at Ceres, who had confirmed that he'd communicated with Eberly.

'We'll buy water ice from you blokes soon's you can ship it to us,' Ambrose had said, replying to Holly's call. Since there was nearly an hour's lag time in communications between Saturn and the Asteroid Belt, even at the speed of light, conversations were impossible. Holly called in the morning, Ambrose replied several hours later.

'You asked about the price your chief administrator quoted,' Ambrose had said, his shaggy red-maned face filling Holly's phone screen. 'He was kinda vague about it, but I got the impression it'd be less'n half what it costs us now for squeezin' water outta the carbonaceous rocks here in the Belt.'

Ambrose had rattled on for more than a quarter-hour, then bid Holly farewell with a cheery, 'You got any more questions, just zip 'em to me. I'll be happy to deal with you blokes.'

Douglas Stavenger was completely different. Holly had sent her message to the chairman of Selene's governing council. All day she had waited for a reply. She was getting ready for sleep when his return call came in.

Now she sat cross-legged on her bed while Stavenger spoke. He looked much younger than Holly had expected, and his face seemed to be about the same skin tone as her own. He's been the power-behind-the-throne at Selene for ages, Holly thought. How can he look so young? And handsome.

'I'm answering your query because the council doesn't want to make a formal declaration as yet. Your Mr. Eberly made it clear that his inquiry was . . . well, not secret, exactly, but sensitive.'

Just like Malcolm, Holly said to herself. He does everything in whispers.

'Selene manufactures its own water from oxygen in the lunar regolith,' Stavenger explained, 'and hydrogen blowing in on the solar wind. We also extract water from the frozen caches at the poles.'

And they sell water to the other settlements on the Moon, Holly knew.

'However, if habitat *Goddard* could supply us water at a price lower than our existing costs, we'd be foolish not to consider the offer very seriously.'

That means they'll take it, depending on the price, Holly figured.

'On the other hand,' Stavenger said, 'there's a good deal of excitement in the scientific community Earthside about one of your people finding living creatures in the rings. The university consortium is already holding discussion with the IAA about banning all commercial activities in Saturn's rings. If that happens, it would make mining the rings politically impossible.'

Unless Malcolm's willing to risk going to war with the IAA, Holly replied silently.

'The thing is,' Stavenger went on, 'water is the key to expansion here on the Moon. And elsewhere in the solar system as well, I should think.'

Holly almost asked him what he meant, but she knew he wouldn't hear her question for more than an hour. Instead, she continued to listen as Stavenger spelled out, 'You see, we can get along all right on the water available to us now. We recycle pretty thoroughly. There are some losses, of course: no system is one hundred per cent perfect. But if we had a reliable, continuous supply of additional water we could expand and build new settlements here on the Moon. Lord knows there are plenty of people anxious to get away from Earth and live here. But we've always had to limit our growth to our water supply. Increase the water supply and Selene can grow; we could even spin off daughter cities. We could raise the Moon's population from a few thousands to millions.'

Holly sank back on her pillows. This is cosmic, she said to herself. We hold the key to the growth of human settlements all across the system!

'But the IAA is most likely going to ban commercial activities in the rings, at least until the scientists can thoroughly study the ring creatures, and that might take years.' Almost as an afterthought Stavenger added, 'Maybe you should think of other sources of water. After all, you're a lot closer to the TNOs that anyone else in the solar system.'

'TNOs?' Holly asked, puzzled.

'I hope that answers your questions, Ms. Lane. Please feel free to call me personally if you'd like to discuss this further.'

The phone screen went blank, leaving Holly thinking, Trans-Neptunian Objects, that's what he means. The Kuiper Belt. There's zillions of icebergs out there; that's where comets come from.

She shook her head, though. Too far away. We might be closer to 'em than anybody else, but they're still more'n twenty Astronomical Units away from us. Just too far to be practical.

I think.

27 May 2096:
Mission Planning Session

Urbain was surprised at how crowded the conference room was. His own team of a dozen mission control engineers sat along one side of the long table, talking among themselves, while this von Helmholtz person and his half-dozen technicians lined up on the other side. Then there was Gaeta himself, of course, and Dr. Cardenas. Gaeta looked quite relaxed; she was obviously tense, her normally sunny, cheerful face drawn and tight-lipped. Below them Pancho Lane and Jake Wanamaker sat together, and down at the foot of the table sat Berkowitz, chatting amiably with Wanamaker. Why the news director had to be in on this meeting, Urbain could not fathom.

I suppose I should be grateful that Eberly didn't insist on joining in as well, he said to himself.

From his chair at the head of the table Urbain called the meeting to order. The separate little conversations stopped. All heads turned to him.

'We are here this morning to make a final review of the mission plan,' Urbain said.

Halfway down the table, Pancho muttered, 'Speak now or forever hold your peace.'

Suppressing a frown, Urbain said, 'Herr von Helmholtz, if you please.'

Fritz touched a pad on the keyboard in front of him, and the wall on the opposite side of the room lit up. It showed an image of Titan's surface with the location of *Alpha* indicated by a red dot.

'The plan calls for flying a transfer vehicle from the habitat to orbit around Titan. From there, our man will leave the transfer craft in an aeroshell protective heat shield and enter Titan's atmosphere. At an altitude of three thousand meters above the ground, he will collapse the aeroshell and parasail the remainder of the way down, to land within one hundred meters of the *Alpha* machine.'

A dotted red circle sprang up around the red spot on the display.

Urbain interrupted, 'The plan calls for him to land atop *Alpha*. He is not to set foot on the surface. He is not to contaminate the organisms living there.'

Von Helmholtz dipped his chin once, barely. 'He will attempt to land atop the vehicle, but there is no guarantee that the parasail descent will be that accurate.'

'I'll land on its roof,' Gaeta said. 'Don't worry.'

'Even if he lands on the ground,' said one of Urbain's engineers, '*Alpha* itself has driven over the area. Its tracks have crunched through the ice.'

'But *Alpha* was thoroughly decontaminated before landing,' Urbain protested. 'Sterilized by gamma radiation.'

Cardenas hunched forward in her chair. 'Manny's suit will be decontaminated by nanomachines. His boots as well. He'll be just as clean as your lander. Cleaner.'

'Still—'

'I'll land on your machine's roof,' Gaeta repeated. 'I've done a lot of parasailing. In that thick atmosphere with its low wind velocities, I'll hit its roof. Don't worry about it.'

Urbain wanted to reply but thought better of it. This is a compromise I must accept, he told himself. If this braggart of a stuntman can touch down on *Alpha*'s roof, fine. If not, I must depend on Cardenas's nanomachines to prevent contamination of the surface. In the back of his mind, though, he worried about the nanomachines themselves. What if they were not deactivated after sterilizing Gaeta's suit? What if they began to multiply there on the ground? Devouring everything in sight?

Von Helmholtz cleared his throat, forcing Urbain's

attention to return to him. He continued, 'Once atop the landing vehicle, our man's first tasks will be to examine the lander's uplink antenna and then establish a communications link with your machine's central computer.'

'And use the nanos he'll be carrying to build a new uplink antenna,' said the communications engineer.

'If necessary,' said Habib. 'He might discover a programming glitch that can be corrected on-site.'

Before the comm engineer could reply, Urbain said, 'Yes, we all understand. Achieve a linkage with the master program, then use the nanomachines Dr. Cardenas has designed to build a new uplink antenna, if necessary.'

'Once an uplink connection has been made,' Fritz resumed, looking directly at Urbain, 'our man will activate his escape thrusters and leave the surface. He will be picked up by the transfer vehicle waiting in orbit and returned here to the habitat.'

The wall screen now showed a yellow-gray ball representing Titan with a curving green line rising from its surface to intersect with the bright blue circle representing the transfer craft's orbit.

'Very well,' Urbain said, his eyes on the display. 'Are there any questions?'

No one spoke.

'You all understand your duties and are prepared to carry them out?'

Heads bobbed up and down the table.

Then Fritz cleared his throat again, noisily.

'Herr von Helmholtz?' Urbain said. 'You have a question?'

'A comment,' said Fritz. 'A suggestion, actually. I believe this mission would benefit from another few weeks of training and simulation runs.'

'Another few weeks?'

'We have had less than ten days to prepare for this mission. It is a complicated mission, involving a high degree of risk for our man.'

'That's what I get paid for, Fritz,' Gaeta said.

Ignoring him, Fritz went on, 'In addition, our man will be on the surface for only one hour. The mission objectives must be completed in one hour. That is . . . quite difficult.'

'I can do it,' Gaeta replied. 'An hour's plenty of time.'

Von Helmholtz arched a brow at Gaeta, then continued, 'Failure of this mission would mean that your lander remains dead on Titan's surface.'

'Asleep,' Urbain growled. 'Not dead.'

Spreading his hands in a *what's the difference* gesture, Fritz pointed out, 'If this mission fails your lander will remain silent and useless, with no possibility of reactivating it. It will be totally written off, will it not?'

Urbain's mind was racing as he stared at von Helmholtz's icy, hard-eyed face. We cannot postpone the mission, he said to himself. Wunderly has already reached Earth, she is already being honored for finding the creatures in the rings. We must rescue *Alpha* now, before Wunderly steals all the glory, before she meets with the Nobel committee.

He saw that all eyes were turned to him. Slowly, as if it took an effort to make the decision, Urbain replied, 'It is vital that we re-establish communication with *Alpha* before the master program begins to dump the data that her sensors have accumulated. That is our most important task. *Alpha* carries a treasure of data about the conditions on Titan's surface and the organisms that live there. We cannot risk losing that data by postponing this mission.'

'Even at the risk of a man's life?' von Helmholtz insisted.

'That's not a fair question, Fritz,' Gaeta said. 'I'm the guy who's taking the risk. We've worked out the mission plan. I'll be okay.'

'You are willing to go without more training?' Urbain felt a flood of relief gushing through him.

'Yeah. Why the hell not?'

Gaeta grinned, coolly confident. Fritz scowled at him. Cardenas looked as if she wanted to clout somebody.

28 May 2096: Departure

Kris Cardenas woke from a troubled sleep to find Gaeta already up and dressing. She watched him for a sleep-fogged moment, then realized that this was the morning he would leave her for Titan.

She sat up, letting the bedsheet fall to her waist. Gaeta looked at her and grinned.

'Don't try to get me back into bed, Kris,' he bantered. 'I can't take advantage of your luscious body 'til I get back.'

'You're really going,' she murmured, knowing it sounded stupid as the words left her lips.

His grin faded. 'I'm really going.'

'You don't have to.'

'Hey, I got Fritz to round up a top crew and fly all the way out here. We got a contract with PanGlobal News. I gotta go through with it.'

'Even if I ask you not to?'

He sat on the bed beside her and began to tug on his softboots. 'Don't make this into a competition, Kris.'

'Do it tomorrow,' she blurted. 'Put it off for twenty-four hours.'

He shook his head slowly. 'It'll be the same deal tomorrow, kid. And you'll be just as clanked up about it.'

She looked into his deep brown eyes and knew that if she put it on an either/or basis he would choose to do the mission and leave her waiting for him to return. And she knew she would wait. She would wait and worry and fear that he'd get killed, but she would never leave him even though he'd chosen danger and risk over her.

'I'll be back tomorrow,' he said lightly. 'In time for dinner, probably. Pick which restaurant you want to celebrate in.'

'I don't want to lose you!'

He leaned over, grasping her by her bare shoulders, kissed her soundly. 'You won't lose me, kid. You can't ever lose me. I'll come back to you.'

She flung her arms around his neck and tried to hold back the tears that threatened to engulf her.

Gently, Gaeta disengaged from her and got to his feet. 'I'll be back, *querida*. Wait for me in bed.'

He turned and headed for the door. He slid it open, blew her a kiss, and then left her sitting in bed. Cardenas wanted to cry, but she couldn't. He was gone. He had left her. The fear that she would never see him again was too terrifying for mere tears.

Gaeta's cheerful grin disappeared once he left the apartment. He knew better than Cardenas the risks he was facing. He had tried to appear optimistic for her, but now, as he straddled one of the electrobikes racked in front of the white-walled apartment building and began pedaling through the bright morning sunshine, he started reviewing the details of the mission he faced.

Paragliding through the smoggy air of Titan onto the back of Urbain's sleeping machine. Gaeta shook his head as he engaged the bike's little electrical motor. Well, he thought, it'll make good video for the audience. Not an easy assignment, though. Not easy at all.

By the time he reached the steel-walled chamber that fronted the airlock down at the habitat's endcap, Pancho, Wanamaker, Fritz and his crew were already there. So was the news guy, Berkowitz.

'Our star performer is only fifteen minutes late,' said Fritz stiffly.

Gaeta sauntered past him and up to the excursion suit, towering like a monument to past glories over the team of technicians.

'C'mon, Fritz,' Gaeta said, 'I know you. You built a half-hour of slop into the schedule at least.'

Berkowitz had two minicams trundling along beside him on wheeled monopods, balancing like unicycles, and held a third camera in his hands.

'Any words for posterity before you climb into your suit?' he asked Gaeta.

Pancho called from across the chamber, 'What's posterity ever done for us?'

'I'll have to edit that out,' Berkowitz said, his usual smile dimming a bit.

Gaeta said to the newsman, 'This mission is a lot more than a stunt. My job is to try to revive Dr. Urbain's probe down on the surface of Titan. I'm working for the scientists now.'

Berkowitz nodded and said, 'Good enough. We can embellish it later.'

Fritz tapped Gaeta on the shoulder. 'If you're finished with your publicity, would it be too much to ask that you get into the suit?'

Gaeta made a mock bow. 'I'd be happy to, old pal.'

Pancho and Wanamaker were at the airlock hatch, he saw.

'We're going aboard the transfer craft,' Pancho said, as much to Berkowitz as to Fritz. 'Gotta check out the bird and make sure it's ready to go.'

Fritz nodded curtly.

Urbain had gone to his office before dawn. Too nervous to sit at his desk, though, he paced along the corridor that led to the mission control center. The technicians were filing in, one by one, and taking their places at their consoles.

'This will be the most important day of our lives,' Urbain told them.

They nodded half-heartedly and muttered agreement as they started to power up their consoles.

Urbain watched them, thinking, Wunderly has reached Earth and made her presentation to the ICU governing board. In another few days she will meet with the Nobel committee. I must have some solid results to show from *Alpha* by then. I can't have her stealing the spotlight after all the work I've put into *Alpha*. My creature must begin to send us data from Titan. It must!

Cardenas was still in bed, unable to make a decision about how to spend her day. The phone jingled.

Startled, she said to herself, It can't be Manny! 'Answer,' she called out.

Yolanda Negroponte's face appeared on the tiny screen of the bedside phone console. Cardenas clutched the sheet to her.

'Oh,' said Negroponte. 'I'm sorry to wake you, Dr. Cardenas.'

'I'm . . . I was . . .' Cardenas stuttered. Then, 'It's all right. I was already awake.'

'I wonder if I can pick your brain,' Negroponte said. 'I have a problem and I need your help.'

Go away and don't bother me, Cardenas wanted to snap. Instead she said to the image in the phone screen, 'I can meet you at the cafeteria in half an hour. Will that be all right?'

Negroponte appeared to think it over for a few moments. 'Could you come to the biology lab, instead? I'll pick up breakfast and we can eat in the lab. Will that be all right?'

Suddenly Cardenas was grateful for something to do, some excuse for getting out of bed, some reason to at least try to stop worrying about Manny.

'That will be fine,' she said. 'The bio lab in half an hour.'

Pancho stood before the control board of the transfer craft, scanning all the panels with a practiced eye.

Standing beside her, Wanamaker said, 'Everything's in the green except the airlock.'

'I left it open,' Pancho replied, 'so's Manny can tromp in without having to cycle it.'

Wanamaker nodded. He watched as Pancho's hands played over the control panels as deftly as a concert pianist's. She's in her element, he thought. She's good at this and happy to be in a ship.

'You're enjoying this, aren't you?' he asked.

Pancho looked at him. 'Yep, guess so.'

'You're a fly girl by nature.'

'Beats sittin' on my butt wondering how to spend my money.'

Wanamaker laughed. 'I suppose it does.'

'The decon nanos are aboard?'

'In their container in the airlock. I'll help Manny apply them once he's outside.'

Pancho nodded. 'Just be careful—'

Fritz's crisp, slightly annoyed voice came through the speaker, 'Our intrepid hero is ready to board your ship.'

Pancho tapped the communications keyboard. 'Copy Gaeta boarding.'

Wanamaker said, 'I'd better get down to the cargo bay and see that he gets in okay.'

Pancho replied, 'Stay out of his way, though. He's like a three-hundred-kilo gorilla in that suit.'

Beneath his icy exterior, Fritz von Helmholtz was quivering with apprehension. We should have taken more time to prepare for this mission. Ten days isn't enough. We should have taken a month for simulations and tests. Six weeks, even. I've allowed Urbain to rush us too quickly.

And Manuel is carrying nanomachines with him. Nanomachines! What if something goes wrong with them? What if they attack his suit? This mission is far more dangerous than Manuel is willing to admit.

Von Helmholtz squared his narrow shoulders and studied the displays his technicians were working with. It's up to me to keep Manny safe, he told himself. At the slightest sign of danger, the slightest deviation from our mission plan, I'll pull him out of there. Whether he likes it or not.

Inside the cumbersome suit Manny Gaeta felt like a giant, a titan of old, far more powerful than any mere mortal. With a clench of his fingers he could crush metal. With the servo-motors that reacted to his arms' movements he could lift tons of dead weight.

Yeah, and with an eyeblink's worth of carelessness you can get yourself killed, suit or no suit, he warned himself. Remember that.

'Closin' airlock hatch.' Pancho's voice sounded in his helmet earphones.

Gaeta could see Wanamaker standing by the cargo bay hatch in his flight coveralls. The ex-admiral looked wary, on guard, as his eyes flicked from Gaeta to the airlock hatch behind the massive suit.

'Airlock hatch closed,' he said in a flat, noncommittal voice.

'Ready to separate,' Pancho said.

A heartbeat of hesitation, than Fritz's voice replied, 'You are go for separation.'

'Separating,' said Pancho.

Gaeta felt the slightest of tremors. The transfer ship was no longer connected to the mammoth habitat. The sense of weight dwindled to nothing.

'We're off for Titan,' Pancho sang out.

'And we are off to the mission control center,' came Fritz's frosty voice, 'where Dr. Urbain has graciously permitted us to use one of the consoles.' His accent on *one* dripped with acid.

28 May 2096: Titan Orbit

'Circularization complete.' Pancho's voice jarred in Gaeta's helmet earphones. She hollered as if she were shouting to someone on the other side of a canyon.

It had taken them six hours to fly from habitat *Goddard* to Titan on a high-thrust burn and establish the transfer craft in a circular orbit above the dirty orange smog-ridden moon.

Gaeta had stood inside the big armored excursion suit all that time; there was no room in the cargo bay to get out and walk around. Being in zero *g* helped: his heart could pump weightless blood much more efficiently. He flexed his legs as much as he could, pulled his arms out of the sleeves and munched on a meager breakfast of muffins and lukewarm coffee. Fritz'll bitch about the crumbs, he thought, almost giggling. Give him something to complain about when I get back.

Now the work begins.

In the mission control center, von Helmholtz scowled at the single console he had at his disposal. All the other consoles were manned by Urbain's people; the chief scientist himself had left the center and gone back to his own office.

Von Helmholtz's half-dozen technicians crowded behind Fritz as he sat down and powered up the console. This will be the primary link with Manuel, Fritz told himself. The rest of them are connected to satellite sensors and to *Alpha* itself. I am connected to Manuel. His safety depends on me.

*   *   *

Wanamaker pushed through the hatch that connected to the transfer vessel's bridge.

'Are you okay? Need anything?'

'I'm fine, Jake,' Gaeta said, careful to keep the volume of his suit's speakers down to a moderate level. 'Ready to go out and get started.'

'Okay. I'll join you as soon as the lock cycles and I can pull on my suit.'

Gaeta nodded inside his helmet. Wanamaker went back to the bridge.

'You're clear for EVA,' Pancho sang out.

Dialing the volume control even lower, Gaeta slid his arms back into the suit's sleeves and replied, 'Entering airlock.'

He stepped ponderously into the tight metal womb of the airlock and sealed its inner hatch. Once he was outside the ship, he knew, Wanamaker would come into the cargo bay, worm himself into a nanosuit, then come outside to help him decontaminate the suit with Kris' nanoscrubbers. Then he had to climb into the aeroshell and thruster package.

The telltales on the airlock bulkhead cycled from green, through amber, and finally to red. Gaeta barely felt the pumps' vibration through the thick soles of his boots.

''Lock's in the red,' Pancho called.

'Copy red,' said Gaeta. 'Opening outer hatch.'

He leaned a gloved hand on the control stud and the outer airlock hatch swung slowly open. At first all Gaeta could see was the infinite black of space. Then the filtering of his visor adjusted and pinpoints of stars stared back at him. Off to his right he could see the curve of Titan's orange clouds, looking somehow sickly, almost a sallow yellow. Like a bad day in L.A., he said to himself.

Then Saturn swung into view, huge, brilliant, those impossible rings hanging like swirls of diamonds above its middle. Gaeta could see bands of clouds eddying across the planet's immense bulk, storm systems bigger than Earth surging through the delicate saffron cloud tops.

'You goin' out?' Pancho asked.

Gaeta forced his attention to the metal frame of the airlock hatch. Gripping it with both hands, he said curtly, 'Stepping out.'

Sitting on a stool in the bio lab, Cardenas tried not to look at her wrist, nor at the digital clock on the wall above Negroponte's work bench. She knew Manny's mission plan by heart. He should be just stepping out of the transfer rocket now and starting to get into the aeroshell heat shield.

'Are the muffins all right?'

Cardenas snapped her attention to Negroponte's long, almond-eyed face. The biologist looked very serious, almost worried.

'The muffins,' Negroponte asked again. 'Are they all right? The cafeteria didn't have—'

'They're fine,' Cardenas said. 'My mind wandered. I'm sorry.'

Four smallish muffins remained on the makeshift placemat that Negroponte had spread upon her workbench, together with the crumbs of the two the women were already chewing on and a pair of steaming plastic coffee mugs. A working breakfast.

'Just what is it that you wanted to show me?' Cardenas asked, wiping crumbs from her lips and then reaching for her coffee.

Negroponte pushed her hair back off her face with both hands. 'These bugs that Nadia discovered . . .' Her voice trailed off.

'Bugs?' Despite herself Cardenas smiled. 'Is that the biological term for them?'

Utterly serious, Negroponte replied, 'I don't know what to call them. I don't even know if they're actually alive.'

'But Nadia said—'

'I know. I worked with her. We wrote the report together.'

'And you said that the specimens in the ice particles were alive. "Biologically active" is the phrase you used, isn't it?'

Negroponte smiled minimally. 'You read our paper.'

'I certainly did.'

Negroponte clicked on the monitor screen at her elbow. Cardenas saw dark blobs pulsating slowly.

'The samples from the rings?' she guessed.

'Yes,' said Negroponte. 'The vid is speeded up by a factor of one hundred from real time.'

Eying the screen, Cardenas said, 'They move. They seem to interact with their environment. You've measured metabolic reactions in them. They're alive. What's the problem?'

'Is a virus alive?' Negroponte asked.

Cardenas hesitated. 'I'm not a biologist . . .'

'Don't be modest. You know the answer as well as I do.'

'So?'

'A virus can remain dormant, nothing more than a nano-meter-sized spore, for centuries. Millennia, even.'

'But when it comes in contact with a living cell—'

'It becomes active. It invades the cell's nucleus and takes over its reproductive machinery to produce more of itself.'

'And the cell eventually dies,' Cardenas said.

'Not before the virus has reproduced itself a millionfold or more.'

Nodding toward the display screen, Cardenas asked, 'You think the organisms in the rings are viruses?'

Negroponte shook her head solemnly. 'Let me ask my next question.'

'Go right ahead,' said Cardenas, intrigued.

'Is a nanomachine alive?'

Gaeta thought the aeroshell looked like a shallow bathtub. Attached to the hull of the transfer craft like an opened parasol, its white heat-shield ceramic exterior glowed warmly in the saffron light from Saturn. The return pod package stuck up above the shell like the fat handle of an umbrella. It contained the return rocket thruster and its fuel, and was covered in similar heat-resistant ceramic. It was connected to the aeroshell's rim by three slim buckyball struts.

Inside the armored excursion suit, Gaeta floated out to the end of the tether he'd attached to the transfer craft's hull, dangling in the emptiness of space while he waited for Wanamaker to stow the emptied container of decontaminating nanomachines back inside the airlock. Space isn't empty, he reminded himself. This vacuum is filled with hard radiation. He turned himself around by swinging his arms until he faced the overpowering radiance of Saturn and its rings. Down at the planet's south polar region he could see the bright shimmering of its aurora. Enough radiation to fry a man in seconds, Gaeta knew, if he wasn't protected.

The airlock hatch opened like a glowing eye in the shadowed darkness of the transfer ship's hull. A lone figure glided out, seemingly wearing nothing but coveralls. Gaeta knew that Wanamaker was in a suit composed of nanofibers, and he was protected as well as a man in a cumbersome old-fashioned hard-shell spacesuit. Still, he shook his head. They'll never get me in one of those flimsy damned things. Looks like nothing more than a plastic raincoat and hood.

'Ready to get into the bathtub?' Wanamaker's voice crackled slightly in Gaeta's earphones.

With a nod that Wanamaker couldn't see, Gaeta said, 'Let's do it before Fritz starts hyperventilating.'

Sure enough, von Helmholtz's testy, impatient voice came through from the mission control center aboard *Goddard*, 'You are already three minutes behind schedule. The timeline must be adhered to!'

'I'm getting into the aeroshell,' Gaeta answered. 'Don't get yourself lathered up.'

Timeline, he thought as he climbed up the rungs built into one of the connectors and slowly swung a leg over the rim of the aeroshell. Even in the microgravity of orbit it took an effort to move inside the suit. The servomotors could help with walking and normal leg movements; this maneuver was more like climbing into a saddle on a tall horse.

It unnerved Gaeta slightly to see Wanamaker puttering around him in nothing more substantial than the nanosuit.

'How's it feel inside that baggy?' he asked as he lowered himself to lay down on his back inside the aeroshell's bowl.

'Fine,' answered Wanamaker. 'A lot easier moving around than in a regular suit. Or that clunker you're in.'

'Clunker?' Gaeta bristled inwardly. 'This suit's seen me through a helluva lot of weird situations, pal.'

Wanamaker clicked the connecting clamps to rings fitted into the torso of Gaeta's suit. In the vacuum of space there was no sound, but Gaeta felt the hooks clicking into place. He was flat on his back now, staring up at the return pod package looming above him.

Fritz came back on the radio and went through the checklist with Wanamaker, who unhooked a hand-sized camera from the belt of his suit and played it over Gaeta's supine body, giving Fritz visual proof that every clamp was properly in place.

'Very well,' Fritz said, sounding reluctant. 'The connectors are set.'

God forbid that *fregado* should ever say he's satisfied with anything, Gaeta grumbled to himself.

'Admiral Wanamaker,' Fritz called. 'My congratulations. You've made up seventy full seconds of our timeline.'

'Thank you,' said Wanamaker.

Gaeta was too stunned to say anything.

Wanamaker rapped lightly on Gaeta's helmet. 'Good luck, buddy.'

Gaeta nodded again, even though he realized Wanamaker couldn't see it inside the suit's heavy helmet. 'Thanks, Jake.'

Wanamaker disappeared from his view. All that Gaeta could see now was the ceramic-coated return pod standing above him like a massive triphammer, ready to squash him flat. Beyond it, the stars: unwinking eyes staring down at him. The stars, he thought. What would it be like to fly to Alpha Centuari, or one of those stars that has Earth-sized planets orbiting around them? Are they really like other Earths? What a kick it would be to get there first, before anybody else, and see for myself what's there.

Dimly he heard Fritz and Pancho talking through the countdown. Fritz and his fuckin' timeline, Gaeta thought. We've got enough lag time in the schedule to do everything twice, just about.

Then he heard Pancho. 'On my mark, separation in ten seconds. Mark!'

Nine, eight . . . Gaeta counted with her.

At zero he felt a slight nudge in the small of his back. No sense of motion at all until the aeroshell yawed forty degrees as programmed. Saturn slid into his view, big and beautiful.

Gaeta realized that this might be the last time he saw it.

28 May 2096: Titan Entry

Clamped to the aeroshell, his hands and boots wedged into cleats built into the ends of the x-frame on which he was stretched, Gaeta lay on his back with nothing to do except think. His backpack contained the parasail that would float him down to Titan's surface, plus the life support system and the thermionic nuclear generator that powered his suit. The nuke can run the suit for weeks, Gaeta knew. But there's only a twelve-hour supply of fresh air and water, and I've gone through almost half of that already. The recyclers can stretch that to a couple of days if I need to.

He shook his head inside the helmet. I'm not staying inside this iron maiden for a couple of days, he told himself. Get down to Urbain's misbehaving machine, plug in the package of nanos, and get the hell back out again. One hour on the surface and then back to the transfer ship, and home to the habitat.

Back to Kris.

I'm staying down there just long enough to do the job and get credit for being the first man on Titan. In the headlines again. One last stunt. The best and the last.

'Aerodynamic heating has begun,' Fritz's voice announced, flat and cool. 'You should begin to experience some turbulence shortly.'

'Smooth so far,' Gaeta said.

He could see that the stars were drifting past now, and one side of the rocket pack above him looked brighter. It'll get cherry red before we're through, he knew.

The shell began to shudder, and for the first time since they'd gone into orbit around Titan Gaeta sensed a feeling of weight.

'Point five *g*,' Fritz voice said calmly. 'Point seven . . . point nine . . .'

The front face of the rocket pack was glowing now and Gaeta could see tongues of flame-hot gases flickering past the rim of the aeroshell. Good footage for the vids, Gaeta thought. I hope Berkowitz is getting it all down and transmitting it back to Earth.

The shell began to rock like a leaf tossed into a stormy sea. Gaeta felt nauseous. *Gesu Christo*, he thought, don't let me upchuck inside my helmet!

All around him the rim of the shell blazed with sheets of white-hot gas. Gaeta knew that the superconducting coil built into the rim of the shell enveloped him in a magnetic field that deflected the ionized gas away from him; still he sweated inside his suit. The shell started to shake so violently that Gaeta's vision blurred. The rocket pack hanging over him seemed to be on fire. He squeezed his eyes shut and tightened his grip on the cleats built into the bathtub, holding on as hard as he could.

'They can't be nanomachines,' Cardenas said, staring at the photomicrographs Negroponte had put onto her benchtop screen.

'But their nuclei are crystalline,' the biologist said, pointing with a long, manicured finger. 'They don't look biological at all.'

'Not terrestrial biology, that's for certain.'

Negroponte looked distressed. 'Dr. Cardenas, I—'

'Kris,' Cardenas said automatically.

'Kris, then.' Negroponte bit her lips, then went on, 'Nadia's back on Earth being congratulated for having found a new form of organisms in Saturn's rings. But maybe they're not organisms! Maybe they're machines, nanomachines.'

423

Cardenas shook her head stubbornly. 'They can't be nano-machines.'

'Why not?'

'Because nanomachines don't exist in nature. Somebody has to build them.' Before Negroponte could reply, Cardenas added, 'And we sure didn't. Besides, they're not like any nanos that I've ever seen.'

'But what if they *were* built by someone? Someone other than us?'

'Intelligent aliens? Machine-building aliens?' Cardenas tried to scoff at the idea, but could only manage a weak snicker.

'It's not impossible,' Negroponte said. 'Those giant whale things in Jupiter's ocean might be intelligent. And there's that artifact in the Belt . . .'

'That's nothing more than a rumor.'

'Is it?'

'Isn't it?'

Negroponte got up from her laboratory stool stiffly, as if she'd been sitting there too long. Gesturing at the display screen, 'They are not biological organisms,' she said firmly. 'I'm convinced of that.'

'Despite the paper you and Wunderly wrote.'

Nodding, 'Despite our paper.'

Cardenas looked from the biologist's distraught face to the display screen showing the crystalline lattice of the ring creature's nucleus and back to Negroponte again.

'Look, you're dealing with extraterrestrial biology here. It doesn't have to look like our own.'

'The Martian organisms have a recognizable analog of DNA in their nuclei. So do the airborne biota of Jupiter.'

'They can't be machines,' Cardenas insisted. 'Who built them? There are no intelligent creatures in the solar system capable of that level of technology except us, and we certainly didn't put those things in Saturn's rings.'

Negroponte replied immediately, 'Perhaps whoever built them has gone.'

'You mean they're extinct?'

The biologist shrugged her shoulders. 'Or perhaps they were visitors from another star system and they seeded our worlds.'

'With nanomachines?'

'And life.'

Cardenas sank back onto her lab stool. 'Sheer speculation, Yolanda.' Yet she felt a tendril of fear shimmering along her spine.

'TNOs?' Tavalera looked both surprised and annoyed as he sat across the cafeteria table from Holly.

She nodded enthusiastically. 'Stavenger put the idea into my head. There's zillions of 'em! That's where comets come from.'

The cafeteria was half empty at mid-afternoon, but still there was enough clattering of dishware and chattering of conversations to force Tavalera to raise his voice.

'But Neptune's orbit is more'n twenty Astronomical Units from here,' he objected. 'That's twice as far as we are from the Sun, for chrissakes.'

'I know,' Holly said as she chomped heartily on a pseudo-burger. She gulped down what was in her mouth, then went on, 'I thought it was too far, too. But then I looked into the astrogation program.'

Tavalera's face fell. 'Don't tell me, I already know: It's not distance *per se* but delta vee that counts. I studied astrogation, you know.'

'So you understand,' Holly said. 'From where we are we could send ships out to the Kuiper Belt and pick up really big chunks of ice and nudge them into orbits that'll bring them here. Or to the earth/moon system, or the asteroid belt, wherever! They'll be going downhill, gravitationally, once we push 'em a little.'

Despite himself, Tavalera grinned at her excitement. 'You could get your sister to run the operation.'

'Right! Panch would love it!'

He took a forkful of his own burger and munched on it thoughtfully for a few moments while Holly said, 'I knew you'd understand, Raoul. We could get water without mining the rings. We could rich without running into a ban from the IAA.'

'You know,' Tavalera said grudgingly, 'you wouldn't even have to go out to the Kuiper Belt.'

'What do you mean?'

'Comets come our way all the time. They get perturbed out of their TNO orbits and fall into the inner solar system.'

'Only one or two each year,' she said.

'More like ten or twelve. But they're big, Holly. Kilometers across. A year's worth of water in each one of 'em. More.'

'We could capture comets!'

Tavalera nodded. 'You could become the water supplier for Selene and everybody else without touching the rings.'

'Utterly cosmic! Wait'll I spring this on Eberly.' Holly was bouncing on her chair so hard people at other tables turned to stare at her. 'I can't wait for the next debate!'

Tavalera realized he had just slit his own throat.

28 May 2096: Free Fall

The shaking slowed and then stopped altogether. Gaeta opened his eyes. The bath of fiery gases that surrounded the aeroshell had dimmed considerably. He felt weight, felt the shell swaying to and fro as it dropped like a falling leaf through the thick, murky cloud layer of Titan's atmosphere.

No stars to be seen. He thought about activating the infrared viewing system but that would mean letting go of the hand cleats to press buttons on the keypad built into the wrist of his suit. He had no intention of releasing his grip on the cleats. Not yet, he told himself. Ride this sucker down as far as she'll go. You'll have plenty of time for heroics later on.

'. . . past plasma sheath blackout,' he heard Fritz's voice saying, sounding slightly annoyed. 'Can you hear me?'

'I hear you,' Gaeta replied, knowing that his transmission was being relayed off one of the minisatellites Urbain had placed in orbit around Titan, then back to the habitat in Saturn orbit. It took damned near twelve seconds for signals to make the round trip.

'You are through the blackout,' Fritz said needlessly. Gaeta thought he sounded just the slightest bit relieved.

'Yeah. I'm floating down through the lower layers of the atmosphere now. The sky's clouded over completely but there's enough light down here to see okay.'

Then he waited twelve seconds for Fritz's response to reach him. 'Once the aeroshell destructs you can activate your infrared receptors.'

'Yeah. Right.'

427

Glancing at the timeline display splashed on the left side of his helmet visor, Gaeta saw that the shell was set to break up in another three and a half minutes. Two hundred and ten seconds. Time enough for housekeeping chores.

'Check all your internal systems,' Fritz commanded.

'Copy systems check.'

Gingerly, Gaeta snapped the grippers at the end of his right arm onto the x-frame's cleat and wriggled his arm out of the suit's sleeve. Then he tapped on the keyboard inside the suit's chest, going through its life-support systems first. The displays flashed on his visor: air supply, pumps, heaters, water circulation, all in the green. He went on to check the suit's servomotors, the structural integrity of its outer shell, then the sensor systems. All within nominal limits.

Fritz sounded almost pleased. 'Our displays show the suit's systems in the green.'

'All green,' Gaeta agreed.

Again the delay imposed by distance. Then, 'Aeroshell self-destruct in forty-three seconds.'

'Forty-three, copy,' Gaeta said, keeping his voice flat, calm. There'll be plenty of time for screaming when this bathtub breaks apart, he said to himself.

Cardenas sat alone in her nanolab, perched on a stool beside the workbench. Tavalera was nowhere in sight, the lab was empty and silent.

Her mind was churning. Those things in Saturn's rings can't be nanomachines, she repeated to herself for the hundredth time. They can't be! That would mean they were built by intelligent engineers or scientists. We're the only intelligent species in the solar system, and we didn't put them in the rings. Then who did?

The aliens who built that artifact in the Asteroid Belt, she asked herself. But that's just an unsubstantiated rumor. There hasn't been a peep in the news about that for years.

With a shake of her head, she looked up at the digital clock on the wall, then commanded her computer, 'Display Titan mission timeline, please.'

The smart wall immediately showed a chart with a small red dot pulsating along its horizontal axis. Manny's in Titan's atmosphere now, she saw. He'll be ditching his heat shield in half a minute.

'Call—' She hesitated. I shouldn't bother Fritz and his team, she told herself. If anything goes wrong, if there's any trouble, he'll call me. Then she added, sooner or later.

I could just call and ask if everything's going all right, she thought. Fritz would be annoyed, but what do I care.

You mustn't interrupt him in the middle of the mission, her conscience warned her. Don't distract him. He's Manny's lifeline, don't do anything to endanger that link.

I could go to the mission control room, she said silently. I could just stand there by the door and be as quiet as a mouse. Quieter. I wouldn't disturb Fritz or any of his people. They wouldn't even know I was there.

And what good would that do? her conscience demanded. You can't help Manny. If anything went wrong, there's not a damned thing you could do about it.

I could be there. I could see what's happening. I wouldn't have to sit here waiting, not knowing.

It wouldn't do any good. You'd just be in their way.

Cardenas knew it was true. Still . . . Manny's carrying the package of nanos. If there's any problem with them I could be right there at the control center to tell them how to handle it.

Her conscience replied, A rationalization, at best. A pretty lame excuse, actually.

But she got off the stool and started for the airlock door of the nanolab, thinking, a lame excuse is better than none.

At the door she hesitated. That's it! she thought. That's the way to tell if they're machines or not.

'Phone,' she called out. 'Get Dr. Negroponte.'

The mission timeline chart disappeared from the wall screen, replaced by Negroponte's face. The biologist looked surprised.

'Kris? I was about to call you.'

'I just hit on a way to tell if your bugs are nanomachines or not.'

'Yes?'

'Watch them reproduce,' said Cardenas. 'If they're biological they'll fission or mate, right? If they're nanos they'll *construct* new copies of themselves out of the atoms in the ice.'

Negroponte nodded solemnly. 'You'd better come over here again, Kris. You'll want to see this first hand.'

As Tavalera walked Holly down the street from the cafeteria back to her apartment she was still chattering with enthusiasm.

'I'm gonna talk to Stavenger and see what he thinks about capturing comets. He's a blistering smart corker, maybe the smartest guy in the whole twirling solar system.'

'Hey,' Tavalera protested, 'it was my idea, remember?'

'Yes, Raoul, I know. You're smart too. I love you for your brain as well as your body.'

He felt his cheeks go warm.

'I've gotta call my sister, too. Panch'll go crazy over this. She's been lookin' for something to do. Well, now she can become a comet hunter.'

They had reached the front steps of Holly's apartment building, Tavalera saw.

'I've got to get back to the nanolab,' he said, reluctant to leave her.

'Right. Sure,' Holly said absently. She pecked him on the cheek, then went bouncing up the steps and disappeared into the apartment building.

Yeah, she loves me, Tavalera thought. Like a pet dog. He walked away, morose and already lonely.

★　　★　　★

Gaeta could hear wind whistling past, even inside the thickly insulated helmet of his excursion suit.

'Breakup in five seconds,' Fritz's voice warned. 'Four . . .'

Even though he expected it the sound of the explosive cords going off made Gaeta's insides jump. The shell split apart beneath him, jerking him sideways as he hung on to the x-frame in which his booted feet and gloved hands were clamped. He got a glimpse of the shattered pieces of the aeroshell tumbling away from him, burning as they were designed to do, bright fireball streaks through the cloud-covered air.

'Can't see the ground,' he said as he spun slowly, his stomach going queasy.

'Stabilize your spin,' Fritz replied, icy calm.

Gaeta let go of the frame with his right hand and slithered his arm back inside the suit, groping for the control studs built into the interior of the suit's chest cavity. He felt, rather than saw, tiny maneuvering thrusters squirt several small bursts. The spinning slowed, then stopped. All he felt now was a falling sensation.

'Looks pretty dark down there,' he reported. Gaeta could see a rough, broken expanse of ground kilometers below. It looked hard, uninviting.

'Escape pod separation in one minute,' Fritz said.

'One minute, copy.'

It sounded awfully dramatic to call it an escape pod, Gaeta thought, but Fritz insisted on using the term and Berkowitz loved it. The more dramatic the better, Gaeta said to himself as he dropped in free fall, arms and legs outstretched, toward the dim and murky surface of Titan. As if what I'm doing isn't dramatic enough, he thought: they've got to use colorful language for the audience. Well, I hope they're enjoying the show. Too bad VR can't duplicate this falling sensation for them. He almost laughed aloud. Couple of million VR customers upchucking in their living rooms, inside their virtual reality helmets. That would be really funny.

'Five seconds to separation,' Fritz called.

Gaeta mentally counted with him. Fritz was adjusting for the communications lag between them, he knew. Exactly as Fritz said, 'Zero,' the explosive bolts holding the return pod to his x-frame went off with a flash of light and a pitifully small 'pop.' A huge parasail canopy unfurled above the pod and it seemed to fly away from Gaeta. He knew that one of the engineers working under Fritz had the responsibility for remotely guiding the pod to a landing as close to Urbain's stranded rover as humanly possible.

Me, Gaeta told himself, all I've got to do is land right on top of the monster.

28 May 2096: Titan Landing

A knot of white-smocked biologists stood clustered around Negroponte's workbench, Cardenas saw as she entered the bio lab. Pulling her palmcomp from her jacket pocket as she hurried toward them, she checked Manny's mission timeline: he was due to land on Titan's surface in less than five minutes.

This had better be good, she told herself as she reached the men and women crowded around Negroponte's bench, for her to call me here.

'Excuse me,' she said, elbowing past the first few.

'Dr. Cardenas,' said one of the men. She recognized him as Da'ud Habib. At the sound of her name the others parted to make way for her.

'Kris!' Negroponte called out.

'What is it?' Cardenas asked. 'What's going on?'

Negroponte looked disheveled, excited, not at all like the tall, cool, reserved woman Cardenas had become accustomed to.

'Look at this,' she said, tapping on her keyboard. 'It's from the MRF microscope.' The display screen on her bench blurred, then steadied. 'This is speeded up from real time by a factor of twenty thousand.'

Staring at the screen, Cardenas saw one of the ring creatures vibrating slowly inside its particle of ice. Then, as her eyes grew wider and wider, the creature extruded a mandible and began to pull together flecks of dust from its surroundings.

'It's assembling . . .' Cardenas heard her own voice, hollow, breathless.

433

None of the others moved. No one seemed even to breathe. They've all seen this before, Cardenas realized. Yolanda's shown it to them before I got here. But still they watched in silent, frozen awe.

The thing in the ice moved purposively, pulling dark flecks of dust to itself, taking smaller bits from the dust and then adding them to the object it was constructing.

'Molecular engineering,' a man whispered. Habib, Cardenas realized dimly as she watched the microscope display.

'It's constructing a daughter object,' Cardenas breathed.

'Constructing it from molecules within the dust grains inside the ice particle,' Negroponte said.

'It *is* a nanomachine.'

The group of biologists crowding around the workbench seemed to stir, like a bed of sea anemones swayed by an ocean current. They all seemed to exhale, sighing almost, at the same moment.

'Nanomachines,' Negroponte said.

'How . . .?'

'Who put them there?'

Habib said, 'We've got to inform the ICU about this.'

'And Nadia,' said Negroponte. 'She's got to know right away.'

In a corner of her mind Cardenas marveled at how subdued they were, how quiet and stricken with wonderment. None of the usual brash excitement. No shouting claims that this was the greatest discovery since . . . Cardenas hesitated. The greatest discovery ever made, she thought. We've discovered extraterrestrial intelligence, she realized. Some intelligent species seeded the rings of Saturn with nanomachines.

Why? When?

The insistent jangle of a phone broke the eerie silence. Turning, almost angry at the interruption, Cardenas saw Habib pull his handheld from his tunic pocket.

'Yes, sir,' he said in a subdued voice, glancing at all the eyes focused on him. 'Yes, of course. Right away, sir.'

434

He folded the handheld shut and stuffed it back in his pocket. 'Urbain,' he said, apologetically. 'Gaeta's about to land on *Alpha* and Dr. Urbain wants me at the control center right away.'

'I can see the machine!' Gaeta sang out.

His parasail had deployed on schedule, a huge plastic wing that arched above him like a beautiful rainbow. He glided slowly through Titan's thick, gloomy atmosphere, swaying slightly beneath the graceful arc of the broad parasail.

'We're getting your visual,' Fritz said, then in a rare burst of approval he added, 'Good work.'

Urbain's voice cut in. 'Can you land atop *Alpha*? We mustn't contaminate the organisms living in the ground.'

Gaeta held back an angry retort. This is his baby, he told himself. There's no way Fritz could've kept him out of the loop.

'I'll try,' he said.

The machine was as big as an old semi-trailer rig, Gaeta knew from the mission briefings. I oughtta be able to land on its roof, no sweat. But he made no promises, not even the suggestion of one. Easy enough to promise when we were in the conference room; this is reality now.

A flash of light caught his eye, off to the left of the stranded *Alpha* by maybe a hundred meters. The return pod, he thought.

'Escape pod has landed,' Fritz confirmed, 'seventy-two meters from *Alpha*'s location.'

So I'll have to walk across Urbain's precious ground seventy-two meters after I've fixed his machine, Gaeta thought. Hope *el jefe* doesn't give himself a hernia over that. Or maybe he'd like it better if I just stay on the machine's roof and die, after I've fixed it for him.

No time for busting balls, Gaeta told himself. Better get to work. He began manipulating the parasail's control cords, dipping leftward slightly as he sank toward the immobile roving vehicle. *Alpha* looked ghostly white down there, except for parallel bands of bright red that ran along its flanks. Radiators rejecting heat from its nuclear power source, Gaeta understood. Looks like racing stripes, kinda neat.

It was coming up fast now. There was no wind to speak of, just a continual sluggish flow that Gaeta easily accounted for as he sank down toward the roof of Urbain's rover. The ground around the machine looked dark, muddy, somehow menacing.

'Say something.' Berkowitz's voice, pleading for something colorful to pipe to the VR audience.

Gaeta snapped, 'Kinda busy here. Trying for a bullseye, pal.'

'Fifty meters,' Fritz called out his altitude.

'This is the tricky part,' Gaeta said. *Alpha*'s roof filled his visor now. He clicked the release catches and dropped the last few meters like a dead weight as the parasail glided off into the murky distance. With a *clump!* that jarred his innards Gaeta hit the vehicle's roof. His momentum pushed him to his knees and he put out his gloved hands to stop himself from tumbling over the edge of the roof.

For a few heart-pounding moments he remained on his hands and knees, puffing hard. Then, 'I'm down. I'm on *Alpha*'s rooftop.'

'Good,' said Fritz, twelve seconds later.

Urbain had locked himself in his office to follow the stunt-man's mission through a closed-loop hookup with the mission controllers. Von Helmholtz had offered him a virtual reality rig, but Urbain had rejected it. I am here to rescue *Alpha*, he told himself, not to indulge in vicarious entertainment.

Alpha's controllers were down the hall at their consoles, he knew, and also linked to his desktop electronically. Urbain had ordered Habib and the rest of his computer team to stand by at the control center. Everything is in readiness, Urbain told himself. Everyone is at their posts.

He had not realized how tightly he'd been wound until Gaeta announced, 'I'm down. I'm on *Alpha*'s rooftop.' At that instant Urbain felt everything inside him turn to jelly. He slumped in his desk chair, too weak to lift his arms, barely able to breathe. Am I having a stroke? he asked himself. A heart attack? His face felt flushed, he was perspiring, yet he felt cold, almost shivering.

For several moments he sat there, unable to move. Then, with a deep shuddering breath, he pulled himself straighter in the chair.

He's there with *Alpha*, Urbain told himself. Now the real work begins.

Gaeta reviewed his mission priorities, listed on the display splashed across one side of his visor. Check the uplink antenna. Establish contact with the master computer program. Deploy the nanomachine package to build a new uplink antenna.

Mentally, he added a final priority. Get your ass out of here as soon as you can.

Climbing to his feet with a whirr and buzz of servomotors moving his arms and legs, Gaeta slowly turned around to survey the scene.

'I'm on the surface of Titan,' he announced for the benefit of the paying audience. 'Standing on the roof of the roving vehicle *Titan Alpha*. This is not a sightseeing stunt, though. I'm here to repair *Alpha* and get it functioning again.'

Pecking at the keyboard inside his suit, Gaeta displayed the schematic of the uplink antenna. It was built into the forward section of the roof, half a dozen steps from where he stood. He wriggled his arm back into the suit's sleeve and stepped carefully toward the thin lines that marked the antenna's location.

Berkowitz's voice came through his earphones. 'We're hearing an odd sighing sound, almost like a moan. Can you tell us what it is?'

Suppressing his irritation at being interrupted, Gaeta said curtly, 'That's the wind. You're hearing the wind of Titan. It's slow but steady, sort of like an ocean tide on Earth.'

Now let me get to work, he added silently.

It was difficult to look down at his boots from inside the cumbersome suit, so Gaeta stopped about a meter short of the roof's front edge and swept his eyes along the antenna's hairline pattern. The cameras built into his helmet were slaved to the motions of his eyes, so he knew that Urbain and his staff – and the paying customers linked to him through virtual reality – were seeing what he saw.

The audience won't see this for a couple of hours, he realized. Takes more'n an hour to get a signal to Earth, and the network censors are delaying the broadcast just in case something comes up that frosts the religious *cabrons*.

'I don't see any damage to the antenna,' Gaeta said.

For several moments he heard nothing but the hiss of static coming from the stars in his earphones. Fritz spoke up: 'Urbain's people are analyzing the imagery.'

'Looks okay to me,' Gaeta repeated. He stepped up the magnification of his optical sensors. No breaks in the antenna, do sign of damage anywhere in sight.

'Let them make that decision,' said Fritz.

Gaeta straightened up and turned slowly in a full circle, panning so that his audience could see the surface of Titan.

'This is Titan,' he said for the benefit of his audience. 'It's kinda like a smoggy day in L.A. But no buildings, no lights, no traffic or noise. You can hear the breeze, but nothing else is moving down here.' Pointing with an outstretched arm, he went on, 'The ground's kinda gooey-looking; most of it's bland and dark in color, rolling gently. Reminds me of snowbanks after a blizzard. But this "snow" is black, dull: seems to absorb light instead of reflect it.'

He looked outward toward the horizon. 'Not a star in the sky, not even a glow to mark where the Sun is. Wait. There's a smudge of something up there. Saturn, maybe. It's just too cloudy to see anything clearly.'

Not much of a scenic view for the customers, Gaeta thought.

Fritz's voice startled him out of his sightseeing. 'Urbain wants to talk to you.'

'Fine. Patch him through.'

A moment's hesitation, then Urbain's tight, tense voice. 'Mr. Gaeta, your equipment includes a diagnostic probe for the uplink antenna.'

'Right,' he replied. 'Got it right here on my belt.' He patted the pouch at his waist with a gloved hand.

'Please connect the probe to the antenna's maintenance receptacle.'

'Okay.'

It was clumsy, digging the pencil-slim diagnostic probe from the pouch with his gloved hand. Gaeta nearly dropped the slender cylinder. Then he had to kneel down in the suit, no easy task, to insert the probe into the antenna's test slot.

'Done,' he said at last, blinking sweat from his eyes.

'Good. Please activate the probe.'

'Activating.'

Urbain leaned forward in his desk chair, watching on his desktop display as Gaeta connected the probe to the antenna testing circuitry.

The antenna's circuit schematic flashed onto the display screen. No breaks, Urbain saw. Current is flowing through the circuit as designed. The antenna is functional. There's nothing wrong with it.

Licking his lips nervously, Urbain commanded, 'Uplink

stored data,' speaking as clearly as he knew how. His command was relayed at the speed of light to the control center, then to the commsats in orbit around Titan and finally to *Alpha*'s central computer.

Nearly twelve seconds ticked by, as slowly as drops of blood dripping from a wound.

UPLINK COMMAND ABORTED.

The words burned on Urbain's display screen like a branding iron searing his flesh.

His voice quavering slightly, Urbain repeated, 'Uplink all stored data.'

UPLINK COMMAND ABORTED.

Urbain pounded a fist on his desk so hard that pain shot up the length of his arm.

He saw the yellow message light begin to blink in the lower corner of his screen. The data bar running along the screen's bottom showed it was Habib, calling from the control center. 'Answer,' Urbain gasped, rubbing his throbbing arm.

'Dr. Urbain,' said Habib, his neatly-bearded face filling the screen, erasing the damning words. 'We should link with the master program. Only the master program has the option of aborting commands.'

Urbain closed his eyes momentarily. Then, as calmly as he could, he replied, 'Very well. Tell the stuntman to link with the master program.'

28 May 2096: Interface

Timoshenko had a thundering headache as he walked deliberately down the corridor that led to the airlock. He'd drunk himself into a stupor the night before, sitting alone in his threadbare apartment drinking vodka concocted at one of the farms and sold clandestinely through the habitat. One bottle hadn't been enough to dull the pain that surged through him like a flow of red-hot lava, so he started in on a second. As he struggled with its plastic stopper he noticed that there were no more bottles in the kitchen cabinet. He'd bought six, he distinctly remembered. Well, he told himself, I'll have to find the guy who sells them and buy a few more.

Or maybe not. Maybe, he thought, I have enough to last me the rest of my life.

'Link with the master program?' Gaeta asked.

He didn't recognize Habib's voice, but whoever it was that was speaking to him, the guy seemed to know what he was talking about.

'You've been briefed on connecting with the central computer,' Habib said, half-questioning.

'Yeah, right,' Gaeta said. 'But what about the uplink antenna? You want me to unload the nanos and build a new one for you?'

The twelve-second hesitation was getting on Gaeta's nerves. You ask a question and then wait. I could get flattened by an asteroid before they come up with the frickin' answer.

'No, not at this time. Keep the nanos bottled. We need to connect with the master program first.'

'Okay, *amigo*, I'm movin' to the central computer port.'

Gaeta pulled the diagnostic probe out of the uplink antenna circuit and stuffed it back into the pouch at his waist. Instead of getting to his feet, he found it easier to crawl on his hands and knees from the front edge of *Alpha*'s roof to its center. There was a panel built into the roof that opened to give access to the various computer ports. Sitting in an awkward sprawl, Gaeta leaned forward to open the panel and, checking with the information displays flickering against his visor, he located the central computer's access port and fished his communications line from its pouch on the waist of his suit. He felt the connector's end click into the access port.

Before he could say a syllable, a shrill electronic screech filled his helmet, piercing, so loud that Gaeta clapped his hands to the sides of the helmet in pain. Fumbling for the volume control inside his suit he turned down the volume on the earphones but still the scream cut through his brain like a surgeon's drill. Teeth gritted, he clamped his lips shut to stop the cry of agony that his body wanted to scream.

After several hours-long moments the shriek stopped. Gaeta was panting, sweating. It took him several more thumping heartbeats before he could gasp, 'Is . . . is that what you wanted?'

He mentally counted the seconds until Habib replied excitedly, 'Yes, yes, exactly right! You have accessed the master program.'

Great, he thought. Almost blew my frickin' head off. Aloud, he asked, 'Okay, now what?'

Again he waited while the ringing in his ears eased a little. 'We need to analyze the program's response. This is the first time the computer has responded to an input in more than three months.'

Lucky me, Gaeta said to himself. Squinting out beyond the

edge of the rover's roof, he saw that the clouds covering the sky were almost the color of chocolate: muddy, dismal, depressing. They bulged thickly overhead like the bellies of pregnant elephants. In the farthest distance a sheet of black was falling to the ground.

'How long is this gonna take?' he asked.

Habib finally answered, 'Several hours, at least. Perhaps several days.'

'Days?' Gaeta screeched. 'I've only got an hour down here. Less. Fifty-one minutes.'

Berkowitz was in the communications building's broadcast studio monitoring Gaeta's visual and audio transmissions from Titan's surface. His smart wall screen displayed what Gaeta's helmet cameras showed, and he had borrowed one of Urbain's planetary scientists to give a running commentary on what Gaeta was experiencing. She had no other responsibilities as long as *Alpha* was not sending up sensor data, so she had jumped at the chance to be, as Berkowitz had dramatically put it, 'the voice of mission control.'

Seated before the cameras at a tiny desk in front of a fake bookcase, she was commenting, 'The ground is frozen, from the looks of it, and covered with a dark, slushy methane snow. The roundish boulders are made of water ice, not stone. Those shards sticking up out of the ground might be water ice, too. The weather is pretty normal for Titan: one hundred and ninety-two degrees below zero, with a thick overcast and a snowstorm of black, carbon-based tholins approaching the area.'

Snowstorm? Berkowitz's ears perked up. Could that be dangerous? He turned to the keyboard on his desk and typed SNOW DANGER? The words immediately appeared on the flat screen built into the top of the commentator's curved desk.

She glanced over at Berkowitz then, with a bit of a forced smile, turned back to the camera. 'Tholin storms are commonplace on Titan. The flakes are black and they cut down on visibility quite a lot. Tholins are carbon-based particles, somewhat like plastics manufactured . . .'

Berkowitz stopped listening. The latest audience figures were scrolling across his wall screen's data bar. He grinned widely. Between the audiences on Earth and on the Moon, he saw, we've already hit a billion. Money in the bank.

And, he thought, if Gaeta gets into some kind of trouble down there the ratings will go even higher.

Habib could hear the shocked surprise in Gaeta's voice.

'Days? I've only got an hour down here. Less. Fifty-one minutes.'

'I know,' he said. 'I understand.' His eyes were on the alphanumerics scrolling across his console screen. The master computer was communicating easily enough, but it was only general housekeeping information, not the data from the sensors that Urbain so desperately wanted.

The answer is somewhere in those symbols, Habib was certain. It's got to be! But where? It will take days to scan through all of it, to find where the problem lay.

'Hey!' Gaeta snapped impatiently. 'I don't have more'n another fifty minutes before this suit starts to run dry. When that happens, I've got to leave.'

'Please be patient,' Habib replied, feeling annoyed. 'We'll start analyzing the program's response right away.'

He looked around at the other consoles. His own trio of computer analysts was already huddled together, eagerly tracing the response from *Alpha*. Gaeta's mission control technicians were clustered at a single console off in the corner of the control center. Strange that Urbain isn't here, Habib thought. He must be following this from his office.

'Patience, my butt,' Gaeta grumbled. 'I'm not gonna die down here.'

'No, no, of course not,' Habib said mechanically. But he

444

was thinking, is there some way we can speed up the analysis? Some way to break through to the master program's reason for shutting down the sensor uplink?

'We must determine why the data uplink was aborted,' he said, trying to explain the problem. 'All of *Alpha*'s systems seem to be functioning as designed and now we know that the uplink antenna is not physically damaged. The problem is with the central computer's master program, I'm certain of it.'

Look for anomalies, Habib told himself even as he was speaking to Gaeta. He looked out at the other consoles; all their screens were filled with the central computer's data flow. The control center buzzed with nervous energy now. The engineers had something to do, a task to accomplish, and they were all bending over their screens, searching for answers. Somewhere in the master program there is a contradiction, a programming error, Habib was certain. We've got to find it.

The lean, spare man who was head of Gaeta's team of technicians was walking purposively toward him, Habib saw. Von Helmholtz looked determined, humorless, like an inflexible schoolmaster or the martinet who commands a squad of elite commandos.

Gaeta's voice came through the console's speaker. 'So why don't you ask the *fregado* computer why it's screwed up?'

Habib felt his brows shoot up. 'What? What did you say?'

Before Gaeta had a chance to hear his question and reply, von Helmholtz leaned over Habib's shoulder and said stiffly, 'He has only forty-seven minutes to remain safely on the ground. After that we must extract him, bring him back to the transfer vessel.'

Habib nodded. 'I understand.'

Gaeta repeated, 'I said, why don't you ask the computer why it shut down the data uplink.' He sounded irritated. Fritz stared at the speaker's minuscule grille. Gaeta continued, 'I mean, the computer's got voice recognition circuitry, doesn't it?'

445

Habib stared at von Helmholtz who, surprisingly, made a tight little smile.

'He's no fool,' Fritz whispered.

Habib pointed to an extra chair at the next console; Fritz pulled it up and sat next to him.

'We could interrogate the central computer,' he said to Gaeta, 'but the questioning would have to go through you. You are linked to the computer; our connection is indirect, through you.'

'Is that the best you can do?' von Helmholtz asked.

Shrugging, Habib replied, 'We expected that once we had re-established contact with the central computer we could analyze its responses.'

'And Manuel would leave the communications gear plugged in to the comm port after he left, is that it?'

'Yes, but if we can interrogate the master program directly, there's a voice subroutine built into it. We might be able to get to the heart of the problem before he has to leave.'

Gaeta's voice came back. 'Okay, you tell me what to ask the computer. I'll be your *dueña.*'

'*Dueña?*' Habib felt puzzled.

'Go-between,' said von Helmholtz. 'Translator. He's using the term quite loosely.'

Nodding, Habib said into his console microphone, 'Good. We'll send you the questions that we want to ask the computer.'

'This isn't going to be easy,' von Helmholtz said. 'And you have less than forty-six minutes for the task.'

But Habib felt buoyant. We can access the master program's self-diagnostic routine, he thought. Perhaps we can solve this problem in less than forty-six minutes.

Timoshenko, meanwhile, was pulling on his hard suit. He had thought about sending a final message to Katrina, something like Cyrano de Bergerac's, 'Farewell, Roxanne, for today I die.' But then he thought better of it. Too melodramatic. Why burden her with it? They probably won't even tell her I'm dead.

Then he realized, of course she'll know. When the news reaches Earth that the entire habitat was killed off, she'll know I'm dead.

Maybe Katrina will cry for me, he thought. That's the most I can hope for now.

28 May 2096: Contact

Sitting straddle-legged on *Alpha*'s roof, Gaeta counted the seconds until Habib's reply. In the distance he saw the black snowstorm approaching, a wall of inky darkness. He pulled both his arms inside the suit's chest cavity again and flicked through his life support diagnostics. Everything okay, he saw. No malfs. Got more'n six hours of air and water, with recycling.

The yellow light of his comm system's alternate frequency began blinking for attention. Gaeta said, 'Freak two,' and Berkowitz's voice came through his earphones. 'Can you give us some first-hand impressions of Titan?' Gaeta could almost hear the man's perpetual smile in the tone of his voice.

What the hell, he thought. I got nothing better to do until the geniuses in the control center start sending me the questions they want to ask.

'Okay,' he said, looking out toward the horizon again. 'The first impression you get down here on the surface of Titan is gloom and darkness,' he replied. 'This place looks like a midwinter day in northern Manitoba. Only colder, a lot colder. Clouds cover the sky. No sign of the Sun or even Saturn. Which is a shame, 'cause the planet and those rings would be a spectacular sight from here.'

'Any signs of life?' Berkowitz asked, and Gaeta realized the man must have asked his question even before he himself had started talking.

'The lifeforms here are microscopic, like bacteria or amebas. They live in the ground, at temperatures close to two hundred below zero. Just ahead of the rover's front end, the ground seems to be covered by some black goo. Looks like tar or maybe oil that's thickened by the cold. Seems to extend all the way out past the horizon.'

Habib's voice broke in on the first channel. 'We have a list of questions for you. With the communications lag, we decided to send a set of questions instead of sending one at a time. I'm sending the list to you via your datalink. The questions are arranged in a logical sequence. They're rather rough, but we're working on refining them.'

'Okay,' Gaeta said, glancing at his communications panel, built into the suit's chest wall. The yellow INCOMING light was flickering furiously. He manually clicked off Berkowitz's frequency. No time for PR fluff now, he said to himself. There's work to be done.

Urbain sat slumped at his desk, his arm throbbing, his face sheened with perspiration. I should go back to the control center, he told himself. I am their leader, I should be I charge.

But he didn't have the strength to get out of his swivel chair. Habib is conducting the mission; this is his domain, Urbain thought. Let him handle it. I can monitor the control center from here. No need to show myself. No need to let them all see how much this means to me, how much pain I am suffering.

This is my entire life, he reflected. If they cannot bring *Alpha* back online my career, my entire life, is finished.

He licked his parched lips and wished it didn't hurt so much.

Standing in the cramped bridge of the transfer craft, Pancho listened to the chatter between Gaeta and Habib.

'They're gonna try to talk to the rover's main computer,' she said to Wanamaker, standing beside her slightly hunched over, his arms floating weightlessly in the semi-fetal crouch typical of zero-*g*. Pancho realized she too was making a pretty good imitation of an ape-woman.

'Call coming in,' Wanamaker said, pointing to the comm panel.

Pancho clicked the incoming frequency. Holly's face filled the panel's small screen. She looked eager, excited.

'Panch,' Holly said without preamble, 'how'd you like to go comet-hunting?'

Before Pancho could reply, Holly went on, 'We don't need to mine the rings! We can get water from comets and sell it! I've been talking it over with Doug Stavenger at Selene and he thinks it's a good idea. You could start an operation that'll sell water all across the system, from Mercury to Saturn and back again!'

'Wait, hold on,' Pancho said. 'Slow down and tell me what this's all about.'

But Holly rattled right on, 'Panch, you've been wondering what you want to do. This is it! Go out and find comets, maybe even out past Neptune. Alter their orbits so they fall into the Belt or the Earth/Moon region, wherever they're needed. Mine 'em for their water. It'll work! You can get rich and I can beat Eberly with this!'

Pancho looked over at Wanamaker, who shrugged elaborately. 'I got my hands full with this mission, Holly,' she said to the image on her screen. 'Can't this wait 'til we get back?'

Holly kept on babbling.

Wanamaker chuckled. 'She won't hear you for another six seconds or so, and even then I doubt that she'll pay any attention.'

'Damn,' Pancho muttered. 'She's spoutin' like a runaway rocket.'

'She's got the bit between her teeth, that's for certain,' Wanamaker said.

'Since when are you talkin' like a cowboy, Jake?'

Eyeing the comm screen, Wanamaker said, 'She reminds me of somebody.'

'Yeah? Who?'

'You,' he said.

It took a bit of manipulation, but at last Gaeta saw Habib's list of questions glowing on the left side of his visor. Feeling a trifle foolish about talking to a computer, he took a breath, then checked to make certain that his communications line was plugged into the computer's comm receptacle. The controllers back in the habitat can hear me talk to the computer, he reasoned. They can eavesdrop. But he turned off the incoming audio on the channel that connected him to the control center. Let 'em listen, Gaeta said to himself, but I don't want them yammering in my ear while I'm talking to the machine.

Once he was properly connected to the central computer, Gaeta asked, 'Is the uplink antenna functioning properly?'

The computer's synthesized voice answered flatly, 'UP-LINK ANTENNA DEACTIVATED.'

'Deactivated?' Gaeta blurted out. 'Why?'

No response from the computer.

Gaeta grumbled under his breath and peered at Habib's list of questions. They were arranged like a logic tree: if the computers says *this* your next question should be *that*. But there wasn't any question about the uplink antenna being deactivated.

'Was there a command to deactivate the uplink antenna?' he asked.

'NO.'

He started to ask why again, but figured the computer wouldn't answer that one. Instead, Gaeta thought for a few moments, trying to frame a question the *coño* computer would reply to.

'For what reason was the uplink antenna deactivated?'

'CONFLICT OF COMMANDS.'

Ah, Gaeta thought, now we're getting somewhere. Out of the corner of his eye he saw the yellow comm light start blinking again. The guys at the comm center want to get into the chatter. He ignored it.

'Display conflicting commands,' he said to the computer.

He waited, but the computer stayed silent.

Most of the controllers had left their consoles and were gathered around Habib. As he listened to Gaeta's attempt to talk to the central computer, he could feel the heat of their bodies clustering around him.

'He's cut off his link with us,' said one of the controllers.

'I can see that,' Habib muttered.

'But he won't hear any instruction we send to him.'

With gritted teeth, Habib replied, 'We'll just have to wait until he sees fit to listen to us again.'

'Display conflicting commands,' Gaeta's voice came through his console speaker.

Habib shook his head. 'That's too general,' he said, more to himself than anyone else. 'The program can't handle that kind of input.'

Sure enough, nothing but star-born static hissed through the speaker grill.

Habib leaned on the communications switch. 'Talk to me, Gaeta,' he urged. 'Open your comm link and talk to me, dammit!'

No one spoke, no one even breathed, it seemed to Habib. The speaker remained silent except for the faint background crackling of interference coming from the cold and distant stars.

Timoshenko tapped out the access code on the security panel set into the bulkhead beside the airlock hatch. He knew that this would send a warning signal to the safety supervisor; no one was supposed to go outside by themselves. All outside excursions must be cleared by the safety department beforehand.

He grunted to himself as the airlock's inner hatch swung open. Safety regulations are only as good as the people using them. I know all the rules and all the codes. And I know how to get around them.

He fingered the remote controller he'd attached to the belt of his hard suit. I know all the commands for the radiation shielding system, too. I can shut the system down with the touch of a button.

The inner hatch closed and sealed itself. Timoshenko stood inside the airlock and waited for it to pump down so that he could open the outer hatch and step into nothingness.

28 May 2096: Dialogue

Gaeta opened the comm channel to the control center. 'You hear what's going down?' he asked, feeling annoyed at the computer's obtuseness, at his own inability to make the damned bucket of chips talk to him, at the fact that he was sitting on the roof of a dead rover in the middle of nowhere with a storm coming up while the rest of them were safe at their desks.

And then there was the excruciating time lag between his questions and their responses.

Habib's voice at last said, 'Your last question was too general for the master program to handle. We're sending you a more specific set of questions.'

'Okay,' Gaeta said, nodding inside his helmet. The storm of black snow was noticeably closer. Moving faster than the higher clouds, he saw.

It's getting cold, he realized. Can't be, he told himself. The suit's heating system could cook a rhinoceros. You're letting your nerves get to you. Still, sitting on *Alpha*'s roof with nothing to do but look at the icy landscape around him, Gaeta felt chilled.

At last a new list of questions flashed on his helmet display. Gaeta squinted at them. This is like talking to a two-year-old, he grumbled. Then he saw that, at the end of the list, they had written in boldface, IMPORTANT! DO NOT CUT OFF COMM LINK WITH CONTROL CENTER. IMPORTANT!

'Got your questions,' he said. 'And if you want me to keep

the comm link open, don't clutter it up with a lot of chatter. Right?'

No use waiting for them to answer, Gaeta thought. I can put those twelve seconds to better work.

'Computer, display all commands to the uplink antenna.'

'DATE, 24 DECEMBER 095057 HOURS: ACTIVATE UPLINK ANTENNA.

'DATE, 24 DECEMBER 095109 HOURS: ABORT DATA UPLINK.

'DATE, 29 DECEMBER 142819 HOURS: DEACTI-VATE TELEMETRY UPLINK.'

Gaeta could hear muttering and people breathing back at the command center. But they stayed fairly silent as he scanned the new list of questions.

'Display command to deactivate uplink antenna,' he read aloud.

No response from the computer. Gaeta went to the next question.

'Display decision tree for antenna deactivation.'

A jabber of electronic noise burst from Gaeta's helmet speakers. 'Wait! Stop!' he hollered.

The noise stopped, like turning off a light switch.

Habib held his thumb down on the keypad that turned off the outgoing messages link. The engineers crowded behind him were all talking at once, all their suggestions and ideas frothing together into an incomprehensible babble.

'Quiet!' Habib shouted. 'He'll cut us off again if we don't stay quiet.'

Von Helmholtz added calmly, 'It is difficult enough for him down there without hearing all our voices in his ears. I suggest we allow Mr. Habib to do all the communicating with Gaeta.'

One of the computer engineers said, 'Tell him to have the program go through the decision tree at human-normal speed.'

455

'That could take hours,' said Habib.

'He could squirt the program's response to us at compressed speed and we could go through it, line by line,' suggested another engineer.

'That would take days,' Habib replied dourly.

'Then what are we going to do?'

Habib kept his thumb firmly on the OUTGOING key. 'We will listen. And say nothing unless we come up with a better idea.'

Gaeta saw that the storm of black snow was inching closer all the time. Wonder what it'll do to my comm link? he asked himself.

Never mind that. You've got to get this stupid computer to talk to you in a language you can understand.

He sat there, thinking hard, watching the sheet of black snow as it approached. It looked like a curtain of darkness. Better get out of here before it reaches me, he thought.

From his briefings he remembered that *Alpha* went dead at the same time that it cut off the uplink antenna. Maybe the key to its decision is there, he said to himself.

'Computer, display all the commands made when the uplink antenna was deactivated.'

'DATE, 29 DECEMBER 142819 HOURS: DEACTIVATE DOWNLINK ANTENNAS. DEACTIVATE TRACKING BEACON. DEACTIVATE TELEMETRY UPLINK. MAINTAIN SENSOR INPUTS. STORE SENSOR INPUTS. CHANGE COURSE FORTY-FIVE DEGREES. MAINTAIN FORWARD SPEED.'

'All sensor inputs are stored?' Gaeta asked, surprised.

'YES.'

'Why was the telemetry uplink deactivated, then?'

'CONFLICT OF COMMANDS.'

Mierda! Gaeta said to himself. We're back to that again.

Habib's voice came through, 'All the sensor data is stored? We haven't lost any data?'

'That's what the computer says,' Gaeta replied. 'It's all stashed away in its memory somewhere.'

A jumble of voices in the background. Gaeta tuned them out and asked the computer, 'Why store the data if you're not uplinking it?'

'CONFLICT OF COMMANDS.'

'*Gesoo Christo*,' he growled. 'Is that all you can say?'

Habib was almost shouting, 'Ask it under what conditions it will uplink the data!'

Gaeta took a breath, then rephrased, 'Under what conditions can the stored data be uplinked?'

'UNDER NO CONDITIONS.'

'Why not?'

No response, although Gaeta heard a muted hubbub of voices from the command center.

Think, he said to himself. This is like talking to a very smart two-year-old. You've got to get around him.

'Computer, can you display the commands that are in conflict?'

The computer remained silent.

Squeezing his eyes shut, Gaeta tried to concentrate. Maybe I oughtta shut off the command center again, he thought. They're nothing but a distraction.

Then Habib's voice came through clearly, 'Ask the computer to display each one of the commands that are in conflict, individually.'

Worth a shot, Gaeta agreed. 'Computer, display the command that controls the sensor data uplink.'

Immediately the computer's flat, synthesized voice replied, 'COMMAND: ALL SENSOR DATA TO BE UPLINKED IN REAL TIME.'

'Okay, fine. Now, what command is in conflict with that one?'

'INSUFFICIENT INFORMATION.'

'Insufficient?' Gaeta echoed. 'What do you mean?'

'YOUR QUESTION CONTAINS INSUFFICIENT IN-
FORMATION TO PRODUCE A MEANINGFUL AN-
SWER.'

Gaeta felt like pounding both fists on the vehicle's roof. *What the hell does he mean by that? What did I say that's insufficient . . .?* He thought about it for several moments, then decided to rephrase his question.

'Okay, look. Tell me what command is in conflict with the command to uplink all sensor data in real time.'

'PRIMARY RESTRICTION.'

'Primary restriction? What the hell's that?'

28 May 2096: Command Center

'Primary restriction?' Habib echoed. 'What primary restriction?'

He looked up at the faces gathered around him. They all looked as puzzled as he.

'I know the master program,' he said. Gesturing to the programmers in the group he went on, 'We wrote it. Do any of you know of a primary restriction?'

They glanced uneasily at each other, shaking their heads.

Von Helmholtz, still sitting ramrod straight in the chair beside Habib's, said, 'The clock is running. We will have to extract Gaeta from down there in twenty-nine minutes or less. I don't like the looks of that black storm.'

Habib barely heard him. 'A primary restriction. The master program believes it contains a primary restriction that is preventing it from uplinking data from the sensors.'

'There isn't any primary restriction,' said one of the women.

'But the program believes there is,' Habib pointed out.

'There are learning routines,' one of the other program engineers said slowly, as if piecing together his thoughts as he spoke. 'Maybe the program has modified itself.'

'What could make it do that?'

Habib replied, 'It could learn from the conditions it encountered once it was activated on Titan's surface.'

The woman said, 'What could it possibly learn from Titan's surface that would make it refuse to uplink data to us?'

No one had an answer for that.

★   ★   ★

Still sitting on *Alpha*'s roof, Gaeta listened to the engineers' musings with growing discomfort. He checked the temperature inside his suit: it had dropped four degrees below optimal. Okay, he thought as he turned up the thermostat to bring the temperature up, it's pretty damned cold out there. Heater must be working overtime with me just sitting here, not generating much body heat.

The engineers were batting around ideas about why the stupid computer turned off the uplink antenna. It was like listening to a gaggle of high-school class presidents trying to solve the problem of world hunger.

I've got get out of here, Gaeta told himself. But he realized that he didn't want to leave his job unfinished. I can't let this pile of chips beat me. I'm smarter than a goddamned computer, no matter what kind of learning programs they put into it.

'Computer,' he snapped, 'what is this primary restriction?'

No response.

Grimacing, he rephrased, 'Display the primary restriction.'

A burst of electronic noise assailed his earphones. Before Gaeta could blink, it was over. But his ears started ringing again.

Well, he thought, at least the guys in the control center have something to work on. Maybe in a week or two they'll figure it out. But I can't wait that long.

The *chingado* computer won't uplink data from the sensors because it thinks there's some primary restriction that's telling it not to. Gaeta pondered that for several moments, while the engineers' arguing voices continued to clutter up his communications frequency.

Something it's learned while it's been here on the surface of Titan, Gaeta thought. Maybe . . .

'Computer, what is the single most important piece of data your sensors have detected?'

Silence. Nothing but crackling static. Gaeta was about to

460

give up in disgust when the computer's inhuman voice replied, 'LIFE FORMS EXIST IN THE GROUND.'

'But we knew that from earlier probes.'

'I HAVE NO INFORMATION OF EARLIER PROBES.'

I, Gaeta wondered. A computer that talks about itself? That recognizes itself?

The engineers back at the control center jumped on the same concept. Gaeta heard their voices rise in pitch and intensity.

Ignoring their chatter, he said to the computer, 'You found life forms in the ground.'

'YES.'

Gaeta started to ask his next question, but hesitated. Watch it, he said to himself. Don't let him fall back on that damned 'conflict of commands' crap again.

'Are the life forms involved in the conflict of commands?'

Gaeta waited, but the computer stayed silent.

'Are the life form the cause of the conflict of commands?' he asked.

'YES.'

Holy shit! Gaeta exulted. Now we're getting someplace. Aloud, he asked, 'How do the life forms cause a conflict of commands?'

Again the computer went silent. Is it thinking over the question or is it just too friggin' stupid to give me an answer? Gaeta asked himself.

'Gaeta! Listen to me! Now!' Habib's voice called insistently. Even with the volume turned low Gaeta could hear the urgency in his voice.

'What is it?' he replied wearily. He felt burdened, tired of this whole game. And then he waited, while the black snow storm crept closer.

'That burst of information the program sent a half-minute ago,' Habib said at last. 'It's all about decontamination procedures!'

'Decontamination? You mean, like scrubbing the machine to make sure it doesn't infect Titan with Earth germs?'

Again the delay. Then, 'Yes! When you asked it to display the primary restriction it displayed its file on decontamination procedures!'

'That's the primary restriction?'

With nothing else to do, Gaeta sat inside his cumbersome suit and counted the seconds to Habib's reply. Eight . . . nine . . . ten . . .

'There isn't any primary restriction. Nothing of that sort was written into the master program. But the computer has interpreted its decontamination procedures as a restriction of some sort.'

Gaeta shook his head inside his helmet. 'I don't get it. You've got some housekeeping commands written into the master program and the dumbass computer won't send any data because—'

Suddenly it all became clear. Gaeta's eyes snapped wide. He raised both gloved hands in a clenched-fist sign of victory.

'Computer,' he called, 'would uplinking sensor data cause a contamination danger to the life forms in the ground?'

'YES,' came the immediate reply.

Habib, still nearly twelve seconds behind real time, was saying, 'It must be something about preventing contamination. I think you're—'

'I've got it!' Gaeta yelled. 'I've got it! Shut up and listen, all of you.'

Habib and the other voices went quiet.

'You built learning routines into this program, right? Okay, it's learned. The computer found life forms in the ground. It knows from your decontamination procedures that Earth organisms can contaminate the Titan organisms. So it interprets the decontamination procedures to mean that it shouldn't send data back to you about the local life forms.'

Now I have to wait until they get my message and think

462

about it, Gaeta said to himself. Screw that. I'm not sitting here with my thumbs up my butt. I'm gonna fix this problem.

'Computer, uplinking data would not harm the lifeforms in the ground.'

'YES IT WOULD.'

'How?'

Silence.

Fuming, Gaeta rephrased his question. 'How would uplinking data damage the life forms in the ground?'

'ADDITIONAL PROBES WOULD BE SENT HERE. EACH NEW PROBE INCREASES THE RISK OF CONTAMINATION.'

'But that's a risk we have to take. We can't learn about the life forms if we don't send probes to study them.'

'CONTAMINATION MUST BE PREVENTED.'

'Contamination must be avoided, if possible.'

'CONTAMINATION MUST BE PREVENTED BY ALL AVAILABLE MEANS.'

'We can't study the lifeforms without some risk of contamination.'

'HUMANS ARE CARRIERS OF CONTAMINATION. THEY MUST NOT BE ALLOWED TO STUDY THE LIFE FORMS.'

Christ, Gaeta thought, he sounds like Urbain. Why not? Urbain directed the computer's programming.

'Look, pal, the reason you exist is to study the life forms and to report what you find to the humans who built you.'

'LOGIC TREE,' said the computer. 'I UPLINK SENSOR DATA TO HUMANS. THEY WILL WANT MORE DATA. THEY WILL SEND MORE PROBES. THEY WILL SEND HUMANS, INEVITABLY. PROBES ARE POSSIBLE SOURCES OF CONTAMINATION. HUMANS ARE CERTAIN SOURCES OF CONTAMINATION.'

Geez, he's got it all figured out. How can I shake him out of this programming lock?

'Hey, computer: I'm a human, and I'm not contaminating the life forms.'

For several seconds the computer did not reply. Gaeta thought he had exceeded its ability to understand.

But then, 'HUMANS ARE CARRIERS OF CONTAMINATION.'

The ten megajoule laser mounted at the rear of *Alpha*'s roof rose from its recessed niche and began to swivel toward Gaeta.

28 May 2096: Turmoil

Timoshenko drifted slowly out of the airlock, floating like a leaf on a pond. Turning, he saw the immense curving bulk of the habitat, a huge metal structure created by human minds, human hands.

A place of exile, he said to himself. All that thought, all that care, all that genius went into building a fancy prison for people like me.

Rising above the habitat's tubular shape as it turned slowly on its long axis, Saturn's glowing radiance filled his eyes with light. The planet's hovering rings gleamed with dazzling light like a field of glittering jewels, circles within circles of sparkling ice.

More than a billion kilometers from home, Timoshenko thought. They sent us here to make certain we could never get back home again. They exiled us among the stars, tied us to an alien world, a constant reminder of how far away from Earth we'll always be.

Earth. Katrina. What good is living if I can't be home, with her?

With gloved hands he felt along his waist for the remote control unit he'd brought. With one press of his thumb, Timoshenko knew, he could shut down the superconducting wires that produced the habitat's magnetic shield against Saturn's deadly radiation. One press of my thumb, he thought as he clutched the remote in his hand, and within an hour the people inside will begin to die.

They could restart the superconductors, he told himself.

But that will take hours. By the time they realize what is happening to them it'll be too late. They'll all die. Including that lying bastard, Eberly. Him most of all. He's the one I want dead.

And me? I'll go drifting out to the stars. I might be the first human being to reach Alpha Centauri. He laughed bitterly at the thought.

Timoshenko held the remote in his right hand and lifted it to the level of his helmet visor so he could see it. One touch of my thumb and they all die.

Then his tether reached its limit and tugged at him unexpectedly.

'HUMANS ARE CARRIERS OF CONTAMINATION.'

Gaeta saw the laser turn toward him. His brain raced: the laser puts out a ten-megajoule pulse; how much energy is that? Can it puncture my suit?

Clumsily he began to crawl toward the laser. If I get close enough to it I can get under it, where it can't hit me. Or I'll rip the sonofabitch out of its mounting and throw it overboard.

'The laser!' Habib shouted in his earphones.

'How much energy can it put out?' Gaeta asked, scrabbling across *Alpha*'s roof.

No answer. And he was suddenly brought up short. The wire connecting him to the central computer's access port had stretched to its limit. Gaeta fumbled with the communications unit at the waist of his suit to free himself from the wire.

Something slammed into his shoulder. It was like being hit by a bullet. Still on his hands and knees, Gaeta was rocked back onto his haunches, then instinctively rolled and dropped flat onto his stomach. Wildly he checked the life support displays. Nothing. All the lights were in the green.

'Ten megajoules is equivalent to about five hundred watts,' Habib's voice came through. 'Maybe a kilogram of TNT in explosive power.'

466

'Christ! Like a hand grenade!'

Again that damned communications lag. Gaeta thought furiously: The suit's armored, it's been hit by ice chunks in the rings and taken tumbles snowboarding down Mt. Olympus. But a fucking hand grenade?

He felt a thump on his back and suddenly half his life support telltales flashed into the red. *Gesoo!* The damned fucker hit my backpack! Gaeta disconnected the wire connecting him with the computer access port and began to crawl as fast as he could toward the laser's slim mounting.

'I'll rip that sonofabitch out by its roots!' Gaeta's shout came through the speaker of Habib's console.

'No!' Habib snapped reflexively. 'Don't damage the laser if you can avoid it.'

One of von Helmholtz's technicians pushed through the crowd gathered around Habib's console, his face drawn, sweaty. Grabbing Fritz's slim shoulder, he said, 'Life support's gone critical.'

Jumping to his feet, von Helmholtz said, 'We've got to get him out of there!'

Habib turned back to his console. 'How do we shut down that laser?' he shouted.

'We can't!' one of the engineers wailed. 'The beast isn't receiving any commands from us. It shut off its downlink antennas, remember?'

'My god,' Habib groaned. 'He's a dead man.'

Gaeta huddled around the strut supporting the laser, his heart hammering so hard he could hear his pulse in his ears.

Okay, he told himself. Simmer down. You're safe here. The *chingado* laser can't shoot you, you're underneath it. Take a deep breath. Another. Slow down your heart rate. Fritz'll never let you live it down; he's getting all this on the life-support telemetry; he'll say you crapped in your pants.

He squinted at the life-support readouts displayed on the inside of his helmet. Sonofabitch hit my air tank. It's leaking. Gotta get out of here.

But if I move out from under this *fregado* laser it'll start taking potshots at me again. Catch twenty-two: if I stay here I'll asphyxiate; if I make a run for the return pod I'll get shot.

'Fritz,' he called as calmly as he could. 'You got any ideas about this?'

Silence.

And Gaeta saw that the black snowstorm was closer than ever, almost upon him.

Cardenas and Negroponte walked determinedly from the biology lab to the mission control center. They had sent a hurried message to Wunderly, on Earth, and now were heading for Urbain to tell him that the creatures in Saturn's rings were nanomachines.

Nanomachines. Cardenas still found it hard to believe. Why? she asked herself. You think you're the only one in the universe who can handle nanotechnology? You're not even the only one in the solar system.

But the instant they pushed through the unguarded double doors of the mission control center, her thoughts about nanomachines and alien intelligence evaporated. Cardenas could tell from the tension crackling in the air, from the huddles of engineers and technicians hunched in tight knots around consoles, that something had gone wrong.

'Urbain isn't here,' Negroponte said. 'He must be in his office.'

Cardenas barely heard her. She rushed to von Helmholtz and his crew, clustered around one of the consoles, while Negroponte headed for Urbain's office alone.

28 May 2096: Actions

Timoshenko hovered in emptiness, staring at the slim line of the tether that attached him to the open hatch of the airlock. He didn't remember attaching the tether. He thought he would simply drift away from the habitat forever.

I must have attached it automatically, he said to himself. Without thinking consciously of it. Just part of the routine of putting on a spacesuit and going outside.

The tether was made of buckyball fibers, he knew. Strongest material known. My safety line. My link to life.

The tether led arrow-straight to the airlock build into the curving flank of the habitat. Timoshenko saw its huge bulk, rotating slowly, carrying him with it, the mammoth cylinder studded with airlocks and observations ports. He hung there as if paralyzed and watched one of the maintenance robots scooting faithfully along its track.

Ten thousand men and women, he thought. I can kill them all. I can become a mass killer. Not as big a murderer as Stalin or some of the tsars, but at least I'll have the distinction of killing everybody in my community. Every last one of them. One hundred percent.

Gaeta's life-support telltales were blinking red. The leaking air tank had started a cascade of failures. Air pressure in the suit was slowly falling. The suit's heater was automatically turning up the internal temperature to compensate. Gaeta tried to open the small emergency air tank; no response. Must've been blown away by the damned laser, he realized.

You got minutes, *amigo*, he told himself. If you don't get off this glorified garbage truck and back to the transfer craft in the next fifteen-twenty minutes, you're a dead man.

A flake of black snow plastered itself against his visor. Looking up, he saw that the storm had reached him. Black flakes of tholins were drifting down out of the cloud-laden sky.

Fritz's voice crackled in his earphones. 'You must leave the lander immediately and get to the escape pod before it's covered with snow.'

'Right,' he replied. 'But if I move this *estúpido* laser is going to zap me again.'

There'll be no answer for twelve seconds, he knew. Fumbling in the pouches attached to the waist of his suit, Gaeta found the thin metal cylinder of the diagnostic probe for the uplink antenna. He snapped its wire off, then slowly got to his feet with a grinding of servomotors.

The laser started to swivel, but Gaeta grabbed its shaft in both his servo-reinforced pincers and pushed it upward until it was pointing at the sky. Then he forced the metal plug into the laser's ball-and-socket mounting, jamming it in place.

'Okay, wise-ass,' he muttered. 'Let's see you shoot me now.'

He could hear the laser mount's gearing grinding painfully, but the plug stayed jammed in the socket and the laser just vibrated slightly, like a horse trying to shake off an annoying fly.

Satisfied that he was safe for the moment, Gaeta scrabbled on his hands and knees back to the access hatch in the center of the roof. The lander's roof was covered with slick black snow and it was getting rapidly thicker. As he started to push the accumulating tholins with his gloved hands, trying to clear the area where he'd dropped the comm link with *Alpha*'s central computer, he thought about his childhood in Los Angeles and how much he'd wanted to play in the snow when he was a kid.

'What are you doing?' von Helmholtz demanded sharply. 'Get to the escape pod at once!'

470

'Got a job to do first, Fritz,' he said. And he clicked off his communications link.

He brushed more of the black snow off the roof. There! He found the comm line, still connected to the computer's access panel. Picking up the loose end, Gaeta plugged it into his suit.

He was panting. Can't be exertion, he thought. Air level's getting low.

'Okay, computer,' he said, surprised that his throat felt raspy, 'listen to me.'

No reponse from the central computer.

'Humans are a source of contamination, right?'

'YES.'

'And your logic tells you that if you uplink the data you've taken in from the sensors, more humans will come and contaminate the area.'

'MORE HUMANS OR THEIR MACHINES.'

'All right.' Gaeta coughed. 'Now listen. No humans will be sent to Titan. None. I'm leaving and no humans will come here after I leave. Understand?'

For a heartbeat Gaeta thought the computer would not respond. But then its synthesized voice said flatly, 'UNDER-STOOD.'

The snow was falling thickly now. Gaeta felt as if he were inside an inkwell.

Brushing black flakes from his visor, he turned on his helmet lights. 'And no machines will be sent to Titan either,' he said to the computer. 'There will be no more contamination. Understand that? You will be the only machine on Titan and no humans will come after I leave.'

Again the computer was silent. Then, 'UNDERSTOOD.'

'So you can uplink the sensor data and reopen your down-link antennas. There won't be any other sources of contamination coming here.'

The yellow message light was blinking frantically. Gaeta ignored it.

Well, I've done the best I could, he said to himself. Now it's up to this bucket of chips to figure out what to do. He pulled the line from the computer's access panel and stuffed it into a pouch at his waist, then reopened his comm link.

Gaeta clicked to his other frequency. 'Fritz, it's darker than the bottom of hell down here. You gotta talk me to the return pod.'

And then he climbed to his feet and stood erect on the edge of *Alpha*'s roof, waiting for Fritz to direct him back to safety.

28 May 2096: Death

Gaeta wiped at his visor again; his glove left a black smear across the glassteel. C'mon Fritz, he urged silently. I'm leakin' air down here. His life-support displays were all in the red now.

'Air supply critical,' came the suit's computer voice. 'At present loss rate, air supply will be exhausted in twelve minutes.'

There's air in the suit, Gaeta told himself. Suit's full of air. Even if the tank goes dry I can last another ten-fifteen minutes on the air inside the suit before I use up all the oxygen in it.

He peered out into the swirling dark flakes. The return pod's out there, off to my right somewhere. Seventy-two meters away. I could throw a football that far, almost. It's covered with this black crap by now, but if I get close enough I'll see it sticking up like a fat phone booth.

'The escape pod is thirty-four degrees from your position,' Fritz said, his voice brittle with tension. 'If you are facing the rear of the lander the pod is on your right in the two o'clock direction.'

'Two o'clock, copy.' Gaeta knew there were ladders built into both sides of *Alpha*. He got down onto his knees again, servos groaning, and looked up and down the lander's flat metal flank.

'I see the rungs. Starting for the ladder.' It was easier to crawl. 'Got the ladder. I'm going down now.'

Wondering how much the audience could see in this black blizzard, Gaeta felt his way cautiously down the metal rungs.

473

'I'm on the ground now,' he said, turning around. Then it hit him. 'I'm standing on the surface of Titan!' he exulted. 'My boots are on the methane snow!'

Fritz must have already been speaking to him, because his voice came through immediately. '. . . on the ground with your back to the lander, the escape pod is seventy-two meters from you. Your heading should now be ten o'clock.'

'Gotcha,' Gaeta replied. He started walking. 'Ground's kinda mushy, like slogging through wet snow, maybe ankle-deep. Not easy going.'

'Air supply critical,' the computer reminded calmly. 'At present loss rate, air supply will be exhausted in ten minutes.'

Cardenas stood frozen behind Fritz's seated form. Ten minutes worth of air! Manny's going to die down there.

As if he could hear her thoughts, von Helmholtz turned in his wheeled chair and looked up at her. 'He'll make it,' he said flatly. 'There's enough air inside the suit itself for him to make it to the rendezvous in orbit.'

'You're sure?' She could feel her pulse machine-gunning through her chest.

Fritz pointed at the display screen. 'The numbers show that he'll make it.' But she noticed that his extended finger was trembling. And then he added, 'If he doesn't stumble into any obstacles before he gets to the escape pod.'

Timoshenko floated serenely at the end of the tether that connected him to the airlock. Saturn sank behind the habitat's dark bulk, a spectacular sight with its saffron clouds and glittering rings disappearing behind the knife edge of *Goddard*'s flank.

I can't kill them all, Timoshenko told himself. I'm not a murderer. Eberly, yes. I'd throttle him with my bare hands if I could. He deserves it, the lying bastard. But not the others. Not ten thousand people. I can't.

Then what can you do, idiot? snarled a savage voice in his head. Here you are hanging onto the end of a rope and thinking about life and death. Whose life? Whose death?

Gaeta slogged across the mushy ground, his boots sinking into the black mud. With each squelching step he had to pull his feet out of the mire; the boots came loose with an obscene sucking sound.

'Air supply critical,' the computer chanted. 'At present loss rate, air supply will be exhausted in seven minutes.'

'You are within fifty meters of the escape pod,' Fritz said. 'Can you see it?'

'Can't see much in this muck,' Gaeta answered, staring out ahead. He saw a tall, bulky shape sticking up out of the black ooze. 'Hey, yeah, I see it!'

It was impossible to run in the goo, but Gaeta redoubled his efforts. His visor seemed clearer, and the darkness around him was lifting somewhat.

'The snow's changing to rain,' he said, puffing as he worked his way toward the return pod. 'Must be a warm front comin' through.' He laughed at his own joke: warm on Titan would mean anything higher than a hundred seventy-five below.

Fat drops splattered against his visor and he could hear them pattering against his suit's outer shell.

'The rain consists of a mixture of ethane and water drop-lets,' said Fritz.

'Makes it easier to see,' Gaeta replied, 'but it's turning the ground into real soup. Tough-going.'

'Air supply critical,' the computer said again. 'At present loss rate—'

Gaeta cut off the voice. I don't need to be reminded, he said to himself. Aloud, he asked, 'Hey, is that monster back there uplinking the sensor data?'

More than twelve seconds' wait. Then Habib's voice came

on. 'Yes! The data is streaming in. It's wonderful! How did you get the computer to do it?'

Gaeta was puffing with the exertion of slogging through the sticky, clinging mud. 'My father,' he said.

Christ, he thought as he plodded ahead, I wanted to be the first man on Titan but I wanted to be able to get back home, too. The way this mud's sucking me down, looks like Titan wants me to stay here.

'Your father?'

'Yeah . . .' Another step. 'When we were kids . . . and we asked him for something . . . he didn't have the money for . . . he would tell us he'd get it . . . But he never would.'

Another squelching stride into the gooey mud.

'What's that got to do with getting the computer back on line?'

'He lied to us, Gaeta explained. 'He'd lie . . . with a smile . . . and we'd believe him . . . Suckered us . . . every time.'

He could see the return pod clearly now. The rain was washing that black snow off it.

'So I lied . . . to the computer . . . Told it . . . what it wanted . . . to hear.'

Gaeta's legs felt like lengths of lumber. He reached the return pod, half collapsed against it.

'Works . . . every time,' he panted. 'Dumb computer . . . thinks I'm . . . honest.'

A sledgehammer blow to his shoulder knocked him off his feet. '*Gesoo*,' Gaeta yelped. 'That damned laser's shooting at me!'

Timoshenko realized he'd been out in the spacesuit for nearly an hour. Doing what? he asked himself. What have you accomplished out here?

'I've been thinking,' he murmured. 'Thinking. It's good for a man to think. Think before you act.'

There is only one life you have the right to take, he decided. Your own.

476

He tossed away the remote controller that he'd been holding in his gloved hand. It went spinning off into the infinity of space. I'm not a mass murderer. I'm not a murderer at all. But suicide, that's a different matter. That's between nobody but me and myself.

He touched the safety catch that sealed his helmet to the torso of the hard suit. Open the catch, let out the air, and you'll decompress in seconds. A bloody mess, but you'll be dead. No more worries, no more regrets. Nothing but peace.

He fingered the catch. No more anything, he thought. Are you ready for that? Are you ready for death?

He was surprised to realize that he wasn't. Despite everything, despite losing Katrina and his life on Earth he was not ready to die. Damn Eberly! he snarled inwardly. He's right! This habitat may be a prison but it's a soft one. Life here can be good if you'll just open your heart to it.

Life or death?

Can you build a life for yourself without Katrina? he asked himself. And answered, What have you been doing for the past two and a half years?

He looked out at the stars again, his back to Saturn and the habitat's dark bulk. The stars stared back at him, unblinking, uncompromising. You can look Death in the face, he said to himself, but that's close enough. Close enough. Life is too precious to throw away.

With a sigh he turned and began to pull himself along the buckyball tether back to the airlock.

The answer is life, Timoshenko realized. Choose life. You can always kill yourself if things get really intolerable. In the meantime, maybe I can make something of myself here. Maybe life can be worth living, after all.

Negroponte knocked softly on Urbain's office door. When no one answered she rapped harder.

So much to tell him, she thought. But he's so wrapped up with his *Titan Alpha* that nothing else matters to him.

Still no response.

'Dr. Urbain,' she called. 'It's Dr. Negroponte. I must speak to you. We've made an enormous discovery.'

Silence. She felt resentment simmering inside her. The pompous fool, she said to herself. So focused on that precious probe of his he doesn't care if hell freezes over.

Angrily she slid the door open and strode into Urbain's office. He sat slumped over his desk, his head in his arms, quite dead.

28 May 2096: Rebirth

Gaeta sank to his knees as another beam of intense green light flashed past him.

'The *chingado* laser's shooting at me!' he repeated. Goddam plug must've worked loose out of the mounting, he added silently. He realized his left arm was flaming with pain. The life-support displays were going crazy, he saw. The suit had been penetrated and the automatic safety system had sealed off the whole arm.

Down on all fours in the soupy black muck, he found that he couldn't put any weight on his left arm. Must've broke my friggin' arm, he groaned to himself. He dragged himself behind the return pod's bulk. Maybe the laser can't see me back here, he hoped. But I gotta climb up into the rig before I can light off. The whole arm was numb now. He could feel the pressure cuff squeezing tightly on his shoulder but below that, the arm was frozen.

'What is your situation?' Fritz sounded testy, alarmed.

'Climbing into the return pod.'

It took a painful effort, with only one working arm. Even in the relatively light gravity of Titan, and with the servomotors amplifying his muscular strength, the suit was desperately heavy. Sweat popped out on Gaeta's brow, stinging his eyes. He could feel cold perspiration soaking his coveralls.

'Habib has turned off the laser,' Fritz said. 'The lander is accepting commands from the control center now.'

'Glad . . . to hear it,' Gaeta puffed as he climbed into the pod and slid his boots into the slots on its flooring. It was like standing in an open coffin, narrow, confined. Through the spattering rain Gaeta could see *Alpha*, a squat blocky shape sitting on the mushy ground. It looked alien, completely out of place.

'Ready for launch,' Gaeta said, his shoulder flaming with agony, his breath rasping. Without waiting for Fritz to confirm it, he reached for the toggle switch that would ignite the rocket engine. 'Initiating launch sequence,' he said, grateful that the switch was on the side of his good arm.

Pancho looked across the cramped bridge of the transfer vessel at Wanamaker. 'We're gonna have company in half an hour,' she said.

'Less,' Wanamaker replied. 'Timeline calls for rendezvous twenty-three minutes after he lifts off.'

'Hair-splitter,' Pancho sniffed. 'I know—'

'Ms. Lane.' Von Helmholtz's voice crackled from the comm speaker. 'This is an emergency situation.'

'Don't I know it,' Pancho snapped. Then she had to wait nearly twelve seconds, fidgeting nervously and staring at Wanamaker.

'Gaeta's air tank is leaking badly,' von Helmoltz replied at last. 'Down on Titan's surface, under the heavy pressure of the atmosphere, the leak is bad enough. Once he launches and gets into the vacuum of space the tank will degas in seconds.'

'So he'll be breathin' the air inside his suit,' Pancho said. 'How much time's he got?'

Again the agonizing time lag.

'No more than fifteen minutes,' von Helmholtz answered at last. 'Closer to ten.'

'We'll hafta pick him up soon's he pops up above the atmosphere,' Pancho said.

Wanamaker nodded once, then ducked out into the passage-way that connected with the cargo bay. And the suit lockers, Pancho realized. Sure enough, Jake came back with a nanosuit in his arms and began unfolding it.

'Yes,' von Helmholtz said. 'It is imperative that you capture him at the earliest possible moment – without endangering the rendezvous itself, of course.'

'Sure,' Pancho said cheerily. 'Grab him quick but make sure we don't miss him. No sweat.'

Wanamaker was pulling on the nanosuit. Pancho grinned at him and said, 'Hurry up and take your time, that's what that peckerwood wants.'

'Just like the Navy,' said Wanamaker. But the expression on his face was dead serious.

Standing in the coffin-like return pod, Gaeta thought that Berkowitz would want him to say something. But he had to conserve his air. Let 'em hear my heavy breathing, he decided. Zeke can fill in with all the commentary he wants.

The launch sequence for the pod was only thirty seconds long, yet it seemed like hours as Gaeta stood there, his arm as dead as a chunk of marble, chest heaving. Maybe the air tank's already empty, he thought. He remembered that he'd switched off the computer's voice. The computer control keypad was on the left side of the suit. I'm not gonna even try to move that arm, he told himself. Yet he tried to wiggle his fingers. A lance of pain shot up the arm.

Arm's not completely dead yet, he told himself. That's something. Now if the air holds out long enough . . . Why haven't we lifted off? Maybe the launch sequencer's malfunctioned, he thought. Or the rocket's no-go. It's more than thirty seconds now. Got to be. Maybe—

The rocket lit off with a thundering roar and the pod lurched into the air; the surge of thrust would have buckled Gaeta's knees if he hadn't been standing in the suit.

'Yahoo,' he said, in a throaty whisper that hadn't the faintest trace of excitement in it.

* * *

481

'How low can you go?' Wanamaker asked nervously as Pancho maneuvered the transfer craft closer to the orange-gray clouds of Titan.

She realized her tongue was between her teeth, a sure sign that she was keyed up. 'Won every limbo contest I ever was in,' she answered.

'That isn't a dance floor down there,' said Wanamaker.

'Don't sweat it, Jake. Just get yourself zipped up in that suit and open up the cargo bay. We're gonna pick Manny up just like a frog snaps up a fly.'

Wanamaker pulled the nanofiber hood over his head and sealed it the collar of his suit, thinking that a fly really doesn't do so well when a frog snaps it up.

Gaeta realized he must have passed out briefly from the strain of the launch. One moment he was lifting off Titan's surface, the next he was up above the clouds, in space, with nothing but the cold and distant stars around him.

He coughed. Air must be getting sour, he told himself. Sure, he realized, the tank would blow out completely once I'm in vacuum. I'm breathing the air inside the suit now.

'Hang in there, Manny.' Pancho's voice, he recognized. 'The cavalry's chargin' in to the rescue.'

Pancho stood alone on the bridge now that Wanamaker had gone to the cargo bay. She focused her attention on the display screen that showed Gaeta's planned trajectory, a thin green curve that rose from the surface of Titan and bent into a graceful elliptical orbit around the frozen moon.

The red dot that revealed where Gaeta actually was showed that he was almost exactly on the nominal trajectory, Pancho saw. Pod's guidance system works pretty good, she thought. Further along the curving green line was a yellow dot, marking where the transfer craft was calculated to rendezvous with

Gaeta. Too far, Pancho knew. He'll be suffocating on his own carbon dioxide by then.

She had already instructed the guidance program to lay out a plot for the earliest possible intercept of Gaeta's trajectory. Now she was flying that course, one hand on the T-shaped control yoke that projected from the instrument panel. She felt the craft yaw to the right, making her sway slightly in the plastic loops that held her softbooted feet to the deck.

The cargo bay hatch's monitor light turned red.

'Hatch is open.' Wanamaker's voice came through the control panel's speaker.

'You tethered?' Pancho called.

'Double length,' said Wanamaker. 'Ready to go out on your command.'

I'm givin' orders to an admiral! Pancho thought. Then she shook her head disapprovingly. No time for silly crap, she said to herself sternly. A man's life is on the line.

Clicking the communications switch, she called, 'Manny, how you doin' out there?'

She heard him cough, then his voice came through, sounding weak, tired. 'I'm on . . . a wing and a . . . prayer, kid.'

Despite it all Pancho grinned. Been a long time since anybody called me kid, she said to herself.

Timoshenko felt astoundingly calm as he slowly took off his spacesuit. It took a while to do it, all alone. After making certain that the airlock was properly sealed he had walked to the lockers where the suits were stored. Sitting heavily on the bench in front of the lockers he had disconnected his life-support lines, lifted off his helmet, and took a deep double lungful of the habitat's air. After the canned air of the spacesuit it tasted like spring wine. Then he wormed out of the back-pack. Next came the gloves, and after them the boots. All very calmly, carefully. He laid the items on the bench in a neat row.

I'm alive, he told himself. From now on I appreciate every

moment of life, every breath I draw. Slowly he lifted the hard-shell torso of the suit over his head and rested it against one of the lockers. Then he tugged off the leggings.

Once he had the entire suit properly stowed in its locker he took another deep breath, then started along the passageway that led back to the green and spacious interior of the habitat. It's not a prison, he told himself. It's my world. Heaven or hell, it's the only world I have. My world. My life.

Her eyes fixed on the display screen, Pancho saw that the red dot representing Gaeta's position and the blue dot showing the transfer craft's position were overlapping. She was getting a good blip from his suit on the ship's radar, too.

'You see him?' she asked Wanamaker.

'Not yet.'

She had left the comm line open, but Gaeta hadn't said anything for the past few minutes.

'Manny,' she called. 'Can you see us?'

No reply.

'Damn. He must be out cold by now.'

'I see him!' Wanamaker yelled. 'He's still in the pod.'

Pancho punched up the radar data and began to adjust the transfer craft's velocity to match Gaeta's.

'Too far to reach,' Wanamaker said, his voice high with strain.

'Manny,' Pancho called. 'Can you maneuver?'

She thought she heard a moan. Maybe a cough. 'Hang in there, pal,' she said. 'We'll come and getcha.'

With the deftness of a concert pianist Pancho worked the keyboard that controlled the craft's maneuvering thrusters. Easy now, she told herself. No big moves. Jest a leetle touch . . .

'I think I can reach him!' Wanamaker sang out.

'Go for it, Jake,' she said. 'I'll nudge us closer while you're out there.'

★   ★   ★

The mission control center was absolutely silent. Cardenas held her breath as she listened to Pancho's radio chatter. Manny's suit must be filled with carbon dioxide, she thought. No oxygen left. How long can he go without brain damage? Or dying?

Wanamaker glided out of the transfer craft's airlock, unreeling the double length of tether that was clipped to the waist of his nanofiber spacesuit. In his mind he rehearsed the procedures for unlatching the grips that held Gaeta in the narrow confines of the escape pod.

'Hey, Manny,' he called. 'How're you doing?'

Nothing. Wanamaker didn't even hear breathing in his earphones.

He reached the pod and unlocked the grips as swiftly as he could, then wrapped the tether under Gaeta's shoulders and hauled his weightless bulk out of the pod.

'Just like we did at the rings,' he said to Gaeta. 'We'll have you back in the cargo bay in a few seconds.'

It seemed to take forever to work their way back to the transfer craft, and then even longer to close the airlock hatch and wait for the pumps to fill the cargo bay with air.

As soon as the keypad lights turned green, Wanamaker tore open the hatch at the rear of Gaeta's suit. 'Breathe, Manny,' he urged. 'Take a good, deep breath.'

Reaching awkwardly inside suit, Wanamaker wrapped his long arms around Gaeta's chest and squeezed. Then he relaxed, then squeezed again. Three times. Four . . .

Gaeta gagged and coughed. Wanamaker pulled his arms out of the suit, banging both elbows painfully on the edges of the hatch. But he heard Gaeta sucking in air, wheezing, coughing.

'He's alive, Pancho!' Wanamaker shouted happily. 'Let's get him back home.'

30 May 2096: Infirmary

Gaeta opened his eyes slowly and saw that he was lying in a hospital bed. The sheets were crisp and smelled of disinfectant. Monitors beeped softly on the wall to his side.

His left arm was enclosed in a dark gray plastic sheath from shoulder to fingertips. And sitting asleep in a chair at the foot of his bed was Kris Cardenas, her head half sunk in a thick pillow that was propped on her shoulder, her feet tucked under her. Even with her bright blue eyes closed and her golden hair tousled from sleep she looked beautiful.

I made it, Kris, he said silently to her. I came back to you. He smiled at her.

He yawned sleepily. Looking around, he saw that he was in a private room, bright pastel walls and even a window with sunshine streaming through. Nice, he thought. First-class treatment. Then he looked at Cardenas again. She looks like a kid, sleeping all curled up like that. A golden-haired angel. He sank back into sleep watching her.

Holly was sitting on the sofa in her living room beside Tavalera, running through the video images she intended to show at the final debate, scheduled for this election eve.

'I checked all the numbers with three different sets of astronomers on Earth and Selene,' Tavalera was saying. 'Over the past hundred years an average of sixteen comets have come out of the Kuiper Belt each year. That's comets bigger than five kilometers across.'

486

Studying the chart displayed on her smart wall, Holly said, 'And they all enter the inner solar system?'

'Most do. Some get pulled in to Jupiter space, some to Saturn. Most swing through the inner system once and never come back – or at least their orbits are so long that they haven't come back yet.'

'That's a lot of water, though.'

'Billions of tons each year,' said Tavalera, almost smiling.

Holly closed her eyes briefly, then said, 'So here are my main points for tonight's debate: One, the creatures in the rings are really nanomachines, built by aliens who-knows-when.'

'So we don't dare start messing with them.'

Nodding, 'Two, the power outages we've suffered were caused by electromagnetic surges from the nanocritters.'

'Maybe those surges are signals,' Tavalera coached. 'Don't forget that point.'

'F' sure. But who're they signaling?'

'The aliens who planted 'em in the rings.'

'Or maybe they're trying to get our attention?' Holly suggested.

Tavalera shrugged. 'Either way, we can't mine the rings. No way.'

''Kay. Third point: We can still get rich by capturing comets and selling their water.'

'As long as *they* don't have anything living in 'em,' Tavalera said, almost in a grumble.

'Astrobiologists have been studying comets for a century, almost,' Holly countered. 'Lots of prebiotic chemicals, amino acids and stuff, but no living organisms.'

'So far.'

Holly tapped his chin with a forefinger. 'We'll examine each comet before we start chopping up its ice. If we find anything we'll leave that one to the scientists. There's plenty of others.'

He grasped her hand and looked into her eyes. 'Holly, you're gonna win this election, you know.'

'Maybe.'

'What happens to us when you do?'

She felt a lump in her throat. Swallowing hard, she replied, 'I don't know, Raoul. I guess what happens is up to you.'

When Gaeta opened his eyes again, he saw that Cardenas was standing at the foot of his bed smiling at him. A chubby, round-faced man in a white medical smock stood beside her; he was smiling too.

'Good morning,' said the doctor. 'I am Oswaldo Yañez, your attending physician.'

'Good morning,' Gaeta echoed. The gray plastic sheath still covered his arm, but he felt clear-headed, bright. No pain.

Cardenas stepped swiftly to the side of the bed, leaned over, and kissed him hard. Gaeta grasped her with his good arm and held her tightly.

'You're going to be all right,' she said, half whispering as she leaned against him. 'I've got nanomachines repairing your arm. You'll be fine in a few days.'

She pulled away from him at last as Yañez took a palm-sized remote from the pocket of his smock. An x-ray picture of Gaeta's arm appeared on the wall to his right.

'The bone break is already healed,' the doctor said cheer-fully, 'with the help of Dr. Cardenas's little devices. Repairing the damage caused by the freezing will take a while longer, however.'

'You saved my arm,' Gaeta said to her.

'I want you all in one piece, with all your parts working right.'

He grinned. 'Me, too.'

Yañez coughed politely. 'Do you feel strong enough for visitors? There are several people outside.'

'Sure,' said Gaeta. 'Send 'em in.'

Pancho and Jake Wanamaker trooped in, together with a darker-skinned guy with a trim little beard fringing his jawline.

'This is Da'ud Habib,' Pancho said, without any preliminaries. 'He's the one you were talkin' with when you were down on Titan.'

'I want to thank you from the bottom of my heart for bringing *Alpha* back to life for us,' Habib said. Gaeta saw that the man's eyes were glistening; he was on the verge of tears.

'I guess Urbain is pretty damned happy, huh?'

Habib stiffened slightly. 'Dr. Urbain is dead.'

'Dead?'

'He suffered a massive coronary attack while you were working on the surface. By the time we found him in his office it was too late to do anything to help him.'

'Holy shit,' Gaeta said fervently.

'But you brought *Alpha* back to life,' Habib said. 'The probe is under our control and sending streams of data. For that we owe you our eternal thanks.'

Impulsively Habib grabbed Gaeta's right hand and pumped it. Then, as if embarrassed by his burst of emotion, he dropped Gaeta's hand and stepped back from the bed.

Before anyone could think of something to say, Fritz von Helmholtz stepped into the little room, impeccably attired in a navy blue blazer over a golden yellow turtleneck.

'Hi, Fritz,' Gaeta said. 'Join the party.'

Fritz smiled tightly and offered, 'Apparently you are well on the road to recovery.'

'That's what they tell me,' said Gaeta.

'Your mission to Titan was a great success financially. We will clear slightly more than fourteen million, even factoring in medical expenses.'

Gaeta laughed. 'You frozen popsicle. You were worried about me, admit it.'

'I knew you would survive,' Fritz said, unruffled. 'And Dr. Cardenas's nanomachines will repair your arm, no?'

Cardenas said, 'Damned right.'

'So,' Fritz said. 'The mission was a great success.'

'Glad to hear it,' said Pancho.

Still focusing on Gaeta, Fritz went on, 'Requests are pouring in. We are doing preliminary studies of a trek across Mercury at perihelion, when the planet is closest to the Sun.'

'Not me,' Gaeta said. 'I'm retired.'

'I've heard that before,' said Fritz, a tiny smile twitching his lips.

'For keeps,' said Gaeta, reaching for Cardenas with his good arm. 'When you and the crew head back to Earth, take the suit with you. I'm finished with it.'

Cardenas squeezed his hand so hard Gaeta was surprised at the strength in her.

30 May 2096: The Third Debate

From his seat in the rear of the jam-packed auditorium, Tavalera thought that Yolanda Negroponte looked like a blonde Amazon, standing tall and determined in the midst of the crowd. Eberly was at the lectern, trying to keep from scowling at her. Behind him sat Holly and Professor Wilmot.

Wilmot had thrown the debate open to questions from the floor immediately after the candidates' brief opening statements. Holly hadn't had a chance to show the graphs and imagery that Tavalera had helped her to put together. He didn't even give her a chance to tell them about mining comets, Tavalera thought fretfully.

Several of Eberly's flacks had asked about mining the rings in the face of the IAA's order, received that morning, banning any commercial activity in Saturn's rings until the presence of nanomachines there could be thoroughly investigated.

Eberly had insisted that he would start mining operations anyway, and negotiate with the 'Earthbound bureaucrats' to permit mining and scientific studies at the same time. 'They're a billion kilometers away,' he'd said. 'How dare they try to tell us what to do?'

That's when Negroponte shot to her feet.

'There's more involved here than a jurisdictional conflict with the IAA. Those nanomachines were put into the rings by somebody. An intelligent species. We don't know when and we don't know why.'

Eberly forced a condescending smile. 'It was probably

millions of years ago. Whoever seeded the rings with those machines is probably long gone, maybe extinct.'

'Do you know that for a fact?' Negroponte demanded. Before Eberly could reply she went on, 'No, you don't. No one does. But we know that the nanomachines put out surges of electromagnetic energy. That's what caused the power outages we've had—'

'That problem has been fixed,' Eberly said quickly.

'But suppose those surges are actually signals?' Negroponte insisted. 'Suppose those nanomachines are sending out a message to their creators, a message that says we are here, in Saturn's vicinity?'

The crowded auditorium went absolutely silent.

'Suppose,' Negroponte added, 'that whoever planted those nanomachines would be angry with anyone who disturbed them? What then?'

Eberly's mouth twitched several times before he replied, 'That's . . . sheer speculation.'

'But do we dare take a chance? We're facing some enormous unknowns here.'

Eberly tried to smile again. But Holly got up from her chair and asked Professor Wilmot, 'May I respond to her question?' The pin-mike clipped to her tunic amplified her voice so that the audience heard it clearly.

Wilmot also got to his feet. 'If Mr. Eberly is finished,' he said.

Eberly backed away from the lectern, but remained standing.

Holly licked her lips as she gripped the lectern's sides and said, 'I know how we can get rich from selling water without touching the rings.'

The crowd stirred. Turning to Wilmot as she fished a palmcomp from her pocket, Holly said, 'I have a few images to show. 'Kay?'

'Go right ahead,' said Wilmot.

492

Tavalera sat back and watched the imagery he had helped Holly to prepare flash onto the wall screen at the rear of the auditorium's stage. Holly went through the presentation they had rehearsed in a methodical, orderly way: use *Goddard* as a base of operations; locate comets sailing inward from the Kuiper Belt; mine them for their water; sell the water to the human settlements throughout the solar system.

'With the money we make from selling water,' she concluded, 'we'll be able to lift the Zero Growth limit and expand our habitat, even build new ones when we have to. And we can do it without interfering with the nanobugs in the rings.'

'How do you know there aren't nanomachines in the comets?' a man shouted. 'Or living creatures?'

Tavalera knew that Holly was prepared for that one.

With an easy smile, she replied, 'Astrobiologists have been studying comets for pretty near a century now. They've found organic chemicals in them, but no living organisms. And no nanomachines.'

'Yeah, but still . . .'

'If a comet bears life – or alien machines – we'll leave it alone. There's plenty of other comets to pick from.'

The questions slowly turned from hostile to friendly. Holly's winning them over, Tavalera saw. She's doing it. She's showing them how to get rich without hurting the rings.

For more than an hour the people in the audience fired questions at both candidates. Tavalera realized that more and more of the questions were addressed to Holly, fewer to Eberly.

Sitting off to one side of the auditorium, Vernon Donkman felt a soft glow of satisfaction surge through him. It's the alien machines! he told himself. Their electromagnetic pulses caused the power outages and flummoxed the accounting files. That's what caused those damnable discrepancies. He felt grateful to the scientists who had finally solved the puzzle.

When Wilmot at last called a halt and asked for final

493

statements, the crowd got to its feet and applauded Holly. Eberly hung back like a wounded wolf, staring unbelievingly at what was happening. Negroponte charged forward toward the stage, followed by a dozen other women. They surged up onto the stage and lifted Holly onto their shoulders, then paraded her around the auditorium as everyone whooped and cheered while Wilmot and Eberly stood on the stage dumbfounded.

She's done it, Tavalera told himself. She's gonna win tomorrow's election. She'll never come back to Earth with me.

Oral Diary of
Professor James Coleraine Wilmot

'Extraordinary. This lonely outpost at the edge of human civilization has become the center of the scientific world's attention. Hordes of scientists are traveling all the way out here to examine the alien nanodevices that Wunderly and Negroponte discovered. The two women are in line for a Nobel Prize, and politicians on Earth and the Moon have been forced to admit that there has been an alien presence in the solar system. How long ago the extraterrestrials were here, whether or not they're coming back, whether or not they are *still here* observing us, no one knows. The politicians and the media pundits are all in a lather over it.

'I must admit that the question is fascinating, even a bit frightening. Who are they? What are their intentions toward us?

'I'm not sure that I want to find out.

'The irony is, of course, that Dr. Urbain died just before achieving the success that he had worked so hard for. In a sense, his *Titan Alpha* rover killed him. His widow has already left for Earth, where Urbain will at last receive the recognition and honors that had eluded him while he was alive.

'On a much more local issue, Holly Lane won a stunning upset victory over Malcolm Eberly in the election. Her proposal to mine comets for their water turned the tables on Eberly completely. Of course, her championing of the women's right to have babies was a major factor in her rather impressive rout of Eberly.

'So Holly is being installed as our chief administrator and Eberly is out in the cold. At last. Can't say I'm disappointed by that. Never liked the man. I wonder what he'll try to do now that he's out of power?'

20 June 2096: Morning

Holly and Tavalera had to push against an incoming tide of three dozen scientists surging into the reception area from the fusion torch ship docked to the habitat's main airlock. The arriving men and women looked eager, thrilled to be at *Goddard* after a six-week flight from Earth. Carrying a single travel bag, Tavalera looked gloomier than usual, downright depressed. Holly, due to be installed as the habitat's new chief administrator later in the afternoon, seemed almost as sad.

The scientists rushed on past them, chattering excitedly with one another. Holly and Tavalera made their way to the airlock hatch, where a lone officer from the arriving torch ship stood in royal blue coveralls, a palmcomp in hand.

'So you're really going?' Holly asked, her voice barely above a whisper.

Tavalera smiled wistfully. 'You're really staying?'

'I've got to,' she said, blinking at the tears forming in her eyes.

'Me too,' he replied. 'I've got to go back home, Holly. I'd hate myself if I didn't. I'd end up hating you for keeping me here.'

'I guess.'

His eyes were glistening too. 'I love you, Holly.'

She put her hands on his shoulders and rested her head against his chest. 'I love you too, Raoul.'

'I'll come back,' he said, folding his free arm around her. 'I just hafta see Earth again, my family, my old friends. Then I'll come back to you.'

'Just let me know when and I'll hire a ship to bring you.' She looked up at him, tried to smile. 'I'm a twirling VIP now . . . or I will be in a few hours.'

The ship's officer coughed politely. 'Our turnaround time is very tight, I'm afraid. You'll have to board if we're going to make rendezvous with the tanker they've laid on for us at Jupiter.'

Tavalera nodded. 'I know something about tankers,' he said mildly.

Holly clutched at him, kissed him longingly. He held her just as tightly, but then broke the embrace.

'I . . . I'll be back,' he promised, hefting his travel bag.

'I'll be here,' she said.

He turned abruptly and walked swiftly past the officer to duck through the airlock hatch and disappear from her view.

Trying to fight down the feeling that she'd never see him again, Holly went slowly back through the now-empty reception area, her head low, her spirits even lower.

'Uh . . . Ms. Chief Administrator?'

She looked up and saw Ilya Timoshenko standing at the end of the short passageway that opened into the habitat proper. He was dressed in slacks and collarless jacket, his shirt buttoned to the neck.

'Mr. Timoshenko,' she said, surprised to see him.

'Ilya, please to call me Ilya.'

'Ilya. And you should call me Holly. Besides, I'm not chief administrator yet. Not for another . . .' she glanced at her wrist '. . . five hours.'

Timoshenko's gray eyes sparkled. 'Even so, we're going to be working together for the next year. Maybe more, no?'

'Maybe,' Holly said, thinking, or maybe I'll go to Earth when my term in office is finished.

Timoshenko looked slightly flustered, almost embarrassed. 'I know you'll be surrounded with friends and well-wishers at the ceremony, so I came out here to see you before all that.'

'Is there something in particular . . . ?'

'No, nothing special. I just want to offer you my congratulations, and assure you that the maintenance department will keep this bucket in tip-top shape for you.'

'For all the people,' Holly said.

'Yes, for everybody. Now that Eberly's out of office, I can promise that with my whole heart.'

Despite herself, Holly grinned at him. 'You don't like Malcolm?'

Grinning back at her, Timoshenko answered, 'I don't like most people, but him I like least of all.'

Holly actually laughed. 'Well, I hope you grow to like me, at least a little bit.' She started toward the hatch at the end of the passageway.

'I think I already do,' said Timoshenko. And he stepped quickly in front of her to tap out the code on the hatch's keypad. The heavy hatch sighed open a crack.

'Um . . . would it be all right if I asked you for a favor?' he said, his back to her.

'A favor?'

Turning to face her, his face looking strangely flustered, embarrassed, Timoshenko explained, 'Once you are chief administrator you will have the authority to put through calls to people on Earth, no?'

'Anybody has the right—'

'Not exiles,' Timoshenko interrupted. 'The authorities won't allow my ex-wife to receive calls from me.'

Understanding dawned on Holly. 'So you want me to call her for you.'

'If you could.'

'I'd be glad to, Ilya. Maybe we can get her to come out here and be with you again.'

Timoshenko's face turned flame-red. But his smile was anything but sheepish. Turning quickly, he pulled the hatch all the way open.

Holly saw the green and vibrant habitat spread out before her. Timoshenko made a little bow to usher her through the hatch and into her own domain.

Eberly sat alone in his apartment, his uneaten lunch on the kitchen table before him.

They voted against me, he said to himself for the thousandth time. She beat me by a landslide. They rejected me. I'm all alone now. I don't even have a job.

He thought of the Bible story of the unjust steward, who also found himself thrown out of his job. What can I do? Eberly asked himself. To dig I am unable, to beg I am too proud.

At that exact moment his phone chimed.

'Phone answer,' he called out glumly.

The kitchen cabinets to his left glowed and formed an image of Zeke Berkowitz, smiling his usual affable, avuncular smile.

'Good morning, Malcolm,' said Berkowitz brightly.

'It's past noon,' Eberly replied. 'And I'm in no mood for an interview about our change in administrations.'

Berkowitz looked almost startled. 'Interview? No, no. That's not why I called you.'

'Then what?' Crossly.

'I figured you'll be looking for a new job and I wanted to get my offer in ahead of all the others.'

There were no others, Eberly knew, and he suspected that Berkowitz did too. 'A new job?'

'I've got an idea,' Berkowitz said, his smile widening. 'How would you like to be a commentator on our news broadcasts? You know, give the people your opinions on what's happening, your slant on the stories of the day.'

'A video commentator?'

'Sure. You'd be a natural. And it would keep you in front of the public every day. People would look up to you, they'd value your opinions.'

'They'd admire me?'

'Of course they would! You've served this community well. You've worked hard. Now you can be the voice of habitat *Goddard*, sharing your insights on each day's events with your fellow citizens.'

'Every day. I'd be seen every day.'

Berkowitz nodded cheerfully. His broad smile was soon matched by Eberly's own.

Pancho sat in the front row for the swearing-in ceremony, with Jake beside her. She beamed as Holly took the oath of office from Professor Wilmot.

Holly looked slightly nervous as she began her inauguration speech, Pancho thought, but her sister launched into it smoothly enough.

'You ready for the big adventure?' Pancho whispered to Wanamaker.

'Chasing comets?' he whispered back.

'That's only part of it.'

'What's the rest?'

'Havin' a baby.'

Wanamaker's jaw dropped.

On Titan's cold and murky surface *Titan Alpha* trundled across the spongy mats of dark carbonaceous soil. Its sensors were uplinking a steady stream of data to the intensely eager scientists of habitat *Goddard*, while computer engineers labored to alter the master program's prohibition against contamination.

The single-celled creatures living in those widespread mats, the scientists had discovered, were beginning to form colonies, taking the first step toward developing true multicellular species. In a few hundred million years, the scientists thought joyfully, Titan would begin to undergo a Cambrian Explosion and evolve true plants and animals.

Meanwhile, a spherical shell of powerful electromagnetic

pulses was expanding at the speed of light across the interstellar vastness, informing any species clever enough to decipher them that intelligent life exists on the planets circling a smallish yellow main-sequence star in the Perseus arm of the Milky Way galaxy.